THE
COLOUR
OF
LAW

MARK
GIMENEZ

sphere

SPHERE

First published in America as *The Color of Law* in 2005
by Doubleday, a division of Random House, Inc
First published in Great Britain in 2006 by Time Warner Books
Paperback edition published by Sphere in 2007
This paperback edition published by Sphere in 2013

3

A CIP catalogue record for this book
is available from the British Library.

ISBN 978-0-7515-5110-5

Printed and bound by CPI Group (UK) Ltd,
Croydon, CR0 4YY

Papers used by Sphere are from well-managed forests
and other responsible sources.

Sphere
An imprint of
Little, Brown Book Group
Carmelite House
50 Victoria Embankment
London EC4Y 0DZ

An Hachette UK Company
www.hachette.co.uk

www.littlebrown.co.uk

Born and educated in Texas, Mark Gimenez attended law school at Notre Dame, Indiana and practised with a large Dallas law firm. He is married with two sons.

Novels by Mark Gimenez

The Colour of Law
The Abduction
The Perk
The Common Lawyer
Accused
The Governor's Wife
Con Law

This book is dedicated to

Frank Gimenez (1926–1990) and Janie Gimenez, my parents.

Jack Hutchison (1931–1998), my father-in-law.

Brigitte, my wife, for reading all those drafts, and
Clay and Cole, my sons, for showing me how smart kids are.

Wm. E. ("Bill") Douglass (1942–1994) and Sheldon Anisman,
the two lawyers I have known who most resembled
Atticus Finch in honor and manner.

Harper Lee, whose great novel inspired me to become
a lawyer and to write this story.

Scout, simply by the nature of the work, every lawyer gets at least one case in his lifetime that affects him personally. This one's mine, I guess.

—Atticus Finch in *To Kill a Mockingbird* by Harper Lee

THE
COLOUR
OF
LAW

PROLOGUE

CLARK MCCALL was thirty years old and the sole heir to his father's $800 million fortune. He was also a major-league screwup. Or so his father often said, usually right before threatening to cut Clark out of his will. Usually because of nights like this—drinking, drugs, and girls.

It was Saturday night and Clark, drunk on whiskey and wired on cocaine, was trolling for a hooker in his father's Mercedes-Benz. He had driven south on Harry Hines almost to downtown without luck. There were plenty of working girls; he just hadn't found the right one. He was now stopped at a light and staring up at the Dallas skyline rising above him: shadowy structures outlined in white and blue and green lights visible for forty miles in the night sky. Looking up like that made him feel a little woozy, so he fumbled for the power switch and lowered his window. He leaned his head out and caught the summer breeze, warm on his face. He inhaled the night air, the sweet scent of sex for sale.

He closed his eyes and might have fallen asleep right there, except a cowboy in the pickup behind him hit his horn like a bugler sounding charge. Which startled Clark. His eyes snapped open—the light had changed. He punched the accelerator and yanked the wheel hard to make a U-turn, but he gave it too much gas and now he couldn't find the fucking brake pedal so he swung across three lanes and one tire of the Mercedes climbed up onto the curb and he almost clipped a street sign. *What the hell was it doing there?* The vehicle bounced hard coming back down.

No sooner had Clark gotten the big German sedan traveling mostly in one lane when he spotted her—a nice girl from the black neighborhoods south of downtown out for a slow stroll on a warm night with her girlfriend. She was just the kind he liked—a slim black babe in a blonde wig, a hot pink miniskirt, matching high heels, and a white tube top, swinging her little pink purse back and forth in perfect tempo with the exaggerated side-to-side movement of her round ass. Her body was fit, her legs lean, her entire essence so sensual and seductive that he knew she was the one—a black hooker from South Dallas specializing in white men from North Dallas.

She would be his date this Saturday night.

Not that Clark couldn't get a date with one of the many gorgeous single white girls seeking husbands in Dallas. He was handsome and his father was rich. In Dallas, rich was required; handsome was optional. Being both, Clark McCall had recently been named one of the city's most eligible bachelors. But he preferred prostitutes for female companionship. Hookers did what they were told and did not file police complaints afterward, and he knew up front how much the relationship would cost his father.

Clark steered the Mercedes over to the curb and slowed alongside the two South Dallas debutantes. He lowered the passenger window and yelled, "Blondie!"

They stopped, so he stopped. The black girl in the blonde wig sauntered over to the car with the kind of sassy attitude he liked in a hooker. She leaned down and stuck half her body through the window. Her skin was smooth and light, more tan than black, and her face was angular with sharp features, more white than black. Her lips and fingernails were painted a shiny red; her pushed-up breasts were round and full and looked real; and her scent was more intoxicating than anything he had ingested that night. She was beautiful, she was sexy, and he wanted her.

"How much?"

"What you want?"

"All you got, honey."

"Two hundred."

"A thousand. All night."

She smiled. "Show me the money."

Clark pulled out a wad of hundreds and waved it at her like candy to a kid. She got in and slid down the slick leather seat and her pink leather skirt crawled up so high he could see her black panties tight in her crotch, and he felt the heat come over him. He hit the accelerator and turned the sedan toward home.

But his thoughts turned to his father, as they often did in times like this. Clark McCall was a political liability to his father and always had been—the drinking, the drugs, the girls. Oh, if the senior senator from Texas could see his only son now, drunk and high, buying a black hooker with *his* money and driving her in *his* Mercedes to *his* mansion in Highland Park! Of course, his father's first thought would be political, not paternal: What damage would be done to his campaign if the press got wind of his son's latest indiscretion?

Clark laughed loudly and the hooker looked at him like he was crazy. At least he came home to Dallas to be indiscreet. Still, if his father found out that he had flown back home again, there would be more angry threats of disinheritance; but Clark would be back in Washington before the honorable senator knew he was gone. He laughed again, but he felt the rage rising inside him, as it always did when he thought of his father, a man who wanted the White House more than he had ever wanted a son.

United States Senator Mack McCall looked over at his second wife and thought what a handsome first couple they would make.

They were sitting in the leather wing chairs, enjoying a quiet Sunday afternoon in their Georgetown town house. Across from them on the sofa sat the two men who would get them into the White House. Their political consultant and pollster were poring over the latest poll results and focus group studies and staking out McCall's positions on the political issues of the day—positions carefully crafted to appease every identifiable voting bloc in America, whether based on race, religion, ethnicity, gender, geography, age, socioeconomic standing, or sexual orientation—anyone who could cast a vote for Senator Mack McCall. The senior senator from Texas held a commanding lead in the preprimary polls.

Mack McCall's lifelong ambition was finally within his grasp. He glanced down at his hands, still strong and calloused from years of working the rigs. He still had the hands of a roughneck and the determination of a wildcatter. And he was determined, as always, that nothing and no one would stand in his way. He would officially announce his candidacy on Monday.

Then he would spend $100 million or $200 million or whatever it took of his own money to win the White House. He had learned long ago that with enough money a man can buy anything and anyone he wants, be it an election or a younger woman. Mack McCall had enough money to buy both. He turned his eyes to his wife again and admired her beauty as if for the first time. He was filled with a sense of proprietorship, the same as years ago when he had gone out into the oil fields and admired his wells, knowing that he owned what other men coveted.

4

McCall was sixty; Jean was forty. He had been a senator for two decades now, and she had been his aide since she graduated from law school fifteen years ago. She was a savvy, articulate, and photogenic asset to his political career. They had been married ten years now, long enough for the messy divorce not to be a negative in his polls.

She had no children and wanted none. He had a son, Clark, from his first marriage—the consummate ne'er-do-well offspring of wealth, a thirty-year-old adolescent. Six months ago, thinking a steady job might bring maturity to the boy's life, and to get him out of Dallas, McCall had pulled some strings and got Clark appointed chairman of the Federal Energy Regulatory Commission. But the boy kept sneaking back home to do God knows what with God knows whom in their Dallas mansion. His son was not a political asset.

"Senator?"

Bradford, the butler, appeared in the arched entry to the living room, holding a portable phone and wearing a dazed expression.

"It's Clark, sir."

McCall waved him off. "Tell him I'm busy."

"No, sir, it's the FBI, from Dallas, calling about Clark."

"The *FBI*? Jesus Christ, what the hell did he do this time?"

"Nothing, sir. He's dead."

ONE

"WHAT'S THE DIFFERENCE between a rattlesnake lying dead in the middle of a highway and a lawyer lying dead in the middle of a highway?" He paused. "There are skid marks in front of the snake."

His bar association audience responded with polite laughter and diplomatic smiles.

"Why did New Jersey get all the toxic waste dumps and California get all the lawyers?" He paused again. "Because New Jersey had first choice."

Less laughter, fewer smiles, a scattering of nervous coughs: diplomacy was failing fast.

"What do lawyers and sperm have in common?" He did not pause this time. "Both have a one-in-a-million chance of turning out human."

All efforts at diplomacy had ended. His audience had fallen deathly silent; a sea of stone faces stared back at him. The lawyers on the dais focused on their lunches, embarrassed by their guest speaker's ill-advised attempt at humor. He looked around the crowded room, as if stunned. He turned his palms up.

"Why aren't you laughing? Aren't those jokes funny? The public sure thinks those jokes are funny, damn funny. I can't go to a cocktail party or the country club without someone telling me a stupid lawyer joke. My friends, we are the butt of America's favorite jokes!"

He adjusted the microphone so his deep sigh was audible, but he maintained steady eye contact with the audience.

"I don't think those jokes are funny, either. I didn't go to law school to be the butt of cruel jokes. I went to law school to be another Atticus Finch. *To Kill a Mockingbird* was my mother's favorite book and my bedtime story. She'd read a chapter each night, and when we came to the end, she'd go back to the beginning and start over. 'Scotty,' she'd say, 'be like Atticus. Be a lawyer. Do good.'

"And that, my fellow members of the bar, is the fundamental question we must ask ourselves: Are we really doing good, or are we just doing really well? Are we noble guardians of the rule of law fighting for justice in America, or are we just greedy parasites using the law to suck every last dollar from society like leeches on a dying man? Are we making the world a better place, or are we just making ourselves filthy rich?

"We must ask ourselves these questions, my friends, because the public is asking the same questions of us. They're questioning us, they're pointing their fingers at us, they're blaming us. Well, I've asked myself these questions, and I have answers, for myself, for you, and for the public: Yes, we are doing good! Yes, we are fighting for justice! Yes, we are making the world a better place!

"And ladies and gentlemen, if you elect me the next president of the state bar of Texas, I will tell the people exactly that! I will remind them that we wrote the Declaration of Independence and the Bill of Rights, that we fought for civil rights, that we protect the poor, defend the innocent, free the oppressed. That we stand up for their inalienable rights. That we are all that stands between freedom and oppression, right and wrong, innocence and guilt, life and death. And I will tell the people that I am proud, *damn proud*, to be a lawyer . . . because lawyers—do—good!"

Now, some might blame the Texas summer heat, but the audience, lawyers all—lawyers who had never protected the poor or defended the innocent or freed the oppressed, lawyers who stood up for the rights of multinational corporations—*believed* his words, like children who were old enough to know the truth about Santa Claus but who clung desperately to the myth anyway. They rose as one from their seats in the main dining room of the Belo Mansion in downtown Dallas and, with great enthusiasm, applauded the tall thirty-six-year-old speaker, who removed his tortoise-shell glasses, pushed his thick blond hair off his tanned face, and flashed his movie-star smile. He took his seat on the dais behind a nameplate that read A. SCOTT FENNEY, ESQ., FORD STEVENS LLP.

As the applause grew louder, the corporate tax lawyer whom Scott was campaigning to succeed as the next state bar president leaned in close and whispered, "You know, Scotty, you've got an impressive line of bullshit. Now I see why half the coeds at SMU dropped their drawers for you."

Scott squeezed the knot of his silk tie, smoothed his $2,000 suit, and whispered back through brilliant white teeth, "Henry, you don't get laid or elected telling the truth."

He then turned and again acknowledged his fellow members of the bar, all standing and applauding him.

Except for one lawyer. Sitting alone in the back of the dining room, at his usual table, was an older gentleman. His thick white hair fell onto his forehead. His bright eyes remained sharp at long distances, but he wore the black reading glasses to eat. He was not a tall man, and his slightly hunched posture made him appear almost short. Even so, he was a lawyer the other lawyers either avoided outright or approached with great caution, like vassals to their lordship, waiting patiently for him to look up from his chicken-fried steak, mashed potatoes, and pecan pie and acknowledge them with a nod or, on the best of days, a brief handshake. But never did he stand. Come hell or high water, United States District Court Judge Samuel Buford remained seated until he was through eating. Today, though, as he dwelled on the young lawyer's speech, a slight smile crossed his face.

A. Scott Fenney, Esq., had just made a tough judicial decision easy.

TWO

THE FORD STEVENS LAW firm occupied floors fifty-five through sixty-three in Dibrell Tower in downtown Dallas. The firm's remarkable financial success was predicated on its two hundred lawyers billing an average of two hundred hours a month at an average of $250 an hour, grossing an average of $120 million a year, and racking up average profits per partner of $1.5 million, putting the Dallas firm on a par with Wall Street firms. Scott Fenney had been a partner for four years now; he pul416led down $750,000 a year. He was shooting to double that by the time he was forty.

One of fifty partners, his perks were many: a personal secretary, two paralegals, and four associates working under him; reserved parking in the underground garage; dining, athletic, and country club memberships; and an enormous corner office on the sixty-second floor facing due north—the only direction worth facing in downtown Dallas. He especially loved his office, the wood-paneled walls, the mahogany desk, the leather furniture, the genuine Persian rug imported from Iran on the hardwood floor, and on the wall, the five-foot-square framed field-level blowup of himself, number 22 on the SMU Mustangs, running for 193 yards against the Texas Longhorns the day Scott Fenney became a local football legend. Keeping all these coveted perks required only that Scott serve the firm's corporate clients with the same devotion the disciples showed Jesus Christ.

It was an hour after his bar association speech, and Scott was standing on his Persian rug and admiring Missy, a twenty-seven-year-old ex–Dallas Cowboy cheerleader who ran the firm's summer clerkship program. In the fall of each year, Ford Stevens lawyers fanned out across the country to interview the best second-year students at the best law schools in the nation. The firm hired forty of the top candidates and brought them to Dallas the following summer to work as summer clerks for $2,500 a week plus room and board, parties, alcohol, and at some firms, women. Most partners in large law firms had been frat rats in college, so most summer clerkship programs had all the markings of fraternity rush. Ford Stevens's program was no exception.

Thus the first Monday of June brought the invasion of forty summer clerks, like Bob here, each trying to catch the eye of powerful partners, the partners in turn trying to divine if these budding legal eagles were the Ford Stevens type. Bob was. From the look on the face of the law student standing next to Missy, he was dreaming of having just such an office one day. Which meant he would bill two hundred hours a month for the next eight years without complaint or contempt, at which time the firm would show him the door—the odds of a new associate making partner at Ford Stevens being one in twenty. But the ambitious students still signed on because, as Scott himself told them, "You want odds, go to Vegas. You want a chance to get filthy rich by the time you're forty, hire on with Ford Stevens."

"Mr. Fenney?"

Scott pulled his eyes off Missy and turned to his frumpy middle-aged secretary standing in the door.

"Yes, Sue?"

"Four calls are holding—your wife, Stan Taylor, George Parker, and Tom Dibrell."

Scott turned back to Missy and the student and shrugged.

"Duty calls." He shook hands with the pale, homely, top-of-his-class student and slapped him on the shoulder. "Bob—"

"Rob."

"Oh, I'm sorry. Now, Rob, my Fourth of July bash, that's mandatory attendance."

"Yes, sir, I've already heard about it."

To Missy: "You bringing some girls over this year?"

"Ten."

"Ten?" Scott whistled. "Ten ex–Dallas Cowboy cheerleaders." The firm paid each girl $500 to spend a few hours in bikinis acting interested in law students. "Bob—"

"Rob."

"Right. You'd better work on your tan, Rob, if you want to snare one of those cheerleaders."

Rob grinned even though he had about as much chance of getting a date with an ex–Dallas Cowboy cheerleader as a one-legged man had winning a butt-kicking contest.

"Mr. Fenney," Rob said, "your speech at the bar luncheon, it was truly inspiring."

First day on the job and the boy was already brownnosing like an experienced associate. Could he possibly be sincere?

"Thanks, Bob."

Missy winked. Scott didn't know if the wink was because she knew his speech was bullshit or if she was flirting again. Like all good-looking single girls in Dallas, Missy had made flirting an art form, always managing to catch his eye when crossing her long

13

lean legs or brush against him in the elevator or just look at him in a way that made him feel as if they were on the brink of an affair. Of course, every male at the firm felt that way about Missy, but Scott was annually voted the best-looking male lawyer at Ford Stevens by the firm's female support staff, not that it was much of a contest. Scott had been a star football player in college; most lawyers were star chess players. Like Bob here.

"Rob."

"Right."

Missy and Bob departed, and Scott went around behind his desk and sat in his high-backed leather chair. His eyes found the phone; four lines were blinking. Without conscious thought, his trained mind instantly prioritized the calls: Tom, Stan, George, wife. Tom had paid the firm $3 million last year, Stan $150,000, George $50,000, and his wife nothing.

Scott picked up the phone and punched Tom's line.

"Mr. Fenney!"

Scott was waiting impatiently for the elevator in the lobby of the sixty-second floor, on his way to see Tom Dibrell on the sixty-ninth floor. He could not restrain a smile. He was blessed with the kind of rich client lawyers dream about: a real-estate developer addicted to the deal; a client who habitually borrowed, bought, built, leased, sold, sued, and got sued, and, most important, who possessed an uncanny knack for getting himself into one precarious legal predicament after another, extrication from which always requiring the very expensive legal services of A. Scott Fenney, Esq.

Sue arrived, her face flushed from running after him.

"Mr. Fenney, you have the partnership meeting at two."

Scott checked his watch: 1:45.

"I can't make it. Tom needs me. What's on the agenda?"

Sue handed him the partnership meeting agenda. Only one

item required his vote: the termination of John Walker as a partner in the firm. Unlike Scott, John was no longer a blessed lawyer. His rich client had just been bought out by a New York company, which meant his client would no longer be paying legal fees to Ford Stevens; and which now meant John Walker would no longer be employed at Ford Stevens. His $800,000 salary had just become an unnecessary expense to the firm. John was a brilliant lawyer, and he and Scott played hoops together twice a week, but this was business: brilliant lawyers without rich clients were worthless to a large law firm.

The elevator doors opened just as Scott reached into his coat for his pen. He stepped inside and Sue followed. Attached to the agenda was a partnership ballot: TERMINATION OF JOHN WALKER. The only partner in the firm who didn't know John Walker would be fired today was John Walker. Dan Ford believed surprise was critical when firing a partner; otherwise that partner might walk out the door with a few of the firm's clients. So in fifteen minutes John Walker would walk into Dan's office, be unceremoniously fired after twelve years with the firm, and then be escorted from the building by security guards. The firm had never lost a single client to a terminated lawyer.

Sue turned and offered her back; Scott put the ballot against her back and his pen to the ballot and started to sign *A. Scott Fenney*— but he froze. He felt guilty, even though his vote was a mere formality, a nod to the illusion that the Ford Stevens law firm was a partnership of equal lawyers. In fact, Dan Ford owned the firm and every lawyer, office, desk, and book in the firm; and Dan had already decided to fire John Walker. Scott could either rubber-stamp Dan's decision or refuse and . . . *what?* . . . join John in the unemployment line? He sighed and signed the ballot in the FOR column, then handed the ballot back to Sue and said, "Give that to Dan."

She stared at the ballot like it was a death warrant and then said, almost in a whisper: "His wife has breast cancer."

15

"Dan's?"

"No. John Walker's wife. His secretary said it's in her lymph nodes."

"You're kidding? Jesus, she's young."

Scott's mother had been young, too, only forty-three, when the same cancer had killed her. Scott had watched helplessly as she lost her breasts, her hair, and her life. He now thought of John's wife and of John, who would soon be standing on the street outside this building, coat and career in hand, cursing his partners for abandoning him and God for abandoning his wife, just as Scott had cursed God as the cancer consumed his mother's body ounce by ounce until she felt like a feather pillow when he lifted her from the bed and carried her to the bathroom.

"Damn."

He could do no more for John's wife than he could for his mother, and no more for John than all the other lawyers Dan Ford had fired without warning . . . but still. Scott stared at himself in the mirrored wall until the elevator eased to a smooth stop and the doors opened on the sixty-ninth floor. The elevator chime snapped him out of his thoughts like a referee's whistle after an injury timeout. He stepped out. The elevator doors closed behind him, and he entered the domain of Dibrell Property Company, the firm's landlord and his most important client, accounting for over ninety percent of the legal fees he generated each year, fees that had bought everything Scott Fenney owned in life, from the bed he slept in to the shoes on his feet.

Eleven years ago almost to the day, Scott, at the time a new associate at Ford Stevens, had been in one of the elevators of this building when the doors opened and in stepped Thomas J. Dibrell. Scott recognized him immediately. Everyone in Dallas knew of Tom Dibrell: an SMU alum and rabid football booster, he had been implicated in the play-for-pay scandal with the governor that resulted in the NCAA giving SMU the death penalty in 1987; he had built the lavish Dibrell Tower with $300 million borrowed from a New York pension fund during the real-estate boom of the '80s; and he had somehow survived bankruptcy in the '90s, a fate so many other developers had suffered when the Texas real-estate market went bust. In fact, how Tom Dibrell had managed to hold on to his skyscraper while all the other big developers lost theirs to foreclosure remained the second greatest mystery of Dallas, right after *Did Oswald act alone?*

But just as Scott recognized him in the elevator that day, Dibrell recognized Scott. His face got that look Scott had witnessed so many times when a grown man had a close encounter with a football hero: it's a child's face on Christmas morning. They introduced themselves, Scott told Dibrell that he was a lawyer at Ford Stevens, and Dibrell invited him to lunch upstairs at the Downtown Club. Over a steak, Dibrell explained that the Dallas real-estate market was in the tank, his company was on life support, and his lawyers—the disloyal bastards he had paid millions during the boom years—had just abandoned him for the Yankee banks that had taken over the insolvent local banks, the ones holding many of his defaulted notes. After lunch, Dibrell bit down on a big cigar, leaned back in his chair, and asked Scott Fenney, local football legend, to be his new lawyer.

A. Scott Fenney, Esq., had his first client.

The rest was history. Eleven years later, the Dallas real-estate market was booming again, Dibrell Property Company was on top of the world, and Tom Dibrell was again a trophy client in Dallas, a client who endows his lawyer with instant respect and social status when the lawyer announces, "I'm Scott Fenney, Tom Dibrell's lawyer." And Scott remained his loyal lawyer to the tune of $3 million a year in fees.

Scott's heels clicked against the mahogany and marble floor until he arrived at the wide entryway. Directly under a longhorn chandelier sat a round wood table on which was perched a two-foot-tall bronze sculpture of an anatomically correct calf on its side, hog-tied and held down by two cowboys, about to lose its masculinity at the hands of a third cowboy wielding a weapon that looked like a giant two-handed toenail clipper. SPRING ROUNDUP was etched in the silver plate attached to the base.

Whenever Scott entered the expansive reception area of Dibrell Property Company, he always felt like he was walking into a western museum. Frederic Remington sculptures sat atop pedestal tables. G. Harvey paintings of cowboys on horses hung on the walls, fine art with names like *When Bankers Wore Boots, Rio Grande Crossing,* and *The Good Lord Willin' and the Creek Don't Rise.* The furnishings were straight out of *Giant*—diamond-tufted leather couches and matching chairs with brass studs and dark wood from floor to ceiling. On the wall above the reception desk hung the museum's masterpiece, a huge portrait of Tom Dibrell astride a big black stallion. He looked like a kid whose parents had forced him to sit on the pony at a petting zoo. It was, in fact, the only time Tom had ever been on a horse. But Tom loved all things cowboy, even though no one in Dallas or Houston or Texas for that matter was ever really a cowboy. Still, it was fun to pretend.

Scott's eyes dropped from Roy Rogers Jr. to perhaps the most beautiful young woman he had ever seen, at least since the last time he had stood here. A blonde, blue-eyed beauty was sitting behind the reception desk and painting her nails over the morning newspaper. Tom Dibrell always said he firmly believed in hiring beancounters from Harvard Business and receptionists from Hooters. Problem was, the receptionists' career path always led from this desk to Tom's office couch, which in turn led to a substantial settlement to avoid litigation.

"God, he was handsome," she said.

She didn't mean Tom. Her blue eyes were focused on the newspaper and a black-and-white photo of a young man under the headlines, "Clark McCall Murdered" . . . "Prostitute Charged" . . .

"Senator McCall 'Devastated' " . . . "Presidential Campaign Delayed."

"That's a mug shot," Scott said, "from when he was busted for dope. He was always in trouble."

She shrugged. "He was rich."

"His daddy's rich."

"That's good enough for me."

"Well, then, he should've picked you up Saturday night instead of that hooker."

"Oh, I would've cost him a lot more than her. But then, I don't carry a gun."

"Girl, from where I'm standing, you're sure packing some heat."

She gave him a coy smile then dropped her eyes back to the newspaper. She shook her head slowly as if pondering a great mystery.

"Rich and handsome. Why would he want a black prostitute when he could have any white girl in town?"

"Cheaper, like you said."

Scott always enjoyed flirting with Dibrell's girls, but he had tired of this conversation. The murder of a senator's son did not concern him this afternoon. He was here to make money. So he said, "Scott Fenney, to see Tom."

The receptionist put down her polish, blew on her nails, and picked up the phone. She held the receiver carefully with the inside pads of her fingers so as not to scuff her fresh paint job, punched a button with the eraser end of a pencil, and said, "Mr. Fenney is here." She hung up, rearranged herself in her chair so as to show off her impressive upper body, and said, "So, are you married?"

Scott held up his left hand to display his wedding ring.

"Eleven years."

"Too bad." She blew on her nails again and said, "Go right

19

back, Mr. Fenney. And call me if that changes . . . or even if it don't."

Grammar skills notwithstanding, she was a fine example of what Texas men wanted most—a gorgeous Texas girl. Texas myths were many, but one was no myth: the most gorgeous girls in the world were found in Texas. Dallas, Texas. Girls like her, they graduate from high school or maybe junior college, and from small towns all across Texas they head straight to Dallas like moths to light. They come for the jobs, they come for the nightlife, they come for the single men making lots of money, the kind of money that buys big homes and fancy cars and fashionable clothes and glittery jewelry guaranteed to bring a smile to any Texas girl's face. Girl wants to marry a refinery worker and live in a doublewide, she moves to Houston; girl wants to marry money and live in a mansion, she moves to Dallas.

Scott walked through the reception area and down a gallery filled with more cowboy art and remembered to put on his glasses. He was slightly farsighted and needed the glasses only when reading in poor light, but he made it a practice to wear them in front of clients because clients like lawyers who look smart. He arrived at Tom's office suite, which consisted of a secretarial area, a private bathroom, a study with a fake fireplace, and Tom's inner sanctum.

Marlene, Tom's middle-aged secretary, looked up from the McCall story, smiled, and waved him in. He found Tom on the far side of the vast space, his head buried in his hands, looking small behind the massive desk under the ten-foot-high ceiling. Scott walked toward his rich client, weaving his way around more leather furniture and a fancy silver-inlaid Mexican saddle on a stand and past photographs of Tom with governors and senators and presidents, and, on the coffee table, the hard hat with DIBRELL stenciled across the front, and the rolled-up blueprints he used as props at groundbreakings, even though Tom Dibrell had never held a construction job in his life.

"We're meeting downstairs on the land deal," Scott said to the top of Tom's head. "Should have it closed soon."

Tom's head started shaking slowly back and forth.

"I didn't call you about that."

Tom was fifty-five, nearly bald so he had recently gone to a comb-over, he stood five seven in his trademark cowboy boots, and he was a pudgy bastard, but for $3 million a year, Scott described him as stocky. He had been married four times to progressively younger women; the current Mrs. Dibrell was twenty-nine. Tom raised his head and Scott instantly knew it was a female problem. He sighed. His best client couldn't keep his hands off the help.

"Who was it this time, Tom?"

"Nadine."

Scott shook his head; he didn't recall a Nadine.

"Brunette, tall, built? Jesus, Scott, she's got hips like a boy!" He paused, and his eyes glazed over, as if reliving the moment. Then: "She's threatening to sue, sexual harassment." Tom held out a letter. "She's got a fucking lawyer!"

Scott grabbed the paper; his eyes went straight to the letter-head: *Franklin Turner, Esq.*, famous plaintiffs' lawyer. Scott exhaled heavily. "Shit." Twenty thousand lawyers in Dallas and she finds Frank Turner.

Scott skimmed the letter. Frank Turner was threatening to file a lawsuit against Dibrell Property Company and Thomas J. Dibrell individually on behalf of his client, Nadine Johnson, unless a financial settlement was reached within ten days.

Tom said, "Is Turner as tough as they say?"

"Yeah, he's a real hard-ass."

Scott said it with a grave tone, much as a doctor might say, *Yes, you have cancer.* It was always best to make the client sweat a little: a worried client will pay more fees with less bitching. So he put a frown on his face and stepped over to the bay window Tom had specially designed for his office just so he could enjoy a panoramic view of Dallas, so he could stand right there and gaze out on the city and breathe it in and think, *God, what a depressing sight!* Gray and dull, like you're watching an old black-and-white TV. A concrete-and-steel landscape as far as the eye can see, all the way to the brown haze of pollution that perpetually rings the city above the loop, treeless and barren, the city's master plan obvious—to pave over every square inch of green in the whole goddamned city. Which might explain Dallas's ranking as the ugliest major city in America. Other than women, Dallas has no natural beauty whatsoever. No ocean or lake or water of any kind except the Trinity River running west of downtown, used for decades as a natural sewage system and today as a big drainage ditch. No Central Park, no Rocky Mountains, and no Miami Beach. No wonderful weather. Nothing other great cities have. All Dallas has is a white X on Elm Street marking the exact spot where an American president was killed. But then, you don't live in Dallas for any of that; you live in Dallas to make a lot of money fast.

"Scott?"

Tom's voice sounded like a child's pleading. Scott turned to his very worried client.

"Tom, going up against Frank Turner, I'll be lucky to hold this one to twice what the last one cost."

Tom shook his head. "I don't care, Scott. Pay two million if you have to, just take care of it. And keep it quiet, I don't want to lose Babs over this. I really like her."

Babs was wife number four.

"I'll take care of it, Tom, just like I took care of the others."

Tom looked like he was going to cry.

"I'll never forget this, Scott. Never."

Scott headed to the door, saying over his shoulder, "Just don't forget it when I send you my bill."

Scott maintained his serious expression past Marlene and back through the cowboy museum—he did give the receptionist a little wink—and into the elevator lobby. But once safely aboard and alone in the elevator, he broke into a broad grin and said to his image in the mirrored wall: "How can one man get himself into so many legal cracks? The guy's fucking uncanny."

In the privacy of an elevator or his thoughts, Scott Fenney regarded his rich client as all lawyers regard the rich clients who subsidize their lives: they're creatures of lesser intelligence who, by the grace of God, have inherited, stolen, swindled, connived, cheated, or simply lucked their way into enormous wealth. So, to restore balance to the natural order, the lawyers are duty bound to relieve their clients of as much of their wealth as possible in legal fees.

A. Scott Fenney, Esq., had always done his duty with respect to Tom Dibrell.

THREE

S COTT RODE the elevator down to the Ford Stevens offices and then walked down the hall to the conference room on the sixty-second floor, past John Walker's office where John's secretary was boxing up his personal belongings and the next lawyer in line was already moving in. Scott was stepping smartly and snapping his fingers, wired on the greatest intoxicant known to man: success.

He threw open the double doors and entered the conference room, a considerable space currently occupied by a forty-foot-long cherrywood table, thirty chairs upholstered in deep brown leather, and a dozen male lawyers fighting over other people's money like lions over raw meat. Today, these ravenous young lawyers were feasting on Dibrell Property Company's $25 million purchase of fifty acres of land adjacent to the Trinity River on which Dibrell planned to build industrial warehouses. Three Ford Stevens lawyers were in the fray, fighting for Scott's client at a combined hourly rate of $850. Scott stepped to the head of the long conference table.

"Gentlemen!"

The room fell silent and all eyes, ties, and suspenders turned to him.

"You guys haven't closed this deal yet? What the hell's the holdup?"

Sid Greenberg, a fifth-year associate at the firm whom Scott had put in charge of this Dibrell matter, said, "Scott, we're still fighting over the environmental escrow."

"That's not resolved yet? It's been what, two weeks?"

Sid said, "Scott, I don't think we can resolve it."

"Sid, there's a solution to every legal problem. What's the problem?"

"The problem is this, Scott: We know—but the government doesn't—that there's contamination on the land, lead from years ago when a battery plant operated there. And there's some leaching into the river whenever it rains—a lot of leaching. So we've got to escrow part of the purchase price to cover the cleanup, in case the lead is discovered before Dibrell can pave over it. The problem is how much to escrow."

"Hell, Sid, hire an environmental consultant. He'll tell us how much to escrow."

"We would've already done that, Scott, except the court ordered us to turn over all environmental reports to those stupid eco-nuts who filed suit to stop the deal."

"Trinity River Allies in Litigation?"

"Yeah, TRAIL. They want the land used as some kind of nature park, where kids can go see a river habitat up close. All they'll see is a bunch of dead fish and raw sewage. Shit, you even stick a toe in that water, you'll get a disease. Anyway, we told the court that neither party had an environmental report. If we get one, we'll have to give it to TRAIL and they'll find out about the lead contamination and use it to stop the deal—the EPA will be all over that land the next day! But without a report, we don't know how much to escrow. We want fifty percent of the purchase price escrowed; the seller wants five percent."

Sid threw up his hands.

"We may have to tell Dibrell to call off the deal."

Scott sighed. Years back he had made the mistake of telling Tom to call off a deal because of some legal nicety. Tom listened patiently to his new lawyer, and then said, "Scott, I'm not paying you to tell me what I can't do. I'm paying you to tell me how I can do what I want to do. And if you can't, I'll find a smarter lawyer who can."

Scott had learned his lesson well. He was not about to tell Tom Dibrell to call off a $25 million deal that would pay $500,000 in legal fees to Ford Stevens, and damn sure not over lead leaching into that cesspool called the Trinity River.

"Okay, here's what we're going to do. Ford Stevens will hire the environmental consultant. He'll deliver his report only to me. Seller's counsel can come to my office to read the report, but no copies will leave my office. That report will belong to Ford Stevens, not to Dibrell or the seller. That way, the report will be protected by the attorney-client privilege, and I can swear to the court that neither party has an environmental report subject to TRAIL's subpoena. And no one will ever know about the lead leaching into the river."

"Will that work?" Sid asked.

"It worked for the tobacco companies, Sid. They kept all that evidence about nicotine being addictive secret for forty years—because their lawyers hired the scientists who conducted the studies. So the studies were protected from subpoenas by the attorney-client privilege. No one ever knew that evidence was out there, because their lawyers hid it behind the privilege. Just like we're going to do."

Sid was beaming. "That's brilliant. We can then close the deal with the appropriate environmental escrow."

27

"Exactly," Scott said. "And those environmentalists can go fuck a tree."

"Frank, how the hell you been, buddy?"

Scott got Franklin Turner, Esq., famous plaintiffs' lawyer, on the phone on the first try. No doubt Frank had instructed his secretary that if Tom Dibrell's lawyer called to put him right through, aware that one phone call might net him a handsome fee.

"Two million, Scott."

Scott had the door closed and Frank on the speakerphone so he could practice his golf swing while negotiating the settlement of a young woman's claim that Tom Dibrell had used his position as her employer to pressure her to have sex with him—which, knowing Scott's rich client, was probably true. Scott swung the 9-iron he kept in his office; he used to swing a 6-iron, but he had punched holes in the ceiling tile on his follow-through, so he had dropped down to a 9-iron. From across his office, Scott said: "Jesus, Frank, we could at least shoot the shit for a few minutes, just out of professional courtesy."

"Scott, Dibrell's a fifty-five-year-old father of five—"

"Six," Scott said while checking his golfing address position in the window's reflection.

"Father of six, married—"

"For the fourth time." Scott checked his takeaway.

"Married and CEO of one of the biggest goddamn real-estate companies in Dallas, he's a member of the business council, the chamber of commerce, and every other important civic organization in this city, and he forces himself on a naïve twenty-two-year-old young woman—"

"*Forces himself?* Give me a break, Frank. Knowing the girls Tom hires, she probably went down faster than Monica Lewinsky."

He chuckled and checked his backswing at the halfway point.

"It's not a goddamn joke, Scott! Nadine was irreparably harmed!"

"But two million bucks would make the hurt go away, right?"

"No, but it would make her go away."

There was a soft knock on the door. Scott turned from the window to see Sue poking her head in. She said in a low voice: "Mr. Fenney, your daughter's on the phone. She says it's an emergency."

An emergency? A jolt of fatherly fear ricocheted through Scott's central nervous system like a pinball setting off alarms. Four long strides and he was at his desk. He said to the phone: "Frank, hang on the line, okay?"

Scott didn't wait for a response. He leaned the 9-iron against the desk, picked up the receiver, and punched the blinking light on the phone, putting Frank Turner on hold and his nine-year-old daughter on the line.

"Hi, baby, what's wrong?"

A tiny voice: "Mother's gone and Consuela's crying."

"Why?"

"They arrested Esteban."

"*Who?* The INS?"

"He said '*inmigración.*' "

"You talked to him?"

"Consuela talked to him first, but she started crying so I talked to him. He said they arrested him where he was building a home, said they're sending him back to Mexico. Can you help him?"

"Honey, there's nothing I can do. Esteban's a tough kid, he'll be all right. They'll bus him down to Matamoros, he'll cross back over the next day, and he'll be back up here in a few weeks, just like the last time."

"Yeah, that's what he said."

"So why's Consuela so upset?"

"She's scared they're gonna come for her, send her back to Mexico, too. She says she has no one in Mexico, that this is the only home she's ever had."

Consuela had come with the house. When the prior owner had filed bankruptcy and could no longer afford the mansion or his Mexican maid, the Fenney family had acquired Consuela de la Rosa like an appurtenance to the property.

"A. Scott, I told her you were fixing things so she can always live with us . . . you are, aren't you?"

"Uh, yeah, I'm working on that." He'd been meaning to hire an immigration lawyer to get Consuela's green card. "Look, tell her not to worry. INS knows better than to conduct raids in Highland Park. Heads would roll."

"Huh?"

"They'd get fired if they took Highland Park maids away."

"Oh. But she's really scared. She shut the front drapes, she won't even go outside in the backyard, and she's saying the rosary. It's just us here and . . . well, it's kind of scaring me, too. No one's gonna come to our house, are they, and bust in the door like on TV?"

"No, baby, no one's coming to our house."

"You promise?"

"I promise. Let me talk to her."

Consuela was an emotional girl, given to sudden bouts of tears over fears real or imagined, which she warded off by wearing three crucifixes, saying daily prayers to various saints, and keeping enough candles lit on the windowsill above the kitchen sink to light a convenience store. But the fear that never left her was being sent back to Mexico. Esteban was her boyfriend; they had met at the Catholic church in the Little Mexico section of Dallas. Scott drove her over every Sunday morning and picked her up every Sunday afternoon, their weekly visit. Esteban worked construction in other parts of Dallas and faced the risk of INS raids, but Consuela was protected by the unwritten rule that the INS did not enter the Town of Highland Park, home to the richest and most politically powerful men in Texas—and their illegal Mexican maids. Scott's illegal Mexican maid was as sweet as she was round, and after three years of tending to the Fenney household, she was like a member of the family, albeit one who reverted to her native tongue when distraught. Consuela's sobbing voice came over the line.

"Señor Fenney, tengo miedo de inmigración."

"Don't be afraid, Consuela. It's okay. *Está bien.* No one's gonna take you away. You'll always live with us."

Scott had picked up some Spanish skills from his Mexican maid, who sniffled and said, *"¿Para siempre?"*

"Yes. Forever."

"Señor Fenney, you make the, uh . . . *promesa a* Consuela?"

"Sí, Consuela, I promise."

A sniffle. "O-kay. *Adiós, señor."*

His daughter came back on. "She stopped crying."

"Good."

"A. Scott, you're not gonna let them take her away, are you?"

"No, baby, that won't happen."

"Okay."

"Look, honey, I'm kind of busy, so if everything's under control there, I need to get back to work."

"We're good. See you later, alligator."

"After while, crocodile."

Scott hung up and made a mental note to call Rudy Gutierrez, an immigration lawyer he had met years ago. He'd been meaning to do that for six months now, or maybe a year, almost two come to think of it, but something had always come up and . . . the blinking light on the phone caught Scott's eye and he remembered Frank Turner holding—not that Scott minded making a plaintiffs' lawyer wait for his contingency fee. The image of his daughter huddled behind closed drapes in their Highland Park home with their Mexican maid faded from his mind and was replaced by the image of a smug-faced Frank Turner, famous plaintiffs' lawyer, leaning back in his chair in his fancy office convinced he was about to win this game and beat Scott Fenney out of two million dollars to buy off sweet Nadine. Not today, Frank. Scott grabbed the 9-iron, punched Frank's button, engaged the speakerphone, and picked up right where he had left off.

"*Two million?* That's an expensive piece of ass, Frank. What, she was a virgin?"

"Her sexual history is irrelevant."

"Yeah, like it was for Kobe." Scott pointed the 9-iron at the speakerphone. "Chances are, Frank, she's been screwing since she was fourteen, so you damn well better advise your client that if she wants to go to trial, we're gonna track down every swinging dick she's ever met up close and personal, we're gonna put their owners on the stand to tell the world about Nadine's many virtues, and by the time we're through with her sweet little ass, she'll make those hookers on Harry Hines look like a bunch of goddamn nuns!"

"Oh, yeah? Well, you'd better advise Tom Dibrell that by the time I'm through with him he'll wish to God he'd stayed faithful to wife number one!"

Scott laughed boisterously, as if that was the funniest thing he had ever heard.

"You wouldn't say that if you'd seen her." He again faced the window and checked his position at the top of his backswing. "Listen to us, Frank, a couple of good ol' SMU boys going at each other like an Aggie and a Longhorn. Look, bottom line, both our clients got some downside here. So to make this go away for both of them, Tom will pay sweet little ol' Nadine half a million bucks, and that's a hell of a lot more money than she was making at Hooters."

"Tips are pretty good there, Scott. One-point-five."

"They ain't that good, Frank. One million."

"Done."

He checked his downswing. "I'll have the release and confidentiality agreement to you first thing in the morning. You get it signed and back to me, I'll have a check waiting."

"Cashier's check, payable jointly to me and Nadine Johnson."

"Frank, you make damn sure Nadine understands that if she talks about her little roll in the hay with Tom to anyone—even her goddamned psychiatrist!—the agreement requires that she return every penny and that you return your fee. And Tom's likely to strangle her."

Frank laughed. "She talks, I'll strangle the bitch myself she costs me three hundred thirty thousand."

"What are you taking, a third?"

"Standard contingency fee."

"Three hundred thirty thousand bucks, not a bad day's work, Frank."

"It's a dirty job, Scott, but someone's gotta do it."

Scott shook his head. Plaintiffs' lawyers. Scott was figuring on making maybe $50 million over his career, but plaintiffs' lawyers, those bastards make that every year, taking 33 percent, 40 percent, sometimes 50 percent of their clients' damage awards, almost always settlements like this because a corporation can't afford to roll the dice with a Texas jury, not when the jurors might pull another *Pennzoil v. Texaco* and come back with an $11,120,976,110.83 judgment, the largest jury verdict in the history of the world. Which made Texas a plaintiffs' lawyers' playground. To date, Franklin Turner, Esq., had amassed over one billion dollars in verdicts and settlements, the bastard.

"Hey, Scott, what do you think about that black halfback we got from Houston? He gonna break your records?"

Frank had been in the Mustang marching band at SMU. Tuba.

"They've been trying for fourteen years now, Frank. No one's come close."

"One day, Scott, one day."

"Yeah, yeah, yeah . . . Good doing business with you, Frank."

Scott reached over with the 9-iron and hit the disconnect button on the speakerphone. A successful ten-minute negotiation, for which he felt duty bound to bill his best client $50,000. The way he figured, Tom Dibrell was prepared to pay $2 million to settle with Nadine; his lawyer had skillfully held the settlement to only $1 million; so, even with a $50,000 legal fee, he was actually *saving* Dibrell $950,000. Studying his reflection in the window, he practiced his full golf swing and held his pose like a pro. Scott Fenney had found that he possessed the necessary skills to excel at three games in life: football, golf, and lawyering.

FOUR

FIVE O'CLOCK. The end of another day of crisis, conflict, and confrontation. A lawyer's life. It isn't for everyone, or even every lawyer. Lawyering either gets into your blood, or it doesn't. If you don't wake up itching for a fight, if you shy away from personal confrontation, if you're not the competitive type, if you don't possess the intestinal fortitude to go mano a mano with a famous plaintiffs' lawyer and beat him at his own game, then the manly sport of lawyering just isn't for you. Go into social work.

Lawyering is a lot like football. In fact, Scott always figured his football career was the best pre-law curriculum the school offered; it certainly made the transition to the law an easy one for him. Whereas football is legalized violence, lawyering is violent legalities: lawyers use the law to pummel each other's clients into submission. And just as football coaches want smart, mean, and tough players, rich clients want smart, mean, and tough lawyers. And they want to win. At all costs. Lie, cheat, steal, just win the goddamned case! In football and the law, winning isn't everything; it's the only thing. Winners reap the rewards; losers lose. A. Scott Fenney, Esq., leaned back in his chair, locked his hands behind his head, and surveyed his world here at the Ford Stevens law firm: he was a winner. And his reward was a perfect life. An absolutely perfect life.

He heard the phone ring at Sue's desk. In seconds, she was standing in the door, purse in hand.

"Mr. Fenney, it's the federal court."

Scott shook his head. "I'll call her back tomorrow."

"It's not the clerk. It's the judge. Judge Buford."

Scott snapped forward in his chair. "Judge Buford's on the phone?"

Sue nodded.

"What the hell does he want with me?"

Sue shrugged, and Scott's eyes fell to the single blinking light on his phone. On the other end of that line was Judge Samuel Buford, the senior judge on the federal bench for the Northern District of Texas. Appointed by Carter, he had presided over every civil rights case in Dallas for the last three decades. He was now something of an icon in conservative Dallas despite being a liberal Democrat. As a federal judge he made less than a second-year associate at Ford Stevens, but lawyers who made a million bucks a year still addressed him as "sir," even outside his courtroom—and Scott had never spoken to him outside his courtroom. Scott took a deep breath, picked up the phone, and punched the blinking button.

"Judge Buford, sir, what a surprise."

"Scott, how you doing, son?"

"Uh . . . fine, Judge. Just fine. Uh . . . how are you doing, sir?"

"Well, I'm not doing so good, Scott, that's why I called you. I've got a big problem, and I need a top-notch lawyer to solve it. I figure you're Tom Dibrell's lawyer and—"

"Does this involve Tom?"

"Oh, no, Scott. It's just that being Dibrell's lawyer, you're accustomed to high-profile work, and your appearances in my courtroom have always been excellent. But, most important, you have the right attitude. Listening to your speech at the bar luncheon today, I knew you were just the lawyer for the job. Scott, I can't tell you how it made me feel, knowing there's still someone who understands what being a lawyer is all about. So many young lawyers these days, seems all they care about is getting rich."

"Yes, sir, it's a crying shame, Judge."

"You know, Scott, seeing you up there, everyone applauding you, made me recall that game of yours against Texas—damn, son, that was the best running I've ever seen. What did you get that day, a hundred fifty yards?"

"One hundred ninety-three, Judge. Three touchdowns. We still lost."

"Hell of a game."

"I didn't know you were a big football fan, Judge."

"I'm a Texan, born and raised, Scott, that makes me a football fan. Did you know I went to SMU?"

Scott chuckled. "Of course, I know, Judge. Every student at the law school knows about Samuel Buford—top grade point average in the history of the school, law review editor, clerk to Supreme Court Justice Douglas, Assistant Solicitor General under LBJ . . ."

"Whoa, son, you're making me feel old."

"Oh, sorry, sir."

"You did pretty well yourself, Scott, top of your class."

"Thank you, sir."

"So, Scott, you up for helping out an old judge?"

"Always happy to help in any way, sir."

Just then his mind's peripheral vision caught a movement, like a linebacker moving in to nail him from his blind side.

"Tough job, Scott, requires a tough lawyer, a lawyer who doesn't quit, who can handle pressure, who can take a hard hit and still get up—you proved all that on the football field. You know, Scott, pound for pound, I always figured you were the toughest player I'd ever seen, except maybe for Meredith."

Before he was the star quarterback for the Dallas Cowboys, Don Meredith had been the star quarterback at SMU from 1957 through 1959, a country boy out of Mount Vernon, one of the greatest athletes ever produced by the State of Texas, and generally regarded as the toughest quarterback ever to play the position. Meredith was still a living legend in Dallas, although he lived in Santa Fe.

"But, Scott, this job also requires a lawyer who believes like you do, that lawyers are supposed to protect the poor and defend the innocent and fight for justice."

"Absolutely, sir."

Back in his playing days, when the game was on the line, Scott Fenney, number 22, always pulled out all the stops to take home a victory. Even though he wasn't sure what he was playing for to-day—perhaps Buford wanted to appoint him independent counsel to investigate a high-profile political scandal, which could make Scott Fenney a very famous lawyer—his natural desire to win took over. He pulled out all the stops.

"Protecting the poor, defending the innocent, fighting for jus-tice—that's not just our professional duty, Judge, that's our sacred honor."

Shit, that sounded good! That's a winner for sure! Scott made a mental note to add that line to his campaign speech.

"Good to hear that, Scott. You've read about the McCall case, the senator's son murdered Saturday night?"

"Yes, sir, by the hooker."

"Yeah, black girl, twenty-four, a dozen priors for prostitution, drug possession . . . says she's innocent."

Scott chuckled. "Don't they all?"

"This case is going to be a media circus—black prostitute accused of murdering a senator's son, and not just any senator, mind you, but likely the next president."

"Yeah, I wouldn't want to be her lawyer."

"Well, Scott, that's why I called."

And what the judge wanted from Scott Fenney hit him with all the force of a linebacker on a blitz. *Blindsided by a federal judge!* Sweat beads erupted from the pores on his forehead. His pulse jumped. He reached up and loosened his silk tie.

"She needs a good lawyer, Scott. She needs you."

That's what he had won? That's the victory he would take home? On the verge of panic, Scott's sharp mind began devising ways to snatch defeat from the jaws of victory.

"But, Judge, what about the public defender's office?"

"Scott, I can't put a death penalty case in the hands of a wet-behind-the-ears PD lawyer who barely got through law school. This girl needs a real lawyer."

"But I'm a corporate lawyer. Why not appoint a criminal defense attorney?"

"I was going to . . . until I heard your speech. Defense lawyers, they're just hired guns. They don't care about defending the innocent or fighting for justice. They just want to get paid. Not like you, Scott. And most of them only work state court; you've got federal court experience."

"Why's a murder case in federal court?"

"Clark McCall was the FERC chairman, courtesy of the senator. Murder of a federal official is a federal crime."

"But, Judge—"

"And besides, Scott, you can make your mother proud."

"*What?*"

"You can be another Atticus Finch."

"But—"

"She has the right to counsel, and you're it, Scott. You're hereby appointed to represent the defendant in *United States of*

America versus Shawanda Jones. Meet your client tomorrow morning. Detention hearing's Wednesday, nine A.M."

Scott was walking quickly—*hell, he was damn near running*—down the carpeted corridors of the sixty-second floor to the marble-and-mahogany staircase leading to the sixty-third floor. He bounded up the stairs and hurried past tiny offices occupied by smart young lawyers churning out their monthly quota of billable hours like blue-collar workers punching a clock on a factory line. Tonight, as every night, the workers were pulling double shifts, much to the benefit of the partners. But that thought did not fill Scott's heart with the usual cheer; tonight his heart was filled with fear as he rushed into his senior partner's office.

Dan Ford was sixty years old. He and Gene Stevens had founded the firm thirty-five years ago, right out of SMU law school. Dan Ford had hired Scott eleven years ago when he had graduated from SMU, taken him under his wing, taught him the profitable practice of law, got him elected to the partnership, got him the mortgage on the house, got him into the dining, athletic, and country clubs, and got him a good deal on the Ferrari. He was Scott's mentor and father figure, and he was at his desk, his station in life from seven A.M. to seven P.M., Monday through Friday, and from seven A.M. until noon on Saturdays, fifty weeks a year. Dan Ford had billed three thousand hours a year for thirty-five straight years, a feat he compared favorably to DiMaggio's fifty-six-game hitting streak. The firm was his life.

Dan's shiny head came up and a broad smile crossed his face.

"Scotty, my boy!"

Scott fell onto the sofa.

"You don't look so good, son. Problem?"

Dan Ford had solved most of Scott's problems over the last eleven years. Scott was hoping this one would be no different.

"Judge Buford just appointed me to represent the hooker who killed Senator McCall's son."

The news took the breath out of Dan. He fell back in his chair. "You're joking."

"I wish."

"Why?"

Scott threw up his hands. "Because I gave my goddamn Atticus Finch speech at the bar luncheon! The judge was there."

"He believed it?"

"Apparently."

Dan ran his hands over his smooth skull.

"This is not good. Not good at all. We can't afford to piss off the next president, and we sure as hell can't afford to piss off Buford. Goddamn murder case, why isn't it in state court? We could work with that!"

State court judges in Texas were always amenable to a call from a powerful partner in a big law firm because state court judges are elected on campaign contributions from big law firms. The threat of moving the firm's contributions to the judge's opponent in the next election has a way of keeping judges in line. Electing state court judges is a constitutional tradition in Texas dating back to 1850 and served to keep the Texas legal system orderly and predictable if not terribly fair. Thus lawyers in big law firms do not fear state court judges just as one does not fear one's own house pet.

But federal judges were a different breed. They're not elected. They're appointed by the president under Article Three of the United States Constitution—for life. They can't be voted off the bench. They don't need campaign contributions from big law firms. They don't fear powerful lawyers. Cross a federal judge and you live with it for thirty or forty years—you'll never win another case in his court. A large law firm like Ford Stevens with an active federal court practice could not afford to offend Judge Sam Buford.

"We've got a dozen pending cases on his docket. Big-dollar

41

cases. We become personae non gratae in Buford's court, we lose our federal practice until the bastard dies."

"Or retires."

"Buford will die on the bench, just like Gene."

Gene Stevens, the firm's cofounder, had died at his desk last year, a pen in his hand, his hand on his daily time sheet, recording his last billable hour. Within twenty-four hours, his office had been cleaned out and Scott had moved in.

"Buford said it'll be a media circus," Scott said.

"Yeah, lots of publicity for the firm—all the wrong kind." Dan's pale face was pinking up like a newborn's. "Goddamnit, this firm cannot defend that whore!"

Dan closed his eyes, placed his hand over his face, and rubbed his temples. His thinking mode. And when Dan Ford thought hard, he always emerged with the correct answer. Scott's senior partner possessed a mind engineered like the Mercedes-Benz he drove: powerful, efficient, dependable, and wholly without a moral component. So Scott sat quietly while Dan's mind worked. He turned his eyes upward and checked out the walls for new trophy kills. Dan was a big-game hunter; mounted on the walls were stuffed heads of the wild animals he had bagged over the years, all looking down on Scott. It was kind of creepy.

After a moment, Dan removed his hand. He was smiling.

"Get her to plead out."

"She says she's innocent, wants a trial."

"So? Look, Scotty, go see her, explain the real likelihood the case will be lost and that she'll be sentenced to death or best case, spend the rest of her life in prison. That by pleading out she'll be released by the time she's fifty and she can still have a life . . . You know, turn on that famous charm, pretend you care."

"And if she doesn't go for it?"

"She goddamn well better go for it! I'm not going to have this firm's revenues damaged by some two-bit hooker!"

Dan's face was now a bright red, and he was pointing a finger at Scott, a sure sign it was time to leave. Scott stood and eased toward the door.

"You tell her she's pleading out whether she likes it or not!"

Scotty nodded and slid out. He was ten paces down the hall when he heard Dan's voice again: "Cop a plea, Scotty!"

FIVE

S COTT STEERED the red Ferrari out of the parking garage, gave Osvaldo, the attendant, his customary salute, and turned north. While most downtown workers commuted to their homes in the distant suburbs via the Dallas North Tollway or the North Central Expressway, hopelessly stuck in bumper-to-bumper traffic for hours and suppressing the road rage that left a number of drivers dead each year on Dallas highways, Scott Fenney drove leisurely up Cedar Springs Road and Turtle Creek Boulevard and Lakeside Drive and then past Robert E. Lee Park, homeward bound over the same route important men of Dallas had traveled for a hundred years. Ten minutes later, he crossed a two-lane swath of asphalt and, as if his fairy godmother had waved her magic wand, his world abruptly changed: land values quintupled, home values quadrupled, per capita income tripled, students' achievement test scores doubled, and the population turned all white.

He had entered the Town of Highland Park.

Developed in 1906 on thirteen hundred acres of high land above downtown Dallas, Highland Park today is a sanctuary of elegant homes, landscaped lawns, and broad avenues canopied by towering oak trees. On its wide sidewalks European nannies and Mexican maids can be seen pushing the heirs of the great Texas fortunes in strollers while their fathers—billionaires and millionaires and the lawyers who tend to them—work in the downtown skyscrapers and their mothers play tennis at the country club and shop at Anne Fontaine, Luca Luca, and Bottega Veneta in the Highland Park Village shopping center, its Spanish Mediterranean architecture and quaint stucco buildings with terra-cotta roofs and decorative wrought iron harking back to a distant time and place when great wealth was reserved for people of a certain class, not just anyone who could dunk a basketball. Visitors from California say the town reminds them of Beverly Hills, and with good reason: the same architect who designed Beverly Hills designed Highland Park. Only difference is, the founders of Beverly Hills did not file deed restrictions that legally limited home ownership in their new town to white people only; the founders of Highland Park did.

Almost a hundred years later, the Town of Highland Park is a two-square-mile island entirely surrounded by the 384-square-mile City of Dallas. It's an island of white in an ocean of color: Dallas, a city of 1.2 million residents, is now only 39 percent white; while Highland Park, a town of 8,850 residents, remains 98 percent white, with not a single home owned by a black person. It's an island of wealth—on any given day over a hundred homes in Highland Park will be listed for sale at prices exceeding $1 million. It's an island immune from the crime and social ills that afflict Dallas—Highland Park kids call their hometown "the Bubble," happy to be insulated from the outside world that beckons at the town boundary—albeit an island without a river or stream or even a moat to keep the outside world out, only the highest home prices in Texas, a well-armed police force, and a long-standing reputation that if you're black or brown and don't live there, you'd damn well better be passing through.

The Highland Park police did not stop the Ferrari: Scott Fenney was white and he lived there. Like other white men of means, he made his money in Dallas but came home to Highland Park, raised his family in Highland Park, and sent his child to Highland Park schools. He turned right onto Beverly Drive and into the driveway of his two-and-a-half-story, 7,500-square-foot, six-bedroom, six-bath, $3.5 million residence. He had bought the home three years ago for $2.8 million when the previous owner had filed bankruptcy and the bank had foreclosed. Dan Ford had called in a personal favor and persuaded the bank to sell the house to Scott with one-hundred-percent financing at prime plus five. Sitting on one acre in the heart of Highland Park, the place had been a steal at that price. Scott had jumped in with both feet, into debt up to his neck. In many towns in Texas, men who owe large sums of money are looked on with suspicion; in Dallas, such men are looked on with awe.

Scott drove up the brick-paved driveway and into the rear motor court. He cut the engine, but he didn't get out. Usually when he arrived home each evening and again admired his residence, he was filled with a sense of pride, that through brains and hard lawyering, he had achieved the perfect home for a perfect life.

But this evening was different.

For only the second time in his life, a distinct feeling of impending doom darkened his mind, just as it had when he was ten and his mother had picked him up early from school and said his father had been hurt. He knew his father was dead.

Butch Fenney had been a construction worker. A cable snapped and a load of lumber fell, crushing him. Scott's mother did the best she could, but they had to sell their small house in East Dallas. She worked for an orthopedic surgeon who lived in Highland Park and owned a teardown over by SMU, a tiny sixty-year-old home that would fall over if given a good push. The house was worthless, but the 75- by 125-foot lot it sat on was worth at least $250,000. The doctor planned to hold the property until his retirement, when he would demolish the house and sell the lot for a substantial profit. The good doctor rented the home to the Fenney family, mother and son.

So Scott Fenney attended Highland Park schools with the sons and daughters of governors and senators and millionaires and billionaires, scions of the great Dallas families like the Hunts and Perots and Crows. He was the poor kid on the block, the kid who didn't wear designer jeans and $100 Nike sneakers, who didn't go to Europe for spring break, who didn't get a $50,000 BMW for his sixteenth birthday. But Scott Fenney possessed something no snotty rich boy could ever buy with daddy's money: athletic ability. Remarkable God-given physical talent revealed with a run the town would never forget. High school football. Friday night fever. Legitimate, structured violence, organized by men, inflicted by boys, cheered by all—and a tried-and-true method for pulling oneself up by one's bootstraps in Texas. Scott was strong and he was tough and he was fast. He became the star running back for Highland Park High, the best since Doak Walker.

After high school, he went to SMU. Most Highland Park kids are deathly afraid of leaving the safety and security of the Bubble, so going off to college for them means moving out of their parents' home in Highland Park, driving the Beemer a few blocks, and moving into a sorority or fraternity house on the SMU campus in Highland Park. Scott Fenney went to SMU because the school offered him a football scholarship. He starred on the varsity for four years; his 193 yards against Texas made him a legend. He was also popular enough to be elected class president and smart enough to graduate first in his class. When the pros passed on the six foot two, 185-pound white running back with jagged scars down both knees, he enrolled in SMU law school.

Now, you don't go to Southern Methodist University School of Law if you plan on pursuing a legal career in New York or D.C. or L.A. or even Houston for that matter: it's not exactly the Harvard of the Southwest. In fact, they say it's a hell of a lot easier to get into the law school at SMU than it is one of the sororities or fraternities at SMU. You go to SMU law school if and only if you want to practice law in Dallas, Texas, because SMU lawyers have begotten SMU lawyers for so many decades now that the Dallas legal community is more incestuous than the Alabama backwoods of the fifties.

Scott graduated number one in his law school class, which earned him job offers from every big firm in Dallas. He chose Ford Stevens because they offered him $5,000 more. Eleven years later, Scott Fenney was no longer the poor kid on the block.

Scott entered the house through the back door that led into a mud room and then into the spacious kitchen, where he found Consuela cooking and the small TV tuned to a Mexican game show.

"*Buenas noches, señorita*. What's for dinner?"

Her brown face turned up from the stainless-steel stove, and she smiled. "Enchiladas, Señor Fenney. *Especial* for you."

He walked over, put an arm around her, and said, "Consuela, don't worry. Esteban will be back soon."

She fought back tears. "*Sí.* He will come."

Consuela de la Rosa was twenty-eight, short, and chubby. She lived in the pool cabana out back, just like countless other illegal Mexican maids throughout the Town of Highland Park, which effectively granted them political asylum from the INS. Their presence was certainly no secret; strolling the aisles of the Highland Park gourmet grocery store on a weekday when the maids did the family shopping qualified as a conversational Spanish lesson these days. The real threat to his maid was not the INS but Esteban's

49

hormones. If her *hombre* got her pregnant, Consuela would have to leave town per the tacit agreement in Highland Park: Spanish spoken in the grocery store was acceptable; Spanish spoken in the schools was not.

"Mrs. Fenney home?"

"No. Señora, she gone all day. She hit the golf ball."

"With all the golf lessons she's taken, she ought to be on the women's pro tour by now."

In keeping with his daily routine, Scott climbed the back stairs two steps at a time to the second floor. He walked down the hall and up another set of stairs to the top floor that was his nine-year-old daughter's domain. Hers was not a kid's room; there were no posters on the wall of Britney Spears or the Olsen twins. There were books, books on the bookshelves, books on her desk, books on her night table, books on the floor. Even at nine, she was a serious child, thoughtful, smart beyond her breeding. Scott found her at her desk tucked under the dormer, barefooted and wearing overall shorts and a green Dallas Mavericks tee shirt, notwithstanding her mother's threats to disown her if she didn't start dressing in designer outfits from Neiman Marcus like the other Highland Park girls her age. But she had steadfastly refused, saying she had her own identity, to which her mother would always retort, "As what, a boy?"

"Hey, Boo."

Barbara Boo Fenney. She was named after his mother, who had died before Boo was born. Scott's mother had not lived to see her son's mansion or her granddaughter. Boo spun around in her swivel chair, her shoulder-length red hair whipping around, and she gave him a smile that shot straight to his heart. Scott loved his wife, but Boo was the love of his life.

"Hey, A. Scott."

He cupped her face, leaned down, and kissed her forehead.

"Did you have a good day, baby?"

"Oh, I read and played computer games, watched TV, cooked with Consuela, you know, the usual . . . until Esteban called. Thanks for calming Consuela down—she'd still be crying."

Scott nodded. "Your mother's been gone all day?"

She gave him a look. *"Duh."*

"It's summer, she ought to spend more time with you."

"Well, I'm not on the Cattle Barons' Ball committee." She smiled. "How was your day?"

"Okay."

"Did you do important lawyer stuff?"

"Oh, yeah."

"Like what?"

Scott recalled his day—billing twelve hours for the nine he was at the office; giving his Atticus Finch speech at the bar luncheon; flirting with Missy while reeling in a law student like a hooked fish; voting to fire John Walker; flirting with Dibrell's receptionist; hiding lead contamination behind the attorney-client privilege; threatening to destroy a young woman by revealing her sexual history at trial in order to obtain a favorable settlement—and quickly decided, as he always decided, that a lawyer's day was best left at the law office. So he said, "Oh, just the things lawyers do."

"Unh-huh." She gave him another look. "You just tell me what you want me to know, don't you?"

He gave her a smile. "Yep."

She frowned. "It's not fair."

"What's not fair?"

"I'm stuck here all day while Mother meets her lady friends for lunch and plays golf and you go to your office and do your lawyer work. Mother comes home and wants to tell me all about her day, but I want to know about your day, and you won't tell me. It's not fair."

Scott sat on the edge of Boo's bed and looked at his daughter, her cute little face contorted into a frown. He knew she wasn't really mad, but it still bothered him. So he thought through his day again and decided he could tell her one thing.

"Okay, I'll tell you something about my day. I got appointed to represent a criminal defendant, the woman who murdered Senator McCall's son."

Her face brightened and all was well again.

"You're not a criminal lawyer."

"Some people say all lawyers are criminal."

Boo smiled. "You know what I mean."

"Well, I'm hoping there won't be a trial, that she'll cop a plea."

"What's cop a plea?"

"Say she's guilty."

"Is she?"

"Probably."

"Are you gonna ask her?"

"Maybe . . . I mean, yeah, sure."

"Why do you want her to cop a plea? I thought you make more money when a case goes to trial."

"Not this trial. I'm doing it for free."

"Why?"

"Judge Buford's making me."

"He can do that?"

"Yeah. I practice in federal court, so he can do that. It's a rule."

"Support his opponent in the next election."

He had taught her well.

"Judge Buford's a federal judge, appointed for life."

"Shit."

"Boo, don't cuss."

"Mother does."

"Well, she shouldn't. And you shouldn't either. It makes you sound trashy."

"They cuss in the movies, even the PGs. And all the other kids cuss."

"That doesn't make it right. Don't be a follower, Boo. Don't do the wrong thing just because everyone else does. Do the right thing."

"I don't say the F-word."

Scott smiled. "Well, that's good."

"I don't even know what it means."

"I hope not."

"Sally down the street, she says her dad says the F-word all the time when he thinks she's not around. And sometimes even when she is. You don't say the F-word when I'm not around, do you?"

"No, of course not."

A small lie.

"So she doesn't have any money to pay you?"

"Who, the defendant? No."

"Doesn't she have a job?"

"She's a, uh . . ."

"Prostitute. I heard it on TV. And a drug addict. What's a prostitute?"

When Boo asked him questions like that, Scott was never quite sure how to answer. She always seemed to know when he wasn't telling the whole truth, but, even though she was born twenty-five years old, he was reluctant to always tell the truth. So he answered like a lawyer. He fudged the truth.

"A personal escort."

"What's that?"

"She entertains men."

"Like you entertain clients?"

A closer analogy than she knew. "Well, sort of."

"Do you have any clients like her?"

"No, Boo, I don't represent prostitutes and drug addicts."

"I mean, black clients?"

"Oh. No, I've never had a black client."

"Why not?"

"Well, because I represent corporations, not people."

"What about those people who call you all the time?"

"My clients are corporations, but my contacts are executives at the corporations."

Boo screwed her mouth up. She was thinking.

"Why?"

"Why what?"

"Why do you represent corporations instead of people?"

"Because people can't afford me. Heck, Boo, I couldn't afford to hire myself, not at three-fifty an hour."

Her eyes got big. "You charge three dollars and fifty cents *an hour*?"

Scott chuckled. "No. Three *hundred* and fifty dollars an hour."

"*For real?* Is that why you work so slowly?"

Nine years old and she was qualified to be the managing partner at the biggest law firm in the country.

She said, "So we're rich because corporations can pay you three hundred fifty dollars an hour?"

"Yes . . . well, no, we're not rich, Boo."

"We live in a big house and you drive a Ferrari."

"Yeah, but I've got to work to keep all this. Rich people don't."

"Cindy's dad got fired and they had to sell their house."

"Don't worry, baby, that'll never happen to us."

From the Jacuzzi tub, his wife said, "You've got to talk to her, Scott, she'll listen to you! How am I ever going to be selected chair of the Cattle Barons' Ball if my daughter dresses like a boy!"

Rebecca Fenney was thirty-three, fit, and gorgeous, still the most beautiful woman in Highland Park—the perfect wife for a perfect life. And she desperately wanted to chair the next Cattle Barons' Ball, the biggest society party put on each year in Dallas, the one night when the sophisticated men and women of Highland

Park get to dress up like cowboys and cowgirls and play Texan to the hilt. The twangs become stronger, the cigars longer, the skirts shorter, and the diamonds bigger; and everyone tries to out-Texan one another, arriving in Hummer limousines, Rolls-Royces, and even helicopters at Southfork Ranch, J. R. Ewing's home on the TV show *Dallas*, or another fitting venue. They drink champagne and whiskey, eat fried alligator and fajitas, ride the mechanical bucking bull, bet on the armadillo races, and dance to the likes of the Oak Ridge Boys or Dwight Yoakam or Willie Nelson.

The men compete with money, betting at the craps table in the casino or bidding at the auction offering diamonds and Porsches. The women compete with clothes. They wear black, blue, red, pink, and white cowboy boots made of lizard, ostrich, elephant, kangaroo, and suede; they wear low-cut satin bustiers, lambskin halters, leather vests, and evening gowns; they wear matching cowboy hats. Last year Rebecca wore a powder blue fringed suede miniskirt, matching cowboy boots, a low-cut pink fringed halter top, and a pink suede cowboy hat—and she was furious because no one noticed her. Scott was always amused by it all, but the Cattle Barons' Ball was deadly serious business to the women of Highland Park, all competing to be the belle of the ball. The lucky woman who chairs the ball is forever enshrined among the society elite of Highland Park—except maybe for one former chairwoman who got nabbed for shoplifting at Neiman Marcus. Providing she kept her criminal record clean, Rebecca Fenney was the front-runner to be the chairwoman of the next Cattle Barons' Ball.

Scott and Rebecca were in the master bathroom on the second floor; she was naked in the Jacuzzi tub, he was irritated in a robe. Scott had tried to talk to his wife about his day, but she had shown no interest at all. The McCall case had him irritated; his wife had ratcheted it up a notch. All she wanted to talk about was the Cattle Barons' Ball and the latest Highland Park scandal, another extramarital affair, which wasn't exactly shocking news to Scott.

Rebecca said, "Muffy, you remember her, from the last party at the club."

Scott didn't recall Muffy and wasn't particularly interested in trying to recall her. He shook his head.

"Bleached blonde, boob job, acts snotty all the time . . ."

"Well, that narrows it down to only ninety-five percent of the women in Highland Park."

"She's married to Bill what's-his-name, old, bald, fat."

"Oh, yeah, I remember her. She was wearing that tight two-piece outfit, nice abs. She's about twenty years younger than Bill. So she was stepping out on him?"

"He caught her in bed with the neighbor."

"Again, not exactly shocking, Rebecca."

She gave him a sly smile, which from prior experience told Scott that she was about to deliver the punch line.

"He didn't catch her with the man who lives next door. He caught her with the woman who lives next door."

"She was in bed with another woman?"

"Yes! I called to tell you, but Sue said you were busy."

"Rebecca, don't bother me at work with gossip."

"It's not gossip if it's true, you said so yourself."

"That's defamation, Rebecca—truth is an absolute defense to slander and libel claims. There's no defense for gossip."

"Not even a lesbian affair?"

"Don't they have a girl about Boo's age?"

"They did. Muffy and her girlfriend ran off to California."

"She left her kid? Why?"

Rebecca shrugged. "Everyone knows. She can't show her face in this town again. Besides, she's a lesbian; the child's better off without her."

"Rebecca, is that all you do at your lunches, gossip?"

"No . . . just during dessert. We call it scandal soufflé."

She seemed pleased with herself, which made one of them. The thought of his wife sitting at lunch gossiping while Boo sat at home alone jacked up Scott's irritation level to a new high. He was about to say something guaranteed to grate on her, but seeing her slick wet body as she climbed out of the tub, her red hair stuck to her face, her full breasts pink from the hot water, her abdomen flat from hours on her Ab Master, and her firm bottom that hadn't dropped an inch since their wedding day eleven years ago, desire drove the McCall case, the Cattle Barons' Ball, scandal soufflé, and all lingering irritation from his mind. He let his robe slip off his shoulders and looked down: he had a full erection. He went over to her, wrapped his arms around her from behind, pressed himself against her, and reached around and cupped her genitals, an act which not that long ago would have produced a soft moan leading to sex on the marble vanity. Tonight it produced only an exasperated sigh.

"Not tonight, Scott. I'm tired."

She had been tired a lot the last six months. He released her and walked into the bedroom and over to the sitting area against the bank of windows. He sat and listened to the *tak tak tak* of June bugs banging against the outside glass, seeking the light like reformed sinners. He used the remote to turn on the television and then he looked down: his erection had melted away like a Popsicle on a hot summer day.

It hadn't always been this way. They had met in his third year of law school, at a party at his old frat house after a football game. She was a senior cheerleader and the reigning Miss SMU. Scott Fenney was a football legend and a campus celebrity, so approaching the most beautiful coed at SMU was easy. They had sex in an upstairs bathroom that night. And at every other imaginable venue in the months that followed: in her car; in his car; at her sorority house; at his apartment; in a stairwell at the law school; in the park in broad daylight; on the eighteenth green at the country club late at night after jumping the fence—to this day he could not putt out

57

on that green without thinking of that night. They were so hot, they couldn't get enough of each other.

But somewhere along the way—when, he wasn't sure—the heat had faded. And now they slept back to back, separated by two feet of king-sized mattress like a demilitarized zone. They weren't mad at each other—they seldom had words—but they seldom had sex. She had just drifted away.

He sat slumped and limp as all the irritating thoughts—the McCall case, his wife's lack of interest in his day, being denied sex again, scandal soufflé, and his daughter home alone all day—came rushing back. He yelled to his wife in the bathroom: "Why don't you spend more time with Boo? Maybe she'll listen to you then."

Rebecca appeared in the bathroom door, still naked, her hands on her hips.

"She's never listened to me. I've got these hideous stretch marks because of her, but she's your child. By the time I was her age, I had won two beauty pageants. She wears overalls. And, besides, I'm busy this summer. Why don't you spend more time with her?"

"I'm working."

"Oh, I see. What I do isn't important."

"Sounds like all you do is gossip."

"Only during dessert. During lunch we plan the ball."

"A big society party."

"Which raises money for charity."

"Which you don't give a damn about. It's just another step up the Highland Park social ladder for you. You're social climbing and Boo's being raised by Consuela!"

She glared at him, whirled, and disappeared into the bathroom. Scott was about to yell after her, *You need to spend as much time with your daughter as you do gossiping with those old society broads*, but then she'd say, *Well, you need to spend as many billable hours with me as you do with your clients*, and then he'd say, *Those clients pay for this house and those cars and your dresses and . . .*

"McCall . . ."

The reporter's voice pulled Scott out of his thoughts and focused his attention on the television.

"His son's murder," the reporter was saying, "has given the senator a sympathy boost in the polls, thus solidifying his position as the clear front-runner for the White House."

SIX

THE NOVEMBER 22, 1963, edition of the *Dallas Morning News* included a full-page black-bordered advertisement titled "Welcome Mr. Kennedy to Dallas." It was not a welcome. It was an indictment of President Kennedy that had been paid for by several right-wing Dallas oilmen, "America-thinking citizens" they called themselves. They accused Kennedy of being soft on Communism, despite the president's successful standoff with the Russians over the Cuban missile crisis. On Air Force One's flight to Dallas, an aide showed the ad to the president. Kennedy read it and remarked, "We're heading into nut country today." The ad identified the mayor of Dallas as a Kennedy sympathizer.

Earle Cabell was the mayor. He met President Kennedy at Love Field that morning and rode in the presidential motorcade, three cars behind the president's blue limousine. As his car turned onto Elm Street, Cabell heard three gunshots ring out from the Texas School Book Depository. He arrived at Parkland Memorial Hospital just as the president was being removed from his limousine. Cabell remained at the hospital until the president's body was taken away. He had hoped to show the president that Dallas was no longer the "Southwest hate capital of Dixie." He had failed. But they still named the federal building in downtown Dallas after him—Cabell, not the president.

Of course, when A. Scott Fenney, Esq., arrived at the Earle Cabell Federal Building on Commerce Street shortly after nine the next morning, he didn't know who Earle Cabell was or why they had named this dull-as-dirt twenty-one-story structure after him. All he knew was that he didn't want to be in Earle's building that day and all he cared about was getting his client to cop a plea and then getting himself the hell out of there. He exited the elevator on the fifth floor, the federal detention center. After passing through the metal detector and having his briefcase searched, he was met by a black guard.

"Scott Fenney to see Shawanda Jones."

"You her lawyer?"

Scott wanted desperately to scream, *Hell, no, I'm not her lawyer!* Instead, he nodded. The guard led him down a narrow hallway to a small room, bare except for a metal table and two metal chairs. Scott entered and stared at the bare walls until the door opened and a black woman entered, bringing with her a foul body odor that filled the room like thick smoke. She looked him up and down, covered her mouth with both hands, and sneezed violently several times. Then she said, "You the lawyer?"

"Yes, I am."

Shawanda Jones was twenty-four but she appeared much older. She was a small woman, rising only to Scott's shoulders. Her hair was neither kinky nor slicked straight; it was brown, hung just over her ears, and appeared soft, although obviously it had gone untouched by a brush for days. Her eyes were creamy ovals with big brown centers, but they seemed hollowed out and vacant. The area below her eyes was a darker brown than the rest of her face, which was tan and smooth and glistening with a light coating of sweat. Her nose was narrow and her lips thin. Her body seemed slim but shapely under the baggy white jail uniform. Her face was angular with prominent cheekbones. She was attractive, but at one time in her life, she must have been beautiful. She reminded Scott of Halle Berry on a bad day. A very bad day.

Scott was not wearing his glasses that morning; he didn't care whether this client thought he looked smart or not. And he did not extend a hand to her even though he always shook hands with a new client: Dan Ford had explained to Scott early in his legal career that a lawyer had only one opportunity to make a good first impression on a new client, so he should always look the client directly in the eye and give him a firm handshake, which, Dan said, would project a sense of forthrightness and honesty, thus making the client less likely to question his legal bills. Instead, fearing that her hand— one of the hands into which she had just sneezed like she had pneumonia—might transmit a communicable disease, Scott gestured for his new client to sit down. But she did not sit. She paced.

She walked from one side of the room to the other and back again. Back and forth she went, again and again, rubbing her arms as if the room were cold instead of warm and kneading her fingers like Consuela saying the rosary. Her eyes darted about the room. Her legs seemed out of sync, and they twitched uncontrollably. Halfway back, she suddenly doubled over and groaned.

"You okay?"

She grunted. "Cramps."

Like most men when a woman speaks of her period, Scott didn't know how to respond. So he said, "My wife has bad cramps each month."

Between groans, she said, "Not from this she don't."

After a moment the cramps apparently subsided, and she resumed her pacing. Scott sat, removed his business card from his pocket, and pushed it to her side of the table. On her next pass by the table, she abruptly pulled out the chair, sat, and flopped her arms on the table. Scott noticed dark spots on the insides of both of her forearms, like someone was going to play connect the dots but had never connected them. Then he remembered: she's a heroin addict. She picked up his business card with her thumb and forefinger and held it before her face.

"What the *A* stand for?" she asked.

"Nothing."

"Your first name be a letter?"

Scott didn't want to discuss his name. He wanted to get this over with and get back to his office on the sixty-second floor of Dibrell Tower where he belonged.

"Ms. Jones, I'm Scott Fenney. The court appointed me to represent you. You've been charged with murder, a federal offense because the victim was a federal official. If found guilty, you could be sentenced to death or life in prison. Which is why I want to talk to you about pleading out to a lesser offense. You could be out in thirty years."

Her hands abruptly shot out and grabbed Scott's wrists. He instinctively recoiled from the woman with the wild eyes, but she was strong for her size and she had a firm grip. She said, "Get me a fix, please? I ain't sleep in two days!"

"A fix?"

"Some H! I need it bad!"

"You mean *dope*? No, I can't do that!"

"Thought you my lawyer!"

"You've had lawyers give you dope?"

"For sex. C'mon, I suck you right here!"

"No!"

She jumped up and resumed her pacing. Scott had to take a minute to gather himself. He'd had corporate clients offer him bribes (also known as legal fees) to destroy incriminating documents, suborn perjury, conceal fraudulent activities, and falsify filings with the SEC, but they were always well-dressed and well-educated white men—and none of them had ever offered him oral sex!

After he recovered, Scott said, "Now, as I was saying, you can plead out and—"

"Say I did it?"

"Yes, but not with the specific intent to murder."

She stopped and stared at him with her hands on her hips and an incredulous expression on her face.

"You telling me, say I killed him? Don't you wanna know if I did?"

"Uh, yeah, sure." He leaned back. "Tell me what happened."

She waved a hand at the bare table.

"You ain't writing nothin' down?"

Scott reached down to his briefcase and removed a yellow legal pad and black pen.

"Go ahead."

Shawanda Jones, prostitute, proceeded to pace the room and tell her lawyer the facts (according to her) of the night of Saturday, June 5.

"We was working Harry Hines—"

Harry Hines Boulevard, named after a Dallas oilman, begins just north of downtown and continues out to the loop, a north–south corridor that is culturally diverse, as they say. On this single stretch of pavement, you can obtain the finest medical care in the country at no fewer than four hospitals, earn a degree at the University of Texas medical school, purchase high fashion and fine furnishings at the Market Center or shop more economically at the Army-Navy store, play golf at the exclusive Brook Hollow Golf Club, eat a wide variety of ethnic food, buy cheap used cars, illegal drugs, fake IDs, and counterfeit designer purses, enjoy topless strip clubs and all-nude salons, lodge overnight at the Salvation Army homeless shelter, get an abortion, or pick up a prostitute.

"Who's we?"

"Me and Kiki."

"What's Kiki's last name?"

"How would I know? That ain't even her first name."

"What time?"

"Maybe, ten."

"P.M.?"

"Shawanda don't work no morning shift."

"What—"

"You want me to tell this here story or not?"

Scott held his hands up in surrender. Shawanda Jones continued her story, extremely agitated and animated, her arms flying about.

"Anyways, we was feeling good and looking good, me wearing my blonde wig, Kiki red. We was strolling, men driving by, whistling, yelling, 'Yo, mama, suck this!' Black dudes, Mexicans, they just window shoppers, can't afford no class girls like us. We wait for them white boys in nice cars. They like us 'cause we ain't dark and we in shape—me and Kiki, we do them exercise tapes most every day, got us a new one, *The Firm*? Use dumbbells. Check this out."

She pushed up the short sleeve of the jail uniform and curled her right arm and flexed her biceps, displaying an impressive bulge for a girl. Great, a heroin addict who worked out.

"So, maybe ten-thirty, white boy driving a Mercedes, one of them long black jobs got them blacked-out windows, he pull up alongside us and roll down the window and look us over. We know one of us is fixing to get picked up. He say, 'Blondie, get in.' Well, Shawanda don't just get in when some trick say get in, so I saunter on over, lean in the window, car smell like a whiskey factory. He say he pay a thousand dollars for all night. I say, 'Show me the money.' I got that from that movie? He pull out a roll of bills could choke a horse, so I get in, almost slide down to the floor, my leather skirt on that leather seat. He reach over, grab my tit, say, 'Them real?' I say, 'Honey, all a Shawanda real.' "

She abruptly groaned, grabbed at her midsection, and doubled over again.

"Shit!"

She remained in that position for a long moment. Scott had often suffered leg cramps back when he played ball, and man, they could really hurt. So he had some amount of empathy for her. Still, he checked his watch and thought of billable hours going unbilled and wished she would get on with it. Finally the cramps abated, and she straightened and started talking nonstop again.

"Anyways, we drive off. I figure we goin' to a motel? 'Stead we go to Highland Park, street sign say. I ain't never been in no Highland Park—black girl know better'n to go there. Pretty soon we drive up to the biggest damn house I ever seen, through big gates, behind a big wall, go round back. Get out, I follows him inside, place is fine. He ask me I want something to drink, I say okay. I'm thinking, white boy got money and place like this and good-looking to boot—what he want with Shawanda?

"We get upstairs, in bed, I find out. He climb on top and start working hard, he say, 'You like it?' Course, I say, 'Oh, yeah, baby, you so big.' Tricks, they like to hear that shit. Then he say, 'Tell me again, nigger, you like my white dick?' Now I don't much like nobody calling me nigger, but for a thousand bucks I don't say nothing but, 'Oh, yeah, baby.' Then he slap me, hard, say he always give it rough to his women. Well, nobody slap Shawanda. I punch that white boy in his mouth, knock him outta me and flat off the bed, jump up and say, 'Ain't gonna get rough with Shawanda, honky!'

"He come at me again, all mean now, so I scratch his face, then I pop him a good one, BAM!" She made a roundhouse swing with her left fist. "Right in the eye. We fall over the bed and he hits me again, with his fist this time, right here." She was pointing to the left side of her face, where a bruise was evident. "But I got my knee right in his balls, he fall off and start cussing me: 'You nigger bitch!' I grab my clothes, my thousand dollars, his car keys, drive back to Kiki and leave the car."

"And that's the last time you saw Clark McCall?"

"That his name?"

"Yeah. He was the son of Senator Mack McCall."

A blank face. She didn't know Mack McCall from Mickey Mouse.

"Last I seen him, Mr. Fenney, he was rolling on the floor, holding his privates and cussing me something fierce."

"He was murdered that night. Police found him Sunday, naked on the bedroom floor, shot once in the head, point-blank, .22-caliber gun next to him, with your fingerprints on it."

"Must of dropped outta my purse."

"So it was your gun?"

"Girl work the streets in Dallas, she gotta carry."

"But you didn't shoot him?"

"No, sir, Mr. Fenney."

"You're innocent?"

"Yes, sir, Mr. Fenney. And I ain't coppin' no plea."

"But, Ms. Jones—"

"Miz Jones my mama. You call me Shawanda. And I ain't pleading out. And what about bail? When I get outta here? I'm in bad need of some—"

"Dope?"

"Mr. Fenney, you looking at me like I ain't nothing but worthless dirt, but you ain't never been where I been."

Scott sighed. This wasn't going as planned.

"I'll check on the bail hearing, but don't count on getting out on a murder charge. And if the court grants bail, it'll be high. Do you have any assets?"

She slapped her butt. "This here Shawanda's only asset."

"A nice ass won't get you out of jail."

"It will in some counties." He thought she was joking, but she didn't smile. "So I be locked up till the trial? Mr. Fenney, I gotta see my baby!"

"You have a child?"

"Name Pajamae, she nine."

Scott put the pen to the pad. "How do you spell that?"

"P-a—j-a—m-a-e. *Pa—shu—may*. It's French."

"Where is she?"

"Our place down in the projects. We been through this before, but only couple days. I tell her, 'Don't even open that door, girl.'"

"Does this Kiki take care of her?"

"No, sir, Mr. Fenney. Kiki, she live with a man. I don't let no man in my place might hurt my Pajamae. Louis, he watch out for her, take her groceries, make sure she okay. He like her uncle but he ain't."

Scott pushed the pad and pen across the table.

"Write down your address . . . and Louis's phone number."

Shawanda stopped her pacing, sat, took the pen in her left hand, and began writing, but her hand was shaking like an old person with tremors. Scott realized the awkwardness of the moment.

"My daughter's left-handed, too."

She stopped and stared at her hand. After a moment, she stopped writing, put the pen down, and looked back up at Scott with wet eyes.

"Mr. Fenney, the smack, it just own me."

Then she doubled over and vomited.

———

Dan Ford was on the phone when Scott arrived at his senior partner's office and dropped his body onto the sofa like a load of cement.

Dan was saying into the phone: "Of course we support your reelection, Governor. Your fine leadership gave the business community everything we asked for from the legislature—no new taxes, tort reform . . . Yes . . . Yes . . . All right, I'll see you tomorrow."

Dan hung up the phone and shook his head in amazement.

"That boy couldn't find oil at an Exxon station." A long sigh. "But he is the governor." Finally, he focused his attention on Scott. "Did she go for it?"

"No. She won't cop a plea."

A knowing nod. "Figured she might not."

Scott had braced himself for one of Dan Ford's profanity-laced tirades, but his senior partner didn't seem all that upset.

"What should I do?"

"Hire her out," Dan said.

"Hire her out?"

"Yeah, hire a criminal defense attorney to take your place. It's a simple mathematical calculation, Scotty."

"Dan, what the hell are you talking about?"

Dan stood and stepped over to the grease board mounted on the wall under the head of an elk, opened the wood doors, and picked up a marker. Writing as he spoke, he said, "Say the case takes a thousand lawyer-hours, worst-case scenario. We pay a defense lawyer—now I'm not talking a summa cum laude graduate; I'm talking anyone with a license—fifty dollars an hour—"

"*Fifty an hour?* We charge a hundred an hour for our summer clerks' time."

"They're top of their class. I'm talking a bottom-of-the-class lawyer, Scott, someone who needs fifty bucks an hour. So a thousand hours at fifty an hour, that's a fifty-thousand-dollar expense to the firm."

Scott knew his senior partner had thought this through because Dan Ford didn't part with fifty cents easily much less fifty grand. He was a lawyer who calculated the profit the firm generated on each copy machine—forty cents per page—and made damn sure the copiers ran around the clock, spitting out paper and adding almost a million dollars to the firm's annual bottom line. Ford Stevens marked up the cost of everything in its offices, animate and inanimate, turning a profit on every associate, paralegal, secretary, typist, courier, copy, fax, and phone call. And Dan Ford kept tabs on everyone and everything.

He was saying, "But that frees up those thousand lawyer-hours for you to work for our paying clients at three-fifty an hour. That's three hundred fifty thousand dollars in revenues for the firm. Deduct the fifty thousand we pay the defense lawyer, and the firm still nets three hundred thousand, versus losing the entire three hundred fifty thousand if you have to work the case."

Scott's spirits started to lift. "Will Buford go for that?"

"Sure. Before the federal court had a public defender's office, we got appointed all the time. Hiring them out was standard operating procedure for the big firms." Dan shrugged. "And besides, it's a win-win situation: she gets a lawyer who knows more about criminal defense than you do, and you get rid of her."

Dan closed the doors to the grease board and said, "You know a cheap criminal defense attorney?"

RO ERT HERR N, ATT NEY-AT-L W, the sign out front read because the landlord was too damn cheap to replace the letters that had been shot off. Didn't matter, it was the only sign printed in English, and most people in this part of town couldn't read it anyway. This attorney's office was not in the best part of town; it was in a piece-of-shit strip center in East Dallas. He was a street lawyer; hence his office was at street level. He would often arrive to find someone sleeping on the stoop. He never kicked them awake as the other business owners in the strip did: hell, the guy might be his next best client. And he never called the police, which would be a monumental waste of a phone call; the police only kept the peace in the parts of town that mattered. He simply stepped over them and entered the law offices of Robert Herrin, Esq.

His professional address was a thirty- by twenty-foot space, one room and a tiny john, lodged between a Mexican bar and a Korean donut shop; he ate donuts for breakfast and drank beer for dinner. The roof leaked, the ceiling tiles were discolored, and the scent of mold permeated the place. The linoleum on the floor was cracked and curling at the corners like elves' shoes. His desk was metal, as was his chair, but it swiveled and had a nice seat cushion. Fortunately, he was a pretty fair typist because he couldn't afford a secretary. And here Robert Herrin, Attorney-at-Law, had eked out a legal living for the last eleven years, representing those members of society who wouldn't get past the security guards at a downtown law firm.

He was a fixture in this East Dallas neighborhood—he was *the lawyer*—same as the bar and donut shop were fixtures. The thin walls of his office afforded him the opportunity to pick up several foreign languages, although his Spanish skills far exceeded his Korean, probably because when he wasn't here he was usually next door in the bar shooting pool. As a general rule, Anglos were not welcome in a Mexican beer joint. But *Señor Herrin, el abogado,* was always welcome because the owner, the bartender, the waitresses, and most of the bar's customers were his clients. Which had the added benefit of keeping his plate-glass window free of bullet holes. He was the go-to lawyer when spouses, offspring, or siblings were busted, either because he showed them respect or because he offered a convenient payment plan. Often he would open the door (after stepping over the aforementioned drunk sleeping it off) and find fives and tens and every now and then a twenty on the floor with a note clipped to each so he could credit the correct client.

It was not the life he had dreamed of in law school.

The phone rang. If experience was any indication, Bobby Herrin would soon be driving over to the county jail to bail out one of his regulars. He reached for the phone.

SEVEN

BOBBY HERRIN felt like a lawyer in an out-of-town court-room.

He was standing in the lobby of the Downtown Club, located on the top floor of Dibrell Tower and hands-down the swankiest eating place in downtown, and watching the richest men in Dallas arrive for lunch, trailed by their lawyers like a rapper's entourage. These were lawyers who owned the biggest law firms in town, who billed three, four, maybe five hundred dollars an hour—Bobby made $500 on a good *week*—and who wore wool suits, starched shirts, silk ties, and shoes shined by the black shoe guy downstairs. Everything Bobby was wearing had been purchased years ago off the sale racks and was made of polyester, except his shoes, which hadn't been shined in months. He rubbed his right shoe against the back of his left trouser leg and repeated the attempt to bring some-thing resembling a shine with the other shoe.

"Bobby!"

He turned and was greeted by the brightest smile on the most handsome face imaginable, the face of the friend he had once cheered and admired and envied and followed like a rock star's groupie—and loved like a brother. Scotty Fenney. Bobby hadn't seen Scotty in eleven years, and now he had to resist the urge to embrace his former best friend. They shook hands.

"Glad you could make it," Scotty said. "You haven't been waiting long, have you, buddy?"

Bobby shook his head. But, in fact, he had. He'd arrived fifteen minutes ago, parked in the underground garage, and rode the express elevator right to the top. Which reminded him. He pulled his parking ticket from his shirt pocket.

"They validate?"

If not, the ten-dollar parking fee would damn near bankrupt Bobby that day. But Scotty didn't answer; he was looking Bobby up and down as if trying to come up with a compliment for his wardrobe. He finally gave up and slapped Bobby on the shoulder.

"C'mon, let's eat."

Scotty led the way to the maître d's station, down a short corridor. One wall was a gallery of framed portraits of the club's founders and board of directors, past and present, a regular Who's Who of Dallas.

"Ah, Mr. Fenney, a pleasure to see you today," a middle-aged Hispanic man said with a practiced smile, as if seeing Scotty was the highlight of his day. He was trim, his hair was parted neatly and slicked over, and his face was smooth and brown, clean-shaven with a pencil mustache. The scent of aftershave hovered over him. He was dressed in a dark suit, dark tie, and white shirt. He could be the local Latino undertaker. He tucked two menus bound in leather under his arm. "Two for lunch, sir?"

"Yes, Roberto."

Bobby followed Roberto and Scotty through the entryway and into a dining room illuminated by fancy chandeliers and floor-to-ceiling windows and filled with dark wood paneling, dark wood columns, and dark wood tables covered with white tablecloths. Young brown men in white waistcoats and black bow ties served old white men. Roberto snapped his fingers at his underlings and gestured at glasses that needed to be filled and plates removed. The alluring aroma of grilled steaks, fresh fried shrimp, and charbroiled fish and the symphony of silver utensils against crystal and china joined together to remind Bobby of what might have been had his life taken a different turn here or there. He usually had lunch at the barbecue joint down the block where you ate at picnic tables on paper plates with plastic utensils.

While Bobby felt like Ralph Nader at a chamber of commerce meeting, Scotty strode through the dining room like the star halfback onto a football field, greeting and shaking hands with everyone he passed—that familiar Scotty Fenney entrance Bobby had witnessed so many times in the old days and from the same vantage point: behind Scotty Fenney. Bobby recognized the faces of the men Scotty was greeting from the business section of the newspaper. These men owned Dallas—the land, the buildings, the businesses, and everything else worth owning in the city. Scotty's attention was suddenly drawn across the room. He said to Bobby, "I'll be right there," and went over to a table of four men.

Bobby followed Roberto to a table by the window through which Bobby could gaze out upon the city where he had lived his entire life. Born poor in East Dallas, he had moved with his parents to a rental duplex near SMU the summer before ninth grade. They wanted a better life for their son, but they couldn't afford private school on his father's truck driver's pay. Instead their son would be educated in the Highland Park public school system just like the sons of the richest men in Dallas.

Bobby had met Scotty Fenney that first year, two renters seeking similarly situated companions—renters occupied a social status in Highland Park only a step above the Mexican household help.

Bobby became Scotty's faithful follower, like Robin to Batman; and as Scotty's status rose with each football game, Bobby was pulled along in his friend's considerable wake, welcomed anywhere in Highland Park, as long as he was with Scotty Fenney.

After high school, Bobby had followed Scotty to SMU. Scotty got a football scholarship; Bobby got student loans. Four years later, he followed Scotty to law school. But a law degree had not led to a better life for him. The money is in the big law firms, and the big firms take only the best of the best, the top ten percent— the Scotty Fenneys, not the Bobby Herrins. All through law school, they had talked about practicing law together, but the big firms came calling and Scotty answered; and suddenly, like a Texas summer storm that dumps two inches of rain and then abruptly disappears, Scotty was gone. For the first time since he was fourteen, Bobby did not have Scotty Fenney to follow.

For eleven years now, Bobby had wandered through life like Moses in the Sinai Desert, trying to find his way without Scotty. He had caught glimpses of his old friend in the society section— Mr. and Mrs. A. Scott Fenney at such-and-such society ball—and sometimes in the business section—another courtroom victory or major deal engineered by A. Scott Fenney, Esq. Each time he read something about his old friend the memories would return and he would feel so completely alone again.

Still, through no real intent, Bobby had fashioned a life of sorts. Not much of a life—his exact thought that morning as he arrived at the office and stepped over a drunk on the doorstep, the start of another day of bailing out dopers at the jail, fighting evictions in J.P. court, eating Korean donuts, and drinking Mexican beer and playing pool in the bar next door. But then the phone rang and the caller identified herself as Scott Fenney's secretary. When she invited him to lunch with Scotty at the Downtown Club, Bobby thought he'd have to call 911 and have them hook him up to a defibrillator. He accepted, hung up the phone, took one look at his clothes, and immediately regretted his decision. He paced the office for an hour, deciding a dozen times to call back and cancel and a dozen times not to. When he finally pulled the old Impala into the parking garage under Dibrell Tower and the attendant looked it over and chuckled, he knew he was in over his head.

Bobby Herrin didn't belong at the Downtown Club.

He realized his finger was tapping the table like he was sending an urgent Morse code message. He craved a cigarette, but the Dallas city council had banned smoking in all public places. He desperately wanted to get up and walk out, to go back to East Dallas where he belonged. *Goddamnit, why had he accepted this lunch invitation?* Only because Scotty's secretary's call had caught him by surprise, he told himself, but he knew the truth: he wanted to see Scotty again.

He missed Scotty more than he missed his two ex-wives.

Bobby looked for Scotty and saw him several tables away, leaning over and whispering in the ear of a man whose face Bobby also recognized. Whatever Scotty said had made the man very happy. He stood and shook Scotty's hand, slapped him on the back, and damn near hugged him. Scotty walked over to Bobby with a big smile on his face and sat down across the table.

"You know Tom Dibrell?" Bobby asked.

"I'm his lawyer. Got him out of a crack yesterday. Literally." Scotty leaned over and whispered, "Tom's got a problem keeping his prick out of the payroll."

"Scotty, he's the guy who paid SMU players, got the football team the death penalty! You hated assholes like him back then. Now you're working for him? *Why?*"

Scotty smiled. "Three million bucks a year in legal fees, Bobby, that's why."

The number took Bobby's breath away: *three million bucks.* Bobby's best year ever, he'd grossed $27,500. Only a few minutes together after eleven years apart, and he was already envying

Scotty's life again. Sure, Bobby had loyal clients—one brought him homemade tamales each week, another had named her illegitimate son after him—and his money was no good at either the donut shop or the bar—free donuts and beer were the only perks his particular position offered—but his best client had paid him $500 last year; Scotty's best client paid him $3 million. In all English-speaking parts of Dallas, money was the only recognized measure of a lawyer's success; consequently, only among the Spanish-speaking population of East Dallas was Robert Herrin, Esq., not considered a total loser.

His mind was prying open the door to depression again, the point in each day when he would walk next door and down a few Tecates, when Roberto appeared with two glasses of iced tea and placed them on the table and then spread napkins in their laps, which made Bobby flinch—where he ate, someone leans in that close they're going for your wallet. After Roberto left, Bobby emptied two sweeteners in his tea, drank half the glass, and said, "Kind of surprised to get your call this morning, Scotty. Your secretary's call, anyway. But you know me, never could pass up a free lunch."

"So, how you been, Bobby?"

Bobby studied Scotty sitting there in his expensive suit and starched shirt and designer tie and looking like the Prince of Dallas and wondered if his old friend really gave a damn how Bobby Herrin had been. Used to be that when Bobby ran into an old law school classmate who had done better—which is to say, any law school classmate—they would both realize the awkwardness of the encounter and manufacture a quick escape. But there was no escaping here.

So Bobby said, "Scotty, when you get up in the morning, do you think good things are gonna happen to you that day?"

Scotty frowned a moment, then shrugged and said, "Yeah, I guess so."

"Why?"

Scotty shrugged again. "Good things have always happened to me."

"The best football player, best student, best looking, marries the most beautiful cheerleader, becomes a rich lawyer, and lives happily ever after?"

Scotty flashed that big smile again. "Something like that."

"Exactly like that."

"Yeah."

"Well, see, Scotty, it ain't like that for everybody. I don't wake up thinking good things are gonna happen that day. I wake up wondering what's the next bad thing that's gonna happen to me."

Scotty was staring at his water goblet with the same expression Bobby had seen on the faces of those other classmates he'd run into over the years, a look of abject embarrassment. But he was too far in to stop now.

"You graduated first in our class, Scotty. I graduated. Remember that old law school joke? What do they call the doctor who graduated last in his med school class? Doctor. What do they call the lawyer who graduated last in his law school class? Infrequently." Bobby lowered his eyes to the silver fork he was fiddling with. "Well, it's no joke."

Scotty did not respond immediately, so Bobby raised his eyes, expecting to see a haughty smirk; instead, he saw a hint of real concern on his old friend's face. Scotty and Bobby had been inseparable in college and law school: they had lived together, studied together, got drunk together, chased girls together (Bobby got Scotty's hand-me-downs), and played hoops and golf together. They were like brothers, right up until the day Scotty hired on with Ford Stevens at a starting salary of $100,000. They had not spoken since.

"Things haven't gone well?" Scotty asked.

"Clients you get from ads in the TV guide don't pay so well." Bobby shrugged and tried to smile. "Hey, life just didn't work out."

Scotty straightened in his chair. "Well, Bobby, let's have lunch and talk about that."

Scotty stuck a finger in the air and a waiter appeared instantly. Bobby was scanning a menu with entrées that cost more than his suit when he heard a thick Latino accent: "Mr. Herrin?"

He looked up at the waiter, a young Hispanic man, well groomed with erect posture. His face seemed vaguely familiar.

"Mr. Herrin, it's Carlos. Carlos Hernandez? Remember me, last year? You was my lawyer? Possession with intent to distribute?"

So many of Bobby's clients looked so much alike—young males, brown or black—and were charged with the same crimes—possession of a controlled substance, possession with intent to distribute, conspiracy to distribute; they were just two-bit users caught in the cross fire of the war against drugs. Sometimes he could remember a particular client by his tattoos—he vividly recalled a client named Hector (conspiracy to distribute) because his entire upper body was one big tattoo, a mural in honor of the Virgin Mary—but since Carlos here was clothed from his neck to his toes, Bobby could not remember Carlos from Jorge or Ricardo or Lupe. Still, he said, "Oh, yeah, Carlos. How you doing, man? You staying clean?"

A big grin from Carlos and a bigger lie, "Oh, yes, sir, Mr. Herrin."

They never stay clean. "Good man."

Scotty ordered salmon, Bobby a T-bone. As Carlos walked off, Bobby gestured after him. "My best client."

"You do a lot of criminal defense work?"

Bobby nodded. "I represent the petty criminal class. Guys like Carlos, they don't need estate plans."

"Federal court?"

"Yeah, since they federalized all the drug crimes."

Carlos soon returned with their food, and they ate and talked and laughed about the old days, old friends, good times, and their families. Scotty didn't know Bobby had been married and divorced twice; Bobby didn't know Scotty's mother had died or that he had a daughter. And for a brief moment it was eleven years ago and they were still best friends. But Bobby knew he was just Cinderella at the ball with the Prince of Dallas, and the fancy lunch at the fancy club would soon be over and he'd be back in his crappy office in East Dallas living his shitty life again representing clients like Carlos.

So when he finished his steak, he pushed his plate aside and said: "Scotty, I appreciate the lunch, man. It's been fun, catching up and all. But I know you didn't invite me up here just to catch up, not after all these years. What's up?"

Scotty glanced around, leaned in, and in a lowered voice said, "Buford appointed me to represent the hooker who murdered Clark McCall."

Bobby almost spit out his iced tea. "You're shittin' me."

"Nope."

Bobby Herrin might not be the brightest bulb in the box, but it didn't take him long to figure out this game: Scotty Fenney was giving him another hand-me-down.

"You want to hire her out?"

Scotty nodded. "Here's the deal. I met with the defendant this morning, Shawanda Jones, black girl, hooker, heroin addict— Christ, she damn near puked on my suit! Says she didn't kill him, but that's bullshit—her gun was the murder weapon. Says McCall picked her up on Harry Hines, offered her a thousand bucks for the night, took her home, started slapping her around, cursing her and"—his voice was a whisper now—"using the N-word." Back to his normal voice. "Anyway, they fought, she kicked him in the balls, took the money he owed her and his car keys, drove herself back to Harry Hines, and left the car. Police got her prints off the gun—she's got prior prostitution charges—and arrested her the next day. She refuses to plead out, wants a trial. Bobby, Ford Stevens can't represent a hooker!"

Bobby nodded. "Okay."

"Okay what?"

"I'll take her. What's the pay?"

"Fifty an hour?"

"Plus expenses."

"Like what?"

"Investigator, forensic experts, DNA tests . . ."

"Okay, but don't go overboard."

"Yeah, what the hell, she's just a nigger."

"I didn't say that, Bobby."

"Sorry. Cheap shot. You got a detention hearing?"

"Tomorrow morning, nine."

"I'll be there."

They stood. Bobby pulled out his parking ticket.

"They validate?"

The athletic club was located on the top floor of the building adjacent to Dibrell Tower, connected by an air-conditioned skywalk so Scott Fenney didn't have to sweat on the way to his daily workout. Most of the office buildings in downtown Dallas were connected by skywalks or underground tunnels, air-conditioned passageways so the lawyers and bankers and businessmen didn't have to venture out into the heat or among the vagrants and panhandlers who called the downtown streets home; it was a prudent practice, particularly after a homeless man jumped a cop a few years back, grabbed his gun, and shot him point-blank in the face, right across the street from the downtown McDonald's.

Scott had just traversed one such skywalk. It was now half-past five and he was looking down on Dallas while running at 7.5 miles per hour up a ten-degree incline on a commercial treadmill and feeling pretty damn special. Which was not a new feeling for him. Scott Fenney had been special all his life. His father, Butch, had told him so when he was only eight, when he first put on pads and discovered his talent in peewee football. "You've got a gift, Scotty," Butch had said. Later his mother said the same thing: "You've got a gift, but I don't mean football," she said. He never understood what she meant, and then she died.

But the notion took hold and grew inside him, nurtured by eight years of high school and college football heroics; the fans, students, cheerleaders, boosters, coaches, and reporters all assured him daily that Scott Fenney was indeed special. It became a part of him, like the blue of his eyes. And it had never left him; it had only grown stronger, through three years at SMU law school and eleven years at Ford Stevens. But now, instead of athletic ability, it was money that made Scott Fenney special. Money enough to buy a mansion, a Ferrari, a perfect life—and even an old friend.

For the first time in the twenty-four hours since the judge's call, Scott's mind was clear, his spirits high, and his eyes locked on the backside of the girl running on the treadmill in front of him, her amazing buns barely shimmying as they pumped up and down like pistons. Scott pulled his eyes off her firm butt and glanced at the mirror to his right; he caught the girl on the treadmill behind him checking out his firm butt. Their eyes met and she winked, and that intoxicating feeling of male virility formed in his brain, coursed through his nerves and veins like a narcotic, and energized his muscles. He increased the speed to ten miles per hour. He loved being special.

When Scott walked into her bedroom that night, Boo was already in her pajamas and in bed, propped up on pillows against the headboard. Her hands were folded in her lap, her hair brushed smooth, and her face scrubbed pink. She smelled like fresh strawberries. She had positioned a chair next to the bed, as she did each night before bedtime, with the current book Scott was reading to her in the seat. Scott picked up the book and sat down, rubbed his eyes, and replaced his glasses.

"Where were we?" he asked.

"Number six," Boo said.

Scott opened the book and turned to the Sixth Amendment to the Constitution. Boo's teacher had mentioned the Bill of Rights in class one day, so naturally Boo wanted to know everything about these special rights she never knew she had.

So he read: " 'In all criminal prosecutions, the accused shall enjoy the right to a speedy and public trial.' " He looked up. "What do you think that means?"

"The cops can't lock you up and throw away the key."

"That's right. And your trial can't be held in secret."

"So if your prostitute doesn't cop a plea, anyone can go to her trial."

"Yes. And she won't."

"Won't what?"

"Cop a plea."

Boo leaned forward, her eyes wide. "You talked to her?"

"This morning, at the jail."

"What's she like?"

Scott shrugged. "Young, not very well educated, strung out, says she's innocent."

"Do you think she is?"

Scott shook his head. "No. Her gun was the murder weapon and her fingerprints were on the gun."

"She had a gun?"

"Yeah."

"*Shit* . . . I mean, *wow*."

She leaned back, thinking, so he read again: " 'By an impartial jury.' You know what 'impartial' means?"

She shook her head. "Uh-uh."

"It means jurors who are fair, not prejudiced against the defendant. 'Prejudiced' means hating people just because they're different."

She nodded. "We talked about that at school last year during Kwanzaa. So if someone hates black people, they can't be on your prostitute's jury."

"That's right."

"How do you make sure?"

"You get to ask potential jurors questions before they become jurors."

"Like what?"

"Well, in the prostitute's case, you'd ask whether they're prejudiced against black people or prostitutes or drug addicts."

"But they'll just say no."

"Well, you don't ask it straight out; you ask subtle questions, like, uh, have they ever been to a black person's home? And you watch their body language, say a white guy is sitting next to a black guy, does he lean away."

"Have you?"

"Have I what?"

"Ever been to a black person's home?"

"Uh, no."

"But you're not prejudiced, are you?"

"No, Boo, of course not. I used to have black friends, guys I played ball with at SMU."

"Like who?"

"Well, like Rasheed . . . and Leroy . . . and Big Charlie—"

She smiled. "Who's Big Charlie?"

Now Scott was smiling. "Charles Jackson. He was my right offensive guard. He blocked for me. He saved me many times on the field . . . and a few times off the field."

"Y'all were good friends?"

Scott nodded. "Yeah. He was a great guy."

"Is he dead?"

"No . . . I don't think so."

"Why aren't y'all friends anymore?"

Scott shrugged. "He went off to play pro ball. I went to law school. We lost touch."

She nodded. "So the only reason you don't have black clients is because you don't represent people, only corporations."

"Exactly."

She pointed at the book. "What's next?"

Scott read again: " 'To be informed of the nature and cause of the accusation,' which means to be told the crime you're charged with."

"Murder, that's the crime your prostitute is charged with."

"Yes." Reading again: " 'To be confronted with the witnesses against him.' That means the prosecution must put the witnesses on the stand in court to testify against the defendant. 'To have compulsory process for obtaining witnesses in his favor.' That means you can call witnesses to help you."

"Your prostitute can get people to say she didn't do it."

"Right. If she can find anyone. And 'to have the assistance of counsel for his defense.' "

"What's counsel?"

"A lawyer."

"Your prostitute has a right to a lawyer?"

"Yes, she does."

"Even if she can't pay you?"

"Yes."

"Why?"

"Why what?"

"Why does she get you for free when everyone else has to pay you three hundred and fifty dollars an hour?"

"Well, George Washington and the other Founding Fathers . . . you know about them?" She nodded. "Well, they didn't think it would be fair for the government to charge someone with a crime but not give him a lawyer to defend him."

"Because he might be innocent and if he didn't have a lawyer to prove he's innocent, he might still go to jail."

"Exactly . . . well, the lawyer doesn't have to prove him innocent, the government's got to prove him guilty. And that's the lawyer's job, Boo, to make the government prove the defendant's guilt beyond any reasonable doubt."

"So the government proved your prostitute is guilty?"

"Not yet. And she's not *my* prostitute, Boo. She's my client."

"But you wanted her to cop a plea, say she's guilty."

"Yes, to confess that she did it."

"So the government wouldn't have to prove she's guilty."

"Right."

"Then why does she need you?"

Scott chuckled. "Well, I'm supposed to, uh . . . I mean, the court appoints a lawyer so she, uh . . . Well, the Bill of Rights says she has a right to a lawyer even if she's guilty and decides to confess. To make sure the rules are followed."

"And the judge appointed you to make sure the rules are followed for her?"

"Yes, but she doesn't want to confess. She wants to go to trial, so I hired her out."

She frowned. "Explain."

"I hired an old law school buddy to take her case to trial."

"Why?"

"Because I'm too busy."

"You're too busy to make the government prove she's guilty?"

"Yes. So I'm paying a friend to do it for me."

"Like if I hired a friend to do my homework?"

"Exactly . . . well, no, not exactly. You've got to do your own homework, Boo."

"Why?"

"Because that would be cheating."

"But it's not cheating if you're a lawyer?"

"Yes . . . well, no. I mean . . . it's complicated, Boo."

She pointed at the book. "Does that Sixth Amendment have one of those things, what did you call it, a pro . . . prov . . ."

"Proviso?"

"Yeah, a proviso."

"What do you mean?"

"A proviso that if the lawyer's real busy, you don't have a right to a lawyer?"

"No. But you don't have the right to a particular lawyer, just a lawyer."

"Any lawyer?"

"Yeah."

"Even a bad lawyer?"

Scott shrugged. "Yeah."

"Is your friend a good lawyer or a bad lawyer?"

"Well . . . I don't really know."

"Is he as good as you?"

Scott smiled. "No."

"So the judge appointed you as her lawyer and you're a great lawyer, but now she's going to get stuck with your friend, who's not so great?"

"Well, yeah. Not everyone can have me as their lawyer."

"Only corporations that can pay you three hundred and fifty dollars an hour."

"Exactly."

She sighed. "That doesn't seem like such a great deal."

"What?"

"That right to a lousy lawyer."

EIGHT

THE NEXT MORNING, Scott was back at the federal building at a quarter till nine, anxious to punt Shawanda Jones to Bobby Herrin and get back to his perfect life. Outside, he was mobbed by TV cameras and reporters sticking microphones in his face and shouting questions. He pushed his way through with several "No comments" and entered the courthouse. He rode the elevator to the fifteenth floor where he found Bobby standing outside Judge Buford's courtroom, wearing the same awful suit and smelling of cigarette smoke. They entered through tall double doors and took a seat in the church pews with the other lawyers awaiting their clients' hearings, arraignments, and sentencings.

For the last three decades, Judge Samuel Buford had presided over this courtroom. And looking at the waiting defendants, the drug dealers up on federal charges, black and brown and nervous, and the white-collar criminals, white and well-groomed and indignant that tax dollars were being wasted prosecuting them for securities and tax fraud—all wondering if they would be going home on probation or to the federal penitentiary for five to ten—Scott couldn't help but consider all the lives that had been changed in this one courtroom by this one judge. For raw power, it was hard to beat the law.

The bailiff called the first case on the docket: "*United States of America versus Shawanda Jones.*"

Scott put on his glasses—he always wore his glasses to court—and he and Bobby stood and stepped past the bar and to the defendant's table. A preppy lawyer, midthirties, walked over to them.

"Bobby, what, you moving up to the big leagues?" the lawyer said. His smirk indicated that it was a smart-ass comment, not a compliment. "I didn't know you were on this case."

"Just trying to help an innocent citizen being railroaded by an overzealous government prosecutor, Ray," Bobby said in a deadpan voice.

Ray chuckled and said, "Yeah, right," then extended his hand to Scott. "Ray Burns, Assistant U.S. Attorney."

Scott shook hands with Burns and said, "Scott Fenney, Ford Stevens."

"I heard Buford tapped private counsel for this case," Burns said. He turned his palms up and glanced from Scott to Bobby and back. "So, what, you bailing on the defendant?"

"No, I'm not bailing. I'm trying to do the right thing, hiring her a real criminal defense attorney."

"*The right thing?*" Burns said with the same smirk, clearly his trademark expression. "Looks an awful lot like bailing to me."

Ray Burns, Assistant U.S. Asshole, returned to the prosecution table, his right shoulder riding low under the weight of the king-sized chip he was carrying around. Government lawyers always have chips on their shoulders when dealing with big-firm lawyers like Scott because the big firms didn't hire them out of law school:

if you can, you do; if you can't, you teach; if you can't teach, you hire on with Uncle Sam.

Bobby leaned in and whispered, "Burns is a dick. Trying to build a conviction record so he can move up to D.C. Asshole's put a couple of my clients away for life, for possession. Course he called it 'intent to distribute.' "

A side door opened and a strange black woman appeared in a white jail uniform. Scott stared at the woman for several seconds before realizing that she was Shawanda. She had looked awful yesterday; today she looked like she was dying. The same black guard escorted her into the courtroom, his arm under hers, almost carrying her over to Scott. By the time she arrived, her face was a brown frown.

"Morning, Shawanda."

Her entire body was trembling, shaking, twitching. Scott almost reached out and embraced her, to warm her like he did Boo when she got a chill after getting out of the pool, but at the last second the thought of his client throwing up on his expensive suit dissuaded him. He eased a step away from her.

"Who's him, Mr. Fenney?" she said in a weak voice, gesturing at Bobby.

"Bobby Herrin, your lawyer."

"Thought you my lawyer?"

"Shawanda, I represent corporations, not criminals . . . I mean, people charged with crimes. I hired you a real criminal defense attorney."

"All rise!"

The bailiff's voice boomed out and everyone in the courtroom stood as Judge Samuel Buford entered from a door behind the bench. He was the very image of a federal judge: the white hair, the patrician face, the black reading glasses, and the black robe. He sat behind the bench, which was elevated, as if to emphasize the supreme power of the law. To look him in the eye Scott had to angle his head up about twenty degrees.

"Be seated," the judge said. He shuffled through papers on his desk and glanced up over his glasses, first at Ray Burns, then at Scott and Shawanda and Bobby. Finally he said, *"United States of America versus Shawanda Jones.* Detention hearing."

He looked at Shawanda again.

"Ms. Jones, are you okay?"

He was a father asking his young daughter if she was hurt after falling off her bicycle. Shawanda nodded and the judge then turned to the lawyers.

"Gentlemen, please make your appearances."

Burns said, "Ray Burns, Assistant U.S. Attorney, for the government."

Then Scott said, "A. Scott Fenney, Ford Stevens, for the defendant. If I may, Your Honor, my firm has retained Robert Herrin, Esquire, to assume representation of the defendant. Mr. Herrin is a well-respected criminal defense attorney in Dallas. He possesses much more experience than I in criminal matters and will be able to provide the defendant a more competent defense. With the court's permission, I ask to withdraw from representation of the defendant and for Mr. Herrin to be substituted in my place."

The judge was eyeing Scott over his reading glasses; a wry smile crossed his face.

"Didn't really want to be another Atticus Finch after all, huh, Mr. Fenney?"

Scott knew better than to respond. The judge's smile dissolved into a look of disappointment that, for some odd reason, bothered Scott. The judge sighed and dropped his eyes. He started writing on what Scott knew was the case docket, officially substituting Robert Herrin, Esq., as counsel for the defendant in place of A. Scott Fenney, Esq. Scott felt like a kid about to get out of detention hall.

The judge said, "Well, since it's okay with Ms. Jones . . ."

Shawanda Jones rubbed her face but her skin felt numb. She hadn't slept in forty-eight hours; the cravings kept her awake all day and all night. She had never been without heroin for this long since she had gotten hooked, and it was killing her. Her mind was fuzzy and she couldn't get her thoughts straight. She had a blinding headache that wouldn't quit. She ached all over. Every muscle and bone in her body was throbbing with pain, and her skin was covered with goose bumps from the chills that swept over her regularly.

Her eyes were dry and gritty as she raised them to the white man standing to her right, this Robert Herrin Esquire. He was short, had a belly on him, and must have had bad acne as a boy because his face was pockmarked. His brown hair clearly hadn't been washed that morning. He was wearing the cheapest suit she had ever seen on a white lawyer—the damn thing *shined* under the fluorescent lights! His white shirt had yellowed a shade and its button-down collar was missing one of its buttons. His tie screamed *Sale at JCPenney!* No doubt, she made more money hooking than he did lawyering.

She turned to the white man to her left, Mr. Fenney. Tall and blond and handsome, wearing a dark pin-striped suit that hung like a silk dress over his broad shoulders, a crisp white shirt with French cuffs, a maroon silk tie, and the overall appearance of a white-boy version of the baddest pimp in the projects, he had a look that said, *I'm a stud.*

A stud or a dud?

Shawanda was twenty-four-years old. She had dropped out of school at age fifteen when she got pregnant. She had only nine years of formal education. But she wasn't stupid. And her prior experiences with the American legal system had taught her an important lesson, one she wasn't ever going to forget: rich lawyer

95

means good lawyer; poor lawyer means bad lawyer. She looked up at the judge and said, "It ain't okay!"

Scott's heart froze as the words from the black woman standing next to him hit his brain. The judge's head shot up. His eyes locked on Shawanda Jones. Scott turned and stared down at her, stifling the urge to strangle this client who refused to go away quietly.

"What?" the judge asked.

"It ain't okay with me," Shawanda said. She pointed a trembling black finger at Scott. "Judge, I'm innocent and I want Mr. Fenney be my lawyer."

The judge yanked his reading glasses off his face and cocked his head at Scott.

"Mr. Fenney, did you not discuss this with your client prior to asking this court to substitute counsel?"

Scott cleared his throat. "Uh, no, sir."

"Well, maybe you should have." The judge returned to Shawanda. "Why?"

"Why what?"

"Why do you want Mr. Fenney as your lawyer?"

"Judge, I believe in him. I feel confidence in him. I know he can prove me innocent."

The judge again turned to Scott.

"Mr. Fenney, it's the defendant's right to counsel, so it's her decision."

"Your Honor, may I have a moment with Ms. Jones?"

The judge gave him a brief wave of the hand.

Scott stepped between Shawanda and the judge, leaned down to her, and whispered through clenched teeth: "Look, goddamnit, my firm is hiring a lawyer for you. I've got better things to do than take you to trial. I'm not gonna be your lawyer. Now you tell the judge it's okay for Bobby to represent you."

Scott straightened up and faced the judge. The judge held his hands up.

"Well, Ms. Jones?"

Shawanda again turned to Robert Herrin—*Dud!*—then to A. Scott Fenney—*Stud!* She pointed at Mr. Fenney and said, "I want him."

"Jesus H. Christ!" Dan Ford was upset now. "A goddamn hooker holding this firm hostage!"

Scott had just come from the courthouse with the bad news. "Can we appeal the appointment?" Scott asked.

"Hell, no! Even if we could, we wouldn't. That'd piss off Buford big-time. We would never be able to set foot in his court again."

"What am I supposed to do?"

Dan stared at his protégé, the finest young lawyer he'd come across in thirty-five years. The boy was a natural: smart, shrewd, articulate, and possessed of the intestinal fortitude to bill a client until he cried uncle. He looked upon Scott as his son.

"Keep Herrin on the case, let him do all the heavy lifting, write all briefs and motions, make all pretrial appearances—that'll keep the firm's name out of the papers and off TV. And no goddamn interviews, make sure Herrin knows that! You"—a finger pointed at Scott—"you work for our paying clients."

Dan checked his watch and walked over to the coatrack. "Keep me posted. I don't want any surprises, Scott."

Scott departed, and Dan slipped into his coat; he was wearing a black suit today. He had to go to a funeral.

NINE

MOST RESIDENTS of Highland Park who knew Clark McCall always assumed he would die young. He was wild and reckless, to the degree only a child of enormous wealth could afford to be. A son of the middle class could not afford to squander his chances at admission to a top college and then law or medical school. But for Clark McCall, those considerations were of no concern: his father possessed a net worth in excess of $800 million.

Dan Ford was sitting in the sanctuary of the Highland Park United Methodist Church situated at the southern end of the SMU campus, waiting for Clark McCall's funeral service to begin. He had known Clark all the boy's life because he had known Clark's father for forty-two years. Dan had met Mack their freshman year at SMU when they had pledged the same fraternity.

With America at war in Vietnam and Uncle Sam drafting more young men to die, Dan Ford had decided to fight the war at a private college and then a private law school. He did not pursue a legal career out of any particular love of the law, only because of a particular fear of dying in some rice paddy ten thousand miles away. He wasn't alone in that fear: enrollment at America's law schools doubled during the war.

But once his future career was fixed, Dan Ford plotted a path to success. He knew lawyers got rich by representing rich clients. So, while most freshmen busied themselves with drinking and screwing, free of mommy and daddy for the first time, young Dan Ford began cultivating future clients.

Mack McCall was at the top of his list. As soon as you met him, you knew Mack was going places. He had that look about him. Born in Odessa, son of a roughneck and one himself, Mack was engaged to his high school sweetheart, the only daughter of an oil company vice president. His future father-in-law paid Mack's way through SMU.

Summers, Dan clerked in Dallas law firms, learning the ways of lawyers. Mack worked on West Texas oil rigs. Back then, oil was going for two bucks a barrel; Mack predicted ten dollars a barrel. Even he didn't dream of oil at fifty dollars a barrel.

By graduation day, Mack knew how to drill wells and, more important, he knew where to drill. Over the four years of college, he had mapped every producing well and dry hole in the Permian Basin. He hit his first wildcat well the summer after graduation. By the time Dan had graduated law school, Mack McCall was worth $20 million. Like H. L. Hunt and other Texas wildcatters before him, Mack McCall soon bored of what he could buy in an oil town, so he moved to Dallas. And Dan Ford, Esq., had his first rich client.

Dan now watched as the senior senator from Texas worked the church crowd as if his son's funeral was just another campaign stop, although he was wearing his version of a grief-stricken face. He was a handsome man, with a full head of starched gray hair, immaculately dressed as always, the kind of man teenagers go "yuk" at, but women of AARP find irresistibly attractive.

Organ music was playing softly in the background, voices were subdued, and Dan was sitting in a pew in the middle of the church, a good vantage point from which to see who came and who did not. Martha McCall, Mack's first wife and Clark's mother, arrived early and sat in the front pew with the other family members. She looked so old next to Jean McCall, but then, who wouldn't? Martha was the family station wagon parked next to a sleek sports car.

Dan's station wagon was parked next to him; she was almost his age and looked it. They had married right out of law school and immediately had a child, added insurance that Dan Ford would not be touring Indonesia courtesy of Uncle Sam. Over the years, Dan had had three brief affairs, if you called making it with a drunk secretary on the sofa in his office after the firm Christmas party an affair, but he had never considered divorcing his wife for another woman. First, there hadn't been another woman who had expressed any interest in becoming his next wife; and second, his true love was and had always been his law firm.

Political animals of every breed were making an appearance at Clark McCall's funeral. They came not out of grief for the deceased, but because it was good for business: CEOs who needed McCall's vote to extend their special tax break or exemption from some onerous environmental regulation; members of Congress who dared not cross the most powerful man in the Senate; the vice president because network news cameras were present; cabinet members who hoped to be in a McCall administration; and judges—district court judges who wanted to be appeals court judges and appeals court judges who wanted to be Supreme Court justices, promotions requiring Senate confirmation. Clark McCall's funeral had brought together a collection of national figures from politics and business the likes of which Dallas had seldom seen. When you're the leading bet to be the next president, people come to your son's funeral.

And the stalwarts of funerals, the old ladies of Highland Park, had come, recalling how handsome Clark had been as a boy. The funeral guests were friends of the family, not friends of Clark. A few young men about Clark's age had come, themselves sons of great wealth who would forever be burdens to their parents. But no young women had come. Clark did not seem to have any female friends who mourned his passing.

Just as Dan's own son would have no female friends at his funeral; he had recently confessed to being gay. God knows, Clark's heterosexuality had never been in question. How many times had the senator called Dan in the middle of the night to bail Clark out of the Highland Park jail? Once a month, it seemed, during Clark's college career at SMU and a dozen times since. Drinking, snorting, screwing—Clark McCall had definitely enjoyed himself. Fortunately, the boy had the good sense to get himself arrested in Highland Park, where money mattered.

The reverend stepped to the lectern, the people took their seats, and the background music faded away. The reverend spoke of God and heaven and peace, that Clark was in a better place; the good preacher was selling eternity, but Dan Ford wasn't buying. Right here, right now, that's all we have. Don't wait for the hereafter. Get what you want here and now.

After ten minutes of the reverend, Senator Mack McCall stood and walked to his son's coffin by the altar, placed his palm on the top, and closed his eyes, as if in prayer. But Dan wasn't buying that either; he knew Mack too well.

Mack went to the lectern and gazed out at the assemblage with a grim expression. He spoke slowly and with great emotion of his only son, of how it was against nature for a son to die before his father, of how he had experienced pain in his sixty years, but nothing like this. Clark had been a troubled boy and for this he blamed himself, which Dan Ford knew was an absolute lie. Mack blamed Martha for not letting him send Clark to a military boarding school when he was ten. But Mack McCall was very good at this

sort of thing, and by the end of his eulogy, most of the funeral
guests were crying or damn close to it.

His only son was dead and buried.

They had never bonded, Mack McCall and his son. Clark had
bonded with his mother; Mack had bonded with money. He
reached into his inside coat pocket and removed and opened his
billfold: not a single photograph of his son or either of his wives,
but thick with the faces of Benjamin Franklin and Ulysses S.
Grant. Money and power had been Mack McCall's lifelong companions, not a wife and son. Now he would use his money to buy
the presidency of the United States of America.

He had spent $25 million to purchase a Senate seat, only to
discover that the sole power senators wielded was the power to deliver pork to their home states, not unlike a mailman delivering
Social Security checks. It was power that served only to ensure their
incumbency.

But Mack McCall wanted to leave his footprints on this earth;
he wanted history to know he had been here. Before the divorce,
Martha had suggested he establish a private foundation, use his
wealth to help the world's poor: AIDS victims in Africa, unedu-
cated children in Mexico, homeless people in America. But even
$800 million was a drop in the bucket when it came to the world's
social problems. And besides, he had never concerned himself with
the plight of poor people; it just wasn't his thing. So he divorced
Martha and married Jean, and now he would spend as much of his
fortune as necessary to buy the power he so coveted, the power to
dispatch the United States Army. Wipe out a few Middle Eastern
dictators, and history damn sure knows you were here.

Mack was standing in the bedroom of his Highland Park mansion where his son had been murdered. His mind began playing

out the last moments of Clark's life according to the police report, moments filled with alcohol and cocaine and lust and rage and fear and a hooker—a nigger, for God's sake! His son had screwed her and fought her and then died right there on the floor where the carpet had been cut out and removed by the FBI. He saw Clark lying dead and felt the emotions welling up inside him and he thought, as he always thought when Clark came to mind:

What a major-league fuckup his son had been.

Anyone else's son and Mack would say the boy deserved it, living a reckless life, bringing a hooker home to Highland Park. But it was his son and that made it different: no one else in Highland Park was running for president. For the last twenty years, Mack McCall's every act, speech, public appearance, Senate vote—*every breath he took*—had been judged against one overriding concern: How would it affect his presidential ambitions? So now no conscious effort was required for his mind to judge his son's murder and all the publicity the hooker's trial would bring against the same concern.

Mack didn't like the conclusions his mind arrived at.

He had threatened to cut Clark out of his will on more than one occasion, an attempt to curb his son's reckless ways by threatening his future. But now it was the son who was threatening his father's future: the circumstances of Clark's death and his many indiscretions posed an imminent threat to Mack's White House dreams. And Mack McCall was not one to wait passively for a threat to become reality.

Two hours later, Mack was standing at the open double doors of the foyer, saying good-bye to those who had come to pay their respects. Dan Ford was the last to leave. Mack watched Dan walk down the long walkway to the circle drive where the valet held open the door to Dan's waiting Mercedes-Benz. Dan Ford would cooperate: a lawyer's loyalty could always be purchased for a reasonable fee.

"This Fenney boy," Mack said, "he played ball at SMU, pretty damn good as I recall."

Mack shut the front doors and turned to Delroy Lund, a big, bald, no-necked slab of beef. Delroy was not the brightest former DEA agent in the country, and he was plenty rough around the edges—subtlety wasn't Delroy's strong point—but he had proved himself a loyal bodyguard and capable private investigator, adept at uncovering dirty little secrets about senators who opposed Mack on various pork barrel bills and his ex-wife during their divorce proceedings.

"Find everything there is to find on Fenney, and I mean everything. I want his transcripts, bank records, debts, tax returns. I want to know his clients, his friends, his enemies, whether he's fucking around on his wife or she's fucking around on him." A pointed finger at his trusted manservant. "Delroy, I want to know how much he craps each morning. Understood?"

Delroy nodded.

"And no rough stuff this time, Delroy. I just want to control him."

Delroy shrugged and said, "You're the boss."

"Get me every newspaper article on the McCall murder case," Scott said to Sue. He gestured at Bobby sitting on the sofa. "Sue, this is Bobby Herrin. He's working with me on the case. Give her your card, Bobby, so she has your numbers."

Bobby dug around in his pockets, pulled out a crumpled card, and handed it to Sue, who was holding out a stack of pink message slips to Scott.

"Reporters and TV producers. They want you to appear on the morning news shows, *Dateline*, *20/20*, and—"

"Trash 'em. And call security: tell them to keep those reporters outside on the street."

"Frank Turner's still waiting."

"Show him in." To Bobby: "I always make plaintiffs' lawyers wait."

Scott slumped in his chair behind the mahogany desk. Last time he felt like this was after the knee injury his freshman season.

"Just when you think you got the world by the balls," Scott said, "you find out the world's got you by the balls."

"Welcome to my world," Bobby said.

Sue escorted Frank Turner into Scott's office. Frank appeared every inch the rich plaintiffs' lawyer, expensively dressed, his hair perfect, looking tanned and rested from another jaunt to Cancún aboard his personal Lear jet, the bastard. Frank had lucked into one major toxic tort verdict a decade ago, and he had never had to take a case to a jury again. His reputation forced every corporate defendant to settle for a substantial sum, one-third of which went into Frank's pocket. So while Scott Fenney had a Ferrari, Frank Turner had a Lear.

Scott did not stand. "Frank, I didn't expect you to come over personally."

Frank grinned and said, "I always show up to collect funds."

"Ah, the personal touch." Scott gestured over at Bobby on the sofa. "Frank, Bobby Herrin. Bobby, Frank Turner, famous plaintiffs' lawyer."

They shook hands, then Frank gestured at the big blowup of Scott Fenney, number 22, on the far wall above the sofa.

"That the day you got a hundred and ninety-three yards against Texas?"

"Yep, that was the day."

Frank's eyes lingered on the blowup, and in Frank's eyes Scott saw the envy of a tuba player. But Frank Turner was now a plaintiffs' lawyer and he was here for money, so he finally turned to Scott and said, "You got the check?"

"You got the release?" Scott asked.

Frank held out a document, which Scott took and scanned to make sure the bastard hadn't changed anything. Satisfied, he turned to the signature page and saw that sweet Nadine and sleazy Frank had both signed in triplicate. He then handed a cashier's check to Frank Turner.

"One million dollars, Frank."

Frank stared at the check a moment and then broke into a birthday-boy smile.

Scott said, "So is this what you do every day, Frank, walk from office to office picking up big settlement checks?"

Frank's face took on an expression of thoughtfulness, then he smiled again. "Yeah, Scott, now that you mention it, that is pretty much what I do."

The smile still on his face and a million-dollar check in his hand, he headed to the door, but stopped abruptly and turned back. He held the check up to Scott.

"Oh, just so you know, Scott, Nadine would've taken half a million."

Frank was turning away again when Scott said, "Well, since we're confessing, Frank, just so you know, Tom would've paid two million."

Frank's smile evaporated like a raindrop on the sidewalk outside and his shoulders slumped: the only thing that makes a plaintiffs' lawyer lose sleep is leaving money on the table. He turned and slithered away, not thinking that he had just *made* $333,333.33, but that he had just *lost* the same amount. Which left Scott with something of a moral victory, at least.

"Asshole," Scott said.

"Who, me?"

Sid Greenberg's head was in the door. Scott motioned him in.

"Sid, meet Bobby Herrin."

Sid stepped over and shook hands with Bobby. "How'd it go this morning? You taking over the hooker?"

"Not exactly," Scott said.

"The judge wouldn't let you out?"

"No. Looks like I'm stuck with her. Bobby's going to carry the heavy end of the log, write the briefs and motions, make all pre-trial appearances—"

Sid smiled at Bobby. "Do all the work, like I do for Scott on Dibrell matters."

Sid's smile disappeared when he turned to Scott and saw that Scott wasn't smiling.

"Yeah, Sid, only difference is, I need Bobby. You can be replaced."

Sid squirmed and forced a sheepish grin. Scott never let on with associates whether he was serious when he made remarks like that, which kept them on their toes and billing hours.

"Why are you standing on my Persian rug, Sid?"

"Oh, we signed up the environmental consultant on Dibrell's land deal. He now works for Ford Stevens. That was a brilliant idea, Scott."

Sid was in damage control mode.

"That it?"

"Well, no. One more thing, Scott." He glanced at Bobby, then back at Scott. "Confidential."

Scott said, "Close your ears, Bobby."

He nodded to Sid to go on.

"Our discovery, production of documents, is due on that Di-brell lawsuit, the one where all the residents in his apartment complex are claiming they were harmed by mold in their apartments and he didn't do anything about it?"

"Yeah, so?"

"So in going through Dibrell's records, we found one letter that might prove troublesome. It mentions some of the symptoms of mold poisoning. But we've taken the position that Dibrell didn't have any knowledge of the dangers of mold."

Scott, to Bobby: "A goddamn lawsuit over mold. One jury in Austin comes back with a thirty-two-million-dollar verdict, next thing you know everyone's dying of mold poisoning."

Back to Sid: "How many pages of production are we giving the plaintiffs' lawyer?"

"Twenty-seven thousand."

"Okay, here's what you do. Double copy everything, so we give them fifty-four thousand pages. And put everything out of order, a real mess. Then make one really bad copy of that letter, you know, like our secretaries do without meaning to, where you can hardly read it. And stick it right in the middle of those fifty-four thousand pages, see if they can find it."

Sid was grinning. "That's brilliant!"

"Aggressive and creative lawyering, Sid."

Among lawyers, employing clever litigation tactics like hiding one damaging document in fifty-four thousand pages of discovery—not to mention just shredding the damn thing—is known as "aggressive and creative lawyering," and it is a skill highly praised by members of the bar. Aggressive and creative lawyering is how successful lawyers become successful, that and not getting caught. A big part of being successful, Scott had learned, was not getting caught.

Sid scurried away, and Scott gestured after him.

"First in his class at Harvard. Might make a lawyer out of him yet."

Bobby was giving him a look.

Scott held his hands up. *"What?"*

"That's what you high-rent lawyers do, play hide the ball?"

"It's just like football, Bobby—if you don't get caught holding, you didn't hold. When you're playing this game against sleazy plaintiffs' lawyers like Frank Turner, you play by the same rules they play by. You do whatever it takes to win—because rich clients don't want ethical lawyers who lose, Bobby. They want lawyers who win."

Bobby seemed unconvinced, so Scott pointed his finger at the open door.

"Bobby, that bastard Frank's got a jet!"

Scott's thoughts returned to Shawanda Jones, like one's thoughts did to a recurring nightmare.

"Oh, and no interviews, Bobby. We want to keep the firm's name out of the press."

Bobby nodded. "I'll get the police report, see what evidence Burns has got, hire a PI. He'll interview witnesses, track down leads, do background checks on Clark and anyone connected to Clark. Name is Carl, he's an ex-cop."

"Dan's gonna crap, paying for a private investigator."

"Scotty, we gotta have a PI. It's a death penalty case."

Scott sighed. "Okay, but hide his fees in your bills to the firm. So Dan doesn't see them."

"Yeah, okay. Uh, Scotty, this case is gonna eat up a lot of my time. I'll have to incur some expenses and . . . well . . . you think I could get an advance on my fees?"

"Sure." To his secretary: "Sue!" She popped in within seconds. "Sue, get Bobby a firm check for twenty-five hundred."

When she left, Bobby said, "Thanks."

Scott waved him off. Twenty-five hundred was pocket change at Ford Stevens.

"Kind of funny, ain't it, Scotty?"

"What?"

"Back in school, we used to talk about working together. After all this time, we are." He shrugged. "Kind of funny."

Scott stared at his former best friend.

"Yeah, Bobby, this is fucking hilarious."

Boo screamed with delight. "A. Scott, you're on TV!"

Her father and mother walked over to the kitchen TV and saw what she saw: on the evening news, A. Scott looking like a reluctant movie star, pushing through a crowd of TV cameras and microphones as reporters shouted questions.

"Did your client murder Clark McCall?"

"How will she plead?"

"What's your defense?"

"This morning," her father said. "The mob at the courthouse."

"You couldn't get out of the case?" Boo asked.

"No."

"You're going to trial?"

"Yeah."

"When?"

"August."

"Well, there goes Vail," her mother said with an exasperated sigh. "We'll be the only family in Highland Park suffering here in August. That'll be embarrassing."

"Can I go?" Boo asked.

"Yeah, you and Mom can still go to Vail," her father said.

"No. To the trial."

"You want to come to the trial?"

"I'll still be out of school."

"No, you may not, young lady," her mother said. "A murder trial is no place for a nine-year-old girl."

"But it'll be like, history in the making."

Her mother gave her another exasperated sigh. "Murder trials happen every day."

"No, I mean A. Scott representing a human being."

Her father looked at her and she at him; they both laughed.

Rebecca was not laughing.

"This won't affect your position in the firm?"

Upon retiring to the master suite, that was Rebecca's first and only question, her way of asking, *Will this affect your income?*

"No, of course not. I'm still Tom Dibrell's lawyer."

Her expression said she wasn't buying it.

"Rebecca, look, I've got Bobby working the case. He'll get me through it, she'll get convicted, and things will go back to normal. Don't worry."

But Scott was worried. That feeling of impending doom had grown stronger. He plopped down in his chair in the sitting area off the master bedroom and used the remote to turn on the TV. The late news. A story about Clark McCall's funeral this afternoon, video of people in dark suits and dark dresses entering Highland Park First United Methodist Church, wealthy people, white people, important people, the vice president, members of Congress, the governor, the mayor, and Scott's senior partner.

TEN

THE REST OF JUNE passed quietly. The temperature climbed steadily as summer set in so that by the end of the month the mercury was pushing one hundred degrees Fahrenheit. Rain became an infrequent occurrence and the sun beat down on the landscape with a vengeance. Native oak trees burrowed their roots deeper into the earth to suck the last drop of moisture from the parched Texas soil, and all God's creatures hunkered down for another merciless summer, except those wealthy Dallas families who could afford to flee to the cool air of Colorado or California. The less fortunate remained behind and relied on air-conditioning and backyard pools to survive the heat.

Rebecca Fenney continued her relentless climb up the Highland Park social ladder; Boo Fenney occupied herself at home with her computer and her books; Consuela de la Rosa was reunited with Esteban Garcia, just back from the border; Scott Fenney billed two hundred hours at $350 an hour for Ford Stevens's paying clients; Bobby Herrin billed one hundred hours at $50 an hour for the firm's only nonpaying client; and the federal grand jury formally indicted Shawanda Jones for the murder of Clark McCall. The federal magistrate set her bail at $1 million, which meant she would remain in custody until the verdict was read, at which time she would be either set free or shipped off to a federal prison to serve her sentence or await execution. She called her lawyer daily, sometimes several times a day, always crying hysterically from the combined effect of craving both her daughter and heroin. Having no idea where he might acquire heroin for her, her lawyer did the only thing he knew to get her to shut the fuck up: he agreed to bring her daughter down to the detention center to see her. Or at least to have Bobby bring her daughter to her.

But Bobby copped a plea: fear. "Shit, Scotty, East Dallas is scary enough for me," he said. "Fat white dude like myself, I wouldn't last five minutes in South Dallas. Sorry, man, but no way I'm risking my life for fifty bucks an hour!"

So it was that on the second day of July and the first hundred-degree day of the summer, A. Scott Fenney, Esq., $750,000-a-year corporate partner at Ford Stevens LLP, found himself driving a shiny red Ferrari 360 Modena slowly through a grim public housing project in South Dallas, past the rhythmic pounding of loud rap music and the glares of tough-looking young black men, and feeling as if he were driving a flashing neon sign that screamed CARJACK ME! Scott had played football with black teammates at SMU fourteen years ago, but he didn't figure that would count for much with these guys. Without conscious thought, Scott slid down the leather seat until he could barely see over the steering wheel.

Thirty-six years Scott Fenney had lived in Dallas and not once had he driven into South Dallas. White people drove south of downtown three times each year and only for events held within the gated Fair Park grounds—the State Fair, the Oklahoma-Texas football game, and the Cotton Bowl game—being careful to stay on the interstate, to take the Fair Park exit, and to drive directly through the park gates without detour or delay. White people never drove *into* South Dallas, into the neighborhoods and mean streets of South Dallas, into the other Dallas of crime and crack cocaine, prostitution and poverty, drive-by shootings and gang-bangers, into black Dallas, where a white boy from Highland Park driving a $200,000 Italian sports car was considered neither welcome nor very smart.

But here Scott was, parking in front of a concrete block building euphemistically called a "garden apartment" by the housing authority, although not a blade of grass much less a garden was evident to Scott's eye. He cut the engine and was working up the courage to get out—the Ferrari had attracted a crowd—when the sun was suddenly blocked out by a Dallas Cowboys jersey on the biggest black man he'd ever seen on or off a football field. Black knuckles rapped against the blacked-out window. Scott lowered the window an inch.

The jersey moved down until Scott saw wide shoulders, a thick neck, and finally a broad black face. The man lowered his sunglasses and peered in.

"You the lawyer?"

"What?"

"You Shawanda's lawyer?"

"Yeah."

"You here for Pajamae?"

"Yeah, how—"

"Shawanda call me. She figured you might need a, uh . . . chaperone, if you know what I mean."

Scott knew what he meant. He looked out both sides of the car at the crowd looking in, black women—girls really—with babies on their hips and toddlers clutching their thick legs and muscular black males, and he thought of Fight Night, the last time he had been in such close proximity to strong young black males. Started during the depths of the great Texas real-estate bust when the Dallas real-estate community desperately needed a distraction, Fight Night had become an annual tuxedo tradition: a boxing ring was set up in the swanky Anatole Hotel and black boxers were brought in to beat themselves senseless for the entertainment of rich white men smoking big cigars, eating thick steaks, drinking hard liquor, and playing patty-cake with beautiful young models hired for the night. Scott remembered thinking that the black boxers might be has-beens in the professional ranks, but they could KO every white guy in the joint with one punch—and probably wanted to.

Scott put on his glasses, not to appear smart, but in the hope that these black guys wouldn't beat up a white guy wearing glasses. He took a deep breath, opened the door, climbed out, and stood pressed against the Ferrari. He felt his face flush and heard the big man's voice boom out:

"Y'all back off, give the man some room! He's the lawyer!"

The crowd eased back several steps. Scott exhaled with relief, then inhaled the air, which felt even hotter down here, not a whiff of breeze or a tree in sight to offer shade from the sun, its full force seemingly directed down on him. Beads of sweat popped out of the pores on his forehead like popcorn and his starched shirt stuck to his skin. He glanced around at the gray bunkerlike buildings, the gray dirt yards, the gray concrete landscape, and the black residents, a strange world in the shadows of the downtown skyscrapers. If Scott's office faced south, his view would be of these projects, hence, the preferred northerly view, toward white Highland Park. Only five miles of pavement separated these projects from Highland Park, but the black kids plastering their faces against the Ferrari's windows to catch a glimpse of the plush leather interior might as well have been living in China.

"That a fine ride, mister," one black boy said with a wide grin.

The big man said, "I'm Louis." He gestured at the crowd. "Don't mind all them. We don't get many lawyers down here."

Louis stood maybe six six and weighed well over three hundred pounds. His huge hands dwarfed Scott's. So Scott didn't offer to shake hands; instead he said, "Scott Fenney," and handed his card to Louis, who examined it intently.

"What the *A* stand for?"

"Nothing." Scott pointed a thumb at the Ferrari. "Maybe I should wait in the car."

Louis said sternly to the boys: "Touch that car, you answering to me." Then he smiled at Scott and said, "Car be okay, Mr. Fenney." Louis turned and the crowd parted. Scott followed Louis a few paces up the sidewalk, but Louis abruptly stopped and turned back. "Still, you might wanna lock it."

"Oh, yeah."

Scott dug the keys out of his pocket and beeped the Ferrari locked and one of the boys said, "Aw, man!" Scott turned and followed Louis through a gauntlet of shirtless young black men bouncing basketballs so hard against the concrete it sounded like high-powered weapons discharging—*boom boom boom*. Their torsos were knotty with muscles and glistening with sweat, their sinewy arms etched with barbed-wire tattoos, their expressions sullen. They were wearing long shorts hung low on their hips and those $100 Nikes Scott couldn't afford as a boy and looking on Scott Fenney as prey, which no doubt he would have been but for the presence of Louis. Scott avoided direct eye contact with them like they say to do with wild animals for fear of inciting them. He wanted to cut and run back to the car and drive full throttle out of here. But he'd never make it to the Ferrari: the image of a pack of wolves pouncing on a fat little rabbit flashed through his mind. So he closed the gap with Louis and followed in the black man's shadow. And he had to admit to himself, he who had never felt fear on a football field felt it now. Scott Fenney was terrified. By the time they arrived at apartment 110, Scott's heart was beating against his chest wall like a jackhammer and he had broken a full-body sweat. Louis knocked on the door.

"Pajamae, it's Louis."

No answer. Louis knocked again. Still no answer. The front window was covered with thick drapes inside and black burglar bars outside. No light was visible from within the apartment.

"Maybe she's not home," Scott said.

Louis's body shook with a chuckle. "She home all right. She afraid to come outside. Don't even open the windows even though ain't no air-condition in there. She ain't come outside since Shawanda arrested." He leaned down and lowered his voice and said, "It's a good thing you doing, Mr. Fenney, taking Pajamae to see her mama."

Scott's mind was busy considering his chances of making it back through the gauntlet alive so the words, "Why didn't you?" were out of his mouth before he realized what he was saying. But Louis didn't react angrily. Instead, his big round face folded into a gold-toothed smile.

"Well, Mr. Fenney, me and the Feds, we got some, uh, outstanding issues, if you know what I mean."

Scott knew what Louis meant. He noticed the peephole in the door turn dark. And he heard a tiny voice: "That the lawyer?"

"Yeah," Louis said.

The peephole went light again and Scott heard the sound of a heavy object being pushed away from the door, then the releasing of five deadbolts. The door opened a crack and a small brown face with big brown eyes gazed up at Scott.

"You gonna save my mama?" she asked.

"Pajamae. That's a, uh, different sort of name."

Her face glued to the Ferrari's air-conditioning vent, the little black girl said, "Mama says it's French, but it's really just black.

118

We don't do names like Susie and Patty and Mandy down here. We do names like Shantay and Beyoncé and Pajamae."

"My daughter's name is Boo."

She smiled. "That's different."

Scott smiled back. "She's different. You'd like her."

Scott had relaxed considerably once they had left the projects and turned onto Martin Luther King Boulevard, the main thoroughfare through South Dallas. His heartbeat was near normal and his body wasn't sweating like a sprinkler hose. He wasn't even slouched in his seat. He was sitting upright, looking around at this strange environment like a Japanese tourist at a rodeo. On one side of the street was the tall black wrought-iron fence that guarded the Fair Park grounds; inside were the Cotton Bowl stadium where the Cowboys had played until they struck out for the suburbs, and the historic Art Deco buildings dating back to the Texas Centennial Exposition of 1936 that now sat abandoned and decaying like an old movie set. On the other side of the street were overgrown vacant lots that apparently served as the neighborhood's unofficial dumps, and boarded-up structures with broken-out windows and black men loitering outside.

"Crack houses," Pajamae said.

Run-down strip centers offered pawn shops and liquor stores. Ramshackle frame houses slanted at twenty-degree angles, their paint peeling like skin from a badly sunburned body. Sofas sat on droopy porches, old cars were jacked up on cement blocks in the yards, garbage was backed up at the streets, and black burglar bars guarded every door and window of every house and storefront as if each structure were its owner's personal prison. The entire landscape was dull and colorless, except for the graffiti adorning every wall and fence and the thick-bodied black women strolling by in colorful skirts and shorts and heels.

"Working girls," Pajamae said. "Mama says they work down here because they're too fat to get white tricks on Harry Hines."

Scott was imagining living in this neighborhood, walking

119

these streets with Boo, or worse, Boo walking alone, when his peripheral vision caught a commotion at the side of the road, and he slowed . . . a little.

"What's going on?"

On the sidewalk outside a dilapidated apartment complex was a massive pile of belongings, everything from a microwave to clothes, a basketball to dolls, as if someone had backed up a truck and dumped the stuff there. Sitting on the curb were two black kids, their elbows on their knees, their chins cradled in their palms, looking like their world had just come to an end. An obese black woman in red stretch shorts and a white tee shirt was yelling and gesturing wildly at a skinny black man wearing a short-sleeve shirt and a tie. Pajamae strained her neck to see, then slumped back down.

"Eviction day," she said matter-of-factly.

"They got evicted from their apartment?"

"Yeah. Happens first of every month."

As a young lawyer, Scott had appeared in J.P. court numerous times on behalf of landlords to evict deadbeat tenants. But he had never witnessed firsthand the law in action—a family's personal property removed from their apartment and dumped on the sidewalk out front, exactly as the eviction statute mandated. He glanced back at the scene and then accelerated away. When the Ferrari's expensive racing tires hit the interstate heading north to downtown Dallas, he breathed a sigh of relief.

"My daddy, he was white," Pajamae said.

He glanced over at the girl in the passenger's seat. She was a cute kid with facial features that were more white than black. Her hair was done in neat rows braided lengthwise and snug to her scalp with long braids hanging to her narrow shoulders; she was wearing a pink tee shirt, jean shorts, pink socks folded down, and white Nike sneakers. Other than her light brown skin, she was no

different from all the little girls Scott had seen in Highland Park—
except for the cornrows.

"Where is he?"

"Dead."

"Oh. I'm sorry."

"I'm not. He hurt my mama."

"How did he die?"

"Po-lice shot him. He was dealing."

She ran her finger lightly over the dash, as if checking for dust, and then she turned to Scott.

"Mr. Fenney, did my mama kill that white man?"

"No, baby, I ain't killed no one," Shawanda said through the glass partition, her right palm plastered to her side of the window and matched by Pajamae's left palm on the other side. Both mother and daughter were crying and aching to hold each other. When Shawanda had said she had a child, Scott had naturally assumed she was a lousy mother—she was a prostitute, for God's sake. But seeing them together now, it occurred to him that this woman loved her daughter as much as he loved his. He turned to the black guard.

"Can't they be together?"

The guard's eyes dropped; he scratched his chin. When his eyes came back up, he said, "You here to discuss her defense?"

Scott caught on quickly. "Yes."

The guard gestured at Pajamae. "She a material witness?"

"Yes."

"Okay."

The guard led them to the small room where Scott and Shawanda always met. He patted Scott down, but he only patted the top of Pajamae's head. When he brought Shawanda in, she dropped to her knees and embraced Pajamae for the longest time. The guard said he'd wait outside. Shawanda finally released Pajamae, then cupped her daughter's face and just stared at her, as if examining every inch of her smooth face. Then she held Pajamae at arm's length and looked her up and down.

"You dress yourself real nice," Shawanda said. "Louis bringing you groceries, watching out for you?"

Pajamae nodded. "Yes, Mama."

"You staying inside?"

Another nod. "Yes, Mama."

Shawanda appeared in much better health than the last time Scott had seen her, more alert, making Scott less worried she might puke on his suit.

"You sleeping now?" Scott asked.

"Yes, sir, Mr. Fenney. I'm over the worst part, except the headaches."

"I brought your medicine, Mama," Pajamae said.

"Good girl."

"I always take Tylenol for headaches," Scott said.

"I need something stronger."

"Ibuprofen?"

"Yeah, Ibu . . . that."

"When are you getting out, Mama?"

"I ain't, not till after the trial. If Mr. Fenney here prove me innocent."

Scott said, "No, Shawanda, I don't have to prove you're innocent. The government's got to prove you're guilty."

Shawanda looked at him like an adult at a naïve child.

"Mr. Fenney, you got a lot to learn."

"When's the trial?" Pajamae asked.

"End of August," Scott said.

Pajamae made a face. "But that's two months from now! What

122

am I supposed to do for that long? Mama, I'm scared to be alone in the projects!"

And the fear Scott Fenney had experienced less than an hour earlier returned with a vengeance. Sweat broke out on his forehead again. His heart beat faster again. His mind played out his odds of survival again, a fat little rabbit chased by a pack of wolves. He did not want to go back into South Dallas, not today, not ever. He did not want to take this little black girl back to her apartment in the projects and get out of the Ferrari and walk her to the door through a gauntlet of strong young black males looking upon him as prey. What if Louis weren't there to chaperone? But he couldn't very well put a little girl on a public bus or in a taxi alone. What the hell could he do with her? While mother and daughter embraced and shared tears, Scott's agile mind worked through all the available options until it arrived at an answer: Consuela de la Rosa.

He figured, Consuela's raising one little girl this summer, why not two? It was a perfect solution: Boo would have a playmate, this little girl wouldn't be scared and alone in the projects, and he wouldn't have to drive back into South Dallas. So in the emotion of the moment, Scott Fenney said words his wife would soon regret: "Pajamae, why don't you stay at my house until after the trial?"

"What the hell am I supposed to do with her?"

Rebecca's face was as red as her hair, her fists were embedded in her narrow hips, and she was glaring at him like he was a Neiman Marcus salesclerk who had brought her the wrong size dress to try on.

Scott had driven home directly from the courthouse. But as luck would have it, he had picked the one day his wife was not out social climbing to bring this little black girl home to Highland

Park. Boo had said, "I love your hair," and then had taken Pajamae upstairs. Consuela had retreated to the kitchen, and Scott found himself facing Rebecca's wrath alone. Of course, Scott wasn't about to tell his wife the whole truth, that he had brought this little black girl home mostly because he was scared to death to take her back to her own home. So he responded like a lawyer. He told her only part of the truth, the part that supported his position.

"She's living alone down in the projects, she's nine years old, she doesn't have anyone else—she doesn't even have air-conditioning! Hell, Rebecca, you go to Junior League and sit around with other Highland Park ladies dreaming up ways to help the less fortunate. This should win you the goddamn grand prize!"

"We help those people, Scott, but we don't invite them home. You said yourself her mother's going to be convicted. What are you going to do with her then, adopt her? Raise her as your daughter? Send her to Highland Park schools? Scott, there's not another black kid at Boo's school!"

Sometimes, as now, the intensity of his wife's anger unnerved Scott, much as when his college coach would grab his face mask and pull him close and chew him out over a blown play. Back then Scott Fenney would stand mute before his coach, and now he stood mute before this beautiful angry woman. Only difference was, little bits of chewing tobacco were not spewing out of her mouth with each angry word and sticking to Scott's face. Still, he would gladly swap this angry woman for wet tobacco in a heartbeat.

"And there's sure as hell not another girl named Pajamae!"

ELEVEN

"S cotty, WITH THIS EVIDENCE, we just might save her life."

Scott had escaped his wife's wrath and found sanctuary in the friendly confines of Dibrell Tower; he and Bobby were having a late lunch upstairs at the Downtown Club. He had filled Bobby in on his visit to the projects and the Fenney family's new houseguest and Rebecca's reaction. Now Bobby was bringing Scott up to date on Shawanda's legal case.

"My man Carl, the PI, he finds this Kiki, she backs up Shawanda's story. No surprise there. But then he talks to some Highland Park cops he's buddies with." Bobby leaned across the table, close enough for Scott to smell his last cigarette on his breath; his voice dropped to a whisper. "Get this: turns out Clark McCall was accused of rape and assault a year ago. SMU sorority girl. She filed a complaint, but it disappeared when daddy—as in Senator Mack McCall—paid her off. Carl talked to the desk sergeant on duty that night, cop that took the complaint. He said the girl was slapped around pretty good."

"How are we going to find her without the complaint?"

"Desk sergeant, he ain't stupid. Figures the senator knows he knows, so he also figures it might come in handy one day: he kept a copy of the complaint."

"Did he give it to Carl?"

"No way. He said it's locked away in a safe-deposit box. Said if he gave it to Carl, they'd know it came from him, he'd get fired, and he's only two years away from a pension. Said he'll deny having it if we call him to testify. But he gave Carl the woman's name, Hannah Steele. She lives in Galveston now."

"Will she testify?"

"Carl's flying down there today to find out."

Scott turned his palms up. "So . . . ?"

"So our defense is twofold. First, she didn't pull the trigger, which is gonna be tough with her fingerprints on her gun and one of her bullets in his brain. And if she didn't, who did? Clark? He suddenly realizes his evil ways and decides to make the world a better place and off himself? I don't think so. Our backup is self-defense. He called her racial slurs, he attacked her, so she shot him in self-defense. But she's black, a hooker, and a drug addict—who's gonna believe her, right? That's where Hannah Steele comes in, corroborating testimony. Nice white girl testifies Clark beat and raped her a year ago, jury figures maybe Shawanda's telling the truth. And the jury's got to include some blacks. We show them that Clark McCall was a racist and a rapist, we might just save her life."

"An acquittal?"

Bobby gave him a look. "No, not an acquittal, Scotty. Life in prison, maybe parole in thirty with good time. You don't get acquitted when your gun is the murder weapon and your fingerprints are on the gun and the gun was fired point-blank into the victim's brain while he was lying on the floor. With that kind of evidence, life in prison is a win for her."

"Goddamnit, Dan, you tell him to drop it and drop it now!"

The senator's voice was so loud in Dan Ford's ear that he pulled the phone away a few inches. Dan had just gotten a status report from Scott on the Shawanda Jones case and, per his agreement with the senator, he had immediately placed a call to Washington. Mack McCall, the senior senator from Texas, didn't like what he heard.

"Bad enough, Dan, a hooker taking the stand and saying Clark beat her and called her nigger. But your boy starts parading white girls up there saying Clark beat and raped them, too, I'm fucking finished! I thought that girl was taken care of! And what if they dredge up that crap from college, Clark and his fraternity?"

Clark McCall had organized a "Minority Night" fraternity party where everyone dressed up as their favorite minority; Clark had gone in blackface as a pimp. Mack had bought off the newspaper to keep the story quiet. Dan Ford had been the bagman.

"The public will think he learned that at home! From me! Press gets hold of that, I'll be branded another Strom fucking Thurmond! I'll never see the inside of the White House!" A pause. "And, Dan, you will never be the president's lawyer."

"George W. Bush?"

"Yes," Scott said.

Sid Greenberg seemed stunned. "The president used eminent domain to take people's land for a baseball stadium?"

"He wasn't the president back then, Sid. He wasn't even the governor yet. While you were at Harvard being taught by left-wing professors, George Bush was running the Texas Rangers. They were playing in a crappy old stadium, so he got the city to condemn land to build a new stadium."

"How is that a public use?"

"It's not."

"Then how could the city condemn the land?"

"Because the law allows it . . . or at least the courts haven't stopped it. They did it for the Rangers stadium, they did it for the NASCAR motor speedway, they're doing it for the new Cowboys stadium . . . Hell, Sid, they're doing it all across the country and not just for roads and parks, but for stadiums and shopping malls and big box stores . . ."

"And now we're going to do it for Dibrell's hotel."

Scott shrugged. "That's the deal Tom made with the city."

"We're going to take poor people's homes so rich people can stay in a five-star luxury hotel?" Sid looked indignant. "Why don't they ever take rich people's homes?"

"Because rich people can afford to hire lawyers and fight it in court. Poor people can't."

"So the city's gonna buy them out cheap—with Dibrell's money, bulldoze their homes, and give the land to Dibrell so he can build his hotel? What's in it for the city?"

"Millions more in property taxes. The hotel will be worth a hundred million, minimum. Those little homes are worth a million, max."

"Dibrell gets his hotel, the city gets more taxes, and poor people get screwed. And it's all perfectly legal."

"Sid, we do what the law allows . . . and sometimes what it doesn't."

"You know, Scott, screwing the government and plaintiffs' lawyers, that's fun, it's just a game. But poor people? My parents were poor. I grew up in a house like those."

"Look, Sid, I don't like it either, but that's our job. At least we're only taking thirty homes. They took a hundred twenty homes for that mall out in Hurst, and they're taking ninety homes for the Cowboys stadium."

"Well, that makes me feel better." Sid shook his head. "This is what I went to Harvard Law School for?"

Scott turned his palms up. "Sid, what do you want me to do? Tell Dibrell we won't do it? If I say no to Dibrell, he'll find another lawyer who'll say yes. This deal is gonna get done, those homes are gonna get condemned, and that hotel is gonna get built. The only question is which lawyers are going to get paid half a million dollars for doing it. If Dibrell takes this deal to another firm, Sid, that means I've got to fire one of my associates. Are you willing to give up your job—and your two-hundred-thousand-dollar salary—so you don't have to condemn those people? So you don't get your hands dirty?"

Sid stared at his shoes. Finally, he shook his head slowly and said, "No."

"Sid, when I was a young lawyer, Dan Ford told me, 'Scotty, check your conscience at the door each morning or you won't last long in the law.' "

Sid looked up. "The law sucks."

"It's just business, Sid."

"They don't tell you that in law school, do they, that the law is just a business, a game we play, with other people's lives and money? No, they need someone to pay tuition, kids who don't have a clue what being a lawyer's all about, kids who think . . ."

Scott sat silently, nodding like a therapist as his patient vented. Every lawyer goes through the same metamorphosis that Sid was now going through, like a caterpillar changing into a butterfly, only in reverse: from a beautiful human being to a slimy lawyer. Scott recalled Dan Ford nodding as a young patient named Scott Fenney vented.

Sid was saying, "Last time I went back home, my parents had

all their friends in the old neighborhood over so they could show me off, their son the big-time lawyer. How am I supposed to tell them what we really do, Scott?"

"You're not. You can't. You *don't*. You walk out that door each night, you leave it here, Sid, your lawyer life. You don't take it home with you. Look, Sid, you've only been at this for five years. It takes a while to learn that you only talk about these things with other lawyers. Regular people just don't understand what we do."

"That's the thing, Scott, I think they do."

"Sid, wait till you get married, have children, you'll see. You'll go home and your wife and kids are gonna say, 'Daddy, what did you do today?' What are you going to tell them, the truth? Hell, no. You're gonna lie. We all lie."

Sid took a moment to consider Scott's words, then slowly stood and walked to the door, but turned back.

"Oh, Scott, we closed Dibrell's land deal. We got the environmental report, escrowed $10 million of the purchase price. We'll start paving over the lead soon. TRAIL will never know about the report, and the EPA will never know about the lead."

"Aggressive and creative lawyering, Sid."

Sid nodded and turned away, but Scott could hear him say, "I should've gone to med school."

After Sid left Scott turned to his computer. He was logging in one billable hour to Dibrell's account for the thirty-minute "office conference" with Sid when he felt a presence. He turned and saw Dan Ford standing in his doorway, about as ordinary an occurrence as going to Sunday morning Mass and seeing the Pope standing at the altar.

"Dan, come in."

Dan entered, his face creased with worry. He started shaking his head slowly and sighed like a man with the weight of the world on his shoulders.

"I knew this case would bring no good."

"What do you mean?"

"I just got off the phone with McCall."

"*The senator?* You mentioned him before, but I didn't realize you knew him personally."

Dan nodded. "Mack and I were fraternity brothers at SMU. I'm the executor of his will, I handle a few personal matters for him from time to time. Haven't done much work for him since he sold the company and went to Washington twenty years ago. But if he's elected and Ford Stevens is recognized as the president's personal law firm . . . Scotty, it'd be a gold mine."

"Great."

"Yes, that would be great, Scotty. We could add fifty lawyers, maybe more, on the new business we'd get, corporate clients who'd beat a path to my door and pay any fee I demanded because I could pick up the phone and get the president to answer. You got any idea what that's worth to a lawyer? I'm a big fish in a small pond here in Dallas, Scotty, but as the president's lawyer, I'd be a big fish in a big pond. I'd be playing on a national stage . . . We could open a Washington office. Think what that could do for me. For this firm. For you. Scotty, you could make a million dollars the first year he's in office, two the year after that, three by the time you're forty. You'd be filthy rich, just like you tell our summer clerks."

Dan paused and caught his breath. "But Mack made it clear that if his son's good name is dragged through the mud at this trial, Ford Stevens will not be his personal law firm."

Scott leaned back in his chair. "He wants me to hide Clark's past."

"Yes, he does."

"But, Dan, Clark McCall was a rapist and a racist. And now with Hannah Steele's testimony, we might save Shawanda's life."

"Yes, you might at that. But you would also destroy Mack's chances to be president. Scotty, if the press can put 'racist' and

131

'rapist' and 'McCall' in the same sentence—even if it's about his son—his chances of winning the nomination are about as good as me getting laid by Miss America."

"Dan, why didn't you tell me you did work for McCall? I could've told Buford we had a conflict of interest, gotten out of the case."

Dan nodded. "I talked to Mack about that option, but he said it would be better to have some, uh, influence with the hooker's lawyer."

"In case her lawyer learned about Clark's past."

Dan shrugged. "Mack McCall didn't make eight hundred million dollars by not thinking out all the angles."

"Clark McCall was a loser, Dan. Rich boy who liked to beat up girls ends up dead because he beat up the wrong girl. Why should we give a damn about his reputation?"

"We don't. But this isn't about Clark McCall, Scott, it's about Mack McCall. And we do give a damn about his reputation because it's in this firm's best interest for him to be the next president. Scotty, we hold his presidency in our hands! Think about it. He'd owe me big-time!"

His eyes got a faraway look and his mouth formed a half smile, which meant inside Dan Ford was turning somersaults. After a moment, he returned to the present and said, "So what do you say, Scotty, my boy?"

Scott said nothing. The two lawyers, separated by twenty-five feet of hardwood floor and almost as many years of lawyering, stared at each other as if they were two kids trying to see who would blink first. Scott knew what his senior partner wanted him to say, that he would follow McCall's orders because what was good for McCall was good for Ford Stevens. But—and Scott couldn't put into thought why—he couldn't bring himself to say those words. Whether born of the mulelike stubbornness he had inherited from Butch or his long-standing general disdain for rich boys like Clark

132

McCall or perhaps something deeper, something inside him wouldn't allow it. Finally, Dan broke eye contact, exhaled loudly, and turned to the door. On his way out, he said, "Scott, I need an answer for McCall. Soon."

Boo sat up in the lounge chair by the pool in the backyard. She was wearing a white bathing suit and sunglasses and drinking pink punch Consuela had made. Pajamae was lying facedown in the adjacent lounge chair, wearing one of Boo's many bathing suits. They were taking turns rubbing sunscreen onto each other's back. It was Boo's turn. She lifted Pajamae's long braids and squirted a line of sunscreen onto her back.

A normal summer afternoon for Boo was spent home alone, reading a book. A. Scott was downtown, Mother was at the country club, and most of the kids her age were at their summer homes or at camp or in Europe. Not that Barbara Boo Fenney had many friends here in the Bubble. Most girls her age wanted to brag about their things. She didn't. She was different. She thought different thoughts and she wore different clothes and she wanted different things. The other girls said she was weird and called her a lesbo because she didn't dress like a girl. So she usually played by herself or swam under Consuela's watchful eye. But today she had a new friend. Who was different, too.

"I love your hair," Boo said. She began rubbing the white lotion into Pajamae's brown skin. "Do black people need sunscreen?"

After a moment, Pajamae said, "I don't know. But Mama always makes me put it on."

"When will she get out of jail?"

"End of summer, if Mr. Fenney gets her out."

"If she didn't do it, she'll get out."

"Don't work that way for us."

"Us who?"

"Black people."

"A. Scott's a great lawyer. He'll get your mother out."

"I hope so. 'Cause my mama, she wouldn't do well in prison."

Boo rubbed until the lotion disappeared into Pajamae's skin, then said, "Why do you talk like we do?"

"What do you mean?"

"Well, whereas—"

"Where what?"

"Whereas."

"Where *ass*?"

"No, where*as*. A. Scott's always saying whereas this and whereas that . . . it's lawyer talk. Lawyers have lots of words like that."

Pajamae was grinning. "Whereas. I like that. Where-*as*!"

"You don't talk like black people on TV talk, like . . ."

"Black English, Mama calls it, like everyone in the projects talks. She says I'm not allowed to talk like that. She says I have to use correct English."

Boo lifted one of Pajamae's braids and let it slide through her fingers. She sat up with a start.

"Come on, I've got a great idea!"

Driving home, Scott was wondering why he wasn't feeling more insulted by Mack McCall's arrogant assumption that he could simply dictate to A. Scott Fenney, Esq., the terms of his representation of a client. The legal code of ethics to which all lawyers swear allegiance (at least long enough to obtain a license to practice law) clearly states (in theory) that a lawyer shall not be influenced by any outside interests in the zealous representation of his client. Of course, in practice the code of ethics is viewed by most lawyers in the same way career criminals view the penal code: more in the nature of suggestions than actual rules governing one's professional conduct.

On the other hand, Scott was also wondering why he hadn't readily agreed to McCall's demands as requested by his senior partner. Scott had never gone against Dan Ford's wishes—that would be like going against his own father. He had rubber-stamped all of Dan's decisions for the firm, whether firing a partner or dumping a client or making campaign contributions to friendly judges up for reelection, because Dan was always acting in the best interests of Ford Stevens and thus in Scott's best interests. Why had he hesitated this time? For the first time?

Back to the first hand: the fact that United States Senator Mack McCall just *assumed* Scott Fenney would drop his client's best defense to a murder charge simply because McCall told him to, that should have brought Scott's blood to a boil. *Who the hell does he think he is?* Back in college, if someone had even dared suggest that Scott Fenney, star halfback, might throw a game, he would have gotten pissed off and punched the son of a bitch in the mouth! Just for thinking he possessed so little integrity as to even entertain the idea of throwing a football game! So why wasn't A. Scott Fenney, Esq., similarly pissed off when asked to throw a trial? Why was he even entertaining the idea? Had he engaged in so much aggressive and creative lawyering that he no longer recognized the difference between making a deal and compromising his integrity? Had he become such a good lawyer that he had no integrity left to compromise?

He was wrestling with these thoughts as he drove past the walled estates along Preston Road that backed up to Turtle Creek, the grand residences of real-estate tycoon Trammell Crow ($13.3 million appraised value), and Dallas Cowboys owner Jerry Jones ($14.1 million), and Tom Dibrell ($18 million), and Mack McCall ($25 million)—and he realized that it had never before registered with him that McCall and his best client owned adjoining estates.

He slowed as he passed the entrance to the McCall estate and was thinking back to the night of the murder, Clark and Shawanda driving in through those gates, only minutes remaining in Clark McCall's life, when his cell phone rang. He answered.

"Scott Fenney."

"Mr. Fenney, this is Louis."

"Louis . . ."

"From the projects."

"Oh, yeah, sure, Louis."

"Well, Mr. Fenney, Pajamae, she ain't come back yet, and I be getting kinda worried . . . She still with you?"

"Oh, Louis, I'm sorry, I should've had my secretary call you. Pajamae's going to stay with us until the trial's over."

"Us who?"

"Me. My family."

"You taking Pajamae in?"

"Well, yeah, you know, until this is over. We were down at the courthouse with Shawanda this morning and I didn't want to drive—" Scott decided not to mention that he didn't want to return to Louis's part of town—"and, well, I've got a daughter her age, and we've got four bedrooms sitting empty, and I just thought it might be better that way. Shawanda thought so, too."

"What about her stuff, clothes and all?"

"Oh, she can wear my daughter's clothes. They're about the same size and, hell, my daughter never wears half the clothes my wife buys her anyway."

"You want, I can bring her stuff to you."

"To Highland Park?"

The phone was silent. Scott thought again he might have angered Louis. But he was wrong again.

"Louis?"

"Projects ain't no place for a little girl living alone, Mr. Fenney.

Tell her I said hey. And if you need any help down my way, you let me know."

"Okay, thanks, Louis."

"Oh, and Mr. Fenney . . ."

"Yeah?"

"I guess I wouldn't expect something like that from a white man. You a good man, Mr. Fenney."

Scott disconnected and wondered if Louis was right.

Boo bounced down the stairs to the kitchen and over to the table, followed by Pajamae. Mother took one look at Boo, put her hands on her hips, and said, "Young lady, what have you done to your hair?"

Boo's long red hair was now braided tight to her scalp with long braids hanging to her shoulders.

"Cornrows. Pajamae did it. Pretty cool, huh?"

Mother turned to A. Scott and said, "Well, Scott?"

He shrugged and said, "She looks like Bo Derek."

"Bo Derek?"

"Yeah, from that movie."

Mother threw her hands up. "Barbara Boo Fenney, Highland Park debutantes don't wear their hair in cornrows!"

"Then it's not a problem, Mother, because I'm not gonna be a deb."

Mother sighed heavily, restraining her anger, and said, "Pajamae, I hope you don't have any tattoos."

Pajamae laughed, but she didn't know Mother wasn't being funny. Consuela held up the salt and pepper shakers and said from the stove, "Is twins, like these." She pointed at Boo—"Is salt"—and then at Pajamae—"is pepper." Consuela chuckled and her body shook like Jell-O. "Salt and pepper."

Mother was shaking her head and her lips were a tight line across her face, normally not a good sign.

"Finish the enchiladas, Consuela."

"Y'all expecting company?" Pajamae asked.

Boo turned to Pajamae, who was standing at the table.

"What?"

"All this food, are you having a party?"

The table was crowded with tacos and enchiladas and gua-camole and refried beans and flour tortillas and hot sauce. Mexican food night.

"No."

"This is all just for us?"

Boo shrugged. "Yeah."

Pajamae smiled and said, "Where-*as*."

Butch and Barbara Fenney had always discussed family matters at the dinner table, in front of their young son: good things and bad things, successes and failures, possibilities and problems. They figured he would learn by listening. Scott recalled one such conversation, not too long before his father died, when Butch said a contractor wanted him to cut some corners on a job to reduce costs and increase the contractor's profits. The owner would never know. Butch was faced with either complying with the contractor's demands or losing the job. He asked his wife for advice. Scott's mother responded without a second thought: tell him no.

So after retiring to the master suite, while Rebecca stood naked before the bathroom mirror and removed her makeup and checked her body for early signs of aging, Scott told her about Dan's visit to his office and Mack McCall's demands and he asked his wife for advice. She, too, responded without a second thought: "Do it! If Dan says drop it, you damn well better drop it. Are you going to give up everything we have for a goddamn—"

"What, Rebecca? A goddamn what?"

She whirled around, incredibly naked, and said, "A goddamn black whore, that's what!"

A. Scott Fenney, Esq., had zealously defended his rich clients against all comers—business competitors, the government, famous plaintiffs' lawyers, and young women claiming sexual harassment. But never against his wife. Of course, he had never had a black whore for a client. Still, his natural lawyerly instinct was to defend his client. So, perhaps because McCall's demands were still weighing on his mind or because he had never thrown a game in his life or because rich boys like Clark McCall had always graveled his butt or because he knew Louis was not right about Scott Fenney or because of the love Shawanda showed for Pajamae that very morning or because of two little girls with their hair in cornrows on the floor above . . . or maybe just because this beautiful woman standing naked before him had denied him sex for over seven months . . . and his heat for her now turned into anger at her—Scott Fenney lashed out at his wife, defending Shawanda Jones with a passion normally reserved for only the richest of clients: "What, she deserves to die just because she's black and a prostitute? What if you had been born black, Rebecca? Would you still have been Miss SMU and chairwoman of the Cattle Barons' Ball? Or would you have ended up a hooker on Harry Hines, too?" He pointed to the floor above. "But for the grace of God, Rebecca, Boo could be that little black girl!"

His naked wife laughed without smiling.

"Don't you get self-righteous with me, Scott Fenney. You wanted money and all the things money can buy as much as I did—this house, that Ferrari . . . How much did you pay for that suit? I married you because you had ambition, you wanted to be a rich lawyer. You didn't go to work at the legal aid so you could help poor black people in South Dallas. You went to a big law firm so you could make lots of money working for rich clients living in

Highland Park. And now you're suddenly growing a conscience? I don't think so."

She pointed a finger at Scott. "You do this, you ruin my life over a whore—who you know goddamn well is guilty as sin—and I swear to God, we're through!" She now pointed upward. "And that little girl will be better off without her mother."

Upstairs on the third floor, Boo and Pajamae were getting ready for bed. A. Scott had read to them, which Pajamae enjoyed. It was fun to have a friend. Boo had insisted they share her room so they could talk. Pajamae agreed. But now Boo was kneeling up in bed and wondering what the heck Pajamae was doing, spreading out a comforter on the floor with a pillow.

"What in the Sam Hill are you doing?"

"Whose hill?"

"It's just an expression."

"Oh. Fixing my bed."

"On the floor?"

Pajamae looked at her bed on the floor, then at Boo in the tall bed. "You sleep in the bed?"

Boo laughed. "Of course, I do. Where do you sleep?"

"On the floor."

"Oh, you don't have a real bed?"

"No, I've got a bed."

"Do you have a bad back? Sometimes A. Scott sleeps on the floor when his back acts up, from when he played football."

"No, I don't have a bad back."

"Then why?"

"It's safer."

"From what?"

"Gunfire."

After some discussion, Boo convinced Pajamae that it was safe to sleep in a bed in Highland Park, and they were sleeping side by side an hour later when Scott climbed the stairs, as he did each night before going to bed, to check on his daughter and to kiss her on the forehead. The two girls were lying so close together that when he leaned over and kissed Boo, he had only to lean over just a little more to kiss Pajamae on the forehead as well. When he did, she stirred and whispered in her sleep, "Daddy?"

TWELVE

THE COMPETITION from other Dallas law firms for the top law graduates each year was fierce. Ford Stevens offered the same starting salary, required the same billable hours, and promised the same personal chemistry between partners and associates. Money and hours were easy sells; personal chemistry, though, took all of the partners' lawyering skills, pretending to care about these students' lives when in fact they cared more about their own shoes. But then, lying to law students was just part of the game.

And that game was being played in earnest today at 4000 Beverly Drive. Scott Fenney was hosting Ford Stevens's annual Fourth of July party for the firm's summer clerks at his Highland Park home. He was standing on the patio under the awning and shaking his head: forty out-of-shape law students in bathing suits, their pale white bodies frolicking in and around his fabulous pool and professionally landscaped backyard, was not a pretty sight. Thank God they had the good sense not to wear Speedos. If not for Missy and the other cheerleaders in bikinis, the view from the patio would have been downright dismal.

"Got some good news, Scotty."

He hadn't noticed Bobby there. "What's that?"

"Talked to Hannah Steele. She'll testify. Told me the whole story about Clark, said he was the nicest guy in the world until he got loaded, then he turned into an animal. His idea of foreplay was smacking her across the face." Bobby took a swig of beer. "Shawanda did the world a favor, blowing his brains out."

"So she's it then, our only defense?"

"Yep. But she wants her name kept quiet until the trial. She's scared shitless of McCall."

"Don't we have to put her on our witness list?"

Bobby shrugged. "We're supposed to. But Buford, he'll cut us some slack, seeing how he hates the death penalty and Burns won't give it up. Did you read my brief on that, why the death penalty doesn't apply to this case under the statute?"

Scott shook his head.

"Have you read any of my briefs or motions?"

"I haven't had time."

Bobby grunted and went in search of the barbecue, leaving Scott to his thoughts, which were of Dan Ford: *Scott, I need an answer for McCall. Soon.*

"Well, if it isn't Johnnie Cochran."

Bernie Cohen had arrived with a beer in his hand.

"What's your whore's defense, Scott?" His next words came out in his version of rap rhythm. "If the condom don't fit, you must acquit?"

Bernie thought he was hilarious. He was a partner in the securities section of Ford Stevens and looked like he was fifty years old even though he was only a year older than Scott. No muscular definition was noticeable anywhere on his body; Bernard Cohen was what in junior high they called a "fat-butted boy." Bernie pointed his beer at Boo and Pajamae sitting on the edge of the far side of the pool.

"That her daughter?"

"Yeah."

"She's living with you?"

"Yeah."

"Saw your client's photo in the paper. She's a good-looking black babe." Bernie nudged Scott's arm and grinned. "She paying you in kind?"

"Shut up, Bernie."

Bernie recoiled, snorted, and walked away, leaving Scott to wonder why at one time he had sort of liked the pudgy prick. And why he wasn't enjoying the party the way he had last year when he had taken great pride in showing off his residence to the impressionable students: the one-acre estate in the heart of Highland Park; the four-car garage occupied by the Ferrari, Rebecca's Mercedes-Benz coupe, and the Land Rover they used for family road trips; and the expansive covered patio overlooking the pool and cabana, beyond which was a vast expanse of grass kept lush and green by the underground sprinkler system. Scott had set up a volleyball net out there and some of the students were now playing. He shook his head—not an athlete in the bunch.

This year he just couldn't get into the spirit of the day. The students were happy, the cheerleaders were friendly, the beer was flowing, and the barbecue was cooking . . . but Scott's thoughts were on Shawanda Jones and the little black girl sitting on the far side of the pool and his wife's threat and Dan Ford's demand. *Scott, I need an answer for McCall. Soon.* The trial was only seven weeks away, and Scott had a big decision to make, a decision he didn't want to make, a decision that had darkened his mind. That feeling of impending doom had become his constant companion.

———

Sitting on the edge of the pool, Pajamae said, "I haven't been around this many white people since last year when Mama took me to the State Fair. Only time we see white people."

"You haven't missed much," Boo said.

Pajamae waved her hand around. "Who are they?"

"Lawyer wannabes."

"Whatabes?"

"Students A. Scott's law firm is trying to hire."

"Those are some homely white boys. But the girls are real pretty. Are they their women?"

"The cheerleaders?"

"They're cheerleaders?"

"They used to be. A. Scott pays them to come to the party and act interested in the students, so they'll hire on. He calls it bait and switch."

"Bait and what?"

"Bait and switch, like when an ad in the paper says certain Rollerblades are on sale, but when you get to the store they say they're sold out so you should buy another brand that costs more."

"Oh, like when a trick tries to get Mama to lower her price after she gets in his car."

"Someone tricked your mother into his car?"

"No, the trick—that's the john."

"The toilet?"

"No, a man who wants to buy Mama."

"Your mother's for sale?"

Pajamae nodded. "By the hour."

"A. Scott sells himself by the hour, too. He calls them billable hours. He charges three hundred fifty dollars an hour."

"Mama makes almost that much and she didn't go to school."

"Awesome. Anyway, these students think if they hire on with A. Scott's law firm they'll get dates with beautiful girls like these, but they really won't."

"If they pay enough, they will. Mama says it's just a question of pricing."

On brutally hot days like today, Bobby would often grab a beer, go out back of his two-bedroom, one-bath lean-to in East Dallas, and sit in a six-inch-deep inflatable pool—his version of a pool party. This pool party was a lot better. For one thing, the pool was bigger. And for another, his eyes weren't closed and he wasn't dreaming of a backyard full of beautiful girls in bikinis; his eyes were wide open and the girls were real. He was really happy Scotty had invited him.

Bobby was standing alone at one corner of the pool, a beer in one hand and a long pork rib in the other, dripping barbecue sauce on his bare belly and trying not to appear too obvious as he ogled the girls. He was wearing only swim trunks. His pale body was not lean and tanned and muscular like Scotty's. Still, compared to the law students, he was feeling like a regular goddamned Adonis when an incredible looking girl in a white bikini sidled up to him, close enough that he could feel the warmth emanating from her skin. Without thinking, Bobby sucked in his gut—a little.

"Noticed you're not wearing a wedding ring," she said.

"That's because I'm not married."

"What a coincidence," she said, turning her big eyes up to him. "Neither am I."

Bobby had already downed several beers, so his courage was operating at its maximum level.

"So what's a gorgeous single girl like yourself doing at a party like this?"

"Looking for a rich lawyer like you."

You can't fault honesty, Bobby thought, as she leaned into him and her breasts pushed together and rose as one until he thought they might pop out of her bikini top. The mere touch of her skin against his raised a distinct feeling in Bobby's trunks.

147

"Well, just so you know, I don't have a home like this, I'm not a rich lawyer, and chances are pretty good I'm never gonna be a rich lawyer. But, hey, we can still slip inside, find a quiet place, and screw ourselves silly."

She pulled back as if she had suddenly discovered poison ivy all over his body. She gave him a thin smile and said, "I don't think so."

And she was gone. Bobby closed his eyes and inhaled her scent one last time. But it was soon gone, too, as was the rise in his swim trunks. He walked over to the only two girls who weren't looking for a rich lawyer that day. Boo and Pajamae were sitting on the edge of the pool, dangling their feet into the water.

"Hey, Bobby," Boo said.

"Girls."

Pajamae said, "Whereas, Mr. Herrin."

Scotty had introduced Bobby to the girls earlier. Bobby now joined them, dropping his feet into the cool water.

"Where's your mother?" he asked Boo. "Haven't seen her since I first got here."

"Back inside," Boo said. "She hates these parties."

"What about you?"

"Oh, I love them. I try to guess what these people's lives are like when they're not sucking up to A. Scott for a job."

Bobby laughed. "Scotty said you're nine going on twenty-nine." He pointed the pork rib at one of the male students. "Okay, tell me about his life, the skinny one with the black glasses."

Boo studied the student for a moment and said, "He's incredibly smart. He went to law school only because his dad is a lawyer, but he wants to do computer stuff. He'll graduate top of his class, hire on with A. Scott's firm, and quit after one year. He's never had a date, he's terribly shy, and he's wishing right now he was back home at his computer, where he's happiest. He's always going to be alone."

Bobby stared down at the child in amazement. "That's pretty

good. Okay, Pajamae, your turn. What about her, the blonde over there with the, uh . . ."

"Store-bought boobs?"

"Uh, yeah, that one. What's her story?"

"She's way dumb, but she doesn't know it. She'll marry a rich lawyer and live happily ever after."

Bobby found himself nodding in agreement.

"You girls are good. Okay, Boo, what about this guy?"

Boo moved her eyes about, scanning the pool crowd.

"Which guy?"

Bobby was now pointing the pork rib at himself.

"Me."

Boo considered him for a moment, then dropped her eyes to the water and shook her head.

"Hey, come on, tell me."

Boo looked back up; her eyes seemed sad.

"No, Bobby."

Bobby laughed and said, "What? I'm a big boy, I can handle it," figuring she was going to say he was a pathetic loser and always would be. Hell, no surprise there. He told himself the same thing every morning in the mirror.

But Boo was quiet. Then, without looking at him, she said: "You secretly loved my mother, but she married A. Scott. You've never gotten over it. You've always wondered what your life would've been like if she had married you instead."

Bobby hadn't figured on that. He had to take a deep breath. He pushed himself up but looked down at her.

"How?"

"I saw how you looked at her when you got here. Your eyes went all over the crowd, kind of frantic like, until you saw her. Then you just looked at her for a long time. Like, forever."

Bobby walked directly to the beer cooler.

From the windows of the master suite on the second floor Rebecca Fenney was looking down on the backyard scene at two of the three men who loved her: Scott, surrounded by law students and cheerleaders and one buxom blonde in a black string bikini giving him the come-on; and Bobby, alone by the beer cooler. Poor Bobby. She had known he loved her back when he and Scott were in law school, but he had kept it to himself, never one to challenge for any of Scott's possessions. Not that he could have won her; everyone knew Bobby Herrin wasn't going places, just as everyone knew Scott Fenney was. So Rebecca Garrett had signed on for the Scott Fenney ride. And it had been quite a ride: eleven years ago she had been living in a sorority house, driving a used Toyota, and leading cheers for the SMU Mustangs; today she was living in a mansion, driving a Mercedes, and vying to be chairwoman of the Cattle Barons' Ball. But now she found herself feeling anxious and afraid and wondering: *Is the ride coming to an end?*

Rebecca Garrett had grown up in a working-class suburb of Dallas. She hated having less; she wanted more. So for her college education she looked no further than SMU. For poor Dallas kids, SMU was their entrée to a better life. It was a way in to Highland Park.

Rebecca was a smart student, in and out of class. In fact, when she drove her old car up and down the streets of Highland Park and fancied herself the woman of the house at one of the fabulous mansions, she was smart enough to acknowledge a fact of life: she would never have a Highland Park home on her own, by using her brain, by pursuing a career. No woman would.

Her future lay in her looks, as it always had. From the time she was ten, other children's mothers would stop and say, "My, what a remarkably beautiful child"; and when she was sixteen and her body had become a woman's, her friends' fathers would stare; and when she was twenty-one and the most beautiful girl at SMU and she interviewed for jobs, men's eyes lit up when they saw her beauty—they wanted it and they would pay for it.

But she would not sell her beauty by the hour or by the night or even by the job. Rebecca Garrett would sell her beauty for community property, for half of everything her husband would acquire over the course of their marriage. As every Texas girl knows by the time she graduates high school, in Texas wives don't have to beg for alimony; in Texas wives are entitled to half of everything—by law.

So she needed a husband. As she saw it, her beauty afforded her three matrimonial options: an older man who had already made his fortune (but such a man always comes with baggage, usually a couple of ex-wives and twice as many kids on the dole); the son of such an older rich man (but an inherited fortune is not community property); or a man with the ambition to make his own fortune, a fortune made during marriage, a fortune of community property. Scott Fenney, a Highland Park and SMU football legend, was just that kind of man. There is no better place in the world to be a football legend than Dallas, Texas. It's as close to an iron-clad guarantee of success as life offers.

So Rebecca Garrett bet her beauty on Scott Fenney.

She loved him back then, but she would not have married him if he had wanted to coach high school football and live in a small house in the suburbs. She could not separate her love from his ambition. She loved him because he wanted what she wanted, because his desire to have all this equaled her own. They were two of a kind. So they married and settled in a small $500,000 home in Highland Park; Scott became Tom Dibrell's lawyer and she became the most beautiful woman in Highland Park.

The early years of the Scott Fenney ride were exactly what she had expected: they bought, they acquired, they went out, they moved up. Scott fought for the family fortune at Ford Stevens; she joined the society clubs and paid her social dues. Success followed success, his and hers. They soon made the Highland Park A-list, the up-and-coming couple, young and beautiful, smart and successful, the SMU legend and Miss SMU. They were the envy of all: men wanted her and women wanted him. But they expended their sexual energies only with each other—success excited her and she excited him. Her husband wanted her with a passion that always burned hot; he needed her more than life itself, a need that never waned or wandered. Success and sex: Rebecca Fenney's life was perfect and getting better by the day.

Until the day she became pregnant.

Which came as a complete shock—motherhood had never been part of her plans—and a recurring one as she watched helplessly as her belly expanded and her body bloated up until she looked like a beached whale. She had always loved to look at herself when she passed a mirror; now she averted her eyes. Rebecca Fenney was not a squat soccer mom in a minivan! She was a sleek white woman in a black Mercedes coupe! Which she drove over to Harry Hines on more than one occasion trying to work up the courage to enter one of the clinics and have an abortion. Of course, she would have blamed the loss of the child on a miscarriage; there are no abortions in politically conservative Highland Park.

But Scott wanted the child.

He alerted all the world that a Fenney child was on the way. Men looked ahead fifteen years to when Scotty Junior would make his football debut at Highland Park High; women showered Rebecca with baby gifts to ease her descent into motherhood. With such attention focused on her pregnancy, a "miscarriage" would have been viewed as a personal failure on the part of Rebecca Fenney, and failure is not socially acceptable in Highland Park. So she resigned herself to the inevitable and became the perfect mother-to-be, eating only organic, no caffeine, no alcohol, exercising daily in the pool, acting oh so happy to be oh so fat.

But Scotty Junior was a girl named Boo. A collective sigh of disappointment went up in Highland Park, from everyone except Scott. He didn't care. When he gazed on his new daughter in the hospital nursery, it was love at first sight. And Rebecca saw that her place in his heart had been stolen.

Sex was never the same.

Rebecca Fenney needed a man who needed her more than life itself; Scott Fenney was no longer that man. But she also needed a man who could give her the life she needed; that man was still Scott Fenney. He had given her this Highland Park mansion, the home she had dreamed about since she was a little girl, the home that told the world Rebecca Fenney belonged in Highland Park. A woman living in a $500,000 house can join the society clubs; a woman living in a $3.5 million mansion can chair the society balls. This home made Rebecca Fenney's life. Her life was perfect and could get no better.

It could only get worse.

Which had become a constant worry for her over the last few weeks: Was her life about to take a turn for the worse? Was the ride slowing down . . . or coming to an end? She had thought and hoped and prayed that the Scott Fenney ride would last a lifetime. But you never know with men. Men can always find a way to fuck up a good thing.

Would Scott Fenney?

Other Highland Park men certainly had, leaving their wives— older women Rebecca knew—for younger women. But those discarded wives were in their fifties and sixties, the family fortunes made and their community halves secure. Rebecca was thirty-three, and the family fortune was still in the making, still owed to the bank that held the mortgage on their home and her life. If Scott left her now, she would have nothing, just as her mother had nothing when her father left them. The Scott Fenney ride had to last until the mortgage was paid off.

She had bet her beauty on Scott Fenney. What if she lost that bet?

When she first became Mrs. A. Scott Fenney and went to the homes of the older lawyers' wives, she would admire their possessions, and she wanted what they had, all the things money could buy. Only recently had she realized that while she was coveting what they possessed, they were coveting what she possessed: youth and beauty—what they needed to compete for their lawyers. But their money could not buy youth and beauty, try though they did with liposuction, tummy tucks, breast implants, and face-lifts; the good doctor could help, but he could not make a fifty-year-old woman look twenty-five again. So they lost their lawyers to younger women.

And now Rebecca, thirty-three, old by Highland Park standards, understood their fear as she observed the blonde by the pool—*what was she, twenty-two, twenty-three?*—giving her husband a come-hither look, competing for her lawyer, more than willing to use her beauty to claim what Rebecca possessed. There was always a younger, prettier, skinnier woman ready to take your place in the mansion. Rebecca Fenney was still remarkably beautiful, still the most beautiful woman in Highland Park, still able to compete with a twenty-two-year-old for her lawyer. But the day would come for her, she knew; and with each passing day, Rebecca Fenney was a day older and a day less beautiful.

If she lost Scott to the girl by the pool—and every Fourth of July there would be a girl by the pool—before the family fortune was made and her community half secure, she would have only one option for a new husband: a man fifty, fifty-five, maybe sixty years old. The thought of a sixty-year-old man climbing on top of her made her shudder. With enough money, a man could always drop down two decades, even three, for a new wife. But a woman? She would have no chance at a man her own age. Men in their thirties or forties were looking at twenty-somethings like the blonde.

Yes, in every woman's life, there's always another woman. But it was different for Rebecca Fenney: the other woman in her life, the woman competing for her lawyer, the woman who was threatening to take everything she had in life—her home, her position, her possessions—was not a twenty-two-year-old blonde with big tits and a tight ass, but a black prostitute accused of murdering a senator's son.

"I'm gonna be a hooker when I grow up."

Consuela let out a shriek from the kitchen, Scott almost choked on a mouthful of barbecued brisket left over from the party, and Rebecca glared at him from across the dining table. He turned to Boo, who had just announced her career plan to her family at the dinner table.

"Excuse me?"

"Yeah," she said, chewing on a barbecued rib, "men pay Pajamae's mother two hundred dollars an hour just to be with her, and if the trick wants her all night, then it's a thousand."

Scott looked at Pajamae, who was nodding matter-of-factly.

"Well, Scott," Rebecca said, "your little social experiment is already making our daughter a more worldly person."

"Rebecca, she doesn't understand what she's saying." To Boo: "And what does Pajamae's mom do with her tricks?"

Boo shoveled potato salad into her mouth and said, "Well, mostly they watch TV and eat popcorn, but sometimes the trick wants to fornicate."

Rebecca dropped her silverware. "Oh, this is just great!"

Calmly: "And what about that?"

Boo said, "Well, that's okay as long as he wears his rubbers, although if it's not raining, why the heck would he need rubbers?"

She turned to Pajamae for an answer, but Pajamae only shrugged, shook her head, and bit into a rib.

155

"Unh-huh. So that's what your mother told you, Pajamae?"

Pajamae was busy with her food, but she said, "Yeah, that's what she said. And she said if a president can make ten million dollars for writing a book about getting blow jobs in the White House, she ought to be able to make a hundred dollars for giving one on Harry Hines." She now looked up from her plate. "Mama talks a lot when she's sick and takes her medicine . . . until she falls asleep."

Boo turned to Pajamae: "What's a blow job?"

Shawanda sucked the bone dry, then licked her lips. She turned her big brown eyes up to Bobby, smiled, and said, "This here some good cooking."

Bobby handed her another barbecued rib from Scotty's party. He had walked out with a dozen ribs, two pints of coleslaw, one pint of baked beans, and two cold beers. He knew he couldn't get the beers into the federal detention center, so he drank them on the way over. Of course, before Shawanda would eat, he had to tell her all about the pool party and Pajamae, how pretty she looked.

She said, "Mr. Herrin, over last month you bring me food what, five, six time?"

"Seven, but who's counting. And don't tell Scotty, okay?"

"Why you come? You sweet on Shawanda?"

Bobby shrugged. "You're my client . . . sort of."

She looked at him like a psychic trying to read his future in his face, then nodded knowingly and said, "You ain't got no one to eat with, do you?"

Bobby stared down at his paper plate. "No."

"Well, you awful nice, bring good food for me . . . 'cept that pizza with them little fishes—"

"Anchovies."

"Yeah, them." She swallowed some coleslaw, then said, "Mr. Herrin, I'm real sorry."

"For what?"

"For thinking you ain't nothin' but a dud . . . lawyer."

Bobby laughed. "That's okay. I feel that way about myself most of the time."

"You just poor 'cause you care. You all soft inside for people like me, workin' for nothin', that's why you ain't a rich lawyer. Can't make no money givin' everyone freebies—where I be, I do that? Nope, Mr. Herrin, that just bad business. Mr. Fenney, he rich 'cause he know to only work for rich people."

"He used to care."

"So you ain't mad, me telling the judge I want Mr. Fenney be my lawyer?"

"No. You need him, Shawanda. He's a lot better lawyer than me."

"Maybe you make him care again . . . maybe about me."

They looked at each other, and Bobby saw the hope in her eyes. "Maybe."

The clubhouse at the Highland Park Country Club wasn't the most expensive building in Dallas or even in Highland Park for that matter, but it was the hardest to get into. To say it was an exclusive club is like saying Michael Jordan was a pretty good basketball player. You don't buy your way into this club; you're born into it, you marry into it, or you kiss so many important asses in town to get in that the American Medical Association could board certify you as a proctologist. Scott Fenney had taken the latter route to membership, a privilege available only because he was a local football legend and Tom Dibrell's lawyer.

Scott stopped the Range Rover under the porte cochere. Before he had cut the engine, the valet had their doors open. Scott gave the boy a twenty, and then walked his family into the club. Boo and Pajamae skipped ahead, giggling like the little girls they were. Scott smiled at the sight. Rebecca did not.

Even when not in the best of moods, as now, Rebecca Fenney was still the most beautiful woman in Highland Park. And Scott felt proud to squire his spouse into the clubhouse at the country club, the tall handsome ex-SMU-football-star-turned-successful-lawyer escorting the gorgeous ex–SMU cheerleader wearing a pale green sundress that showed off her fabulous figure, and to see each man discretely glance at her, wishing that she and not their wrinkled dinosaur wife was going home with them tonight. Rebecca was a big part of Scott Fenney's perfect life, albeit a severely pissed-off part tonight.

"This is a big fucking mistake," she said through her teeth.

"Oh, you worry too much. We're here for the fireworks. No one's going to pay attention to a little black girl."

"Yeah, right. The women here notice if your breasts are half an inch bigger or your butt's half an inch smaller. How am I going to explain her to them? She's sure as hell not a member's kid!"

The country club opened its doors to the members' children twice a year, for the annual Christmas Party featuring Santa Claus and for the fireworks on the Fourth of July. Otherwise, children were banned from the premises. Not that kids would find the place inviting. The average age of the members was seventy-four; Scott and Rebecca were two of the young members, "young" meaning under sixty. The decor was contemporary—for 1952; the members saw no reason to update the club, the only concession to the last fifty years being a big-screen TV in the men's grill. There was simply no sense in trying to convince a seventy-four-year-old member that change could be good; to a man that age, change could only be bad. No change could make him young again.

So, other than those two annual events, there were no kids at the country club. Or blacks, except for the caddies and the help. Or

Hispanics, or anyone else who could qualify for affirmative action. Or Jews. Even though the Bible-beating Baptist members got their medical care at Zale Lipshy Hospital and their wives shopped at Neiman Marcus, they wouldn't let a Jew join their club. Go figure. Not that there was a written policy to that effect—you don't write stuff like that down. You just know how it is, like you know not to give a cop the finger: there's no law against it, but it will get you a ticket for reckless driving just the same.

The Fenneys continued into the clubhouse and down the main corridor, detained briefly by several wrinkled dinosaurs who congratulated Rebecca on her certain selection as the next chairwoman of the Cattle Barons' Ball—"She's a Junior League project!" Rebecca blurted out when the women noticed Pajamae—and then out the back doors and to the elevated grassy area behind the eighteenth green where the club had set up lawn chairs so the members could enjoy the club's fireworks show.

They found four empty chairs next to a group of geriatrics who boasted a combined net worth in excess of a billion dollars. They didn't blink an eye at Pajamae's presence; but then, they probably couldn't see her in the darkness. The two girls sat in front, with Scott and Rebecca behind. Scott leaned into Rebecca.

"See, nobody cares."

They sat quietly, enjoying the summer evening and the spectacular view of the lights of downtown Dallas. The girls were huddled together and whispering when the first fireworks suddenly exploded, a giant Roman candle—*boom*!—and Pajamae dove out of her chair and hit the deck like a soldier under incoming attack. Scott jumped to her.

"Pajamae! What's wrong?"

"Get down, Mr. Fenney! Get down! It's a drive-by!"

Some nearby kids started laughing, dredging up some bad childhood memories for Scotty Fenney, the poor kid on the block—"Scotty, where'd your mommy buy your clothes, at *Sears*?"—and jacking up his blood pressure to pregame level. Highland Park kids enjoyed taunting their poorer peers, the most recent occasion being last year's playoff game at Texas Stadium against a team from a working-class suburb: the Highland Park kids had chanted, "Cold cash versus white trash!" and tossed dollar bills down on their opponents from their daddies' skyboxes. Scott glared at the snotty brats, fighting an overwhelming urge to slap the bunch of them into the ninth fairway. But smacking the heirs of the richest men in Dallas wouldn't be good for his law business, so instead he helped Pajamae up.

"Honey, it's okay, we don't have drive-by shootings in Highland Park. It's just the fireworks."

Pajamae sat up, looked around, and said, "Oh." Scott helped her back into her chair and sat down behind her. The geriatrics were now staring intently at Pajamae.

Rebecca sighed and said, "Well, that should make the club's newsletter."

THIRTEEN

CARLOS HERNANDEZ, Bobby's favorite waiter at the Downtown Club, got busted on the Fourth of July. He went to a party in East Dallas, figuring on firing off a few fireworks. It's illegal to even possess fireworks in the City of Dallas, but since Carlos was also in possession of cocaine and marijuana, he wasn't thinking about the city's fireworks ordinance—or much else, for that matter—as he stood drunk and stoned out of his mind in the middle of Grand Avenue blowing off bottle rockets at passing vehicles. When a Dallas police cruiser happened by, Carlos put a bottle rocket right in the cop's lap. Carlos was busted for possessing two dozen bottle rockets, five strands of firecrackers, fifty Roman candles, ten grams of cocaine, and two Baggies of weed. Due to his prior experience in the federal system, he was turned over to the Feds. They charged him with possession with intent to distribute—the dope, not the fireworks. With his five priors, Carlos was looking at ten to life in a federal prison.

Which is what brought Bobby downtown four days later. Carlos's mother had hired him to represent her son for the total sum of $500, $100 down and $100 a month until paid in full. Bobby parked six blocks down from the federal building to avoid a parking fee and to smoke another cigarette. By the time he arrived at the U.S. Attorney's office on the third floor, he reeked of sweat and cigarette smoke. After stating his name and purpose to the receptionist, Bobby took a seat in the waiting room. He had come to negotiate a plea bargain with the Assistant U.S. Attorney handling Carlos's prosecution. He tried not to look surprised when Ray Burns walked through the door.

"Bobby!" A big smile from Burns, as if he were happier to see Bobby Herrin this morning than any other person on the planet. "Good to see you, man."

"Ray."

Ray sniffed the air, then gave Bobby a funny look.

"You run over a skunk?"

"You're the AUSA on Carlos's case?"

"Yeah. Some coincidence, huh?" A slap on his newest best friend's shoulder. "Come on back, Bobby, let's talk about your main man Carlos."

Ray's genial disposition got Bobby's mind to churning. It occurred to him that it was a pretty goddamn big coincidence that Ray Burns was the Assistant U.S. Attorney on this case, too. He followed Ray down a corridor and into his office. It was standard government issue, but compared to Bobby's office, it was lavish: a leather chair, a wood desk, two guest chairs, and Sheetrock walls thick enough so you didn't hear Jin-Jin cussing Joo-Chan for messing up a batch of Korean donuts. On the walls were Ray's diplomas, licenses, and photos of important politicians. Ray gestured Bobby to a chair, then he sat behind his desk, leaned back, and said, "What would you think about two years for Carlos?"

"*Two years?* You're reducing the charge to simple possession? No intent to distribute?"

A shrug between friends. "Sure, why not?"

"Why?"

The two lawyers stared at each other across the wide wood desk; a thin smile crossed Ray's face. And Bobby knew his instincts were on the mark.

"What do you want, Ray?"

No pretense now. "I want the bitch's guilty plea. You get Shawanda to plead to second-degree murder, we'll agree to forty years."

"*Forty years?* She'll be eligible for Medicare by the time she gets out."

"Thirty. And that's as low as we're going."

Bobby studied Ray Burns. "Why the change of heart, Ray? You were gung-ho for the death penalty."

"I still am—a death sentence would round out my résumé nicely. But we're political appointees, at least the U.S. Attorney is, and he doesn't want to spend the rest of his career in this hellhole, a hundred and ten in the goddamn shade. He's thinking maybe California. This case might be his ticket west."

Bobby Herrin was not a lawyer whose clients were beneficiaries of political power. So it took a moment for the motive behind Ray's generosity to dawn on him.

"You know about Clark's past?" he said.

"Yep."

"And Senator McCall wants to keep it quiet?"

"Yep again."

"So he calls up the United States Attorney General and asks for a small favor. And the Attorney General calls up the U.S. Attorney in Dallas and asks for a small favor. Which the U.S. Attorney will grant, for a small favor in return. And, just like that, a person's life is suddenly changed."

Ray smiled and turned his palms up.

"What, you complaining? Two of your clients are getting good deals because of McCall's power."

"Ten years, Ray. Ten years for Shawanda, or you can tell the good senator to forget the White House and your boss to forget California. And I want Carlos's charges dismissed."

Ray grinned. He was such an asshole that he actually liked the game, two lawyers negotiating over other people's lives. Liking the game is an annoying character trait in a lawyer; liking the power is a dangerous one.

"Twenty, and that's a great deal, Bobby, and you know it. But if she rejects this deal, I won't back off the death penalty, understand? And if that information about Clark becomes public, the offer is withdrawn. So get the bitch to agree, fast."

Bobby stood and walked to the door, but he turned back.

"Ray, one more thing: if you call my client a bitch again, I swear to God I'm gonna punch you in your fucking mouth."

Scott, I need an answer for McCall. Soon.

"You called, Scott?"

Karen Douglas was standing in front of his desk.

"What? Oh, yeah, sit down, Karen."

Scott pushed Dan's voice out of his mind. Karen sat in one of the chairs on the other side of his desk and tucked her legs under so as not to reveal any thigh. She was twenty-six, pretty enough to be noticed on the street, and the youngest of the four associates working under Scott. She had graduated first in her class at Rice with a degree in literature and first in her law class at Texas. Book smart, but she was having a difficult time adjusting to the practice of law. As a supervising partner, Scott felt a responsibility to teach his new associates the necessary practice skills they weren't taught in law school. If Dan Ford hadn't taught Scott those same practice skills, he wouldn't be the lawyer he was today.

"Karen, I know you've been with us only a few months, but it seems like you're having some problems. Am I right?"

She nodded and Scott worried she might cry.

"Okay, let's see if I can get you back on track. First thing, your billable hours. You haven't met your monthly quota once. Karen, my associates *exceed* their quotas."

"But, Scott, two hundred hours a month? Ten billable hours a day? That's impossible, if I'm honest."

"Karen, this is a law firm, not a seminary."

He smiled; she didn't.

"Look, here's how billable hours work. First, you always round up. Twenty minutes becomes half an hour, forty minutes becomes an hour, an hour and a half becomes two. Second, every phone call you make and every letter you read is a minimum quarter-hour. You read ten letters, a quarter-hour each, that's two and a half billable hours. Heck, I usually bill four or five hours just reading my mail each morning. And travel—didn't you fly to San Francisco with Sid last month?"

She nodded.

"Did you bill your flight time?"

"Two hours. I worked on another matter."

"How long was the flight?"

"Four hours."

"Then you should bill eight, four hours to the client you're flying to San Francisco for, and another four to the client whose work you're doing during the flight. See? That's six hours you didn't bill last month. If every lawyer here dropped six hours each month, Karen, that's twelve hundred hours that wouldn't get billed. That's three hundred grand we wouldn't collect. *Each month*. Twelve months, that's three-point-six million. See how it adds up? See why every hour counts? Billable hours are a law firm's inventory, Karen, so when you don't bill your quota, it's like you're working at McDonald's and giving away hamburgers."

Karen was looking at Scott like a freshman coed watching her first porn flick at a frat party.

"Scott, you're telling me to pad my hours. Isn't that cheating?"

"Every place except a law firm."

Bobby entered the Ford Stevens lobby and was waved through by the smiling receptionist. Each time he walked into the Ford Stevens offices, he smelled something in the air. Like a funeral home, a downtown law office has its own unique smell; but instead of formaldehyde, this place smelled of money.

Bobby walked down the carpeted corridor to Scotty's corner office. Scotty was sitting behind his desk and addressing a young woman. He noticed Bobby and waved him in.

Bobby stepped into the office. The young woman stood and when she turned to face Bobby, he was struck by her appearance: she was very attractive and from her sharp suit, a lawyer.

"Bobby, this is Karen Douglas. Karen, Bobby Herrin."

Her eyes widened. "You're working the Shawanda Jones case with Scott. That must be very exciting. When I was in school, I always thought I'd work in the public defender's office."

"But we pay better," Scotty said. He pointed at the sofa. "Sit, Bobby, I'll be right with you." He picked up a thick document and turned back to Karen. "Now, Karen, you're clear on billable hours?"

Karen sighed heavily and nodded. "I guess so."

"Okay, the other thing I wanted to talk to you about is your memo. I've read it and it's great. You researched the law perfectly, you applied the facts, you did everything exactly right . . . except—"

"Except what, Scott?"

"Except you didn't answer my question."

"But you asked whether Dibrell could sue that little town over its denial of his rezoning request. The answer is no."

Scotty was shaking his head. "Karen, I didn't ask you *whether*

Dibrell could sue the town, I asked you *how* Dibrell could sue. We're going to sue; we've already decided that. It's part of our strategy to get the town to give us the rezoning we want. And believe me, after their lawyer tells them how much the litigation will cost in fees and expenses even if they win, the town will crater. What I wanted from you is a legal position we can take to justify our lawsuit. You answered whether. I asked how."

Karen's face expressed that dismay unique to a new lawyer learning the ways of lawyers.

"I . . . I didn't understand, Scott. I'll try again."

"Good girl."

Karen departed and Scotty said, "Nice body, but she'll never make it as a lawyer. What's up?"

Ten minutes later, they were driving to the federal building.

"Scotty," Bobby said, "twenty years is a good deal. I've had two-bit dealers go down for life."

But Scott wasn't thinking about what was good for his client; he was thinking about what was good for himself. Which was Shawanda's pleading out, for twenty or thirty or forty years, he didn't give a damn. Because if she pleaded out, he wouldn't have to make a big decision. *Scott, I need an answer for McCall. Soon.*

"*Twenty years?* Mr. Fenney, Pajamae, she be twenty-nine by then, I won't even know her. She all I got."

Shawanda was pacing the small room, around and around, circling Scott and Bobby in their chairs.

"I understand, Shawanda, but if you're convicted of first-degree murder, you might get the death penalty."

"Twenty years in prison, I die anyway. Mr. Fenney, why don't you believe me? I didn't do it! I didn't kill nobody!"

In civil litigation, judges routinely order the parties to mediate their disputes before going to trial. Mediation allows the lawyers to hammer their clients into settlements they don't like, force them to pay amounts they don't want to pay, and make them end lawsuits they don't want to end. But there is no court-ordered mediation in criminal cases. So all Scott could do to try to convince his client to take the plea deal was stand and shout: "Shawanda, please think about this!"

She stopped short.

"I don't gotta think no more about it, Mr. Fenney. I told you before, I ain't coppin' no plea!"

Ray Burns was not happy when Scott and Bobby informed him of their client's decision to reject the plea offer.

"That bi—" Ray's eyes met Bobby's. "That woman is making a big mistake. And her lawyers are making an even bigger mistake if they go public with Clark's past."

"What about ten years?" Scott asked.

"No way. We don't give ten-year deals to people who stick a gun to a guy's head and blow his fucking brains out!"

Scott was back in his office, sitting behind his desk, his elbows on the top, his head in his hands, his eyes closed, and his mind a jumble of thoughts and images: Scotty Fenney, number 22, racing down the field, scoring the winning touchdown, the campus hero . . . two little girls, one white, one black, sleeping side by side in the big bed, their faces smooth, their hair in cornrows . . . Rebecca, beautiful and naked and angry . . . Shawanda, alone in her cell, crying for her daughter and heroin . . . and Dan Ford, who had replaced the father who had died when Scott was just a boy. What son wouldn't do what his father asked? *Scott, I need an answer for Mc-*

Call. Soon. But the boy had a mother, too, and just as the image of a mother reading to her son flashed across his mind's eye, Scott opened his eyes to find Dan Ford standing over him. And he knew what his senior partner had come for.

"She turned down the deal?"

Scott leaned back in his chair. "Word travels fast."

"The U.S. Attorney called Mack, Mack called me."

"And now you're calling on me? What's that saying, shit rolls downhill?"

"Something like that."

Dan strolled around the office and stopped at the huge framed photograph of Scott Fenney, number 22 for the SMU Mustangs, running the ball against Texas. "One hundred ninety-three yards . . . unbelievable," he said. After a moment, he broke away and sat on the sofa. Finally, he turned to Scott.

"Scott, I need an answer for McCall. Now."

"I don't know, Dan."

"What's there to know? We know what Mack wants."

"And I know what my client wants."

Dan chuckled. "Your *client?* Clients pay us fees, Scott. Ms. Jones isn't paying us anything. She's costing us. She's an expense to this firm. And she's expendable."

"Dan, I'm her lawyer!"

Dan stood. "Scott, do you really believe she's innocent? Do you really believe she didn't kill Clark?"

Scott shook his head. "No."

"Then what's the problem?"

"The problem is, Dan, if I don't introduce that evidence about Clark's past, she's gonna die!"

A look of absolute puzzlement came over Dan's face. He said, "And how does that affect your life?"

_____

169

And that had been the guiding principle of A. Scott Fenney's professional life since the day he joined Ford Stevens: How would it affect his life? Or, more to the point, his income. Any event—a lawyer fired, a client dumped, a case won or lost, a law enacted or repealed, a natural disaster, a stock market crash, a war, a presidential election—that affected his life and income was, by definition, important. Any event that did not affect his life or income was unimportant, irrelevant, as inconsequential to him as another gang murder in South Dallas. Now, driving home to his $3.5 million mansion in a $200,000 automobile, Scott found himself wondering: How would Shawanda Jones being sentenced to death affect his life and income?

The answer was obvious: not at all. The day after her conviction, he would be back at his desk, working to make rich clients richer and bringing home $750,000 a year. As he would the day after her execution. She would quickly become part of his past. A year from now he wouldn't even remember her name.

Scott had always followed Dan Ford's advice, and he knew he should follow Dan's advice now. He should chalk up Shawanda's pathetic heroin-addicted life as unimportant and irrelevant and inconsequential to his life. He should lose her case and move on, as he had with other clients whose cases he had lost. Even Scott Fenney couldn't win every case. Those few times he had lost, he had moped around, cursing the judge and jury for a few days, but once the client paid his final bill and the check cleared, he had gotten over it and moved on.

But there was a difference.

Scott Fenney had never thrown a case. Or a contest. Or a game. He had always played to win. Every game he had ever played—football, golf, lawyering—had been a test of his manhood, so he had played every game to win. All-out, no-holds-barred, win at all costs—that's what made him a winner. Every cell in his body was infused with the desire to win, a desire that had taken him from being the poor kid on the block to owning a mansion on Beverly Drive in the heart of Highland Park. But Dan Ford was now telling him to play to lose. Could Scott Fenney play to lose and still be a winner?

That thought bothered him all the way home. But as he pulled into the motor court behind his mansion, a new more bothersome thought had invaded his mind: How would Shawanda's death affect Pajamae's life?

Scott had said bedtime prayers with the girls, tucked them in snugly, and was standing to leave, but he needed to ask Pajamae a question.

"Pajamae, do you think your mother could hurt anyone?"

"No, sir, Mr. Fenney. Mama, she's got a good heart. She cares about people. Her problem is, she doesn't care enough about herself. She's always telling me to love myself, but she doesn't love herself. My daddy made her like that, hitting her, making her sick. So don't blame her, Mr. Fenney, it's not her fault."

Then she turned her big brown eyes up at Scott and asked him a question.

"Mr. Fenney, are the po-lice gonna kill my mama, too?"

FOURTEEN

*E*XECUTION OF THE DEFENDANT *would violate her civil rights under the Eighth Amendment to the Constitution of the United States . . .*

The defendant. Her mother. Execution. Damn.

Pajamae was playing in the pool with Boo; they were standing in opposite shallow ends and tossing a Frisbee back and forth across the deep middle part of the pool. Scott was sitting on the patio reading Bobby's brief that argued Pajamae's mother should not be put to death if found guilty of murdering Clark McCall.

It was another blazingly hot Sunday afternoon in Highland Park. The girls were cool in the pool. Scott was sweating in the shade of the patio awning. Rebecca was down in the exercise room climbing the Stairmaster to nowhere in air-conditioned comfort. Consuela was in Little Mexico being courted by Esteban Garcia. Scott had driven her down that morning to the Cathedral Santuario de Guadalupe Catholic Church located at the northern boundary of downtown Dallas, which was also the southern boundary of Little Mexico. Esteban was waiting at the curb, dressed in black boots, black trousers, and a long-sleeve white shirt starched crisp; he was clean shaven and his hair was slicked back. He looked like a Mexican matador. He greeted Consuela de la Rosa like a princess, taking her hand to help her up and out of the low-slung Ferrari. She turned and waved good-bye to Scott, then walked to the entrance of the church like a teenager in love. She was brown and beaming.

Scott was white and worried.

Scott, I need an answer for McCall. Now.

What if he said no to McCall? What could Mack McCall do to *Scott Fenney, Tom Dibrell's lawyer?* McCall might be the senior senator from Texas and Dan Ford's former fraternity brother, but he paid no legal fees to Ford Stevens. So saying no to McCall would not harm the firm; of course, it wouldn't help the firm either. But still, no harm, no foul. Sure, McCall could block A. Scott Fenney's future nomination to the federal bench, but that did not concern Scott; he had no intention of taking a pay cut to only $162,000 a year. Saying no to McCall would result only in a pissed-off U.S. senator; Scott could live with that.

But could he live with a pissed-off senior partner?

How would Dan Ford take no for an answer? Saying no to Dan would be breaking new ground for Scott; he had never said no to Dan, never even considered saying no. Now Dan wanted to be the president's lawyer, which required that Mack McCall be elected president, which required that Scott Fenney hide Clark McCall's past, which required that Scott say yes.

Dan would not be happy if Scott said no.

But Scott brought in over $3 million in fees for the firm each year, and that always had a way of brightening Dan's mood. And if Scott promised to increase his billings to Dibrell to $4 million this year—*which would require some seriously creative accounting*—surely Dan would forgive Scott (who was like a son to him) this one act of rebellion. Surely.

Still, Scott Fenney had never said no to a coach, a client, or his senior partner. If the coach called an end sweep on third and 20, he ran it. If a client wanted him to coerce a sexual harassment settlement by threatening to bring up the woman's sexual history, he threatened it. If a senior partner wanted him to rubber-stamp a decision to fire a fellow partner, he did it. But now a U.S. senator and his senior partner wanted him to hide critical evidence and watch his client be executed. Could he do it?

What if he did? What if Scott Fenney said yes to Mack McCall and Dan Ford? Both men would be very happy. McCall would be elected president, Ford Stevens would be the president's law firm, and Dan Ford would be the president's lawyer. The firm would open a Washington office, new corporate clients would pay millions in legal fees to the firm, and the partners would double their income. Scott Fenney would be filthy rich. All of which sounded good until he heard Pajamae's little voice: "Catch it, Boo!"

Mr. Fenney, are the po-lice gonna kill my mama, too?

Scott heard the French doors behind him swing open and felt the rush of cool air against his warm neck. Rebecca stood beside him and he smelled her sweaty scent. She was wearing a tube top and short running tights that clung to every surface of her lean body. Scott felt the urge to pull his wife onto his lap and hold her close; but like a dog who had gotten smacked the last hundred times he had gone after a bone, Scott did not make a move in that direction. They watched the girls play.

"It's good she has a friend now," he said.

"She has friends," Rebecca said, "girls from the best families in Highland Park. She just refuses to do anything with them."

"Then they're not her friends, Rebecca."

They watched in silence again. After a moment, Rebecca said, "A black girl for her best friend. That'll be such a positive on her debutante application."

She abruptly pivoted and went back inside. Scott shook his head. *Her debutante application.* Barbara Boo Fenney would never be a Highland Park deb; she just wasn't the right type. Neither would Pajamae Jones; she just wasn't the right color. She had been born on the wrong side of life, just as Scott had been, but she could not run with a football to the right side of life as he had. Maybe that was why Scott felt a bond with this little black girl, because they were both from the poor side of the tracks; or maybe because Scott had always taken up for the weak kids, like Bobby. Back in high school, Bobby would've been beaten up daily if he hadn't been under Scott's protection.

Pajamae Jones was now under Scott Fenney's protection.

She threw the Frisbee over Boo's head. Boo retrieved it and flung it from far across the yard. The Frisbee landed in the middle of the pool, in the deep section. Pajamae climbed out of the shallow end and walked around to the far side where the Frisbee floated on the water. She knelt down and reached out for it, just out of her grasp. She leaned farther over the pool and before she fell in and sunk below the surface of the blue water, Scott had already dropped the brief and was running toward the pool.

Boo screamed, "She can't swim!"

"Stay there, Boo!"

Scott dove into the pool, not even thinking that he was still wearing sneakers and shorts. He went straight to the bottom and grabbed Pajamae around her waist. He pushed hard with his legs; they broke the surface with a splash. Pajamae was coughing up water. Scott lifted her out of the pool and onto the deck, then climbed out and knelt beside her. She rolled over and heaved more water. She slowly sat up.

"Are you okay, baby?"

Pajamae looked up at Scott. "I thought I was gonna die, Mr. Fenney."

"Not on my watch."

She wiped her nose and leaned into Scott. She buried her face in his wet shirt and wrapped her arms around him. He patted her back.

"Girl, you're getting swimming lessons."

FIFTEEN

Scott Fenney led a double life: at the law firm, he was a successful lawyer practicing law like he played football—winning at all costs, working the margins, gaming the system, bending the rules, mastering the art of aggressive and creative lawyering, and making lots of money. At home, he was a good man, a faithful husband to Rebecca and a loving father to Boo, in whom each night at bedtime he tried to instill the virtues of living a good and decent life. Rebecca didn't want to know what he did each day at the office and Boo didn't need to know. The only part of his lawyer life he brought home each night was the money.

All lawyers lead such a Jekyll-and-Hyde life, diligently maintaining a strict separation between their dual lives, lying to their wives and children, and hiding their lawyer lives like a drug addict hides his illegal habit. Scott always told everyone he was a lawyer, but he never told anyone what he did as a lawyer. A lawyer learns that such matters are best left at the law firm. You walk into the office each morning and become a successful lawyer; you leave each night and become a good man again. But with each night, the transformation back—from Hyde to Jekyll—becomes harder. The lawyer in you doesn't want to let go. But you beat it back because you cannot allow the boundary between your two lives to be breached. Scott Fenney had never brought his lawyer life home— *never!*—until the day he brought home a nine-year-old black girl.

Pajamae Jones was now part of his life—both lives. She was part of his home life, her mother part of his lawyer life. She loved her mother, and he was her mother's lawyer. His decisions as her mother's lawyer would determine if she had a mother much longer: if he said yes to Dan Ford, he was sending Pajamae's mother to death row. The boundary between his dual lives had been breached, and now, like the last two teams standing at the end of a long season set to play for the championship, his two lives—Dan Ford versus Pajamae Jones—were locked in a life-and-death struggle for Scott Fenney's soul.

I need an answer for McCall. Now.

Are the po-lice gonna kill my mama, too?

Would he be the lawyer Dan Ford wanted him to be? Or the man Pajamae needed him to be? He could no longer be both. He had to choose between his two lives. He had to face it head-on, like all those times when the blocking broke down and number 22 found himself alone on a football field facing five defenders. Then, as now, he had a choice to make: step out of bounds before getting hit or charge forward and take the hits and make the extra yards. Football coaches call those moments "gut checks," because it is in those moments when you find out what you're made of.

Scott Fenney was facing a gut check.

The trial date was one week closer, and Scott was sitting at the small table in the small room at the federal detention center next to Bobby and across from Shawanda. She was happy, upbeat, and full of energy. Bobby was showing her photos from Carl's background checks.

"This is Clark in his better days. He ever try to pick you up before that night?"

She shook her head. "No, sir. Course, drunk white boys all look the same on Saturday night."

Bobby held up another photo. "The honorable senator."

Shawanda stared at the image of Mack McCall and said, "He make my skin crawl."

"Yeah." Bobby pointed to a big bald man standing in the background of the same photo. "You ever see this guy?"

"No, sir . . . and I wouldn't forget that face."

Scott said, "Who's he?"

"Delroy Lund, McCall's bodyguard. His goon, according to Carl. Ex-DEA. Carl says he can smell a dirty cop a mile away."

"So what's he got to do with the case?"

Bobby shook his head. "Nothing."

"So Carl came up empty?"

"Yeah, but he never quits looking."

With that news, Scott decided to make one last attempt to convince his client to accept the plea offer. "Shawanda, all we have is this Hannah Steele woman. Clark raped her a year ago." Scott turned to Bobby. "Did Carl get a photo of Hannah?"

"No, she's real shy, wouldn't let him. Carl said she's like a piece of china, a real fragile girl. Said he wouldn't bet a six-pack on her holding up under a tough cross. And Ray Burns is gonna be damn tough, he'll try to make her look like a . . ." Bobby's eyes cut to Shawanda. "He'll explore her sexual history."

"Yeah." Scott turned back to his client. "Shawanda, if you made a deal, at least you wouldn't be facing a death penalty."

"Mr. Fenney," she said, "if I can't be with Pajamae, I just as soon die."

Scott sighed and nodded at Bobby.

"Okay, Shawanda," Bobby said, "we'll go to trial. But you've got to understand, the evidence against you is substantial, more than enough to put you on death row. Our only hope is Hannah. We'll put you on first, then we'll put her on. She'll corroborate . . . back up your testimony, which gives the jury more reason to believe you."

"Why can't I take one of them lie detector tests, prove I ain't lying? I seen them on that TV show—they make the boy wanna marry the daughter take a lie detector test, ask him if he was cheating." She laughed. "Them white boys lie every time."

Bobby was shaking his head. "That's not a good idea, Shawanda." He turned to Scott. "Scotty, I was thinking about those reporters calling you, asking for TV interviews with Shawanda? Maybe we should do that, let her tell the world what happened. That'll condition the jury pool. And after she's told her story, you can ask that any other woman who was beaten or raped by Clark McCall come forward so Shawanda doesn't go to jail for a crime she didn't commit."

"That sound good to me, Mr. Fenney," Shawanda said.

Scott dropped his eyes and said, "I don't know, Shawanda, that might not be the best strategy."

Scott's eyes were still down when Bobby said, "Shawanda, Scotty and I need to talk outside."

Bobby stood and knocked on the door. The guard opened the door, and Scott pushed himself up out of the chair and followed Bobby into the hall. They had walked ten steps down the corridor when Bobby stopped and leaned against the wall.

"She's doing a lot better," Scott said.

"She's high."

"What?"

"She's feeling the rush."

"You mean heroin?"

Bobby nodded.

"How do you know?"

"Scotty, my best clients are dopers. You can see it in their eyes when they're on it. It's like they own the world."

"How'd she get it in here?"

Bobby shrugged. "Guard, janitor, who knows."

"She looked good the last time. I figured she was over it."

Bobby shook his head. "A junkie's never over heroin. The cravings are always there. I get them probation conditioned on treatment, they get the methadone, stay straight a couple weeks, a couple months, then go right back to it like an old lover."

"Her life's on the line and she can't stop shooting up? My wife's pissed off at me, Dan's pissed off at me, I'm taking all this grief so she can get high? All this for a goddamned junkie?"

"Scotty, if you lived her life, you'd probably shoot up, too. You got the best of life, she got the worst. But she can still be happy when she's high. And now the stuff on the street is so cheap, she can spend every waking minute high—until she dies." Bobby sighed. "And she'll die from the stuff one day."

"We're trying to save her from the death penalty so she can kill herself with heroin?"

"Yep, that's exactly what we're doing. I can see it in her eyes, Scotty, she's a junkie for life. And hers will be a short life." He stared at his shoes a long moment, then stood straight. "But not as short as Ray Burns wants it to be. So, you catching some heat over this?"

Scott nodded. "Big-time. Why not a polygraph?"

"My junkie clients always think they can beat the machine. Course, when they're high, they think they're fucking Einsteins. But they always fail. She takes it and fails, she's history."

"Polygraphs aren't admissible. Burns can't use it against her."

"Not in court. But Ray'll leak it to the press, it'll be front-page news. Every juror will know she failed."

"Maybe she'll plead out if she fails."

"Look, Scotty, I know this is a tough decision for you and I know you don't want to make it, but hey, man, that's why you make the big bucks. What do you want to do?"

"McCall's pressuring Dan Ford to get me to drop this defense, not to drag his dead son through the mud."

"Clark lived in the mud, Scotty. He was a bad boy." Bobby checked his shoes again. "So Dan told you to drop it?"

"He advised me to. He wants to be the president's lawyer. Good for business."

"But bad for Shawanda. Is your job on the line?"

"*My job?* No! Dan wouldn't fire me. I'm like his son."

Bobby nodded. "Three, four years ago, I represented a father who killed his son over a football game." He chuckled softly. "Look, Scotty, I'm not a big-time lawyer like you, I don't represent important people, I don't make much money, . . . but I've never screwed a client. I've always done my best for every client, even if my best isn't much. Clark beating her up, raping Hannah Steele, maybe more women—Scotty, that evidence might be the difference between life and death for her."

Bobby ran his hands over his head of thin hair.

"All my clients are just like her, poor, black or brown, living in an alternate world where daddies are dealing and mamas are hooking. Difference is, all my clients are guilty, no bones about it. But she may really be innocent—or at least have acted in self-defense. We drop Clark's past, we're sentencing her to death by lethal injection—you and me, Scotty, not a jury. We'll be responsible, same as if we push that needle into her arm." He shook his head. "Scotty, I need the money you're paying me for working this case, but I can't live with that."

"What do you mean?"

"I mean, you drop this evidence, I'm out."

"Bobby—"

"Scotty, I followed you every step of the way—high school, college, law school. Back then, I would've followed you anywhere. I was weak and you were strong and you protected me. But you ain't Batman no more, and I ain't Robin. I can't follow you on this. It just ain't right. She may not be a white society girl . . . she may be a junkie hooker, living in the projects, but her life means something, too. Maybe not to you, maybe not even to herself . . . but to me. And to her little girl. She needs someone strong to protect her . . . someone like you used to be." He paused. "When your secretary called that day, said you wanted to have lunch, man, I about cried. All those years, I really missed you." His eyes were watering. "And being around you again now, it's been great . . . just to breathe your air again." He breathed in and out. "But, Scotty, you do this to that girl, I don't want to see you no more."

"Come on, Bobby."

"Scotty, the court appointed you. You're her right to counsel. You do what you think is right."

Scott turned away, wishing this gut check could be answered by simply running into five frothing-at-the-mouth testosterone-charged linebackers.

Scott got into the Ferrari, but he couldn't go back to the office. Downtown suddenly felt claustrophobic. So he drove onto the Dallas North Tollway and hit the accelerator hard. He felt the power of the machine beneath him as he took the engine through the gears. The 360 Modena topped out at 180 miles per hour, but Scott eased off the accelerator at eighty, the customary highway speed in Dallas. No one drove the speed limit in Texas, not even women putting on their makeup. Northbound traffic was light at this time of the morning, so he drove unimpeded in the left lane. He often drove aimlessly about the 4,000 miles of roads in Dallas when he needed to think. For some reason, he thought better in a Ferrari.

Without thinking, Scott suddenly veered across three lanes of traffic and exited at Mockingbird Lane, cut over to Hillcrest, and drove north. He turned left, stopped three doors down on the right, and stared at the new two-story monster house, arched entry, dormers, vaulted roof. But in its place he saw the small one-story cottage that had once occupied this lot, the home he and his mother had rented from the good doctor. Living room, kitchen, two bedrooms, two bathrooms, less than one thousand square feet including the porch where they often sat after dinner and waved at neighbors taking their evening walks. He remembered crawling into bed, lying back on the pillow, and waiting for his mother to come in, sit down, open the book, and read a chapter. And when she finished, she'd close the book and say, "Scotty, be like Atticus. Be a lawyer. Do good."

It's hard to do good when your clients are bad.

Lawyers never believe their clients because clients lie. They lie to the IRS and the SEC and the FBI. They lie about their taxes, they lie about their financial statements, and they lie about their lies. Most of the time, they don't get caught. When they do get caught, usually for lying about their lies to the FBI—a felony called obstruction of justice—their lawyers stand outside the courthouse and proclaim their client's innocence right up to the moment the client plea-bargains, pays a fine, and lives to lie again.

A lawyer always assumes his client is lying.

So Scott naturally assumed his heroin-addicted hooker-client was lying. But maybe he would believe a nice white sorority girl. He had gotten Hannah Steele's unlisted phone number in Galveston from Bobby. Now he sat in the Ferrari and listened to the call ring through. A soft voice answered.

"Hello."

"Hannah Steele?"

"Who's calling?"

"Scott Fenney. I'm Shawanda Jones's lawyer. My cocounsel, Bobby Herrin, spoke with you."

"Yes, Mr. Fenney."

"Hannah, I need to hear your story. I need to hear you tell me what Clark McCall did to you."

A long sigh. "I've told Carl and Bobby, I don't—"

"I know this isn't easy, Hannah, but Senator McCall is pressuring me not to bring up Clark's past at the trial, not to call you as a witness. For me to make a decision, I need to hear for myself what happened."

"All right."

Hannah Steele told Scott of her encounter with Clark McCall. She had met him on the SMU campus after a football game. He asked her out for the next night. He picked her up at her sorority house. They had dinner at a Mexican restaurant in the Uptown section of Dallas, the nightlife area between downtown and Highland Park. They had a few drinks and they went to the McCall mansion, where Clark attacked her, beat her, and raped her. Afterward, he acted as if nothing out of the ordinary had happened. He gave her a ride back to the sorority house and even smiled at her when she got out of his car. She got in her car and drove straight to the police station and filed a complaint. She was taken to Parkland Hospital for a rape analysis and then returned to the sorority house. The next morning, a man came calling for her, saying he was Senator McCall's lawyer. He handed her a document and a pen, said it was a release and confidentiality agreement, and he gave her a cashier's check for $500,000 to settle all claims against Clark and cover her relocation costs.

"Relocation costs?"

"He said I had to leave town. He said my life would be better that way. He said I didn't really have a choice, that if I pressed charges against Clark, his father would destroy me. He said they

187

would bring out my prior sex life at trial, make me look like a whore."

"What was his name, this lawyer?"

"I don't think he told me."

"What did he look like?"

"Like a lawyer. Old. Bald. Creepy. The way he looked at me and talked to me—my God, I'd been raped! He acted like it was just business."

Scott ended the call and he knew. Lots of old lawyers he knew were bald and most were creepy. But he knew one such lawyer who would view paying off a rape victim as just business.

"You knew about Hannah Steele?"

"Of course."

Scott had driven directly back to the office, parked in the underground garage, taken the elevator straight to the sixty-third floor, and hurried down the hall to Dan Ford's office. He was now staring in disbelief at his senior partner, who was looking at Scott with a bemused expression.

"Scotty, you think this is the first time something like this has happened—college girl claiming a rich boy raped her? Maybe he did, maybe he didn't, but she wanted money, she got money, everyone's happy."

"She didn't seem so happy when I talked to her."

Dan shrugged. "Seller's remorse."

"And you just bribed her to drop her complaint? Threatened to destroy her by bringing out her sexual history at trial?"

"Bribed her? Threatened?" Dan laughed. "How many girls have you paid off for Tom Dibrell? How many times have you threatened to bring up their sexual histories at trial if they didn't settle? Do you still use my 'every swinging dick' line?"

When Dan had first taught him that tactic, it had seemed so clever, so goddamn lawyerly clever. As it had when Scott used it on Frank Turner, famous plaintiffs' lawyer, negotiating a settlement with Tom's last girl—what was her name, Nadine? Now, after talking to Hannah Steele, it didn't seem so clever.

Scott sat down on the sofa and said weakly, "Tom's girls didn't claim rape. They claimed sexual harassment."

Dan dismissed Scott's comment with a wave of his hand.

"Semantics. Sexual harassment, rape—bottom line, someone got screwed. Scotty, my boy, you did exactly what a lawyer's supposed to do, exactly what I taught you to do: you settled a legal dispute for your client. Just as I did."

Even more weakly: "Doesn't make it fair."

Dan laughed again. "*Fair?* Fair ain't got nothing to do with the law, son. Fair is where you go to see farm animals and ride the rides."

"Why didn't you tell me about Hannah?"

"You didn't need to know, Scotty. Why didn't you tell me you hired a PI to go digging into Clark's past?"

"Dan, I really believe Clark beat and raped Hannah."

"Well, if it makes you feel any better, so do I. Of course, I believed all the others, too."

"The *others?* There were more?"

"Seven, counting Hannah." Dan shook his head. "That little fuckup cost his dad almost three million, just buying off girls. Plus, of course, my fee: twenty-five thousand dollars."

"Twenty-five thousand dollars to buy off a rape victim?"

Another bemused look from his senior partner. "As I recall, you charged Dibrell fifty thousand to buy off his last girl."

Scott's face felt hot. "I thought it was just business."

"It is, Scotty. It's just business. Clark's girls were just business, Dibrell's girls were just business, and this is just business."

"Not to Shawanda. It's her life." Scott met Dan's gaze. "I can't drop it, Dan."

"Sure you can . . . because I'm asking you to. Scotty, are you going to say no to Mack McCall—to *me*—for a goddamn heroin junkie? For a prostitute?"

"No . . . for her daughter."

"Her *daughter*?"

"Yeah. She needs her mother and her mother needs me. And I might be able to save her life."

"Don't start believing your own bullshit, Scott."

"What are you talking about?"

"Your campaign speech. You're not Atticus Finch. No one is. Hell, who would want to be? He lived in a middle-class home, drove a middle-class car—what was it, a Buick?"

"Chevrolet."

"You drive a Ferrari." That amused Dan. "Scotty, that movie did more damage to the legal profession than Watergate. Lawyers of my generation, we went to law school to dodge the draft. But the generations that followed us didn't have a war to worry about, so they went to law school to be some kind of goddamn hero. But that's not what being a lawyer's all about. And truth is, they don't want to be another Atticus Finch any more than I do, any more than you do. He had nothing. But they—and you—and me, we want it all—the money, the house, the cars, all the things a successful lawyer can have today. And how does a lawyer become successful? By doing his job, which is making rich people richer. And we get paid very well indeed for doing our job, and not in chickens and nuts like Atticus. Our clients pay us in cash. Which is a very good thing, Scotty, 'cause you can't buy a Ferrari with chickens and nuts."

Dan walked over to the window and gazed out.

"When I graduated from law school, Scotty, a wise older lawyer gave me some good advice. He said, 'Dan, every new lawyer must make a fundamental choice from which every other decision in his professional life will follow. And that choice is simple: Do you want to do good or do well? Do you want to make money or make the world a better place? Do you want to drive a Cadillac or a Chevrolet? Do you want to send your kids to private schools or public schools? Do you want to be a rich lawyer or a poor lawyer?' He said, 'Dan, if you want to do good, go work for legal aid and help the little people fighting their landlords and the utility companies and the police and feel good about it. But don't have regrets twenty years later when your classmates are living in nice homes and driving new cars and taking vacations in Europe. And you have to tell your kids they can't go to an Ivy League school because you did good.' "

Dan turned from the window.

"My son went to Princeton and my daughter went to Smith."

Dan sat on the edge of his desk and folded his arms.

"That's the choice every lawyer makes, Scotty, and you made your choice eleven years ago when you hired on with us. You chose to do well. You stood right there, said you were tired of being the poor kid on the block, said you wanted to be a rich lawyer. Now you want to be a good guy? I don't think so.

"Scotty, this law firm exists for one reason and only one reason: to make as much goddamn money for the partners as humanly possible. And how does this firm do that? By representing clients who can pay three and four and five hundred dollars an hour for our services. By doing what our clients want, when they want it. By never saying no to our clients. Because we know they can always take their legal fees to a law firm across the street or across the state or across the country. Because there's always another law firm ready to take our place at the trough."

"Dan, she's got a little girl. I've got to do right by her."

191

"You've got a little girl, too. You want to do right by her?"

He rose and came over to Scott, sat beside him, and put his hand on Scott's shoulder. His voice was now fatherly.

"Scotty, you've always followed my advice, and you've done okay by my advice, haven't you?"

Scott nodded. "Sure, Dan, but—"

"Then follow my advice now. C'mon, son, don't do this. Not to yourself, not to this firm . . . not to me. I need an answer for Mc-Call, Scott. Now."

Scott buried his hot face in his hands as the battle within raged on, Dan Ford versus Pajamae Jones fighting for his soul:

I need an answer for McCall. Now.

Are the po-lice gonna kill my mama, too?

And he heard Bobby's voice: *She needs someone strong to protect her . . . someone like you used to be.* Gut-check time for Scott Fenney.

"No, baby, they're not gonna kill your mama. I'm not gonna let them."

"What?"

Scott removed his hands from his face and turned to Dan, who was looking at him oddly. Scott realized that when his gut had answered the call, it had done so out loud. He said, "Tell McCall no."

Dan removed his hand. "That's not the right answer, Scott. Try again."

"My answer is no."

Dan stood, walked across the room, and sat behind his desk. He folded his hands on the mahogany top.

"Scotty, Mack McCall's a U.S. senator now. He dresses nice and talks nice on those Sunday morning political shows . . . but underneath that politician's demeanor, he's still just a Texas roughneck. He grew up poor in the West Texas oil fields, started working the rigs when he was fifteen. It's a hard life, it makes a man hard—it makes some men mean. Mack's one of those men."

Dan picked up a pen and studied it a moment; then he said,

"Back in college, we were at a party at Martha's sorority house. She was Mack's fiancée then, a pretty girl and wealthy. She was Mack's ticket, and he wasn't about to let someone else punch it. Well, a football player got drunk and made the mistake of flirting with Martha. Mack told him to leave, but he said no. So Mack told him to step outside. Now, that boy outweighed Mack by fifty pounds, but he didn't stand a chance. Mack beat him with brass knuckles, might've killed that boy if I hadn't pulled him off. I said, 'Mack, why the hell did you do that?' All he said was, 'No one takes something that belongs to me.' "

Dan shook his head in apparent disbelief at the memory.

"Scott, I learned three things about Mack McCall that night: he doesn't take no for an answer; he doesn't fight fair; and he's the meanest son of a bitch I've ever met."

Scott let out a nervous chuckle. "So what's he gonna do, beat me up?"

Dan sighed. "I don't know what he's going to do, Scotty. Forty-two years, I've never said no to him." He paused, then said, "But I do know one thing, Scott: Mack McCall thinks the White House belongs to him."

SIXTEEN

*¡U*STED ME LO PROMETIO, *Señor Fenney! ¡Usted me lo prometio!"*

Consuela's brown face was wet with tears and contorted with fear as she cried out—*You promised, Señor Fenney! You promised!* Her eyes were begging for help, her round body was shaking uncontrollably, and her arms were held behind her colorful Mexican peasant dress by handcuffs. INS policy, the agents had said.

Two agents from the Immigration and Naturalization Service had arrived at the Fenney residence at exactly 6:30 A.M. that Monday morning. Consuela had collapsed into Scott's arms when they flashed their INS badges. The fear that had haunted her always now possessed her. All her protections had failed her: the crucifixes, the prayers, the candles, the Town of Highland Park . . . and Señor Fenney.

Ten minutes later, the agents were departing with Consuela de la Rosa in federal custody. Scott stood by helplessly as the agents escorted her to their waiting car. He shouted, "INS doesn't come into Highland Park, that's the deal! This is gonna cost you your jobs!"

One agent smiled and said, "I don't think so, sir."

"Half the homes in Highland Park employ Mexican maids! Why'd you come to my house?"

"Anonymous tip, sir," the same agent said over his shoulder.

Scott gave the agent the best glare he could work up in his boxer shorts.

"Anonymous tip, my ass!"

Boo pushed past Scott and ran barefooted in her nightie down the walkway shouting, "Consuela! Consuela!"

Consuela turned back just as Boo threw her arms around the older woman's wide waist and clutched her tightly. Consuela bent over and said, "Oh, *niña*." Boo reached up and wiped tears from Consuela's face. After a moment, one agent tugged at Consuela's arm, so she kissed Boo and motioned for her to return to the house. Boo ran straight into Scott's arms, her face frantic.

"You promised they wouldn't come to our house! You promised! Where are they taking her? What's gonna happen to her?"

Pajamae was now standing next to them. "That's how they do it," she said. "They just come and take you away."

Finally Rebecca appeared. She punched her fists into her hips, sighed, and said, "That's just great. Who's gonna cook now, *me*?"

One agent put Consuela in the backseat of the dark sedan while two morning joggers stopped and gawked. Down the street, less noticeable than a soft breeze on this warm summer morning, a truckload of brown men, young and middle-aged and old, arrived for work, just as a hundred other truckloads of brown men were arriving at grand residences on quiet streets throughout the Town of Highland Park: the yardmen. Mexican men just up from Matamoros or Nuevo Laredo or Juárez, willing to toil under the cruel summer sun for the chance at a better life.

The second agent was standing at his open door, but turned back when Scott yelled at him: "You want to bust illegals?" He pointed down the street at the yardmen. "Go arrest them! You can drive all over Highland Park this morning and arrest a hundred more Mexican nationals! But they mow the lawns of the richest men in Dallas, so you're not going to their homes, are you? I know why you came to my house! I know the asshole giving you orders!"

"It's McCall."

An hour later, Scott was standing in front of Dan Ford's desk, his adrenaline still pumping hard.

Dan sighed and said, "Perhaps. Perhaps you should reconsider your decision."

"What, this is a warning from McCall, that he can hurt me? He didn't hurt me, he hurt a poor Mexican girl! Who didn't do a god-damned thing to him!"

Scott headed to the door, but stopped and turned back. "Oh, Dan, when you call the senator, tell him I said to go fuck himself."

Scott stormed past Sue and into his office where he found Bobby stretched out on the sofa.

"Mr. Fenney?" Sue was at the door, pink phone slips in hand. "Reporters. They won't stop calling."

"No reporters." Sue disappeared. Scott wiped sweat from his forehead, looked over at Bobby, and said, "They took Consuela."

Bobby sat up. "Who?"

"INS. They showed up this morning, anonymous tip."

"From McCall."

Scott slumped. "Jesus, Bobby, her face. She was so scared."

His anger rose again, and he desperately needed to hit something, so he kicked the trash basket across the room.

"That son of a bitch doesn't know who he's messing with!" He pointed a finger at the blowup of himself on the wall. "I got a hundred and ninety-three yards against Texas!"

"Football's got rules, Scotty. Game McCall plays, ain't no rules."

"We'll see about that."

Bobby climbed up from the sofa and said, "I'll be in the library if you need me—briefs for Shawanda. Lunch?"

Scott nodded. Bobby turned to leave but stopped dead in his tracks when Karen Douglas appeared in the door. They looked at each other like two preteens, then Karen broke eye contact and entered the office. Bobby left and Karen said to Scott, "He's cute."

"Yeah, that's what I always tell him."

Scott sat down hard in his chair and tried to get his breathing under control.

"You okay?" Karen asked.

"No." After several deep breaths: "What's up?"

"We're ready to file the Dibrell zoning lawsuit." Sid walked in as Karen continued: "But Richard down in litigation says Dallas County state court isn't a favorable venue for this type of action. He says the judges are all Republicans and aren't inclined to overrule a city's zoning decisions."

Sid winked at Scott and said, "Karen, what's the single most important fact a lawyer needs to know before going into court, the one fact that will determine whether you win or lose?"

Karen seemed confused. Finally, she shrugged and said, "Which party was in the right and which was in the wrong?"

Sid chuckled. "Not exactly. This wasn't on the bar exam, Karen, but the single most important fact to know is whether the other lawyer contributed more money to the judge's last campaign than we did. Right, Scott?"

Scott nodded at Sid, but his thoughts were on Consuela . . . and the look on her face . . . as if Señor Fenney had betrayed her.

Sid said, "Only problem is, Scott, cases are assigned randomly. How can we be sure of getting one of our judges?"

Scott's mind, though clouded with Consuela, remained ever aggressive and creative.

"Karen, tell Richard to file the lawsuit six times back to back. The six suits will be assigned to six different judges. We'll pick the judge we gave the most money to, proceed with that suit, and non-suit the others."

Sid was duly impressed. Karen had that same freshman-coed-watching-her-first-porn-flick expression. Scott thought of his maid . . . he had betrayed her. He yelled out to his secretary:

"Sue, get me Rudy Gutierrez's number! He's an immigration lawyer!"

Karen asked, "Scott, is that ethical? Filing the same suit six times?"

"It's a code of legal ethics, Karen, not the Bible."

"Where's the goddamn coffee?"

In the commercial-style kitchen at 4000 Beverly Drive in Highland Park, Rebecca Fenney was opening and slamming cabinet doors, trying to find the coffee beans and the grinder so she could make her own coffee for the first time in three years, angry and agitated because her anxiety and fear had increased exponentially. Had her husband fucked up a good thing? Was losing Consuela just the beginning—the beginning of the end? The arrest of the Fenney maid would be the main topic at every luncheon of Highland Park ladies this Monday. What would they think of Rebecca Fenney now? How would it affect her chances to chair the Cattle Barons' Ball?

"What's gonna happen to Consuela, Mother?"

Sitting at the table were the two little girls.

"I don't know, Boo. Eat some breakfast."

Pajamae jumped up. "I can cook, Mrs. Fenney. I cook for Mama all the time, eggs, bacon, biscuits, grits—"

"Skip the grits." Rebecca tried another cabinet. "Where's the coffee?"

Pajamae was now pulling out frying pans and utensils and dragging a chair to the range. She climbed up.

"Where-as. This is a cool stove."

Rebecca gave up on coffee. "I'll be downstairs on the Stairmaster. You girls try not to start a fire. We've got to get another maid. Soon."

"INS came to your home in Highland Park? Jesus, Scott, who'd you piss off?"

Scott had called Rudy Gutierrez, the immigration lawyer.

"Her name is Consuela de la Rosa. Get her out today."

"No way, Scott. INS won't let go of her."

"Why not? She's just a maid."

"Scott, since 9/11 every Mexican here illegally is an international terrorist as far as INS is concerned. They play hardball. They were pricks before—now they're goddamned pricks."

"I'll pay whatever it takes, Rudy, just get her out."

"Scott, it'd be cheaper not to fight deportation. Let INS bus her across the border, then she can cross back over and work her way back up here."

"Consuela can't handle that."

"Okay, but it ain't gonna be cheap."

"How much?"

"Twenty-five . . . thousand."

"I'll send you a check today. You find her today, Rudy, tell her everything is gonna be okay, that we're her family and she'll be back with us . . . and Rudy, tell her I'm sorry."

200

Bobby had returned from the library shortly before noon. They were now taking the elevator upstairs to the Downtown Club. Scott was still aching to punch something. Or someone. He straightened his tie in the mirrored wall and said, "Bobby, we're gonna show the world what kind of boy Clark McCall was."

"For Shawanda or because McCall got your maid arrested?"

Scott stared at himself in the mirror a moment.

"I don't know."

"Let me know when you do."

The elevator doors opened and Scott led the way down the corridor to the maître d's station.

"Two, Roberto."

Roberto stood frozen, his brown eyes wide, as if the Virgin Mary herself stood before him. Scott expected him to make the sign of the cross.

"Roberto?"

"Uh, Mr. Fenney, I, uh, I, uh . . ."

"What, Roberto? We want lunch."

"Mr. Fenney, I no can do."

Roberto was suddenly no longer the suave maître d' of the Downtown Club; he was a *no habla inglés* immigrant just up from the border.

"You no can do *what*?"

"Give you seat."

"Why not?"

Roberto's forehead shone with a layer of sweat.

"You no member."

"What the hell you mean I'm not a member?"

"Mr. Fenney, is no more."

"You're telling me I'm not a member anymore?"

Roberto nodded. *"Sí."*

201

"Get Stewart."

Roberto hurried off in search of the club's manager. Scott turned and nodded at the three men waiting behind him to be seated. In less than a minute, Stewart appeared, trailed by Roberto—and the club's security guard.

"What the hell's going on, Stewart?"

Stewart regarded Scott with the same disdain he would a homeless person seeking a handout at the swanky Downtown Club.

"Mr. Fenney, your membership has been revoked by action of the board of directors, effective immediately. I must ask you to leave the premises." He gestured at the members in line behind Scott. "Roberto, seat these gentlemen."

The three men followed Roberto into the dining room, but not before giving Scott a curious glance and whispering among themselves, "That's Scott Fenney, Tom Dibrell's lawyer."

"You're joking?"

"No, Mr. Fenney."

Stewart held out an envelope. Scott snatched it, opened it, and removed a letter from the board of directors of the Downtown Club informing A. Scott Fenney, Esq., that his membership had been terminated. Scott's blood pressure ratcheted up until the veins in his forehead felt like they would blow any second.

"Please leave, Mr. Fenney. Or Darrell will escort you out."

Darrell, the security guard, took a step toward Scott. Darrell was young, early twenties, maybe two hundred pounds, wearing a clip-on tie and a brown polyester sports coat the sleeves of which were straining against his thick arms. Sporting a flattop, he had a square jaw and the protruding brow of a weight lifter fashioned from steroids. Scott had played football with what God gave him; he hadn't bought it in a goddamned drugstore. But he had played against many such freaks. Problem with drugstore muscles, though, was they weren't real, they weren't strong, they weren't powerful. They just looked good. At least that was his theory. Scott

Fenney was still 185 pounds of natural muscle and he could still kick Darrell's ass up and down the seventy floors of this skyscraper. He now took a step toward Darrell, so close he could smell Darrell's foul breath. Scott said through clenched teeth: "I wouldn't recommend trying."

Scott wadded up the letter and tossed it in Stewart's face, then he turned and walked away. They were ten paces down the corridor when he heard Bobby's voice: "Scotty."

Scott stopped and turned back. Bobby was pointing to a portrait on the wall, one of the club's founders: Mack McCall.

If Mack McCall had appeared before him at that moment, Scott Fenney might well have found himself sleeping in a cell like Shawanda Jones that night. He had never before been this mad at another human being, not even on a football field. He knew he couldn't return to the office in that state, so he and Bobby took the skywalk across to the athletic club.

"They got a juice bar," Scott said.

They were met at the front desk not by the trim little blonde Scott normally saw after work but by Han, a hulking bodybuilder who made Darrell look like a runt. Han greeted Scott like a stranger.

"Please wait here, Mr. Fenney."

"Oh, shit," Bobby said. "Déjà vu all over again."

Han returned with a cheap little gym bag the club gave to guests. He held it out to Scott.

"What's this?"

"The contents of your locker."

"Why?"

"Your membership is terminated."

"As of when?"

"This morning."

"Why?"

"Orders."

"From whom?"

"The club manager."

"And who gave him orders?"

"I don't know."

Han crossed his arms over his chest, creating a mass of muscle, bulging biceps and triceps and forearms and pectorals. Scott wasn't sure he wanted to test his theory about steroid-induced muscle on Han. Scott had been in his share of bar fights in college, but never in a juice bar and never sober and never with anyone as big as Han. And he had always been backed up by one or two offensive linemen; those guys were crazy enough to fight a grizzly bear hand to hand. So when Bobby grabbed his arm and said, "Let's get out of here," Scott did not resist.

For the first time since he made partner at Ford Stevens, A. Scott Fenney, Esq., ate a hot dog for lunch, purchased from a street vendor, in the company of people whose collective net worth was less than the price of his suit.

After choking down two dogs, which he was beginning to regret, he and Bobby walked down Main Street, something else Scott hadn't done in years. Or ever. And for a good reason.

Five minutes in the July heat and Scott was soaked from head to toe in sweat. His hair and face were wet, and his crisply starched shirt now clung to him like wet tissue. The sweat from his chest and back was rolling down and collecting in his underwear; the sweat from his legs was collecting in his socks. Hoping to at least save the coat of his $2,000 suit, he removed it and draped it over his shoulder. Bobby was saying something, but to Scott it was just background noise. Scott's mind was on Mack McCall.

Bobby said, "Can you believe those civic boosters, actually

thinking the Summer Olympics might come to Dallas? Half the athletes wouldn't make it out of this blast furnace alive."

A block later, Bobby said, "Used to be whorehouses and saloons all up and down Main Street. Doc Holliday practiced dentistry and killed his first man right here."

And later: "You know Bonnie and Clyde grew up here? They're both buried here. Clyde's grave is over in West Dallas. I don't know where Bonnie's is at."

They walked like that, Bobby giving Scott a brief history of Dallas and Scott responding with only nods and grunts the same as if he were listening to Rebecca telling him about her day. They arrived at Dealey Plaza on the western edge of downtown, a tiny triangle of green grass wedged between Houston, Commerce, and Elm Streets, the Triple Underpass to the west and the School Book Depository and the grassy knoll to the north. The place remained exactly as it had been on November 22, 1963.

Bobby said, "You ever been up to the Sixth Floor, looked out the window?"

Scott shook his head.

"No way Oswald did it alone," Bobby said. "Had to be a shooter on the grassy knoll. You want to go over?"

Scott shook his head again.

Bobby pointed down the street. "Right over there, that's where Ruby shot Oswald, down in the basement of the old jail."

Scott grunted. Oswald shot Kennedy, Ruby shot Oswald, Shawanda shot Clark, Scott shot Mack. It was a thought.

Bobby said, "Right here, this is where Dallas got started, a hundred and sixty years ago, at the exact spot Kennedy got shot. Kind of creepy, ain't it? Anyway, guy named John Neely Bryan set up a trading post right on the banks of the Trinity River—you know it used to run right here? Every spring it flooded downtown, so eighty years ago the city leaders moved the whole damn river a mile west, built big levees so it wouldn't flood downtown. Course, ever since it's flooded black people's homes in South Dallas. They didn't build levees down there."

They started back toward Dibrell Tower.

Bobby said, "People that started Dallas, they were running from their creditors back East. 'Gone to Texas,' they said, which is like saying 'chapter seven bankruptcy' today. They figured their creditors might be brave enough to chase them into Indian territory, but they sure as hell weren't stupid enough to follow them into this hellhole."

When they arrived at the six-story Neiman Marcus flagship store at Main and Ervay, Scott stopped and watched an old homeless woman pull her shopping cart full of junk over and admire the window display, designer clothes on skinny white mannequins, while inside the fine ladies of Highland Park were attending the Estée Lauder Focus Week, or so the sign in the window said. The old lady looked up at Scott and gave him a big toothless smile.

They walked on and Scott began to notice the other strange people populating downtown, the people who walked the streets amid the heat and the noise and the nauseating exhaust fumes of buses and cars, so thick in the air he could taste it, the vagrants and the panhandlers, the old women without teeth and the old men with beards, Hispanic girls with little children in tow, black boys looking tough, and the cops walking the beat. There was another world down here on the streets. Driving by in his Ferrari, Scott had noticed these people no more than he did the inanimate objects of downtown, the light poles and parking meters and trash cans. His life was lived 620 feet up, in air-conditioned comfort. Scott was terribly uncomfortable down here on the street. Bobby was passing out business cards.

"What the hell are you doing, Bobby?"

"Trolling for clients, man. Scotty, I'm a street lawyer and this is the street. You look at them and see homeless people, vagrants, dime players, bottom-feeders—I see clients! This is my Downtown Club."

Bobby quickly realized his error.

"Shit, I've been trying my best for an hour to get your mind off that, now I bring it up. Sorry."

But Scott's thoughts had already returned to his perfect life sixty-two stories above them. He now knew that Mack McCall was not going to beat Scott Fenney senseless with brass knuckles. He was going to do something much worse. He was going to take Scott's perfect life away.

That feeling of impending doom enveloped Scott Fenney.

If she made this putt, Rebecca Fenney would finish with a 74, her lowest score ever. She stood behind the ball and took two practice strokes, then walked over and assumed her putting stance, carefully placing the putter behind the ball and adjusting her weight until she was comfortably balanced. She knew Trey, the young golf pro whom she was paying $500 for today's playing lesson, was watching her closely, but he wasn't eyeing her putting stroke. He was eyeing her butt. He always managed to stand directly behind her when she putted.

Trey had already holed out for a 62. He was twenty-six, gorgeous, and a former All-American golfer. He had just received notice from the PGA that he was eligible to play in the remaining tournaments that year. This was his last week at the club.

She made a smooth stroke, sending the ball on a true line six inches outside the cup, and watched as the ball broke left and rolled into the hole.

"Yes!"

Trey walked over to her. They high-fived on the eighteenth green of the country club. He looked at her like he always did, and she saw the need in his eyes: he needed her more than life itself. They had been having sex for the last seven months.

They turned and walked up the grassy slope to their cart and climbed in for the short drive to the clubhouse. Trey parked the cart, and the black bag boy appeared.

"Your car be the black Mercedes coupe, Miz Fenney?"

"What?"

"Your car, it the black coupe?"

"Yes, what about it?"

"Make sure I take your clubs to the right car."

"Don't take my clubs to my car. Put them in the clubhouse, like always."

"Mr. Porter, he tell me take them to your car."

"Why?"

He shrugged. "Don't know, ma'am."

Rebecca turned to Trey. He shrugged. She walked inside the clubhouse, into the golf shop, and directly to the head pro's office, where Ernie Porter was sitting. Ernie couldn't make it on the pro tour, so he had spent the last twenty years giving golf lessons, running tournaments, and pocketing a percentage of every club, golf ball, and pair of shoes sold in the pro shop.

"Ernie?"

He looked up. "Yes, Mrs. Fenney?"

"The bag boy, you told him to take my clubs to my car?"

"Yes, ma'am."

"Why?"

"If that's inconvenient, Mrs. Fenney, I'll have them delivered to your house."

"I don't want my clubs at my house. I play here every day."

Ernie suddenly appeared sick. "Mrs. Fenney, you don't know?"

"Know what?"

Ernie shuffled some papers, squirmed in his chair, then said, "Your husband, Mr. Fenney . . . Well, he's . . . He's, uh . . . He's no longer a member here."

"*What?* We've been members for four years."

"Well, technically, Mrs. Fenney, your husband is the member. You have playing privileges as his spouse. Since he's no longer a member, you no longer have privileges. It's in the bylaws."

"Since when isn't Scott a member?"

"Since today."

She found her husband sitting at the kitchen table, their daughter cradled in his lap and sobbing into his shoulder as he stroked her braids. Pajamae was sitting across the table, her face glum, her chin resting on her hands on the table.

"Mother, Consuela's gone and she's never coming back!"

Rebecca put her hands on her hips and tried not to scream.

"Didn't Sue pay our club dues this month?"

Scott raised his eyes to her. He nodded blankly.

"Ernie said you're no longer a member."

His hand slowly came up and fell on a piece of paper on the table. She recognized the club's letterhead. He pushed it her way. She picked it up and read:

Dear Mr. Fenney:

    The Membership Committee believes that your continued presence at the club will detract from the collegial social atmosphere of the membership. Therefore your membership has been revoked effective this date. Please do not return to the premises. Your personal belongings will be delivered to your residence, along with your final bill.

"It's McCall," he said. "He got me kicked out of the Downtown Club and the athletic club, too. He's trying to pressure me to drop our defense."

"Goddamnit, Scott, I told you!" Her arm dropped and the letter floated to the floor. The Scott Fenney ride was coming to an end. The only question now was whether the end would be a soft landing or a fiery crash.

The girls were sitting up in Boo's bed when Scott picked up the book and sat down in the chair next to the bed. All the strength had drained out of his body. In one day, he had lost his maid and his memberships at the dining club, the athletic club, and the country club. Just the idea of it, that Mack McCall possessed that kind of power, that he could sit in Washington and pull strings in Dallas, make a few phone calls and affect Scott's perfect life, made Scott realize his relative place in the world. Maybe 193 yards against Texas didn't make Scott Fenney so special after all.

"You broke your promise," Boo said, her voice stern, "and now Consuela's gone."

Scott had suffered all manner of physical pain, but none compared to the pain he felt now for letting his daughter down.

Scott removed his glasses. "I'm sorry, Boo."

"Get her back."

"I'm trying to." Scott replaced his glasses and opened the book. "Where were we, the Thirteenth Amendment?"

Boo said, "We want to talk about something else."

Scott shut the book. "Okay. What?"

"What's a will?"

"A will is a legal declaration evidencing a testamentary intent to dispose of one's property upon one's death."

Boo had a blank expression. "In English," she said. Pajamae was nodding.

"A will says who gets your stuff when you die."

The girls glanced at each other and nodded. Boo said, "So who gets your stuff if you die?"

"Your mother."

"Who gets her stuff if she dies?"

"Me."

"Who gets your and Mother's stuff if you both die?"

"You."

"Who gets me?"

"Oh."

"My grandparents are dead, I don't have any uncles or aunts or older brothers or sisters . . . and now I don't even have Consuela."

"Well, first of all, Boo, your mother and I don't plan on dying anytime soon, so this is all hypothetical."

"All what?"

"Hypothetical. You know, what if. But don't worry, your mother and I are going to be here to take care of you."

Pajamae said, "Mama says all my kin are dead or in prison."

"So what if?" Boo said.

"What if what?"

"What if you and Mother die?"

"I don't know, Boo. I guess I haven't thought much about it."

Boo held out a handful of one-dollar bills and assorted coins. "We want to hire you as our lawyer, but we've only got thirteen dollars between us, so you'll have to work really fast."

"And what do you want me to do?"

"Write us a will that says if Pajamae's mother dies, we get her and she gets to live with us, and if you and Mother die, her mother gets me and I get to live with them."

"In the projects?" Scott said before he could catch himself.

"No. I'll get this house, we'll live here."

Both girls were nodding now. And Scott smiled for the first time that day, at the image of Shawanda Jones as the woman of the house at 4000 Beverly Drive in the heart of Highland Park.

SEVENTEEN

M cCALL'S AN ASSHOLE."

"Tell me something I don't know."

It was nine the next morning, and Scott was slumped on the sofa in Dan Ford's office. His senior partner was sitting behind his desk, his hands folded, like a priest taking a confession.

"But he's rich and powerful, Scott, which makes him a very dangerous asshole."

"He's your friend."

"I didn't say he was my friend. Fact is, I wouldn't turn my back on the bastard. But he's going to be the next president, and we want him to be this firm's friend."

"Dan, you tell him I can live without the Downtown Club and the athletic club and the country club—taking my membership . . . okay, fine, that's playing hardball. But taking Consuela, hurting a poor Mexican girl who never hurt a soul in her life . . . that ain't hardball, Dan, that's just plain fucking mean. You tell him he's a mean son of a bitch to do that." Scott had awakened that morning itching for a fight. "Matter of fact, why don't you give me McCall's number, I'll tell him myself."

Dan smiled. "I don't think so, Scotty."

"You know, Dan, I was never carried off the field. I took the best shot any team could give me, and I always got up."

Dan nodded. "You were tough."

"I'm still tough." Scott tapped his index finger to the side of his head. "Up here. That's where real toughness is, in your head. Everyone hurts physically, but the guys who are mentally tough get up off the ground and keep playing. McCall gave me his best shot, and I got up. You tell him that. I'm still playing—and I'm gonna play harder now. You tell him that, too."

Scott stood and walked to the door but stopped when Dan said, "Scotty?"

"Yeah?"

"How do you know that's his best shot?"

Five minutes later, Mack McCall was saying to Dan, "The boy don't break easy."

"No, he doesn't," Dan said.

"Well, he will . . . or everyone in Dallas is gonna know his wife is screwing the assistant pro at the club."

"*Trey?* Jesus, that boy's cutting a wide swath through the wives out there. He ought to be paying us. How'd you find out?"

"Delroy's been snooping."

"Damn, Mack, hold off on that, see if Scott gets on board. His wife cheating on him . . . that's gonna be tough on him."

"You sound like you care about Fenney."

"He's the best young lawyer I've ever met . . . he's like a son to me."

"Dan, a son can be a dangerous thing."

214

The morning mail was waiting for Scott when he returned to his office. But instead of billing a thousand dollars for reading his mail, today's mail was going to cost him many times that sum: one letter was from the Internal Revenue Service, demanding $75,000 for back nanny taxes, penalties, and interest in the matter of Consuela de la Rosa. And Scott knew Dan's words had been a warning: Mack McCall was not yet through with Scott Fenney.

Scott sat at his desk and assessed his financial condition. He had $100,000 cash, more or less—actually, $25,000 less since he had sent a check over to Rudy Gutierrez yesterday—in his savings account, which was generating almost nothing in interest income, and another $200,000 in his 401(k) account, all in tech stocks, all under water, all worth half what he paid for them.

He owed $2.8 million on the house, $175,000 on the Ferrari, and another $150,000 on the Mercedes and Range Rover, and $25,000 on credit cards. Three million one hundred fifty thousand in debt. The cars were probably at breakeven, debt to value, and the house was worth maybe a million over the debt, although the high-end housing market in Dallas had slowed recently.

His only income was his monthly partnership draw, $62,500 gross, but only $42,000 after taxes, which disappeared faster than a raindrop on the sidewalk in July: $4,000 in monthly payments on the Ferrari, $3,000 on Rebecca's Mercedes and the Rover, $16,000 in monthly interest payments on the house note, $10,000 a month in property taxes and insurance premium escrows, and $4,000 a month in utilities and upkeep. Which left only $5,000 a month for groceries, clothes, eating out, entertainment, and club dues—at least he wouldn't have to pay club dues anymore. He had never worried about saving money; the house was his savings account, retirement account, and rainy-day fund. Of course, he could access those accounts only by selling the place or refinancing the mortgage, which was not a likely option since Dan Ford had called in a personal favor with the bank president to get the $2.8 million loan in the first place.

So Scott wrote a check on his savings account for *Seventy-Five Thousand and no/100 Dollars* to the "Internal Fucking Revenue Service." And then he sat back in his chair and wondered what McCall would take next.

From the sofa in Scott's office, Bobby said, "Seventy-five thousand bucks? Shit, I sell everything I own and pay my debts, I'm still seventy-four thousand shy of that. And you wrote a check?"

Bobby had arrived and Scott had brought him up to date.

"Yeah. But it was all of my cash."

"You know, Scotty, McCall's taken this way further than I thought he would. I mean, being pissed off is one thing, but trying to destroy your life, man, he's into Stephen King territory now."

"He can't destroy my life, Bobby. He can take my maid, my memberships, and my cash, but he can't destroy me. I've still got clients that pay me three million dollars a year."

"Mr. Fenney?"

Sue was standing in the door.

"Yeah?"

"Mr. Dibrell called, said he needs to see you ASAP."

The beautiful blonde Dibrell Property Company receptionist did not inquire about Scott's marital status today, and Marlene did not smile at Scott. Instead she averted her eyes as he walked past her workstation and into Tom Dibrell's inner sanctum. From Tom's pained expression, Scott figured he would have to negotiate sexual harassment settlements with two receptionists this time. And he wondered if he could.

"What's up, Tom?"

Tom motioned to the sofa. "Sit down, Scott."

Scott stepped around the coffee table, a long glass top set on a base of horseshoes laid flat and welded together. He plopped down on the soft leather and spread his arms along the top of the back. Attorney and client regarded each other across twenty feet of expensive finish-out.

"We've been together a long time, Scott."

"Eleven years, Tom. As long as I've been a lawyer."

"You're the best lawyer I've ever had, Scott, and I've had more than a few."

"Well, thanks." He chuckled and smiled. "You know, Tom, back in college when I broke up with a girl, I'd always tell her how beautiful she was first."

Tom nodded and exhaled. But he didn't smile.

"We're breaking up, Scott."

"What?"

"You're no longer my lawyer."

Fear shot Scott up off the sofa and across the void to Tom's desk. He was now looking down at his rich client, at three million in legal fees, his heartbeat increasing with each second as all the ramifications of losing Tom Dibrell as a client raced through his mind like a runaway locomotive.

"Tom . . . *why?*"

"It's best not to go into it, Scott. It's done."

"But . . ."

"Don't, Scott."

Scott felt wobbly and confused, like he'd taken a blow to the head. He turned away from Tom and took several steps toward the door, and he saw something he had never seen before or had never taken the time to see. He blinked hard, his eyes and mind coming into focus simultaneously. On the wall was a framed photograph of Tom Dibrell and Senator Mack McCall at a golf tournament. He turned back to Tom, but pointed at the photo.

"It's him, isn't it? McCall. He made you do this."

Their eyes locked for a long moment, then Tom's face sagged and he nodded his head like it hurt.

"Scott, you want to know the answer to the mystery?"

"What mystery?"

"Did Oswald act alone? . . . What the hell mystery you think I'm talking about? How Tom Dibrell survived the real-estate crash and kept his building when everyone else failed and lost theirs."

Scott nodded.

"McCall. He saved me. The pension fund in New York, the bastards holding the mortgage on this building—which they were trying to foreclose—they wanted legislation passed in Congress, some kind of special tax break on their investments. Mack told them if they foreclosed on me, he'd shit-can their legislation. They dropped the foreclosure. And Mack got me the contracts on the new post office building and the justice center, gave me some cash flow. He saved me, Scott, just because we're neighbors and I send my gardener over to mow his grass. And he's never asked me for a goddamned thing . . . until now. He's like the Godfather, Scott—when he finally asks you for a favor, you don't say no. I owe him."

"What about me? I started working for you when other lawyers dropped you like a load of shit. I've been loyal to you for eleven years. Don't you owe *me*?"

Tom recoiled and his expression changed from pained to bemused.

"I paid you what I owed you, Scott. In full, every month. As a matter of fact, more than in full. You've been overbilling me for years. You think I didn't know that? Billing me for your law students, training new lawyers on my tab, marking up your cost of copies and faxes and phone calls, charging your hourly rate for our lunches, padding hours—why'd you think I hired all those MBAs from Harvard, for my health? I know where every goddamned penny in this company goes! I figure over the years you're probably into me for two, three million in overbillings. But that's what you wanted from me—my fees, not my friendship. So that's how I paid you back, Scott, in cash. Not in loyalty. I'm loyal to my friends, damn loyal. But you weren't my friend. You were my lawyer."

"Yeah, Tom, and as your lawyer I've bent some rules for you. I've pushed the ethical and legal envelope for you, to make your deals happen!"

Tom held his hands up, as if surrendering. "Whoa, I don't know nothing about that, Scott. I'm just a dumb ol' dirt developer. I leave that complicated legal stuff to my real smart lawyer."

He smiled.

"Not a month ago, Tom, I was standing right here, and you needed me to pull your ass out of a crack again . . . what was her name, Nadine? I did. You said you'd never forget."

"I won't. I'll never forget that, Scott. But this is business."

He's Ross Perot's lawyer.
He's Jerry Jones's lawyer.
He's Mark Cuban's lawyer.
He was Tom Dibrell's lawyer.

A lawyer would much prefer his wife run off with another man than his client run off with another lawyer. A wife's betrayal makes him question her. But a client's betrayal makes him question himself; fact is, a client's betrayal is the *only* thing that can make a lawyer question himself, what he is and who he is. Because a lawyer without a wife is still a lawyer, but a lawyer without a client is just a man.

A lawyer's identity is derived from the clients he represents. A lawyer's power, prestige, influence, wealth, reputation, and standing in the community—*what he is and who he is*—are determined by the clients he represents. You're only as good as your clients are rich.

Scott had ridden the elevator up as an important lawyer in Dallas, a lawyer with a rich client; he was *Scott Fenney, Tom Dibrell's lawyer*. Now he rode the elevator down as . . . who? He didn't recognize the man in the elevator's mirrored walls.

His first known identity was as Butch's son. Then, from the time his football skills became apparent, it was as a football player. And for the last eleven years it had been as Tom Dibrell's lawyer. He had always had an identity. But who was Scott Fenney now? Just another lawyer without a rich client, no better than Bobby, whose best client was a Latino waiter?

For the first time in his life, he didn't know who he was.

Scott was still in a state of shock when he returned to his office and found Bobby on the sofa and a certified letter on his desk. The name on the envelope—First Dallas Bank—barely registered in his mind. He used the letter opener to slice the top of the envelope with no more thought than if it were junk mail. He removed the letter, four pages of crisp bond paper, and unfolded and smoothed the pages flat on his desk. And he read. And as he did, a slow realization came over him: he was reading his own obituary.

The bank was calling the notes on the house and the cars. He had ten days to pay off $325,000 on the three automobiles and thirty days to pay off $2.8 million on the house. Failure to make timely payment would result in immediate repossession of the cars and foreclosure of the house. Scott Fenney would lose his mansion and the Ferrari.

His perfect life would be gone.

A sense of defeat tried to take hold in his mind, but Scott Fenney had never been defeated, even when he lost. Because when he lost, he did not accept it. Instead, he got mad. As he did now. His respiration accelerated, his jaws clenched, and anger energized his mind and body. He picked up the phone and hit the speed dial for the private number of Ted Sidwell, the bank president. Ted answered on the first ring.

"Ted, Scott Fenney. What the hell's going on?"

"Demand notes, Scott. And we just made demand."

"Why?"

"These loans were made to you as a favor, Scott. To get favors, you've got to give favors. That's how the game's played."

"I see. McCall. Fine, I'll refinance with another bank."

Ted laughed. "In today's market? And without Tom Dibrell as your client? I don't think so."

"News travels fast."

"I knew before you did."

"I'll sell the damn place, it's worth a million more than the debt."

"Fire sale in thirty days? You'll be lucky to get what you owe."

"I'll throw it into bankruptcy. I can hold you off for six months, maybe a year."

"Also not likely. The bank holds a note on Judge Schneider's home in Highland Park. He's the bankruptcy judge. And he understands favors."

Scott had run out of lawyerly rebuttals, so he fell back on the universal football retort: "Fuck you, Ted."

He slammed the phone down.

Bobby was sitting up. "What was that about?"

Scott realized his face was damp with sweat. "The bank called my notes, on the cars and the house."

"How can they call your mortgage?"

"Because it's not a mortgage like you think. You don't get a thirty-year five percent Fannie Mae mortgage for two-point-eight million, Bobby. You get a demand note callable on thirty days' notice."

"*Jesus*. Can you refinance?"

"Not likely. I got this note only because Dan used his influence with the bank president, that asshole."

"Guess who's influencing the bank president now?"

Scott nodded.

"You could sell the place."

"Rebecca would die. That house means everything to her."

"Shit, Scotty, you got three million in fees. You can swing something."

Scott could barely give voice to the words: "Dibrell just fired me."

Rebecca said, "If you're not Tom Dibrell's lawyer anymore, who am I?"

All the way home, Scott had bucked himself up for this moment; he hoped his performance was more convincing to his wife.

"I don't need him."

"No, but you need his three million in fees. Look, Scott, most lawyers' wives don't have a clue what their husbands do at the office, but I do. God knows you've educated me over the last eleven years. I know how things work in a law firm. And I know that a partner who just lost a three-million-dollar client won't be a partner for long. And what are we going to do then, Scott? How are we going to pay for this house?"

Scott walked to the windows of the master suite. He could not bear to look at his wife when he said what he had to say.

"Well, that's the other thing, Rebecca. The house. The bank called the note. I've got to pay off two-point-eight million in thirty days or lose it. Unless we sell it first."

He turned and saw the color drain out of Rebecca's face and her legs give way; she sat down hard on the bed and stared blankly at the wall in front of her. After a moment, she spoke as if to herself: "Without this house, I'll never be chairwoman of the Cattle Barons' Ball." Her eyes, vacant and lost, turned to Scott. "How will I ever show my face in this town again?"

Scott Fenney felt the sting of his wife's disappointment. He had let her down, failed her, betrayed her. He had promised her this life, a life in this house, with these things, driving those cars. Now he had broken that promise. For the first time in his life, he felt the pain of failure. And behind the pain, he felt something else, an anger building deep inside him, not the anger of a lawyer at a client who doesn't pay his bill or a judge who rules against him, but the kind of anger he had previously felt only on a football field, a base anger that had been in man since Adam, an anger that clouded your mind and strengthened your body, that made you say things you shouldn't say and do things you shouldn't do, the kind of anger that usually resulted in Scott Fenney being flagged for unsportsmanlike conduct. The kind of anger that meant some son of a bitch was fixing to feel some Scott Fenney payback.

EIGHTEEN

OVER THE COURSE of four seasons of Division I-A college football, playing against teams like Texas, Texas A&M, Nebraska, and Oklahoma, teams with players that outweighed the SMU players by forty or fifty pounds per position, Scott Fenney, number 22, had taken a beating. At 185 pounds, he was strong, fast, and tough; but when a 250-pound linebacker tackled him and drove him into the hard turf, he still hurt. He suffered two knee surgeries, a dislocated shoulder, five broken ribs, four broken fingers (the same one twice), two broken noses, one concussion, numerous abrasions and contusions, and a cumulative total of 117 stitches. But he never missed a single game.

Scott Fenney got up every time they knocked him down. And when he did, he always gave them payback, breaking a long run, returning a kickoff, scoring a touchdown. The payback helped make the hurt go away.

Senator Mack McCall had shown Scott the true meaning of

hurt. He had hit Scott like no linebacker had ever hit him. Now it was time for payback.

Scott checked his watch and stood. He glanced out at the night lights of downtown. It was almost nine the next evening and Scott was in his office.

"Scotty," Bobby said from the sofa. "I know this was my idea, but maybe it ain't such a good idea."

"You coming or not?"

Bobby stood. "Oh, yeah, I'm coming. Course, I feel like I'm boarding the *Titanic*."

Mack McCall's eyes roamed over the naked body of Jean McCall, and he recalled the first time they had had sex, fifteen years ago, not a month after she had graduated law school and joined his Senate staff. She was young, she was lean, she was sexy, and she was not his wife. His wife was not sexy or lean or young; she was old, forty-five, same age as he was back then, but he did not feel as old as she looked. Martha looked like her mother—not a woman he was particularly interested in having sex with.

At age forty-five, Mack McCall still felt young and randy, and he needed a woman who was young and randy, like Jean. They had sex nearly every day, anytime and anywhere—his private bathroom, the backseat of the limousine, the Senate cloakroom. She had an incredible body, a body that made him feel twenty-five again and brimming with testosterone. And she possessed a sex drive that could permanently disable a man half his age.

She was also a TV camera's dream, beautiful, articulate, charming, and intelligent. When Mack began dreaming of the White House, he had to make a decision: Did he want a first lady who looked like a grandmother or a fashion model? The decision took less than a minute to make. He divorced Martha.

She hired an asshole for a lawyer and threatened to confirm

what the tabloids had suggested: that Senator Mack McCall was having an affair with a member of his staff. Not that that was any big news on Capitol Hill, a member of Congress screwing around on his wife. But it was a sensitive issue when the particular member ran on a conservative family values platform and had his eye on the White House. Of course, Mack McCall could cut a business deal when the need arose. For $100 million, Martha kept her mouth shut and went home to Texas.

Jean had been worth every penny.

But the years had taken their toll on Mack McCall. Now, at age sixty, he didn't feel twenty-five anymore; he didn't feel forty-five, or even fifty-five; he didn't feel young and virile and brimming with testosterone. So he did what any self-respecting sixty-year-old man with money and a wife twenty years younger than him would do: he went to the doctor. Every morning now, Senator Mack Mc-Call showered, shaved, and slapped on aftershave and a testosterone patch, and every night he popped a Viagra pill, all in an effort to satisfy his sexual fantasies and Jean's sexual desires.

That evening she was stretched out naked on their bed. Her body was still incredibly shapely and inviting; her black hair was draped over her shoulders and fell onto her firm breasts; her belly was flat with no stretch marks from pregnancies; her lean legs didn't look like road maps. She was wearing her Clark Kent glasses and working on her laptop; the TV was on but the sound was muted. He was taking no chances tonight: he had replaced this morning's testosterone patch with a fresh one an hour ago when he had swallowed the Viagra pill. The patch was secreting that elixir of youth into his bloodstream and the little blue pill was expand-ing the arteries leading to his penis, physiological actions that re-sulted in an impressive erection. Feeling pretty damned proud and young and virile (albeit chemically and momentarily enhanced), Mack went over to Jean and stood by the bed until her eyes left the laptop and found him. Her eyebrows rose, and she smiled.

"I take it we're not going to watch *Dateline* tonight."

Mack could not know his wife was thinking, *Or at least the first five minutes of* Dateline, as she removed her glasses, set the laptop on the night table, slid down onto the bed, and spread her legs. Mack Mc-Call's version of foreplay had always consisted of checking the oil futures, so he climbed on top of Jean and entered her without so much as a howdy-do. She felt incredible, her legs pulled up and wrapped around his waist, her fingernails biting into his butt, her large breasts suffocating him with pleasure, as he pushed into her again and again and again with the steady rhythm of an oil well pump and he wondered what oil futures had closed at today when—

"Mack! Mack, stop!"

Jean reached for her glasses and the remote control. She put her glasses on with her left hand and pointed the remote with her right. Mack slipped out of her, panting heavily.

"What?"

Jean pointed at the television. "Look!"

Mack turned to the TV and saw his dead son's face.

"Tonight, from the federal building in downtown Dallas, an exclusive live interview with Shawanda Jones, the woman accused of murdering Clark McCall, the son of Senator Mack McCall, the leading candidate to be the next president of the United States."

On the screen, Mack saw the black face of Shawanda Jones, prostitute, drug addict, and murderer. Sitting next to her was A. Scott Fenney, Esq.

"He's a hunk," Jean said, which ignited the anger already smoldering within Mack.

On the TV: "With Ms. Jones tonight is her court-appointed lawyer, Scott Fenney. Mr. Fenney, every news show in the country has been trying to get an interview with you or your client ever since she was arrested—why tonight?"

"Because certain information has come to our attention that requires a public appeal. And because certain actions of Senator McCall constitute obstruction of justice."

"That's a serious charge, Mr. Fenney. But let's first go back to the night of Saturday, June fifth. What happened?"

Mack McCall's blood pressure rose steadily as the black bitch told her story: That Clark had picked her up, offered her a thousand dollars for a night of sex, took her to the McCall mansion in Highland Park, engaged in sex acts with her, and then beat her and called her nigger; that she fought him off, kneed him in the groin, and left, taking the money he owed her and his car keys; that the last time she had seen Clark, he was alive, lying on the floor, in pain and cursing her; that the murder weapon was in fact her gun, but that she had not held the gun to Clark's head and pulled the trigger and put a bullet through his brain. When she finally stopped talking, the program went to commercial.

During the break, McCall paced the bedroom, naked and angry. And when Mack McCall got angry, someone got hurt. That someone would be A. Scott Fenney. The only question was how McCall would hurt him this time. He had just about decided when the show returned to the air and the reporter turned to Fenney.

"Mr. Fenney, your client is alleging that Clark McCall was a racist and a brutal rapist. But he's not here to defend himself. How can you expect a jury to believe the word of a drug-addicted prostitute?"

"Because she wasn't the first woman Clark McCall beat and raped."

All the anger Mack McCall had experienced in his sixty years of life combined—anger against business competitors, political opponents, his ex-wife—could not compare to the anger that now controlled his being. He wanted desperately to kill Scott Fenney.

"Clark McCall beat and raped another woman a year ago. She filed a criminal complaint against him, but dropped it under pressure and a half-million-dollar payment from Senator McCall. She has agreed to testify at Shawanda's trial."

"To corroborate that Clark McCall was a rapist?"

"Yes. And there were other women, six others, who were raped and beaten by Clark McCall. I'm asking those women to come forward and testify so that an innocent victim of Clark McCall will not be sentenced to death for a crime she did not commit."

Another commercial break had Mack pointing to Jean's laptop and asking her if she had Dan Ford's home phone number on it. She did.

When the program resumed, the reporter asked: "Now, Mr. Fenney, let's turn to your allegation that Senator McCall obstructed justice."

Fenney said, "Obviously, the trial of the person accused of murdering Clark McCall will be a media circus. The federal court did not believe that the public defender's office could provide an adequate defense for Shawanda under those circumstances. So the court appointed me to represent her."

"That must have been a shock."

"Sure, at first. I'm a partner in a large Dallas law firm and I'm very busy with our paying clients, but I've always believed that lawyers have a professional duty to represent people who can't pay. So when the judge called, I readily accepted the appointment."

"But as they say, no good deed goes unpunished."

"So I've learned. I expected some adverse publicity, perhaps a few clients who didn't like what I was doing, but I did not expect Senator McCall to try to destroy me."

"And what has Senator McCall done?"

"First he called my senior partner and asked him to get me to exclude any evidence at trial about Clark's past criminal conduct. He said he did not want his son dragged through the mud. But Clark McCall lived in the mud."

"You refused to drop that evidence?"

"Absolutely. To do so would have been unethical conduct by a lawyer and unfair to Shawanda. She's entitled to the very best defense I can muster. And that's exactly what she will get."

"What did the senator do next?"

"He got the U.S. Attorney in Dallas to offer a plea deal, twenty years for Shawanda if we kept quiet about Clark's past. Of course, we rejected the offer. My client is innocent."

"Then what happened?"

"INS agents showed up at my house and arrested my maid, a Mexican national. Consuela—that's her name—had been with us for three years. She's part of our family."

Fenney's eyes looked wet.

"She didn't have a green card?"

"No."

"She was here in America illegally?"

"Yes."

"And you knew that?"

"Look, we can debate the merits of the immigration laws, but the point is that Senator McCall used his political power in Washington to have my maid in Dallas arrested."

"To pressure you?"

"Yes."

"Did he succeed?"

"No. I will never be pressured to act to the detriment of my client. Senator McCall only hurt a poor Mexican girl."

"Not a smart political move given the percentage of Hispanic voters in America. What happened next?"

"Senator McCall then got me kicked out of my dining club, my athletic club, and my country club."

The reporter offered a shocked expression.

"The man who wants to be president stooped that low?"

"Yes, he did."

"So is that all?"

"No, unfortunately, that's not all. Since I still refused to accede to his demands, Senator McCall used his power to get the bank to call the notes on my cars and my home. I now have ten days to pay off the car notes and thirty days to pay off the house note, or I'll lose everything."

"My God, you're not serious!"

"I'm afraid I am."

"I hesitate to ask, but is there more?"

"Yes. Since all of that did not succeed, McCall called in some favors with a client of mine, Tom Dibrell, a real-estate developer in Dallas and—"

"What kind of favors?"

"Well, Tom told me that ten, twelve years ago, McCall threatened to hold up legislation desired by the lender holding the mortgage on his downtown office building unless the lender held off foreclosure. And that McCall used his influence to swing several federal construction projects to Tom."

"And now he asked Mr. Dibrell for a favor in return?"

"Yes."

"And what was that favor?"

"To fire me as his lawyer."

"And did he?"

"Yes, he did."

"And how does that hurt you?"

"Tom was my biggest client. He paid my firm three million dollars in fees each year."

"That's a lot of money. So when Mr. Dibrell fired you, your professional career was harmed in a very significant way."

"Yes, it was. But I'm here to tell Senator McCall, on national TV, that despite his efforts to destroy me, I will defend Ms. Jones to the best of my ability. And evidence about his son's racism and rapes will be introduced at trial. Shawanda Jones will have a competent defense. I'll make sure of that."

The phone rang just as the program went to commercial again. Mack picked up the phone and answered. It was Delroy calling from Dallas. "You watching this?" Delroy asked.

"Yeah."

"You still just want to control him?"

"Now I want to hurt him. Leak it about his wife and the golf pro."

"Okay, but we can hurt him worse than that . . . and control him."

"You mean . . ." Mack decided not to complete his thought with Jean present. But he didn't need to with Delroy.

"Yeah, I mean. It worked with a Mexican drug lord. It'll damn sure work with a lawyer."

"I don't know, Delroy, that sort of thing . . ."

Mack turned back to the TV. The reporter was speaking directly into the camera: "What kind of man would try to destroy a lawyer for doing his professional duty? For defending a black woman accused of murdering a white man? Apparently, Senator Mack McCall is that kind of man."

Mack's blood pressure and anger spiked again. He said into the phone to Delroy: "Do it."

He could almost see Delroy grinning when he hung up.

On the TV the reporter turned to Fenney: "Mr. Fenney, thank you for coming on tonight so the American people can know what kind of man Senator McCall is before they decide to elect him president. You're a brave man. But Senator McCall is a rich and powerful man. Aren't you afraid he'll hurt you again?"

Fenney said, "McCall can't hurt me anymore."

Mack McCall walked into the closet, returned with a Smith & Wesson .357 magnum pistol he kept up on the shelf, pointed it at the image of A. Scott Fenney on the television, and pulled the trigger.

"The hell I can't."

233

After leaving the federal building, Scott drove the Ferrari through the dark and deserted downtown. It was eerily quiet. And it reminded him of his senior season, after his last game, when he walked from the belly of the stadium onto the dark and deserted field, stood on the 50-yard line, and just looked around, knowing it was over.

Rebecca was in the kitchen, staring at the TV, when he entered the house. The late news was on; a reporter was saying, "A flash poll taken immediately after the Shawanda Jones interview shows Senator McCall's poll numbers plummeting. He's fallen to single digits among likely voters, from first place to last, perhaps spelling the end to his White House ambitions."

Scott said, "I showed that son of a bitch."

Rebecca turned from the television; on her face was an expression of utter devastation.

"You just threw our lives away for a whore."

NINETEEN

THE NEXT MORNING, Scott Fenney felt like he had the morning after he had run for 193 yards against Texas: he hurt less because his opponent hurt more. Sure, he had lost his rich client, all his cash, his dining, athletic, and country club memberships, and his Mexican maid, and he would soon lose his Ferrari and his mansion. But Mack McCall had lost the White House. Scott Fenney had beaten a Texas roughneck at his own game.

How about those brass knuckles, McCall?

How's that for hardball, you mean son of a bitch?

So as he pulled the Ferrari into the parking garage beneath Dibrell Tower a little after nine, Scott was smiling. And why not? He was still a partner in Ford Stevens LLP, the most profitable law firm in Dallas. He still made $750,000 a year (although he would have to recruit new clients to replace Tom Dibrell's fees). He was still a local football legend, still able to bring a smile to any SMU alum's face, still able to turn on the famous charm and flash that movie-star smile.

Scott Fenney was still a winner.

He stuck the key card into the slot on the entrance gate and waited for the gate to rise. And waited. He stuck the key card in again and waited. Still nothing. He punched the button that rang Osvaldo over in the exit booth twenty feet away. When Osvaldo turned and saw him, Scott waved him over. Osvaldo exited the booth and walked over. Scott held up the key card.

"Card won't work," Scott said. "Raise the gate."

Osvaldo retreated a step and said, "No card."

"No, I've got a card. It's not working. Open the gate."

Osvaldo was now shaking his head. "No gate."

"Open the goddamned gate!"

Osvaldo held his hands up. "No card. No gate."

"Jesus Christ!"

Scott backed out and parked the Ferrari on the street, pumped a few quarters into the parking meter, pissed off until he remembered that the Ferrari would be his for only nine more days. Fuck it. Two-hundred-thousand-dollar car gets scratched, it's the bank's loss. By the time he hit the front door of Dibrell Tower two blocks away, he was whistling.

Rebecca Fenney was crying. She was still in bed, hiding from Highland Park. She had bet her beauty on Scott Fenney and lost. Her house. Her car. Her status. Her life. Everything she had acquired over the last eleven years would soon be gone. And it hadn't been lost to a twenty-two-year-old blonde with big tits and a tight ass—to a girl by the pool—but to a heroin addict, a whore, a . . . Rebecca never said that word because even in Highland Park such words are best said only behind the brick walls at the club, but she thought that word now: *nigger.*

Her husband had sacrificed her life for a nigger's life.

There. She had said it. Or at least thought it. As everyone in Highland Park was thinking at that very moment—the town is so small, so insular, that nothing escapes notice. Not that this could have escaped the notice of anyone in America, her husband on national TV, for God's sake! And today at lunch, her (former) society girlfriends would order Caribbean salad, tortilla soup, sparkling water, and for dessert, Rebecca Fenney. She would be today's scandal soufflé.

Oh, how they would gossip! And how they would laugh!

There's nothing the girls love to sink their sharp teeth into more than a juicy scandal: a lesbian affair; a good Highland Park girl knocked up by a black SMU athlete; botched cosmetic surgery; drinking, drugs, and STDs at the high school; criminal fraud committed by a scion of an old Highland Park family; a Democrat in Highland Park; failure in Highland Park. They lapped it up like the family dog laps up leftovers.

Rebecca Fenney had gossiped so many times about other women's scandals. Now everyone in Highland Park would be gossiping about her—at the Village, at the club, at the gym, at every restaurant and in every dressing room. They would all be gossiping and laughing—at her expense.

How could she ever show her face in this town again?

She was crawling back under the comforter when the phone rang.

Boo quietly pushed open the door to her parents' bedroom and stuck her head in. She saw her mother sitting on the far side of the bed and heard her talking on the phone. Her voice sounded strange.

"*What?* . . . Sleeping with Trey? . . . Where'd you hear that? . . . It's all over town? . . . Everyone knows? . . . *Oh, my God!*"

She hung up the phone and put her hands over her face.

"Mother?"

"Oh, God."

"Mother?"

"Oh, God." Finally she turned to Boo. Her mother looked like a frightened little kitten. "What, Boo?"

"Are you okay?"

"No."

"Can I help?"

"No. What do you want?"

"Is it okay if Pajamae and I go to the Village? We'll be real careful crossing the street."

Mother waved her hand. "Fine, whatever."

"Okay. See you later."

Boo started to shut the door, but her mother said, "Boo, wait. Come in. I need to talk to you."

As soon as Scott stepped inside the lobby of Dibrell Tower, he stopped whistling. A tidal wave of reporters and cameramen came rushing toward him, all shouting questions on top of each other.

"Mr. Fenney, what's her name, the woman Clark raped?"

"What are the names of the other women he raped?"

"You brought down Senator McCall—are you happy?"

"Do you think Senator McCall will be indicted?"

"What about Tom Dibrell—will he be indicted?"

Scott squinted at the bright camera lights and ducked and weaved his way toward the elevator bank. But at the speed at which he was advancing against the mass of reporters defending their ground, he wouldn't get into an elevator before noon. He was about to retreat when two enormous blue blazers stepped in front of him. Two black men, Dibrell Tower security guards, were now running interference for Scott Fenney. The reporters had a choice: get out of the way or get run over.

They got out of the way.

The two guards pushed forward until they arrived at the elevators where a third guard stood blocking the doors of an empty elevator. He stepped aside to allow Scott entrance, then again blocked the way. He was joined by the other two guards, three huge bodies in blue blazers protecting Scott Fenney from the reporters and cameras, black guards whom Scott had never before even acknowledged; they were just inanimate objects in the lobby, like the big bronze Remington sculpture. Scott reached over and punched the FLOOR 62 button, then fell to the back of the elevator. Just before the doors closed, the middle guard turned to him and said, "Thanks, Mr. Fenney."

"For what?"

"Standing up for that girl."

Pajamae followed Boo out the front door and down the walkway to the sidewalk. Boo said, "Boy, my mother was acting really weird this morning. The stuff she was saying."

"Is she sick?"

"I don't think so. Why?"

" 'Cause Mama says weird stuff when she takes her medicine."

They turned left down the sidewalk. Boo was talking, but Pajamae was watching. Mama had taught her to keep her eyes peeled when she went outside in their neighborhood, watching for strange people. Of course, in their neighborhood grown men hung around outside the liquor stores on every corner and drank malt liquor out of brown paper bags and peed right into the street whenever nature called, so strange here in Boo's neighborhood was a different thing altogether. But Pajamae still noticed something strange.

A man in a car.

He was sitting across the street and down one house from Boo's. He stared at them as they came down the sidewalk. He was a big man with a bald head in a black car. When she and Mama were outside and a white man looking like him drove into the projects, everyone would stop what they were doing and shout, "The man!" The police. The bald man in the black car looked like a policeman.

Pajamae noticed the car door open partway and the bald man's black shoe come out. She was about to grab Boo and hightail it back to their house when an old man stepped out the front door of the house they were walking in front of. He came down the path toward them, but he stopped and picked up a newspaper on the grass.

Boo said, "Good morning, Mr. Bailey."

The old man smiled and said, "Why, good morning to you, Miss Boo Fenney."

Pajamae looked over at the black car. The bald man's foot was back in the car and the door was shut, but he was still staring. They continued down the sidewalk and came to a busy road named Preston and turned right. Pajamae glanced back and saw that the black car was gone. She shook her head at herself for being so silly: *You're not in the projects, girl!*

They walked on and Pajamae soon found herself enjoying the stroll through Boo's neighborhood, what she called the Bubble. She always felt nervous and scared if Louis was gone and she and Mama had to walk alone through their neighborhood to the nearest liquor store to buy some bread or eggs, even in the middle of the day. Mama always told her, "If I say 'run,' you run, girl." But she wasn't nervous or scared at all in this neighborhood. The sidewalks were so clean, no beer cans or liquor bottles or syringes or those funny long balloons Mama told her never to touch. And no men hanging around outside liquor stores—in fact, there were no liquor stores. No pimps or pushers trying to recruit her or sell to her, no older boys driving by and yelling out nasty words, no loud rap music from cars and boom boxes, and nobody cussing each other 'cause they just got evicted. It was so quiet!

Boo's Bubble was nice.

They stopped at an intersection and waited for the light to change. When it did, they looked carefully both ways and hurried across four lanes of traffic and a short parking lot and onto the sidewalk of—

"Highland Park Village," Boo said.

They were standing outside a store named Polo/Ralph Lauren in a fairyland place Pajamae had never imagined existed, fancy cars lining the sidewalk shaded by little trees and fancy white women getting out of those cars followed by pretty little white girls looking like princesses and giving her second and third glances like they had never seen a black person their whole lives, and leaving behind a smell so sweet that Pajamae breathed it in several times and was reminded of the old fat ladies at church each Sunday morning—only these ladies weren't fat and they didn't gush over her and pinch her cheek. The white women and white girls just hustled by and into the store, the cool air from inside rushing out, making Pajamae's face feel like it did when she stuck her head in the freezer to cool off, as she often did down home in the projects.

Boo said, "Do y'all have shopping places like this?"

"We don't have any place like this."

When she and Mama went shopping, it was generally at yard sales and the Goodwill store, not someplace where she couldn't begin to pronounce the names, and sometimes one of their neighbors would get a good deal on sneakers or stereos or TVs and sell them right out of his car trunk, at real good prices 'cause the stuff was a little warm, Mama would say, although Pajamae was never exactly sure what she meant. And before school started each year, Mama would work extra and Louis would take them to buy her school clothes at the JCPenney, but it wasn't like this.

"Where-*as*," Pajamae said.

They walked down the sidewalk in the shade of the awning, Pajamae feeling like it was Christmas, checking out every window display, fancy clothes on skinny mannequins wearing makeup, and past a kid's store—

"That's Jacadi Paris," Boo said. "My closet is full of clothes from here."

"Does this stuff cost a lot?"

"Mother bought them, so they must."

When they arrived at a store called Calvin Klein, Boo said, "Britney was here a few months ago."

"Britney who?"

"Britney Spears, the singer. Everybody went crazy."

"White girl?"

"Yeah."

"Oh. We don't listen to white girls down in the projects."

Boo shrugged. "I don't listen to her up here either."

And on they went, past stores named Luca Luca and Escada and Lilly Dodson—"Mrs. Bush bought her red party dress here, when George W. got elected the first time," Boo said—and Banana Republic—only they sold clothes not bananas—and they crossed the parking lot and got ice cream cones at Who's Who Burgers.

They walked outside and Pajamae stopped short. A bad feeling swept over her small body: the bald man in the black car was driving by slowly and giving her a creepy stare. She got really scared, and Pajamae Jones didn't get really scared easily.

"Boo, that man's following us."

"What man?"

"That man who just drove by, in that black car. See him? The bald guy?"

Boo laughed. "This is Highland Park. Nothing bad happens here."

Boo tugged on her arm and Pajamae followed reluctantly. They walked past more stores then went inside a store with the same name as the old wino with no teeth who lived three apartments down. Harold.

"This was my mother's favorite store," Boo said.

A saleslady was on them before they made it five steps, and Pajamae thought at first she was going to run them out. But the lady smiled and said hi like she was really happy to see them. She was very pretty for a white girl, with hair that bounced and smooth skin and lips that were painted red. She looked at Pajamae and leaned down, putting her knees together and her hands on her knees, and said, "My, aren't you the cutest little thing!"

Pajamae was wearing Boo's denim overalls, a white tee shirt, white socks, and white sneakers; her hair was in cornrows; and she was licking her ice cream cone.

She said, "Thank you, ma'am."

"So how do you like living in Highland Park?"

Pajamae glanced at Boo, who shrugged. How did this woman know that she was living with Mr. Fenney?

"I like it just fine, thank you."

"You tell your mother to come see me, my name's Sissy. I'll make sure she's as well dressed as any woman in Highland Park."

"My mama's in jail."

The lady snapped up straight with a confused look on her face. "*Jail?* Aren't you the new black family's little girl?"

"I don't have a family. I only have Mama. And Louis, he's like an uncle only he's not."

Boo said, "What new black family?"

"The black family that just moved into town, the first black homeowners in the history of Highland Park." The saleslady was now staring at Boo when a hint of recognition crossed her painted face. "You're the Fenney girl, aren't you?"

"Yes, ma'am."

"I almost didn't recognize you with that hair. Where's your mother been lately"—her thin eyebrows raised a notch—"and your handsome father?"

"My mother's being weird and A. Scott's been real busy."

"Helping my mama," Pajamae added, and the lady's head swiveled to her. "They say she killed the McCall boy, but she didn't."

The saleslady slapped her hand over her mouth. *"She's your mother?"*

Pajamae licked her ice cream cone and said, "Unh-huh. Mr. Fenney, he's her lawyer, so everybody's mad at him."

The saleslady's face suddenly looked like that boy's face that day in the projects when he tried to get a freebie from Mama and when she refused, he called her a "white man's whore." As he turned to run away he ran smack into Louis—and that black boy's face turned white. Just as this lady's face had turned two shades whiter. She must not have known what to say, so she said, "Maybe you girls should leave now."

"Mr. Ford wants to see you," Sue said.

Scott grabbed his message slips and walked to the staircase. He greeted his fellow partners along the way, but all he got in return were odd stares, averted eyes, and shaking heads. No doubt they had seen his network interview last night and didn't care for it. Fuck 'em. He found Dan standing by the window in his office.

"Dan, what's up?"

Dan turned; his face looked like he hadn't slept last night.

"Come in, Scotty. Shut the door."

Scott did as instructed and said, "Dan, can you talk to Ted at the bank? He's being a real asshole. He called the notes on the Ferrari and my house."

"I'm afraid I can't."

"Why not?"

"Because, Scotty, as of right now, you're no longer a partner in the firm."

"You're demoting me?"

"I'm firing you."

Dan's words knocked the air out of Scott as fully as a football helmet in the solar plexus. Scott stumbled back and fell onto the sofa. Dan returned to the window and stared out, his hands clasped behind him. Scott struggled to find words.

"You said I was like a son to you."

Without turning from the window: "You were. But when my son embarrassed me with that homosexual nonsense, I disowned him. Now I'm disowning you."

"Why?"

Dan turned to face Scott; he was now an angry father figure.

"Your little spectacle last night! For Christ's sake, Scott, what the hell were you thinking?"

"McCall tried to destroy me, that's what I was thinking!"

"So you go on national TV and accuse the senior senator from Texas of obstruction of justice? Extortion? Bribery?"

"I was just trying to do the right thing!"

"The hell you were! I know you too well. You were giving McCall a little Scott Fenney payback. You weren't doing it for the hooker; you were doing it for yourself. And even if you were doing the right thing, it's no better. I told you, Scotty, this firm doesn't exist to do the right thing; no law firm does. We don't do the right thing; we do what's right for our clients. And destroying Mack McCall's presidential ambitions isn't right for our clients. But you took care of that, didn't you?"

"What was I supposed to do, let him take everything I have?

My club memberships, my car, my house, my best client? McCall did all that."

Dan Ford was now staring at Scott with an expression Scott had seen only once before, five years ago. Scott had stood next to Dan in a state district court as the judge read his ruling, a ruling against their client, against Ford Stevens, against Dan Ford, who had made a substantial contribution to the judge's last campaign. Dan's expression then and now was that of a man betrayed, but a man with the power to do something about it.

"No, Scotty, he didn't do any of that. I did."

"You?"

"Yes, me. When you refused to do what I asked, I wanted you to see what your life would be like without all the things success buys—*It's a Wonderful Life* starring Scott Fenney. But you're stubborn, Scotty, too stubborn for your own damn good. McCall asked me for a small favor, to get you to leave his son's past in the past where it belongs, so he could be president. And I asked you for a small favor, so I could be the president's lawyer. And after all that I've done for you, how did you repay me? You betrayed me."

"A small favor? Dan, without that evidence, Shawanda will be sentenced to death!"

"So?"

"What, she's just a nigger?"

Dan laughed. "Oh, yeah, I'm a racist. My son grew up wanting to be Michael Jordan and my daughter's in love with Tiger Woods . . . No, it's the other way around, my daughter wanted to be Jordan and my son's in love with Tiger. Anyway, I'd love to have both of them as clients. Because they're rich. Because they pay their lawyers lots of money. Scotty, the color of law isn't black-and-white, it's green! The rule of law is money—money rules! Money makes the law and the law protects the money! And lawyers protect the people with money!"

Dan's face was red and his neck veins were purple cords. He paused and gathered himself.

"Scotty, this firm is my life. I built it from nothing to the richest firm in town. No one makes what we make. No one! And no one's gonna hurt this firm, not your hooker, not you, not anyone. I'll run over anyone who gets in my way."

"What about me, Dan? You gonna run over me, too?"

Dan sat down in his chair, reached over and buzzed his secretary, then looked back up at Scott and said, "I think I already have."

Scott stood in the middle of the office, surrounded by Dan's trophy heads. Their sad eyes seemed to look down on him, as if they were saying, *We've saved a place up here for you.* And now Scott knew how John Walker and the others had felt standing right here when Dan had fired them without warning. He had chuckled when another lawyer had shown him John's ad in the TV guide—one day a successful lawyer in a big firm and the next day just another shyster trying to sleaze out a living. Now his mind conjured up his own ad, situated between ones for a psychic and an escort service: CAR ACCIDENT? DIVORCE? BANKRUPTCY? CALL A. SCOTT FENNEY, ATTORNEY-AT-LAW. WE CARE. E-Z TERMS. SE HABLA ESPAÑOL.

This can't be happening, not to me!

The door behind Scott opened and two of the three black Dibrell Tower security guards from downstairs were standing there, puzzled looks on their faces.

It was happening to him.

"Your personal belongings will be delivered to your house, Scott," Dan said. "Firm policy."

The game was over. Scott Fenney had lost. There was nothing more to do but to walk off the field. The guards parted and Scott walked down the corridors that he had so proudly strutted just days before, A. Scott Fenney, Esq., Tom Dibrell's lawyer, wired on success. Yesterday, the other lawyers had greeted him like a star; today they averted their eyes as from a patient dying of AIDS. Dead lawyer walking. Scott Fenney's legal career as he knew it was over.

He and his escorts walked down the staircase to the sixty-second floor and ran into Missy walking up, looking sexy in a tight knit dress. But she did not wink at Scott Fenney today; she did not act like they were on the brink of an affair; she acted like he had a contagious disease. They continued down to the landing, where Sue stood, holding out his briefcase and 9-iron. Before he reached her, Sid Greenberg walked up to Sue with a stack of documents.

"Sue, I'm putting these documents on your desk. Copy them and get them up to Dibrell ASAP. Put the originals in Scott's . . . I mean, in my office."

"Yes, Mr. Greenberg."

"*Sid?*"

Sid spotted Scott and said, "Oh, hi, Scott. Sorry to hear the news. Good luck."

"You're taking my client, my secretary, my office? I taught you everything you know!"

"Yeah, Scott, you did. You taught me practicing law is just business. Nothing personal."

"I wasn't talking about me!"

Sid shrugged lamely and walked off. Scott turned to Sue, her hands extended toward him. Scott took his briefcase and 9-iron from her.

"Good-bye, Mr. Fenney."

"That's it? Good-bye? Eleven years you've been my secretary. Don't you care?"

Sue got a look on her face he had never seen and she seemed to grow six inches.

"For eleven years I've fetched your dry cleaning and coffee, run your personal errands, paid your personal bills, shopped for gifts for your wife and child and clients, lied to clients for you . . . Did you care about me? About my life? You never once asked about my life. Do you know I have a handicapped child and that's the only reason I've put up with you for all these years? Because I needed the money? You didn't know and you didn't care. Did you care when Mr. Walker got fired? No. Like every other lawyer here, you care only about yourself."

Scott turned from this stranger standing on the marble floor in the lobby, talking to him like that in front of a gathering crowd. Followed by the two guards, he walked to the elevators and pushed the down button. The doors opened and they stepped in. One of the guards said, "What happened, Mr. Fenney?"

"I got fired."

" 'Cause of what you did, standing up for that girl?"

"Yeah."

"I know where Mr. Ford parks his Mercedes down in the garage. You want I should flatten his tires?"

"Yeah." Then Scott shook his head. "No."

The doors started to shut, but at the last second a hand pushed in and the doors receded. Standing there was Sue. She said, "John Walker's wife died last week."

They stepped outside the store and Pajamae froze.

"Boo, there he is again."

"Who?"

"The bald man in the black car."

"Where?"

Pajamae motioned with her head to the parking lot. Boo turned that way, but Pajamae said, "Don't look!"

They turned and faced the store window. In the Village, cars

249

could park in slanted spots right at the sidewalk. Then there was a little one-way road for cars to drive around the center and then two more rows of parking in the middle of the open parking area. The bald man in the black car was parked there, maybe thirty feet away. Boo acted casual and kind of looked around at different things and finally got around to glancing at the bald man in the black car: he was staring straight at them. Boo turned away.

Pajamae was frantic. "Let's run, Boo!"

Boo took Pajamae firmly by the arms. "No. Act normal. He can't grab both of us, not here. He's just trying to scare us."

"Honey, it's working!"

Boo started patting around her pockets.

"What are you doing?" Pajamae asked.

"I'm pretending I'm looking for something." She threw up her hands and pointed inside the store. "Now I'm acting like I left something inside. Come on, we'll go back in and I'll call A. Scott. He'll come for us."

"He better get here fast."

"He drives a Ferrari."

They walked back inside and Boo went directly over to the same saleslady. "Ma'am, may I use a phone? It's an emergency. I need to call my handsome father."

Scott had always enjoyed the ride home at the end of each day, jumping into a $200,000 automobile, exiting the parking garage, saluting Osvaldo like the president saluting the Air Force One attendants, and pointing the Ferrari north toward Highland Park . . . Driving leisurely through the Uptown area just north of downtown where the singles commingled, young men and gorgeous girls, their heads swiveling his way as he passed by, envy written all over their faces, wondering what it must be like to be living a perfect life like the handsome man in the Ferrari . . . And finally entering the Town of Highland Park, where the kids are smart, their parents are successful, and everyone is safe and secure.

But today was different.

He wasn't enjoying the ride home. Because at the end of the ride, he would have to tell his wife and daughter that he had been fired, that he was no longer a partner at Ford Stevens, that he would no longer be bringing home money each night, that he had lost the family fortune. That Scott Fenney was now a loser.

How could he face his wife as a loser? His daughter? His neighbors in Highland Park? Scott hit the right turn signal and braked to turn onto Beverly Drive . . . but at the last second he changed his mind and accelerated straight through the intersection and continued north past Highland Park Village. He couldn't go home. Not yet. A few blocks later he turned left and pulled over in front of the Highland Park High School football stadium, where life as he knew it had begun the first day of fall football practice his freshman year.

Inside a stadium that shamed many college stadiums, this year's team was practicing on the artificial turf. Scott cut the engine and got out of the Ferrari. He walked over to the fence and watched the boys working out on the field while the cheerleaders went through their routines on the sideline, white boys dreaming of being another Highland Park football legend like Doak Walker or Bobby Layne or Scotty Fenney and white girls dreaming of being another Hollywood starlet from Highland Park like Jayne Mansfield or Angie Harmon, but knowing that if their dreams were not realized they could always fall back on their daddies' money, fortunes that assured them futures as bright and certain as the blue sky above. And he wondered if he had fooled himself all these years, thinking he belonged here, that his football heroics were enough to make him one of them. Maybe the son of a construction worker is always the son of a construction worker. Maybe a renter is always a renter. Maybe the poor kid on the block is always the poor kid on the block, even if he lives in a mansion. Maybe you are what you've always been.

His dream had begun right out there, on that very field, twenty-one years ago when he was fifteen. And that dream had ended today. And he found himself wondering, for the first time since that day so long ago, what he would do with the rest of his life.

He walked back to the Ferrari. Now he would drive home and tell his wife and daughter that he had lost everything, his only consolation being that there was nothing more for Mack McCall and Dan Ford to take, nothing more for Scott Fenney to lose.

When he opened the car door, his cell phone was ringing.

A. Scott said he'd be there in less than a minute. He didn't lie. They were standing on the sidewalk outside the store again when Boo heard the familiar roar of the Ferrari's engine. She turned and saw the bright red vehicle veer sharply into the Village and accelerate through the parking lot. She held her arms above her head and waved wildly and jumped up and down. And then she pointed directly at the bald man in the black car. He sat up quickly when he saw her pointing; then he saw the Ferrari coming toward him. He started his car and drove out of his parking place and turned left, but another car was backing out of one of the slanted spots by the sidewalk.

His car was blocked.

The red Ferrari screeched to a stop behind the bald man's black car. A. Scott jumped out. He didn't even shut his door. He ran up to the black car with a golf club in his hand.

Why did A. Scott have a golf club in the Ferrari?

Boo's lawyer-father, wearing one of his starched white shirts and a silk tie flapping over his shoulder, reared back and swung the club at the driver's window.

WHACK!

The glass cracking sounded like an explosion and froze everyone within earshot. A few old people ducked. Ladies from inside the store rushed outside. Now it was the bald man's turn to be scared. A. Scott yanked on the man's door, but it was locked. So he stepped forward and swung the golf club again and again at the windshield of the car and screamed words Boo had never heard him say:

"You're following my girls, you sonofabitch!"

WHACK!

"McCall sent you, didn't he!"

WHACK!

"You come around my girls again, I swear to God I'll fuckin' kill you!"

WHACK!

The car in front drove off. The bald man gunned the black car and sped away and around the corner. A. Scott stood there in the middle of the Village parking lot, red-faced, breathing hard and sweating, and holding the golf club over his shoulder like an ax. He looked like an action figure. Shoppers were staring, shocked at such a commotion in Highland Park. Boo was grinning: it was great! The same saleslady was standing next to her.

"God, he's handsome," she said.

Boo Fenney had never been so proud of her father. She ran to him, wrapped her arms around his waist, and clutched him tightly. Pajamae joined them.

"You girls okay?"

"We are now. Who was that man?"

"Delroy Lund."

Pajamae said, "Mr. Fenney, you're the man!"

Boo said, "A. Scott, you said the F-word."

"Yeah." His breathing was calming. "I'm sorry."

253

The adrenaline rush had receded by the time Scott turned the Ferrari into the driveway at 4000 Beverly Drive and drove into the back motor court. The girls were doubled up in the passenger seat.

Pajamae said, "That's why Louis walks with me and Mama. No one messes with him, not even in the projects."

Scott cut the engine, grabbed his cell phone, and hit a number he had recently added to the speed dial. When a familiar voice answered, he said, "Louis, this is Scott Fenney. I need your help."

He hung up and they climbed out of the car. There was still his wife. He still had to tell Rebecca the bad news. They entered the house through the back door. It was quiet.

"Rebecca?"

Boo said, "Oh, I forgot. She's gone."

"Gone? Gone where?"

"On a trip."

"Where?"

"I don't know. She just said she had to leave."

Scott took the stairs two steps at a time and ran down the hall to their bedroom. He found Rebecca's letter on the bed, a handwritten good-bye. He had lost her home, her cars, and her chair of the Cattle Barons' Ball. In short, he had ruined her life, she said, so they were through, just as she had promised. And since she could no longer hold her head high in Highland Park, she was leaving with the assistant golf pro at the country club. He was going on the PGA tour. She would be a golfer's groupie.

"When is she coming back?"

Scott looked up to Boo standing in the door.

"She's not."

Boo was crying facedown in bed. *Every girl she knew had a mother—even Pajamae!* She felt Pajamae's arms around her, hugging her tightly.

"Boo, I don't have a daddy and now you don't have a mama, maybe your daddy and my mama could get married. We'd be sisters."

"Pajamae, A. Scott can't marry your mother, she's . . ."

Pajamae's hug went soft. Boo felt her pull away. Boo wiped her face and sat up. Pajamae had a funny look on her face. Her fists were on her hips, like Mother when she got mad.

"She's *what*?"

Boo shrugged. "She's twenty-four. That's way too young for him. He's really old."

Louis arrived an hour after Scott's call. He pulled his old car around back. Scott met him in the motor court. They shook hands this time.

"Thanks for coming, Louis."

"Ain't no problem, Mr. Fenney. I been watching over Pajamae most of her life. Been missing her." He looked around. "Course, you probably don't get as much shootin' up here."

"Come on inside, Louis, I've got a bedroom for you."

"Aw, no, sir, Mr. Fenney, I don't feel right with that."

Scott could tell that Louis was uncomfortable with the idea, so he didn't press him.

"You can stay in the cabana. Consuela, our maid, lives out there, but she's gone for a while. INS."

"No, sir, that her place. I sleep in my car. In the garage. I can keep a better eye out back here."

"It's air-conditioned, there's a full bath. I can fix up a bed for you . . . and I'll bring out a TV and a recliner."

"TV and chair be nice, but not the bed. Back seat of my car work just fine." Louis smiled. "And, Mr. Fenney, don't you worry none. Ain't no one gonna hurt them girls now."

Scott would not be spending the rest of his day in his fancy office on the sixty-second floor doing the things lawyers do and eating lunch at the swanky Downtown Club and working out among gorgeous girls at the athletic club. He did not feel special today, sitting in the den at home and staring out the windows at the pool and the professionally landscaped yard. His career was gone, his wife was gone, and his house and cars would soon be gone. Mack McCall had won. And his prize was Scott Fenney's perfect life.

For the first time in his life, Scott felt defeated. He didn't know if he could get up off the ground this time.

Twice Boo came downstairs and crawled up into his lap and they cried together. The third time Pajamae came with her. The two girls sat on the wide arms of the big leather chair and buried their faces in his broad shoulders and cried until his shirt was wet. They never said a word.

Scott sat there as the sun's rays moved slowly from one side of the den to the other. He heard the girls in the kitchen, and Pajamae brought him a scrambled egg sandwich, but he had no appetite. When the sky turned dark, he pushed himself out of the chair, climbed the stairs, and put a brave face on for the girls. He found them huddled in bed and his chair next to the bed. He sat and they said prayers.

Then Boo said, "I don't want to read tonight. I want to talk."

Pajamae said, "We want to talk."

Scott removed his glasses. "Okay. What about?"

"We saw you on TV last night," Boo said, "with Pajamae's mother. I know I'm not supposed to watch TV at night, but I went downstairs and saw Mother watching you on TV, so I had to, you know that."

Scott nodded. "And?"

"And you have some explaining to do, A. Scott."

"Ask your questions."

Scott knew better than to launch into a narrative with Boo. He always made her ask the questions. He figured if she asked, she was ready to know.

"What's sex?"

He hadn't figured on that question. That was a question for a girl to ask her mother, but when her mother runs off with the assistant golf pro, it falls to the father. And now he had two girls facing him, their legs curled under them, hands in their laps, apprehension on their faces, asking about sex.

"That's a boy's thing, right, Mr. Fenney?"

"A boy's thing?"

"You know, a boy's privates. Like, when I go outside in the projects, some boy's always saying, 'C'mon over here, little girl, an' I shows you my sex.' "

"Oh. Well, sex is when a boy and a girl . . . I mean, a man and a woman . . . when they, uh . . ."

"Do the nasty?" Pajamae blurted out. "That's what the big girls call it. I told Mama what they said, and she said I couldn't play with those girls anymore."

"Look, do either of you have any idea what sex is?"

The girls shook their heads.

"Why do you want to know?"

"Because Mama said the dead man gave her money for sex."

"Oh."

"Then he hit her, and boy, that was his first mistake. My mama, she doesn't let any man hit her, not since my daddy. So she kicked his butt good." She smiled. "Like you beat up that man's car, Mr. Fenney."

Boo said, "That was awesome! You were great! Did you ruin your golf club?"

Their attention thus diverted, Scott did not have to explain sex to two nine-year-old girls. After the girls had relived the scene at the Village, Boo said, "Clark wasn't very nice, was he?"

"No, he wasn't."

"And now his father, the senator, he's mad at you because you're trying to help Pajamae's mother?"

"Yes."

"To keep the po-lice from killing Mama?"

"Yes."

"That man today, he works for the senator?"

"Yes."

"Is he going to come after us again?"

"No, baby, he's not."

Pajamae smiled. "He'll have to come through Louis."

Boo said, "Do we have to sell our house?"

"Yes, Boo, we do."

"Why?"

"Because I got fired today."

"You're not a lawyer anymore?"

"No, I'm still a lawyer, just not with the firm."

"And that means what?"

"That means as of right now, I don't have any income."

"No money?"

"We have some money, but not enough to keep this house."

Boo nodded. "When Cindy's dad got fired, they had to sell their home. You said that would never happen to us."

"I was wrong."

"And you've got to sell the cars?"

"The bank will just take them."

"Are we poor now?"

"No, Boo, we're not poor. Poor people are like—"

"Mama and me," Pajamae said.

"So all these bad things, Consuela, the cars, the house, your job, Mother leaving, it's all because McCall's mad at you?"

"Yeah . . . well, maybe not your mother."

"Mama always says she's bad luck."

"Pajamae, your mother's not to blame. I made a decision. And decisions have consequences. Sometimes bad consequences."

They were quiet for a long moment then Boo said softly, "Mother was crying. She said I'd be better off without her."

TWENTY

JULY EXITED THEIR LIVES and August entered, ushering in the dog days of summer when hot air masses called Mexican Plumes settle in over Dallas like mushroom clouds, fending off cool air from the north and rain from the south and trapping the occupants of the land below in an unmerciful mixture of 110 degree temperature and 80 percent humidity, day after day after sweltering day. The winds subside and the air is so still that even the slightest breeze feels like a blue norther. Pollution watches reach level purple, which means just breathing the air can kill you. Sidewalks are vacant of pedestrians, dogs lie all day in the shade, too weary even to engage their tails to swat the flies buzzing about their hindquarters, and TV reporters inevitably fry eggs on the sidewalk as stunts for the evening news. Time seems to slow to a crawl. Women's hairdos and their prize-winning gardens wilt, car radiators and drivers' tempers boil over, and incidents of road rage rise dramatically, as do domestic violence calls to 911. The reservoirs supplying Dallas's drinking water run precipitously low, the city rations lawn watering, the green grass bakes to a crisp brown, and the pest control business picks up as the entire rat population emerges as one from their nests in search of a drink, usually from the family pool. Poor people without air conditioners die.

The only thing Dallas has going for it in August is knowing it's worse in Houston. Houston's a goddamned swamp. If the heat and humidity don't kill you in Houston, mosquitoes the size of small birds will.

"It's hot," Scott said.

Life in Dallas in August is lived indoors and in pools. Where Scott Fenney now was, sitting on the steps of the backyard pool in the cool water and wearing sunglasses, a sombrero-style straw hat, and a number 50 sunblock to protect his fair skin from the deadly UV rays. He sucked iced tea through a straw from a big plastic mug like he was siphoning gasoline while Bobby sucked on a cigarette. Boo and Pajamae were playing with a Frisbee in the shallow end of the pool, Louis was sitting in the shade of the patio awning, and out front the FOR SALE BY OWNER sign was slowing traffic on Beverly Drive.

Scott had decided to sell the place himself, without a real-estate agent, an unheard-of transaction in Highland Park. Selling your own house was way too similar in job description to mowing your own grass or washing your own car, manual labor that no Highland Park homeowner with pride, money, and a religious upbringing dared engage in, for to do so called into question the whole concept of divine infallibility: "If the good Lord wanted us to mow our own grass and wash our own cars, then why did He make Mexicans?" Or so the prevailing thought went. Bottom line, if you're too damn cheap to pay a real-estate commission, then you're too damn cheap to live in Highland Park. But as he watched his income evaporate before his eyes, Scott had become damn cheap lately.

His asking price was $3.5 million, the market value. But market value didn't mean squat when the seller was desperate and everyone in the market for a Highland Park home knew it. The best offer to date was $3 million, only $200,000 more than he owed. A broker's six percent sales commission would take $180,000 and leave Scott only $20,000 in sales proceeds. Once closing costs were deducted, he'd be lucky to break even. After doing the math, Scott drove to the nearest hardware store, purchased the red-and-white FOR SALE sign, and hammered the son of a bitch into the front lawn.

"How's Boo handling it?" Bobby asked.

Scott slapped a June bug off the water and wondered why June bugs hung around through August. Rebecca had been gone fifteen days today.

"Okay, I guess. Hell, I think Boo misses Consuela more—she was more of a mother to her than Rebecca."

"Rudy gonna get her back?"

In spite of Rudy Gutierrez's best efforts, the INS had deported Consuela de la Rosa to Mexico. She was now living in the four-star Camino Real Hotel in Nuevo Laredo on Scott Fenney's American Express card and waiting for Rudy to secure her green card so she could return to the Fenney family in Dallas. A week ago, Scott had put Esteban Garcia on a bus south to keep her company.

"She cleared the background checks, I'm sponsoring her for citizenship, guaranteeing her employment . . . but the INS is slow-balling her green card." He shook his head. "But I'll get her back. I promised her. And Boo needs her more than ever now, her mother running off with a goddamned golf pro."

"I understand Rebecca leaving you"—Bobby shot Scott a smile—"but how could she leave Boo?"

Scott shrugged. "The humiliation, I guess. This is a tough town if your life is less than perfect. Failure is not an option in Highland Park." Scott paused and looked over at the girls. "Thank God she didn't take Boo."

"Maybe she just changed."

"Maybe. Maybe I never really knew her. Back then, we were exactly the same, that's why I married her. We were young and ambitious, two poor kids on the block trying to make it big in Dallas. When we stood in that church and said 'for better or for worse,' we weren't thinking for worse. Things were good and getting better fast. I never figured on things getting worse."

He shook his head.

"It's just like football. You never really know your teammates until you start losing."

"One problem with that, Scotty."

"What's that?"

"She started up with that guy while you were still winning."

Scott nodded. "So the home, the cars, the clothes, none of it made her happy." He looked over at Bobby. "What the hell do women want?"

Bobby chuckled. "Like I would know? Shit, Scotty, *two* women have walked out on me."

"The last seven months, she didn't want to have sex."

Bobby caught an errant Frisbee flung by Boo and said, "My wives didn't want to have sex on our wedding night."

"I'll probably never have sex again," Scott said.

Bobby flipped the Frisbee back to Boo and said, "*You?* Shit, Scotty, half the married men in Highland Park are worrying their wives are gonna want a second shot at you. It's me who's never gonna have sex again. Been almost three years." Bobby took a drag on his cigarette. "Course, I can crush an armadillo with my right hand."

"That's going to kill you one day, Bobby."

"Nah, it'll only make you go blind."

"Not that. Smoking."

"Oh. One can only hope."

264

"Don't start that depressed crap with me, Bobby. I'm the one who's lost everything."

Bobby exhaled smoke and said, "Yeah, but at least you had everything for a while. At least you know what it feels like."

Scott sucked his tea and said, "You loved her back then, didn't you?"

"Yeah, but mostly I loved your life."

"Me, too. Right up until two months ago. If Buford had called anyone but me, my life would still be perfect."

"It wasn't perfect, Scotty. You just didn't know it."

Scott felt the emotion building inside him again and the tears forming and thought he would burst out crying as he had each night in the shower until Bobby said, "You think he'll make it?"

His tone was that of asking whether a patient would survive a life-threatening operation.

"Who make what?"

"Her golf pro—you think he'll make it on the tour? It's pretty tough out there."

Bobby maintained his deadpan expression until Scott jumped on him and dunked him, Bobby holding one arm aloft to keep his cigarette dry. Scott released him when Boo yelled, "Oh, boys— we've got company!"

Over by the entrance to the motor court stood a burly man wearing mirrored sunglasses and a cap turned backward, his greasy hair and black tee shirt stained with sweat, his huge belly lapping over his waist like a lava flow over a cliff. He was looking around at the Fenney estate like a kid at Disneyland.

The repo man.

He was here to take away Scott's beloved $200,000 Ferrari. Two days ago, knowing this moment would come, Scott had cashed out his 401(k) and purchased a replacement vehicle: a $20,000 Volkswagen Jetta.

Scott walked over to the motor court. Two more tow trucks were idling at the curb, here for the Range Rover and Rebecca's Mercedes-Benz. The repo man held out a clipboard and said, "Nice hat." Scott signed the document acknowledging the repossessions on this date and watched as the red Ferrari 360 Modena two-seater with Connolly leather interior and an engine capable of hitting 180 miles per hour was hoisted onto the flatbed by a winch and secured in place. Even though he knew he was losing something he never really had, it still hurt like hell to see his perfect life being dismantled and carted off piece by piece.

An hour later, Scott, still hurting, was stretched out on the chaise lounge by the pool.

"Mr. Fenney," Louis said.

Scott looked over at Louis, who nodded his head in the direction of the motor court. Scott twisted around and saw a young couple standing there. The man was slim, in his early thirties, and dressed in a starched, long-sleeve, button-down blue shirt, khaki slacks, and black loafers. His hair was dark and curly, his skin pale and pasty. He was wearing wire-rimmed glasses. He seemed vaguely familiar.

The man said, "We had an appointment to see the house at three. We rang the doorbell, but no one answered."

Scott checked his watch and climbed out of the chair.

"Sorry, I lost track of time."

Scott walked over in his swim trunks, bare-chested and barefooted, and held out his hand.

"Scott Fenney."

"Jeffrey Birnbaum. And my wife, Penny."

Standing next to him was a pretty young Highland Park Junior League wife, perfectly made up and wearing a red sundress and red sandals. Her hair was jet black, her legs were bare and tanned, her body trim, and her lips matched her dress. Jeffrey had married up in looks, way up.

Penny said, "You're famous."

"Infamous is more like it."

She smiled, that flirtatious smile so familiar to Scott Fenney, and he immediately knew Penny, because he had dated so many Pennys during high school and college: a nice Highland Park girl who had taken a walk on the wild side and was now ready to settle down with a nice Highland Park boy who could provide a nice Highland Park mansion. Scott motioned around at the motor court, garage, and backyard.

"Four-car garage, heated and air-conditioned, pool and spa, one-bedroom, one-bath cabana, all on one acre in the heart of Highland Park. Come on, I'll show you the place."

Scott led Mr. and Mrs. Birnbaum through his house, starting with the commercial-grade kitchen with the Italian tile floor, the mural of a French bakery scene on one wall, hand-painted on hundreds of six-inch tiles, and the walk-in freezer big enough to hold a side of beef. He proceeded through the butler's pantry, the formal living and dining rooms, the den, and then down to the basement for the wine cellar, the home theater, the game room, and the exercise room with the framed blowup of himself running the ball against Texas, the one that had hung in his office for eleven years, leaning against the far wall.

"You're a legend," Penny said. "Did you really get a hundred ninety-three yards against Texas, like the paper said?"

"Sure did. You a big football fan?"

"Oh, I love football," Penny said.

Jeffrey glanced at the exercise machines with indifference and walked out. Penny lingered behind, and as she squeezed past Scott at the door, she gave him a look and whispered, "But I love football players more."

They found Jeffrey in the game room rolling billiard balls

267

across the pool table, then they proceeded upstairs to each of the six bedrooms and six baths. The tour ended in the master suite with the stone fireplace separating the bedroom and the bathroom, the steam shower suitable for three adults, the Jacuzzi tub, and the sitting area overlooking the pool. Jeffrey was proving himself a royal pain in the ass, complaining about something minor in every room of the house and acting as if he could take it or leave it. But he wasn't fooling Scott; Scott saw it in his eyes. This was the house Jeffrey had dreamed of owning his entire life. Scott knew because he had seen the same look in his own eyes three years ago, in the mirror of this same master bathroom. Jeffrey asked for the third time if the theater in the basement had Dolby Surround sound. Scott assured him it did, but Jeffrey said he was going downstairs to make sure.

Jeffrey departed and Penny said, "He likes to watch action movies," then went into the master bathroom. Shortly, he heard Penny's voice again: "Scott, what's this, in the steam shower?"

Scott walked into the bathroom and over to the shower. The door was open; Penny was inside, sitting on the built-in bench.

"What?"

"This."

Scott stepped inside to look, and without another word, Penny grabbed his swim trunks, yanked them down, and took him in her mouth like she knew what she was doing. She did. He was wrong about Penny: she hadn't finished her walk on the wild side. Scott had not had sex in more than seven months and had been too depressed to masturbate since Rebecca left, so he did not last long.

"Jesus!"

Scott's face was now plastered to the tile wall and he felt like a nap but—

"Penny!"

Jeffrey was back. Scott pulled up his trunks and Penny wiped her red lips with her hanky just as Jeffrey stuck his head in the steam shower and said with a big grin, "Wow, you do have Dolby down there!"

Scott stepped out of the shower, followed closely by Penny, who squeezed his butt as she passed. Fifteen minutes later, they were all standing at the front door.

Jeffrey said, "You don't remember me, do you, Scott?"

Scott said, "No. Should I?"

"We worked a real-estate deal a few years ago. You were representing Dibrell, a garden office project in North Dallas."

"Oh, yeah. You're with Dewey Cheatham and Howe."

"Dewey *Chatham* and Howe."

"Oh, right."

"You were pretty tough on us. But I learned a lot about negotiating from watching you in action."

"I'll send you a bill." Jeffrey smiled and Scott said, "Just business. Nothing personal."

"Then you won't take my offer personally."

"What's your offer?"

"Three million one hundred thousand."

"No, I won't take it personally, Jeffrey, because I won't take it."

Jeffrey smirked. "Come on, Scott, your life story's been in the paper. Everyone knows you've got to sell. You can't expect top dollar."

Scott reached over to the entry table and picked up a big brown envelope that contained his final bill from the country club for the last month, during which Rebecca had run up over $4,000 in charges. Scott held the envelope up to Jeffrey.

"I've already got an offer for three-point-three million."

Jeffrey's smirk vanished. "You're kidding?"

Scott put on his most sincere look and said, "Nope."

Jeffrey glanced at Penny. She gave him that pouty face mastered by Highland Park girls by middle school, a face that walked a fine line between obnoxiously whiny and incredibly sexy, between making her man want to slap her into next week or rip her clothes off and ravage her. Penny was very good. And Scott knew Jeffrey would find the extra money to make Penny a happy Highland Park wife.

"Three million three hundred ten thousand."

Scott smiled. "Jeffrey, it's nothing to be ashamed of if you can't afford this place."

Scott had learned years ago, when he was the poor kid on the block, that you could insult a Highland Park boy's mother, his sister, his girlfriend, his athletic ability, and even the size of his dick without getting a rise, but question his financial standing in the community, and the fight was on. Jeffrey's face was getting redder by the second, and not just from Scott's needling; Penny was squeezing his forearm like she was checking his blood pressure.

"Can't afford? I can afford this place! Three million four!"

Jeffrey should've paid closer attention to Scott during those negotiations because the boy obviously hadn't learned much. First rule of negotiating, don't bring your ego to the bargaining table. Second rule, don't bring your wife. Jeffrey had violated both rules; now he would pay dearly. Scott stuck his hand out.

"You just bought yourself a house."

Jeffrey said, "I want the appliances, the window treatments, and the black man."

"*What?*"

"The appliances—"

"You can have the appliances, Jeffrey. What do you mean, you want the black man?"

"Doesn't he come with the house? He's your help, right?"

"No, he's my friend. And he doesn't go with the house. Slavery ended a few years back, maybe you read about it."

Jeffrey frowned, but Penny smiled and said, "I'll have to measure for furniture, maybe Monday morning? Will you be available, Scott? I'd really like to come."

"I can't believe none of Clark's other victims have come forward," Scott said.

It was after dinner. The girls were upstairs, Scott and Bobby were sitting on the kitchen floor drinking a beer, and the trial was only two weeks away.

"They're scared," Bobby said. "They've seen what McCall did to you."

"Our whole case rests on Hannah."

"And my briefs," Bobby said. "You read them yet?"

"Yeah. You're a good writer, Bobby."

"That's the only thing about the law I really like doing."

"Why do you stay in it?"

Bobby shrugged. "Too late to do something else. And debts—I can't afford to quit. And, dumb as it sounds, I care about my clients, probably because no one else does."

"You were always taking in stray dogs."

"I was at that."

"I remember that brown-and-white mutt, you called him Shitface. What ever happened to him?"

"Got run over by a delivery truck."

"Ouch."

"I liked that dog." They sat in silence, and then Bobby said, "When this is over, maybe you should get out of Dallas."

"McCall's not running me out of town. I'm staying."

"Good." Bobby drank his beer, then said, "Let's subpoena Dan Ford, make him give up the names of the six other girls he paid off for McCall."

Scott shook his head. "No way he gives them up. And the judge won't bust through the attorney-client privilege. I've hidden enough damaging evidence about my clients behind the privilege to know."

"Then Hannah's our only witness, other than Shawanda."

"Did you tell Carl to check into Delroy Lund?"

"Oh, yeah. Way into Delroy."

"What about the prosecution witnesses?"

"I got Ray's list, shows how the trial's gonna go."

"And how's that?"

"It's a circumstantial case, most cases are. Ray'll first put on the Dallas cops who found Clark's car and called it in. Then he'll put on the Highland Park cops who went over to the McCall mansion and found Clark. Next, the FBI agents who processed the crime scene and took the photos, which he'll put up on the big screen. Then the Dallas County medical examiner will testify as to cause of death and time of death. And last up will be the crime lab guys who lifted Shawanda's prints from the gun and the car, test-fired the gun, and matched the ballistics, and a forensics expert to give his opinion as to how the crime was committed. Scotty, by the time Ray's through, the jury's gonna believe she did it for sure."

"And then we'll put Shawanda on, a heroin-addicted hooker."

"She has to testify, Scotty. Fifth Amendment sounds great, but juries expect an innocent person to take the oath, look them in the eye, and swear she's innocent."

"She looks like hell."

"You would too, Scotty, if you were injecting Mexican black tar heroin three times a day."

Four miles due south, Shawanda Jones withdrew the needle from her right arm, leaned back on her cot in her cell, and waited for the heroin to enter her bloodstream, travel to her brain, cross the blood-brain barrier, and bind itself to the opioid receptors on her brain's nerve cells. When the heroin hit the receptors, it triggered a euphoric rush that swept over her slim body like an orgasm, only better. Then the rush dissolved and she drifted off into a peaceful little dream world.

She thought of her short life. She had turned her first trick at twelve. Unless you counted her uncle, who fingered her when she was six, then gave her fifty cents for a snow cone. She was using cocaine regularly at fourteen, pregnant at fifteen, and hooked on heroin at sixteen. Twelve years a prostitute, eight years a smack addict.

The only time she felt good about herself was times like this. When she was on the stuff, she felt like a little girl again, all happy and light and clean. She wasn't poor or a white man's whore. She was young again and didn't know anything about drugs or hooking on Harry Hines or white men wanting black girls. She was just a happy little girl like Pajamae.

And thinking of her baby made her cry. She cried because she pictured her Pajamae shooting smack into her arm and lying down for money and never being loved for anything else. She wanted her baby to have better than she'd had. She wanted her to have a good life, marry a good man, and live in a good home. She wanted someone to love her Pajamae as much as she did. The only thing Shawanda Jones loved more in life than heroin was her daughter.

TWENTY-ONE

S COTT, LOUIS, and the girls arrived at the federal building at noon the next day, Saturday. Louis stayed outside in the car because of his outstanding issues with the Feds. Scott carried the big picnic basket inside, which the weekend security guard manning the metal detector checked thoroughly, as he always did. Now that Scott was no longer eating lunch at the Downtown Club, they had gotten into a regular habit of eating lunch with Shawanda at the federal lockup.

"Another picnic, Mr. Fenney?"

"Yep. How 'bout some fried chicken, Jerry?"

Jerry, an overweight white man about fifty, smiled and took a drumstick. They rode the elevator to the fifth floor and were met by the black guard.

"Ron," Scott said. "Picnic time, buddy."

Ron led them down the hallway to the same small conference room, but he seemed different today, silent and solemn. He had already moved the table and chairs to one corner. Boo and Pajamae spread the blanket on the cement floor and plopped down in their places. Ron left and returned shortly with Shawanda, who hugged Pajamae first and then Boo. She turned to Scott.

"Mr. Fenney, your woman leave you?"

"Yeah."

" 'Cause of me?"

"No, Shawanda, because of me."

"We've got chicken, Mama, from the Colonel!" Pajamae said. "And potato salad and beans and rolls, the kind you like."

Ron scratched his head and said, "Mr. Fenney, I, uh—"

"Ron, how many times I gotta tell you? It's Scott. You can't eat fried chicken with me and call me Mr. Fenney."

"Scott, I've, uh . . . I've got to search everyone."

"What? *Why?*"

"We searched Shawanda's cell and found some, uh"—he glanced down at Pajamae—"some controlled substances."

"You think I'm bringing it to her?"

Ron shook his head. "No, sir, not you."

When the meaning of Ron's statement finally registered with Scott, they both slowly turned to Pajamae. Scott said, "Pajamae, when we stopped by your apartment, did you get something for your mother?"

With Louis riding shotgun, Scott felt no fear returning to the projects. But the Jetta did not attract a crowd. The few residents who did notice them were actually friendly. One young boy asked, "Louis say you run for a hundred ninety-three yards against Texas—that true? A white boy?" When Scott assured him it was true, the boy said, "You the man." He waved when they drove off.

Pajamae shrugged. "Just Mama's medicine."

"And where was it at?"

"In the medicine cabinet in the wall under the sink in the kitchen."

"Please give it to me."

She stuck her hand in her pocket and retrieved a plastic Baggie filled with a black substance. Scott handed it to Ron.

"Mexican black tar," Ron said. He looked at Shawanda. "This stuff is eighty percent pure. It can kill you, girl!"

Shawanda lunged at Ron and snatched for the Baggie.

"Give it here!"

Scott grabbed Shawanda and held her until she gave up and slumped in his arms.

Ron said, "I'm sorry, Mr. Fenney. I'll leave now." He opened the door, but stopped. "Shawanda, why don't you let the judge put you in the prison hospital in Fort Worth? They'll put you on methadone."

Shawanda said nothing, so Ron left, shaking his head. Scott released Shawanda, and she dropped to the floor. He sat in one of the chairs and looked down at this young black woman.

"Why do you do it?"

Shawanda's eyes came up. " 'Cause it make me feel special."

"You don't need that. You are special."

She laughed. "You sound like Louis. He always saying 'Shawanda, you God's special girl.' "

"He's right."

"No, he ain't, Mr. Fenney. Nobody never give a damn 'bout Shawanda, not my daddy, not my mama, not no one."

"Pajamae does." He turned to her. "You love your mother, don't you?"

"Yes, sir, Mr. Fenney, I love her very much."

"So that's me, Louis, Pajamae, Boo, Bobby . . . and Ron. Six people who think you're special."

"That sound real nice, Mr. Fenney, but if I get out, I don't figure me and you gonna see much of each other."

"Sure we are. Our daughters are best friends. They're like sisters."

She turned to Pajamae. "That right? Boo like your sister?"

"Yes, Mama."

She turned to Boo. "Pajamae like your sister?"

"Yes, ma'am."

And she smiled the sweetest smile Scott had ever seen on her face. "That's good." She looked up at Scott. "Mr. Fenney, if I don't get out of here or if they . . . well, you know . . . you promise me something?"

"Sure. What?"

"Take care of my Pajamae."

Five weeks ago, when Scott had taken a little black girl home to Highland Park, his wife had asked him what he was going to do with her when her mother was convicted: Adopt her? Raise her as his daughter? Send her to Highland Park schools? He did not answer his wife that day because he wasn't thinking of Pajamae that day; he was thinking only of himself, his fear of returning to the projects. But this day he answered.

"Yes, Shawanda, I promise."

"It's perfect!" Boo said.

They had looked at six houses, Scott and the girls, each cheaper than the prior one, until they walked into this tiny fifteen-hundred-square-foot, two-bedroom, two-bath cottage over by SMU with a backyard that had a rope swing and a pool the size of the master bathtub at 4000 Beverly Drive. It was priced at only $450,000, within Scott's reduced financial reach, and it was in the Highland Park School District, so Boo wouldn't have to start over at another elementary school.

"One bedroom for us," Boo said, "and one for you. You can have the big bedroom."

Pajamae ran into the backyard, and Scott said to Boo, "Honey, you understand, if her mother gets out of jail, Pajamae's going back to live with her."

Boo turned her green eyes up at him. "Well, we've been thinking."

"I bet you have."

"She doesn't have a father and now I don't have a mother, so we thought maybe you and her mother could get married or something."

"*Married?* But she's—"

"Only twenty-four, I know. But Pajamae said it's okay for a man to marry a younger woman. She said they do it all the time in Hollywood."

"But, Boo—I'm still married to your mother."

Scott was running at 7.5 miles per hour up a ten-degree incline on a commercial treadmill. But he wasn't at the athletic club in downtown Dallas; his mind was not clear, his spirits were not high, and his eyes were not firmly attached to the backside of a beautiful young woman running in front of him; there was no girl running on a treadmill behind him checking out his butt; he did not feel young and successful and virile—or special. He was running on the treadmill in the exercise room of his Highland Park house, which would be his for only two more weeks.

Their visit to Shawanda that morning had raised the same questions in his mind: Had he done the right thing? Had he made the right choice? Was saving Shawanda's life worth sacrificing his perfect life? Was a heroin addict's life worth his lawyer life? He couldn't save her life, not with the evidence Ray Burns had against her. She would be convicted and sentenced to death or a long prison term. But he had already made the sacrifice; his life was already ruined. There was no quid pro quo, no something for something, to this bargain. He had given up his perfect life and would get nothing in return. And thinking about that brought the darkness back into his mind. So he did the only thing he knew to do when he was down: he exercised. Hard. Twice a day. Every day. He had begun working out as if he were getting in shape for another football season, running and weight lifting, torturing his body to ease his mind.

But working out made him think about football, and thinking about football made him think about the cheerleaders, and thinking about the cheerleaders made him think about Rebecca. He thought about their life together, the incredible sex, their vacations to Hawaii and San Francisco and London, and, of course, Boo. They had had eleven years together, and now she was gone. Had their marriage been a mistake from the beginning? Had she ever really loved him? Of course, it had never occurred to him that she might not have loved him because everyone—fans, coaches, cheerleaders—had always loved Scott Fenney.

He had so many questions, and no one to ask for answers. His mother would have said, "It's God's plan, and God has a reason, even if we don't understand." Butch would have said, "She's a selfish bitch, running off like that." The truth lay somewhere in between. But one truth he knew: if he hadn't married Rebecca, there would be no Boo. And without Boo, there would be no life for Scott Fenney.

"What the hell was I supposed to do, kill him?"

"Jesus, Delroy, in the Highland Park Village?"

Delroy Lund was standing in the den of the McCall town house in Georgetown. The senator was standing at the window. He wasn't happy to hear Delroy's report about the incident with Fenney at the shopping center.

"I was just trying to send him a message, but Fenney went fuckin' nuts . . . Oh, by the way, you bought a rental car."

The senator dismissed that news with a wave of his hand. Delroy particularly appreciated that aspect of working for a guy worth

$800 million: He didn't blink an eye at an unexpected $35,000 expense. He just wanted results and screw the costs. Delroy Lund got results.

"Now he's got a big black dude playing bodyguard. But I'll try again if you want."

"No, leave it alone. You and the black guy get together, someone will get killed. And that's all I need, another murder connected to me. So Fenney's wife left him?"

"Yeah, she ran off with the golf pro."

The senator smiled for the first time that day. "Good."

"Look, Senator, Fenney talked big on TV, but he ain't got nothing to back it up. Those other girls, they're not testifying. All they got is Hannah Steele."

"She's enough, goddamnit!"

The senator turned from the window and paced the room, talking like he was thinking out loud.

"Fifteen months until the election. If the hooker's convicted, everyone will figure what Fenney said on TV was just the lies of a lawyer. It'll all be forgotten a few months from now . . . The public's got the attention span of a two-year-old. I can still get into the White House, Delroy, if she's convicted. But if Hannah Steele walks into that courtroom and testifies that Clark beat and raped her . . ."

The senator started shaking his head.

"But, Senator, if she don't testify, it's just the word of a whore."

The senator stared at Delroy a long moment.

"Delroy, go see if the fish are biting in Galveston."

Scott Fenney hadn't cried since his mother died. And the only time before that was when his father died. He didn't cry when they drove his body into the ground, he didn't cry when they broke his fingers or his ribs, he didn't cry when they tore his knee ligaments. You don't cry on a football field.

But Scott Fenney wasn't on a football field now; he was in bed and he was crying.

His wife had left him for a golf pro. The final humiliation in a long list of humiliations, every detail of which had been duly reported in the local newspaper. All of Dallas knew about Scott Fenney's fall from grace. A few weeks ago, he had had the perfect Highland Park family: a trophy wife and a smart daughter and an illegal Mexican maid and a fast Ferrari. Today his family consisted of a white girl with cornrows, a street-smart black girl, a jailed prostitute, a lawyer who advertised in the TV guide, and a six foot six, 330-pound black bodyguard who lived in the garage.

"A. Scott, you okay?"

Boo's voice in the dark. Scott wiped his face on the bedsheet and said, "Yeah."

She climbed up onto the bed. "It's okay. I cry, too."

Scott sat up and pulled his daughter close. He felt her little body sag slightly in his arms. He thought she was falling asleep, but she spoke quietly.

"I've always been different. Now I'm really different."

"How so?"

"I'm the only kid I know without a cell phone *or* a mother. Pajamae says none of the kids she knows have dads, but they all have mothers. Rachel and Cary, they don't have dads . . . well, they have dads, but they don't live with them. They're divorced. But they see their dads on weekends." She was quiet again. Then she said, "I don't think we're gonna see Mother on weekends."

Scott held her tightly.

"It's just us now, baby."

And they cried together.

TWENTY-TWO

Bobby came by at nine on Monday morning. He gave Scott the once-over and said, "You're wearing jeans and a polo shirt to a pretrial conference with the judge?"

"What's Buford gonna do, fire me?"

"Good point."

They walked out the back door just as Louis was walking in. After almost three weeks living in the garage and nonstop pleading by Scott, Louis had finally relented and agreed to come inside the house for his meals. Pajamae was cooking breakfast.

When Scott turned the Volkswagen south on Turtle Creek Boulevard, Bobby asked, "How do you like the Jetta?"

"Well, the Ferrari could do zero to sixty in four-point-five seconds and the Jetta takes half a day, but hey, this little baby gets great gas mileage." Bobby laughed, but turned sober when Scott said, "Why aren't you mad at me?"

"For what?"

"For quitting on you back then."

"Oh." He shrugged. "What good would that do? You were gone. Didn't know what to do, so I married the first girl who said yes. Lasted less than a year, took her that long to figure out she'd married a loser. Second wife, we got married four years after the first divorce. She's the sister of the guy who owns the bar next door to my office, Mexican girl, most beautiful woman I ever saw naked. Problem was, I wasn't the only guy seeing her naked. She was stepping out with most of the guys at the bar. Some of them were my clients. Still are."

Bobby made a face.

"Is that a conflict of interest?"

"They repo your suits, too?"

Ray Burns had that same smart-ass expression on his face. Scott and Bobby had met him outside Judge Buford's chambers, where the pretrial conference would take place.

"Shit, Scott, why didn't you just stick a gun to your head and blow your brains out like your girl did to Clark? Would've been a hell of a lot less painful."

"What are you talking about, Ray?"

"Throwing your career away for her. Jesus, were you really making seven-fifty a year? And driving a Ferrari? What, you got a death wish or something?"

Scott glared at Ray Burns as he stepped past him and entered Judge Buford's chambers, but he heard Bobby say, "Ray, your mouth is writing checks your body can't cash."

———

"Jury selection on the nineteenth, opening statements on Monday the twenty-third," Judge Buford said. "Anything else, gentlemen?"

"Yes, Your Honor," Scott said. "Mr. Burns is persisting in claiming that the alleged crime is eligible for the death penalty when that is clearly not the case."

Ray Burns shrugged. "Our position is that the victim was an officer of a federal agency, and the defendant killed him in the perpetration of a robbery."

"Give me a break, Ray. Clark McCall was with a prostitute. The statute requires that the officer be engaged in the performance of official duties. And she didn't commit robbery. She only took the thousand dollars Clark owed her. He had another sixteen hundred on him. She didn't take that or anything else in the house."

"She took his car."

"Only to get back to her part of town."

"She had his skin under her fingernails."

"She scratched him when he attacked her. She's not denying she was there."

"But she's denying she pulled the trigger, even in self-defense. See, Scott, if she'd come clean about that, maybe we'd be willing to discuss dropping the death penalty."

"Using the death penalty to coerce a confession—that's prosecutorial misconduct, Ray."

Ray shrugged. "We call it prosecutorial discretion, Scott."

"You're full of shit, Ray," Scott said.

"And you're unemployed."

"Gentlemen," Judge Buford said as Scott fought back the urge to punch the Assistant U.S. Attorney. "The death penalty has been well briefed by Mr. Burns for the government and by Mr. Herrin, I presume"—Judge Buford eyed Scott over his reading glasses—"for the defense. We will address that issue if and when it becomes necessary. Anything else?"

"No, sir," Ray Burns said.

"No, Your Honor," Scott said.

"Fine. We'll reconvene on the nineteenth."

The three lawyers stood to leave, but the judge said, "Scott, may I speak with you alone?" Buford turned to Ray. "If you have no objection, Mr. Burns?"

"No, sir, I have no objection."

Ray and Bobby exited the chambers and shut the door.

"Sit down, Scott."

Scott sat. Judge Buford stared at him like a psychiatrist addressing his patient. "You holding up okay?"

Scott lied: "Yes, sir."

"I've read what's happened. I suppose all of Dallas has. They really deported your maid?"

"Yes, sir. She's down in Nuevo Laredo, waiting on a green card. I've done everything, but the INS says they're backlogged."

"Scott, if I had any idea all this would happen, that you'd lose your job, I would've never appointed you. I'd expect something like that from McCall, but Dan Ford . . ." His shoulders slumped and he shook his head. "I don't know what's become of the legal profession. When I was practicing, handling a case like this, it meant something. Now it's to be avoided because it might hurt the firm's business."

He looked at Scott with an expression of genuine puzzlement. "Do lawyers today care about anything except money?"

Scott spoke the truth: "No, sir, not in my experience."

The judge grunted. "Scott, may I ask you a personal question?"

"Sure, Judge."

"Your speech, that day at the bar luncheon . . . did you mean it, what you said about defending the innocent, protecting the poor, fighting for justice?"

Lie or tell the truth? Scott saw in the judge's eyes the desperate hope that he had meant it, so his first inclination was to do what experienced lawyers do often and well: lie. But the judge

286

needed to hear the truth today. So A. Scott Fenney, Esq., went against fourteen years of legal training and told the truth, the whole truth, and nothing but the truth.

"No, sir. Not a word. I said what those lawyers wanted to hear."

The judge nodded solemnly and said, "I appreciate your honesty, Scott. I'm letting you off the case." The judge's eyes dropped to his docket sheet. He began writing. "I'll substitute Mr. Herrin. He seems capable. He's certainly written some good briefs."

Two months ago, Scott would have jumped for joy at the judge's words. But now he sat stunned and suddenly afraid of losing his last client, even a nonpaying client, because a lawyer without a client is just a man.

"Judge, I know I'm not the lawyer you are, or the lawyer my mother wanted me to be . . . hell, I'm not even the lawyer I wanted to be. But I'm not a quitter. I never quit in a game, I've never quit on anything in my life. I'll play it out."

The judge's eyes came back up, and now he glared at Scott.

"This isn't a goddamn football game, Scott!"

Scott recoiled at the judge's harsh voice.

"This case isn't about you, your life, you proving something to yourself or Dan Ford or Mack McCall! This case is about Shawanda Jones, about her life! She's the defendant! It's her right to counsel, goddamnit!"

The judge stood abruptly, stepped to the window, and stared out. After a time, he spoke softly.

"I'm an old judge who needs to retire and tend to his garden. But a case like this comes along, and I know I can still contribute to justice, one human being at a time—and that's how justice is served, Scott, one person at a time. Today we're here to protect Shawanda Jones. That woman is my responsibility as long as she's in the custody of the federal government. Which arrested her, took her from her home and child, and is putting her on trial for her life. Now, maybe she did it, maybe she didn't, I don't know. But until the jury speaks, she's innocent in the eyes of the law—and thus in my eyes. And I will protect her. That's my duty. And her lawyer's duty is to defend her, to make damn sure the government proves she did it, beyond all reasonable doubt. That's what the Constitution requires, a lawyer standing up to the government on behalf of a citizen. That's what it means to be a lawyer, Scott."

The judge returned to his desk and sat.

"When I was practicing, I had half a dozen cases like this, where the defendant's guilt was truly in doubt, and in each case I made damn sure the government had to prove its case. Which the government did not do. They were innocent, and they were acquitted. Six people, Scott, six human beings whose lives I saved. I cared about those people, and I care about Ms. Jones. I'm not gonna die rich, Scott, but those few cases, they're my contribution to justice. They're what made my life worthwhile. Ms. Jones needs a lawyer who cares about her, someone to stand up for her, someone who understands the honor of defending an American citizen facing a death sentence. She needs her hero. You were such a football player, I thought you might be such a lawyer. I was wrong." The judge picked up his pen. "You're off the case. I'll appoint Herrin and postpone the trial."

Scott jumped up and leaned over the judge's desk.

"Judge, you can't postpone the trial! It'll kill her! She's barely hanging in now. I've been telling her it'll be over soon. If you postpone the trial, she'll die in her cell!"

The judge sat back, a curious expression on his face.

"What's this, concern for your client?"

"You're right, Judge, I haven't thought about her. But I'm a damn good lawyer, and she needs me."

Judge Buford removed his reading glasses and wiped them with his white handkerchief. He replaced them and gazed at Scott.

"She's a heroin addict, you know that?"

"Yes, sir."

"Why didn't you file a motion to have her transferred to the prison hospital, for drug treatment?"

"I . . . I never thought about it."

"Well, I did. She refused. She wants to be close to her daughter. You ever see a heroin addict go through withdrawal?"

"No, sir."

"Go downstairs and look. She's going through hell, alone in her cell, so she can see her daughter. What's that tell you about her? Tells me there's something good inside that woman, that maybe we need to look past the prostitution and the heroin and not just assume she's guilty, that maybe we ought to give her the benefit of the doubt. Beyond all reasonable doubt, Scott." He sighed. "So I've got Burns trying to send her to death row on his asinine legal position, which the appeals court will probably uphold, and I've got you. There's no hope for him—he's the worst kind of lawyer, a political animal, using the law to gain power over the people. And you, A. Scott Fenney . . . what's the A stand for, anyway?"

"Nothing."

The judge grunted. "You don't want power; you just want money. So the question I've got to answer is, Is there hope for you? I know you bring her daughter up here to see her, the guards say three, four times a week. That's good. And that you took her in, to live in your Highland Park home. That's very good."

The judge paused; a chuckle escaped.

"You're probably not up for citizen of the year in Highland Park, are you? But that tells me there's something good inside you, too, Scott, that perhaps there's still hope for you, that maybe you won't become another Dan Ford. That one day you might make your mother proud."

The judge fell silent and stared at Scott in the same way all those college coaches who had come to the Fenney rent house to recruit him had stared, seeing him in the flesh, trying to size him up, figure him out, decide if he was the real deal. Then Buford abruptly waved Scott off and said, "Go away."

"Wh . . . *what?*"

"Go think about it. I've got hearings until noon. You come back then—but only if you're ready to be her lawyer. If you don't show, I'll substitute Herrin and postpone the trial."

Outside, Bobby and Ray were waiting.

"What's up?" Bobby said.

Scott shook his head. "Personal." Then he addressed Ray Burns. "You're being a prick, Ray."

"Yeah, Scott, a prick with a career. A death penalty gets me an office in D.C."

"How do you sleep with yourself?"

Ray laughed. "Uh-oh, a born-again lawyer. Eleven years you spend every waking minute billing hours, making boatloads of money, living in a mansion, driving a Ferrari—how much did that cost your clients? Then you get fired and suddenly you see the light like a dying man: *I wanna do good, Lord!* Bullshit, Scott. You don't give a flying fuck about her. She's just a nigger, right? Two months ago, you were trying to bail on her faster than you can spit, now you're gonna be her hero? Tell it to Oprah. Oh, and I don't sleep by myself, Scott, I sleep with a gorgeous redhead from accounting. Who you sleeping with? Not your wife; she's sleeping with her golf pro."

Scott lunged for Ray, but Bobby jumped in between them.

"Hell, Scott," Ray said with a little laugh, "don't worry. The bitch probably won't live through withdrawal."

In one quick movement, Bobby released Scott and punched Ray in the mouth. Ray fell back against the wall.

Bobby said, "I told you, Ray."

"I'm real worried about her, Mr. Fenney," Ron the guard said. "I'm thinking maybe I made a mistake, taking her H."

They were standing outside Shawanda's cell. Inside, she was lying on her bed facing the far wall, curled up in a ball, her entire body shivering uncontrollably. She was groaning as if she were dying, her skin glistened with sweat, and her legs kicked involuntarily.

"That's why they call it kicking the habit," Bobby said. "Right now, she'd give everything she has in life for one fix."

Bobby was rubbing his right fist. "Hitting someone hurts."

"I'm proud of you, Bobby." Scott pointed the Jetta toward Highland Park and said, "You know what pisses me off the most?"

"The Ferrari?"

"No, about Burns."

"What?"

"The prick's right. About me."

Bobby worked his hand and said, "What did Buford want?"

"He wanted to take me off the case. Said he was going to appoint you."

"You still want out?"

"No. I told Buford that, but he told me to think about it, come back at noon, tell him if I'm ready to be her lawyer."

They were silent until they exited downtown. Then Bobby said softly: "I can't try this case, Scotty. I'm not good enough. She needs you."

An hour later, Scott left the house by the back door and ran west on Beverly Drive. It was exactly eleven A.M.; he had sixty minutes to make the biggest decision of his life.

Scott turned south on Lakeside Drive and ran past the stately old mansions that had stood for almost as long as Highland Park had existed. The homes sat higher than the street and looked down on a little park and Turtle Creek, where Scott often took Boo to skip rocks across the water.

Scott headed west on Armstrong Parkway a short distance, then turned north on Preston Road and ran up the sidewalk, the road to his left and to his right the massive wall that shielded the grand estates of Trammell Crow and Jerry Jones and Mack McCall and—

Tom Dibrell.

Scott had damn near run right into the long silver Mercedes as Tom exited his estate and stopped to check for traffic, blocking the sidewalk. They stared at each other across a distance of just a few feet, Tom wearing a suit and tie but cool in the air-conditioned luxury of a German sedan, Scott wearing only shorts and running shoes and sweating profusely in the hundred-degree heat. For eleven years they had talked daily; they had traveled the country, negotiating deals, making deals, and closing deals; they had celebrated victories and lamented defeats; they had eaten together and gotten drunk together; but they had never been friends. Successful lawyers, Scott now knew, have rich clients, not loyal friends.

Now, seeing this man who had given him his identity and had taken it away, Scott saw a sad man. This man had had four wives, but none of them had made him happy. He had six children by three of those wives, children who chose not to live in this fabulous estate with their father, because their father loved his skyscraper more than he loved them. He was a man who had lawyers, but not friends. Who had money and everything that money could buy, but little happiness. Three weeks ago, after Tom had fired him, if they had crossed paths like this, Scott Fenney might have shot him the finger.

Today Scott only nodded and smiled at the sad man in his Mercedes-Benz.

Tom opened his mouth as if to say something, then abruptly broke eye contact and hit the accelerator hard, sending the silver sedan roaring out onto Preston Road. Scott watched Tom drive away in a cloud of exhaust fumes, then started running again. He ran north past the Village and across Mockingbird Lane. A mile later, he turned east on Lovers Lane. He knew now where this run would end.

His journey took him along the boundary of the Highland Park Country Club, its tall brick wall discouraging gawkers. But there was one break in the wall where wrought iron spanned a few feet, and Scott stopped and looked in. A foursome of old white men was putting out on the seventh green, getting a round of golf in before the summer sun sapped their strength.

Growing up in Highland Park, Scott had often looked in through this opening at the old white men playing golf; it was like window-shopping with his mother at Highland Park Village, where she couldn't afford to shop. He'd always said that one day he would be rich enough to own a mansion in Highland Park, play golf at the country club, and buy his mother anything her heart desired at the Village. She had died before he could buy her anything at the Village, but four years ago, when Scott Fenney was admitted to the membership of the country club, he thought how proud his mother would have been of her son. For the last four years, he had played golf with pride inside these walls and looked out at others looking in.

Today the view was different.

From inside the walls, these old white men had seemed so special because they were so rich. But from outside, they just seemed old. And Scott realized that just as he was looking in at them, they were looking out at him. And in their eyes he saw their envy: they would gladly give every dollar they had to be young again, to have a head full of hair and sharp eyes and a clear mind with a memory that did not play tricks on them several times a day; to again live in a strong muscular body instead of the broken-down body they were left with; to run down the street instead of barely making it back to the golf cart; to again have a prostate gland instead of having to wear a diaper because the surgery had left them permanently impotent and incontinent; to again feel the pleasure of sex. They were looking out at a young man with his life in front of him; he was looking in at old men with nothing in front of them except the end of their lives.

The old men were tended to by their caddies, middle-aged black men wearing white canvas overalls, black men who caught the bus each morning before dawn in South Dallas and rode north to Highland Park to work at a club where they could never be a member because they had been born black. They were good men, like Louis, but they weren't good enough for the club, these black men who fixed old white men's divots, found their lost balls, and carried their clubs, all the while performing like actors in *Gone With the Wind*—"Yassuh, Mistuh Smith, that there swing sure 'nough make you look like Arnold Palmer hisself"—because making these old white men feel like Southern plantation owners meant a bigger tip. Scott had always been uncomfortable with the whole black caddie thing, but he had always employed a caddie for every round because it was club policy.

After each round, he would retire to the men's grill for drinks and cards with these old white men, and he had felt so proud to be accepted by them, to be seen in their company, to share their special space and breathe their rarefied air. He would hang on their every word—usually jokes and commentary about "niggers" and "wetbacks" and "kikes" made without regard to the presence of the black waiters hovering about. But Scott's eyes would always meet those of his waiter, and he would feel the heat rise within him. Yet Scott Fenney, who had played football with black guys, showered with black guys, roomed with black guys, and partied with black guys, had never stood up and told those old white men that he would no longer be available for a game of golf with a bunch of racist anti-Semitic sons of bitches in shorts. No, A. Scott Fenney, Esq., had smiled politely at their jokes and nodded approvingly at their commentary so as not to offend them. Because to offend these old white men would have been bad for business.

One day a year or so ago, Scott had asked Dan Ford whether these old white men just hated blacks, Mexicans, and Jews. Dan had laughed and said, "Oh, no, they hate lots of people, not just blacks, Mexicans, and Jews. They hate Democrats, Yankees, Californians, Asians, feminists, Muslims—anyone who's different from them. See, Scotty, the glory days for these old farts were the fifties, back when they were young and white men ruled Dallas and the only black in their world was their oil, and the Texas Railroad Commission controlled the price of oil in the whole goddamn world. Now the best golfer in the world is black, the mayor of Dallas is a woman, and the price of oil is controlled by a bunch of Arab sheikhs. The only part of their world that's still run by white men is this club. Drive through those gates and it's 1950 again. And they aim to keep it that way until the day they die. Like it or not, these bastards own most of Dallas, so if you want to be a rich lawyer in this town you've got to join their club. Scotty, my boy, it's just business."

Dan Ford was wrong: it wasn't just business; it was just bigotry. And A. Scott Fenney was wrong: his mother would not have been proud of her son.

Scott gave the members and their caddies one last glance—and noticed one of the caddies staring at him. The caddie's face changed; he recognized Scott. He smiled and gave Scott a discrete thumbs-up. Scott thought he recognized the caddie but he couldn't remember his name—he had never asked his caddies their names—but he returned the gesture, then ran on.

A few blocks later his thoughts were still on the club and the caddies and his good mother when he heard a high-pitched voice: "Scott! Scott!" He slowed, turned, and saw an arm waving out the window of a red Beemer: *Shit, Penny Birnbaum!*

"Scott! Wait!"

Penny was heading in the opposite direction down Lovers, so Scott cut through Curtis Park, two backyards, hit an alley, ran a few more blocks, and came out on Hillcrest Avenue. He turned south and ran along the western boundary of the SMU campus. He entered the campus at University Boulevard right in front of the law school.

He stopped.

Three years he had spent in that building, three years studying the law—torts, taxes, contracts, conflicts, procedure, property, and ethics, a subject he studied in school and quickly forgot in practice. The practice of law isn't about ethics; it's about money.

Scott began running again, past the sorority houses placed all in a row, conveniently, he had thought back then, so he wouldn't have far to walk between girls. And he recalled all the pleasures he had experienced in those houses with those girls, and he found himself wondering, as he had never wondered before, if their lives had turned out well.

He ran along University Boulevard into the heart of the manicured campus, then turned south on Hilltop Lane, which became Ownby Drive and led him directly to the new Gerald Ford Stadium, named after the billionaire Dallas banker, not the former president. He found an unlocked gate, entered the stadium, walked to the nearest ramp, and emerged from the concrete underbelly onto the green grass.

He was alone on the field.

The best times of his life had played out in this small arena—

120 yards long, 53⅓ yards wide. And the worst times, too, he used to think. Glorious victories and crushing defeats. Moments of immeasurable joy and unspeakable sadness. He could still close his eyes and see the crowd. He could still hear them cheering and smell the freshly cut grass. He could still taste his blood. He could still feel football.

Scott climbed the steps to the spectator stands and abruptly did what he had done so often back then: he ran the stands. His arms pumping, his legs burning with pain, he ran all the way to the top. He turned and looked at the downtown skyline in the distance, the skyscrapers silhouetted against the blue sky. Dibrell Tower stood above them all, and on the sixty-second floor, Sid Greenberg was standing in Scott's office. Sid couldn't see Scott four miles away, but Scott shot him the finger anyway, just on principle.

Back in college, he had often run the stands at night just so he could sit at the top of the stadium and gaze at the lights of downtown, the Emerald City rising out of the endless Texas plains: Dibrell Tower outlined in blue argon lights; the lighted ball above Reunion Arena looking like a Christmas tree ornament; and Pegasus, the neon red flying horse above the old Magnolia Building. Like so many other young white men, Scott Fenney had been seduced by the lights, by dreams of getting rich in Big D. That's what they call Dallas—"Big D"—because it's a mecca for men with big dreams. Big dreamers come to Dallas like sinners to Jesus: you want to get saved, come to Jesus; you want to get rich, come to Dallas. Sitting right here, Scott Fenney had dreamed big.

"That ain't bad for an old man!"

The booming voice startled Scott out of his thoughts. He searched the stadium until he saw a big black man standing on the sideline below. He looked familiar. Scott walked down the stands toward him. As he came closer, he recognized the man.

"Big Charlie, is that you?"

"Scotty Fenney, how you doing, man?"

Scott arrived and stuck out his hand, but Big Charlie wrapped his huge arms around Scott and bear-hugged him, as if Scotty Fenney had just scored the game-winning touchdown.

Charles Jackson stood six four and weighed 285 pounds—when he was an eighteen-year-old freshman. By the time he was a senior, he weighed 325. He played right guard, which required that he pull and lead running plays around either end, removing any obstacle from Scotty Fenney's path. Scott scored the touchdowns, but Big Charlie led the way.

Big Charlie came from Tyler, an East Texas town known for its red roses and black football players. Earl Campbell was the best known, but Big Charlie was the biggest. He attended SMU instead of Texas because he didn't want to be too far from his mama and his sisters. He drove the two hours home every Sunday morning for church and came back every Sunday night for curfew.

The last Scott had heard, Big Charlie had been drafted by the Rams. Charlie now told him that he had played two seasons and had been a knee injury away from fulfilling his dream. He had returned to SMU, where he had coached the offensive line for the last ten years. Scott had attended most of those games but he'd never noticed Big Charlie. It was a long way down to the sideline from Ford Stevens's private skybox.

"We could always use a good running back coach," Big Charlie said. He had read about Scott's troubles.

"Thanks, but I've still got some lawyering left in me."

"You gonna win?"

"I don't know."

"You think she's innocent?"

"Of murder, but not of killing Clark."

"Which means?"

"Worst case, she gets the death penalty. Best case, they convict her of second-degree murder, give her twenty years in prison. But she won't live that long, without heroin or her daughter."

"Read you took her in."

Scott smiled. "Yeah, her name's Pajamae; she's a great kid. You got kids?"

Big Charlie nodded. "Two girls, seven and ten."

"I bet you're a good dad."

"I love those two kids more than football."

"They're lucky then. Anyway, Pajamae was down in the projects by herself, so I went down there and got her—"

"You went into the projects? By yourself?"

"Yeah, in a Ferrari."

Big Charlie's head rolled back, and he let out a belly laugh. "White boy in a Ferrari down in the projects—that must've been a sight! I'm amazed you got out alive!"

"I had a friend, Louis. He ran interference for me, like you used to. He's living with us now, too. Anyway, first night, Pajamae did my daughter's hair in cornrows. Rebecca damn near fainted."

Big Charlie smiled. "How you doing since she left?"

Scott shook his head. "I only cry at night."

"That's 'cause you got heart, Scotty. You cried when we won and you cried when we lost. You cried 'cause you cared, about winning, about your team, about me. You know, Scotty, I never told you, but you were my hero."

Scott must have appeared shocked, because Charlie said, "No, man, I mean it. A hundred ninety-three yards against Texas—nobody does that! You wouldn't quit and you wouldn't let me quit. Twenty-three end sweeps that day, pulling my big butt around right end, then left end, then right end: I thought I was gonna die right out there on the field. But I'd look at you, getting the crap beat out of you every play but getting up and never quitting . . . man, you were tough."

Scott sighed. "Life is tougher."

"No, it ain't. You're forgetting your heart. Look inside yourself, it's still there. Scotty, God gave you a gift back then, your athletic ability. But what we did out there, that was just a game. That girl's life, that ain't no game." He put his hand on Scott's shoulder. "Scotty, don't you see? God's given you a better gift than being a football star. You've got the ability to save that girl's life."

Scott looked at Big Charlie, who had given everything he had to Scott Fenney on a football field; and now, on a football field again, he had given Scott even more. At that moment, Scott realized that he needed Shawanda Jones as much as she needed him. He needed to be her hero. It was who he was. It was who he wanted to be again. It was what had been missing in his life. Scott was brought out of his thoughts when the bells at the Methodist church on the campus rang out.

"Shit, what time is it?" Scott asked.

"Noon, straight up," Big Charlie said.

"Damn, I'm late!" Scott held his hand out, but Big Charlie bear-hugged him again. Scott said, "Thanks, my friend."

And he ran toward the Emerald City.

United States District Court Judge Samuel Buford was sitting in his chambers behind his desk checking his watch. Twelve-thirty. No Scott Fenney. He wasn't going to show.

Sam Buford sighed. He had thought there was hope for young A. Scott Fenney, Esq. But he had thought wrong. Fenney had the brains to be a hero, no doubt; and Buford had hoped he still had the heart. But now he saw that he didn't. There was no hope for Scott Fenney . . . or for Shawanda Jones . . . or for the law.

At that very moment, Sam Buford decided to retire.

His time had come. He would retire and tend to his garden. Clear out those weeds, till the soil, plant carrots and squash and cabbage and tomatoes, maybe go organic; get that garden in good shape, something he hadn't had time to do since . . . well, ever. Yep, time to put down the gavel and pick up the hoe.

He buzzed his secretary on the intercom and said he needed to dictate several orders. First order, postpone the trial date in *United States of America versus Shawanda Jones*. Second order, substitute counsel for Scott Fenney. But who? Herrin? The boy was a good writer, no doubt about it; but the defendant needed a hero, not a writer. He wished he were still Samuel Buford, attorney-at-law. He'd take her case. He'd be her hero. But he was Judge Samuel Buford. Soon to be a retired judge. Third order, dictate his resignation letter. As usual, Helen was prompt. In seconds the door swung open and—

Scott Fenney stood in the doorway, wearing only running shorts and drenched in sweat.

"Judge, I'm ready to be her lawyer."

Sam Buford damn near got out of his chair and walked over to embrace the young lawyer, but that would probably violate some rule of judicial ethics, so he reined in his emotions.

"All right, son. Her life is in your hands. I hope you're man enough to handle that responsibility."

"I am. And, Judge, I'll make her proud. My mother."

Scott Fenney turned and walked out the door. Helen stepped into his place, dictation pad in hand.

"Ready, Judge?"

Buford waved her away. "Go back to your desk, Helen. I've got judging to tend to." Helen turned away. "Oh, Helen, wait." She turned back. "Get me Bob Harris on the phone."

"Bob Harris?"

"He's the INS regional director." Buford leaned back and smiled. "My mama always said, one good deed deserves another."

301

TWENTY-THREE

O N SATURDAY the circus came to town.

Men and women, boys and girls, young and old, the wealthy residents of Highland Park came in droves. They parked on the side of the street, without the benefit of valets. They braved the 110-degree pressure cooker of a day and walked a block or more up the sidewalk to 4000 Beverly Drive. They had come to see something that only happened in other parts of Dallas County, in *those* neighborhoods into which they did not venture.

A yard sale.

But this was not a yard sale offering used toasters, beat-up couches, hand-me-down clothes, and an assortment of toys, baby strollers, car seats, and golf clubs. No, this yard sale boasted a walnut sideboard by Francesco Molon, a mahogany bookcase by Bevan Funnell, a pecan armoire by Guy Chaddock, a leather chair by Ralph Lauren, and a billiard table by Brunswick. It promised an assortment of sofas and tables and lamps and bedroom suites and Oriental rugs, an eclectic mix of furnishings with only two things in common: the former lady of the house once fancied them, and they were terribly expensive. It offered designer clothes, footwear, and accessories for women—dresses by Rickie Freeman and Luca Luca, handbags by Louis Vuitton and Bottega Veneta, shoes by Dior, Donna Karan, Marc Jacobs, and of course Jimmy Choo, shirts by Anne Fontaine, and silk scarves by Hermès. And there were girls' clothes by Jacadi Paris. In all, over $500,000 worth of pricey personal possessions were on sale. And while Highland Parkers might joke about white trash and minorities engaging in curb shopping and Dumpster diving, a bargain purchase is a basic human desire that transcends race, color, creed, national origin, political affiliation, or socioeconomic position.

So they came.

They came up the brick-paved driveway and arrived at the rear motor court and backyard and four-car garage where the Fenney family possessions were on display and for sale. For cash. Pajamae told Scott you don't take checks or credit cards at yard sales.

At dinner a week before, Boo had asked Scott what they were going to do with all of their stuff. They had enough things to fill the little house by SMU five times over. Scott said he didn't know, but Pajamae said she did: "Have a yard sale, Mr. Fenney." Pajamae had volunteered to run it because of her prior experience as a customer at numerous South Dallas yard sales. So the day of the event Scott was sitting at a makeshift checkout counter at the entrance to the motor court and taking cash from buyers while Pajamae and Boo made the sales.

"Two hundred," said the old lady in the sun hat who had introduced herself as Mrs. Jacobs.

"Now, Miz Jacobs," Pajamae said, "Miz Fenney, she paid two thousand dollars for that couch, and you want to buy it for two hundred? We priced it at seven hundred but"—she glanced around and lowered her voice—"long as you don't tell Mr. Fenney, I'll let you have it for six."

"I'll take it."

With her Sharpie, Pajamae wrote "SOLD" and "JACOBS" on the tag and changed the price to $600. She pointed at Mr. Fenney.

"Pay the man."

Mrs. Jacobs walked toward Mr. Fenney.

"Yoo-hoo, little colored girl!"

An old biddy was waving at Pajamae from over by the garage. Pajamae walked over. The woman was pointing at a leather chair.

"Is that a Ralph Lauren?"

"Lady, I'm not colored, I'm black. Well, I'm a quarter black, at the most. See, my mama's daddy was white and so was my daddy. So that'd make me a quarter black and three-quarters white." She smiled at the woman. "Why, I wouldn't be surprised if we were related! And no, ma'am, that's not Ralph Lauren, that's a chair."

"That's a Ralph Lauren."

Pajamae shrugged. "Whatever."

"The price is six hundred fifty, but I only have hundred-dollar bills," the lady said. "Do you have change?"

"No, ma'am, sure don't."

"But I want this chair!"

"So does that man over there."

The woman turned. "What man?"

"Bald dude in the blue shorts, with the big belly, talking to the fat woman in the striped shirt? He said he was bringing his wife over to look at it."

In fact, Pajamae had not spoken to the man.

"Don't you let him have this chair!"

"Ma'am, first rule of yard sales is, cash rules."

The woman again studied the chair, then the bald dude, then the chair. Finally she said, as Pajamae knew she would say, "I'll pay seven hundred."

Pajamae removed her Sharpie from behind her ear and wrote as she spoke: "Sold to Miz . . ."

"Smythe, with a *y* and an *e*. S-M-Y-T-H-E."

"Pay the man."

"I live just down the street. Can you deliver?"

"No, ma'am, but Louis can carry."

Pajamae waved at Louis standing off to the side like he was trying to go unnoticed, as if a six foot six, 330-pound black man in Highland Park could blend in. When he arrived, she said, "Louis, this nice lady needs this chair carried to her house."

Louis leaned down, spread his arms, grabbed the sides of the big chair, and lifted it without effort. He began walking toward Mr. Fenney like he was carrying a sack of groceries.

The lady said, "Do I have to tip him?"

"No, ma'am," Pajamae said, "just don't make him mad."

Mrs. Smythe with a *y* and an *e* looked at Louis's broad back walking away with her chair, frowned, and said, "I'll tip him. Twenty. No, fifty." She followed Louis over to Mr. Fenney.

Pajamae shook her head: *White people wouldn't last a day down in the projects*. When Boo walked up, Pajamae said, "Mama would love this."

"What?"

"Rich white people at a yard sale."

"Do you shop at yard sales often?"

"Yard sales are our shopping malls."

"Do you get good stuff?"

"Nothing like this. Course, we don't look for designer labels. We just make sure the clothes don't have blood stains, and no one's thrown up on the furniture."

Just then a woman wearing big sunglasses walked over holding out a handbag. "Is this a knockoff?" she asked.

Boo gave her a look. "Ma'am, my mother would rather have died than be seen with a knockoff. That's a Louis Vuitton original, retails for seven-fifty. We're offering that bag for two-fifty. My mother never even took it out of the house."

"I'll take it."

"Pay the man."

The woman left and Pajamae said, "Your mama has some fine stuff."

Boo nodded. "Mother always said, any girl says money can't buy happiness just doesn't know where to shop. But I guess she was wrong."

Boo pulled a black party dress off a rack. "A thousand dollars. She wore it one time to a party at the club." She replaced the dress and picked up a red spike-heeled shoe. "Three hundred dollars."

"For shoes?"

"Dior."

"Dee who?"

"Christian Dior. Women kill for these shoes."

Pajamae took the shoe and examined it. "My mama could wear these to work."

Scott had moved Rebecca's entire closet down to the backyard, hundreds of dresses and shoes and pants and shirts and garments of every kind and color. He had never once ventured into her huge walk-in closet so he had never realized just how many clothes she owned. He wondered now how much they had cost. Scott smiled as he accepted money from another customer buying his wife's clothes.

Pajamae was holding up a powder blue fringed miniskirt.

Boo said, "That was Mother's Cattle Barons' Ball outfit."

"Wearing this, she'd fit right in with Mama and Kiki working Harry Hines."

Pajamae replaced the skirt and picked up red pajamas.

"Neiman Marcus," Boo said. "One hundred thirty dollars."

"You think Mr. Fenney would sell these to me? I can pay seven dollars."

"You want red silk pajamas?"

"For Mama, so she doesn't have to sleep in that jail uniform."

"Oh." Boo thought for a moment, then said: "A. Scott put us in charge of pricing because he doesn't have a clue how much Mother paid for this stuff—he'd stroke out if he knew—so I'm going to mark these down to seven dollars. Pay the man."

"The little black girl said to pay you."

"Yep."

Scott looked up to see Penny Birnbaum.

"Oh, uh, hi, Penny. Did you find something you like?"

"I found something I liked the first time I was here." She smiled that smile and licked her red lips wet. "You want to go inside and see if I can find it again?"

"Well, uh, Penny, I've, uh, I've got to tend to the cash register, see?"

"You don't need cash. I'm giving it away."

She leaned in and her shirt gaped, revealing the top of her tanned breasts. Scott inhaled her perfume and he remembered that day in the steam shower and he became weak. He thought of feeling Penny's naked body against his and his hands on her and hers on him and her mouth on . . . but he thought of Boo. She wouldn't be very proud of her father if he gave in to his weakness.

Penny said, "I've come by every day and you haven't been home. Don't you want to see what else I can do?"

In fact, Scott had been home, but when he had seen who was standing on his front porch, he had hidden until she left.

"Oh, well, I know you're a very talented girl and—"

"Girl with the cornrows, she said to pay you."

Thank God. An old lady had walked up with a handful of clothes. Penny dropped three hundred-dollar bills on the counter and sashayed down the drive with two of Rebecca's purses, her narrow bottom in the tight shorts moving side to side so temptingly.

Bobby couldn't afford to buy any of the stuff Scotty had for sale—not that any of the furniture would go with the East Dallas flea-market decor of his little house—and he wasn't helping Boo and Pajamae sell the stuff because he'd probably punch out the first rich bitch who tried to negotiate him down on a price. So he was shooting pool in the garage, hoping the GQ dude checking out the pool table wouldn't buy it because he was hoping Scotty might give it to him in lieu of some of his fees. He could put it in his combination living/dining room.

"Your wife shopping outside?" he asked Mr. GQ.

"Yeah." Mr. GQ picked up a cue stick and said, "Wanna play?"

Bobby shrugged. "Why not."

Bobby played pool at the Mexican bar next to his office in the strip center two, three hours a day, sometimes more. Okay, usually more. In fact, his regular clients knew to call there if they had an emergency, which is to say, if they were unexpectedly arrested by the vice squad.

Bobby racked the balls and pulled out a twenty-dollar bill. "For a twenty? Or is that too much?"

Mr. GQ recoiled. "Too much?" He slapped a twenty on top of Bobby's bill and busted the rack. Not a ball fell.

Bobby chalked his cue tip. On his eighth straight stroke, he rolled the eight ball into the side pocket for the win. He reached over for the two bills when Mr. GQ said, "Double or nothing?"

Bobby smiled. The GQ dude didn't make his money playing

pool in a Mexican bar. Two games later, when his wife came looking for him, Bobby had netted $140, more than he made lawyering most days.

Boo saw a familiar face and said, "See that woman over there, the blonde?"

Boo pointed and Pajamae followed her finger. "Wearing the short shorts and heels? The real skinny girl?"

"She's a lollipop."

"A lollipop? You mean, like a sucker?"

"Unh-huh. See how her head looks too big for her body?"

Pajamae studied the woman. "She does look like a lollipop. That white girl needs to put some meat on her bones."

"Mother said she eats and then she throws up."

" 'Cause she's sick?"

"No, on purpose! So she doesn't gain weight."

"Boo, you pulling my leg?"

"No! She was Mother's sorority sister. She married money."

Pajamae frowned. "How do you marry money?"

"You look like her and you find an old man with money."

"Oh. Kind of like Mama does, only it lasts longer."

"Mother said she's only thirty-three, but she's had breast implants, a tummy tuck, a butt lift, and liposuction. Mother said the only part of her that's real is her brain, and that's only because they don't do brain implants." Boo shrugged. "That's what Mother said, anyway."

"Is her old man here?"

The lollipop turned and walked over to a white-haired man sitting on the love seat from the formal living room that was selling for $1,000. She sat down and he patted her skinny thigh.

"That's him. Mother said he's a billionaire."

"He looks like her granddaddy. Mama would charge double to

entertain a man as old as him. He must've paid a lot of money for his lollipop."

Scott was taking cash faster than he could count for clothes he had never seen Rebecca wear, furniture he had never sat on, and rugs he had never stepped on. Rebecca had filled every square foot of the 7,500-square-foot residence with her stuff. Now Scott was selling six thousand square feet of her stuff. And he was enjoying it.

"Your daughter said to pay you."

A middle-aged black woman had walked up to Scott.

"Hi, I'm Scott Fenney."

"I'm Dolores Hudson. We just moved in down the street"— she smiled—"the first black homeowners in Highland Park history?"

"Oh, yeah, I read about you. Welcome to the neighborhood, although I won't be here much longer."

She gave him a sympathetic look. "I've read about you, too."

"Yeah, well, you should believe everything you read."

"I don't think so. When are you moving?"

"I close on the sale of this place Thursday, then on the new place Friday. We'll move right after the trial."

"Well, if the timing doesn't work out and you need a place to stay, you and the children come stay with us. And I bet those girls haven't had any home cooking since your wife—"

She was embarrassed. But Scott smiled and said, "My wife didn't cook."

"Well, I do. I'll bring something over."

"Thank you, Dolores."

"No, thank you, Scott. For what you're doing. You know, we weren't sure we were doing the right thing buying a home here. I didn't know if I wanted to be the Rosa Parks of Highland Park, whether we'd be accepted here."

"You did the right thing, Dolores. Most of the people here, particularly the younger ones, they'll be fine. Some of the old-timers won't accept you, but take it from me, you don't want to be friends with them anyway."

Dolores paid and said thanks again.

Boo was holding up a flowery sundress for a young woman.

"Luca Luca, you've heard of him, the Italian designer?"

"Of course. Who hasn't?"

She took the dress from Boo and held it against her body. It was a perfect fit.

"Almost as pretty as it looked on my mother."

"You know, I pledged the same sorority as your mother. She was six years before me. But she's still a role model for all the girls—Miss SMU marries a football star who becomes a rich lawyer. It's like Cinderella."

Boo nodded. "I must've missed the part where Cinderella walks out on her family for a golf pro."

Bobby was lining up a shot when someone stepped directly into his line of sight at the opposite end of the pool table. He raised up to tell the idiot to get the hell out of the way—

"Hi, Bobby."

—and damn near hit himself with the pool cue.

"Karen, what are you doing here?"

"I quit."

"What?"

"Ford Stevens."

"You're shi . . . You're kidding me? Why?"

"I didn't like the way they were making me think."

"Like a lawyer?"

"Yeah."

"Smart girl. What are you gonna do?"

"Work with you and Scott on your case."

When the summer sun set on the yard sale at 4000 Beverly Drive in the heart of Highland Park, nothing was left—not a shoe or a dress or a lamp or even the pool table. In less than nine hours, Scott had sold most of the material possessions he had acquired during eleven years of marriage, all the things that evidenced his existence, his ambitions, his career, and his wife.

The girls were at the other end of the kitchen, adding up their profits on the floor. Louis was counting his tip money—"Six hundred dollars for carrying stuff"—and sitting with Scott, Bobby, and Karen Douglas on the floor and eating fried chicken Dolores Hudson had brought over. The table and chairs had sold for $1,500.

"Karen," Scott said, "forget everything I ever told you about being a lawyer. I was wrong."

"You're a great lawyer, Scott, everyone at the firm says so, even since you left."

"I didn't leave. I got fired."

"Well, even after that."

"No, Karen, I was a corrupt lawyer. I cheated my clients, I cheated the law, and I cheated myself. I did whatever it took to win. I practiced law like it was a football game. It isn't."

"Karen wants to help us," Bobby said.

"Why?"

Karen said, "Because you need help. And I like Bobby."

Bobby dropped his drumstick.

Boo yelled over, "Sixty-seven thousand, four hundred fifty dollars."

313

TWENTY-FOUR

"VOIR DIRE" is a legal phrase meaning "to speak the truth." In the American legal system, "voir dire" refers to the process of picking a jury, perhaps because of all the players in a criminal trial, only the jurors are truly interested in the truth. Everyone else just wants to win.

In federal court, jurors must be citizens; at least eighteen years old; proficient in reading, writing, understanding, and speaking English; not be physically or mentally infirm; not have been convicted of a felony; and not have felony charges currently pending against them. Finding twelve people who meet such qualifications is easy; finding twelve people you would want to sit in judgment of your life is not.

That's where voir dire comes in. The judge and lawyers question the prospective jurors to uncover biases, prejudices, and predispositions that might prevent them from rendering a fair and impartial verdict. At least that's the theory. The reality is that every juror comes to court with his or her personal biases, prejudices, and predispositions that will absolutely prevent that person from rendering a fair and impartial verdict—which is precisely the kind of jurors both sides want. The real goal of voir dire is to find twelve jurors who are biased, prejudiced, and predisposed in your favor.

A trial in a court of law is not about truth, justice, and the American way. It's about winning. Prosecutors want a conviction so that they can build a track record of putting criminals in jail, a prerequisite for election or appointment to higher political office; defense attorneys want an acquittal because acquittals in high-profile criminal cases bring fame and fortune. Thus neither the prosecutor nor the defense attorney is concerned with truth or justice: truth is whatever they can get a jury to believe, and justice is when they win.

As he sat in a federal courtroom in downtown Dallas on a hot day in August, Scott Fenney believed his client had put the barrel of her .22-caliber gun to Clark McCall's head and pulled the trigger. He also believed she had done so in self-defense. Now he had to question the men and women sitting before him in the hope of finding twelve jurors who might agree with him and, if not acquit his client, at least not send her to death row.

Judge Buford had already questioned the prospective jurors concerning their legal qualifications and dismissed only one, a man who, when asked if he had any pending felony charges, answered, "They haven't been able to prove anything yet!"

Ray Burns had then questioned the prospective jurors about their willingness to find the defendant guilty knowing she might be sentenced to death. Seven prospective jurors said they were morally opposed to the death penalty and were excused.

Now twenty-nine prospective jurors were staring at Scott Fenney and Robert Herrin, waiting for the defendant's counsel to question them. In every prior voir dire, sitting next to A. Scott

Fenney had been an expensive psychologist trained in the art of jury selection, not a lawyer who practiced street law in a strip center next to a Mexican bar. For fees up to $1,000,000, such jury experts conduct mock trials, focus groups, and pretrial polling to develop a detailed psychological profile of the ideal juror. They investigate the prospective jurors' employment, income, religion, hobbies, and politics. They study their clothes, their body language, and their answers during voir dire. They coach the lawyers on what to drive to the courthouse (leave the Mercedes-Benz at home because jurors might see you in the parking lot), what to wear to trial (no Rolexes or double-breasted Armani suits), and how to act in front of the jurors (try to "humanize" yourself; that is, pretend to be a normal human being in front of the jurors, a more difficult assignment for most lawyers than merely dressing down). They give the lawyer a thumbs-up or a thumbs-down on each prospective juror.

A lawyer learns with his first jury trial that the case is won or lost during jury selection. Today, with enough money, you can legally fix a jury. But since neither Scott nor his client had enough money to hire a jury expert, there was no paid consultant sitting next to Scott, only Bobby.

So Scott said to the men and women before him, "I'm nervous, about this. I've never represented a person accused of murder. Are you nervous, too?"

Heads started nodding.

"Well, rather than me asking you a lot of questions, maybe we'll just visit for a while. Forget what we're here for, forget you might be jurors, forget we're lawyers—as you might have read, my former law firm's been trying to forget I'm a lawyer."

A few chuckles from the jury box, which gave Scott an idea.

"What's the difference between a rattlesnake lying dead in the middle of a highway and a lawyer lying dead in the middle of a highway?"

A female juror: "Skid marks in front of the snake."

The jurors laughed.

"You know why New Jersey got all the toxic waste dumps and California got all the lawyers?"

A male juror: "New Jersey got first choice."

Louder laughter from the jury box.

"What do lawyers and sperm have in common?"

A male juror: "They both have a one-in-a-million chance of turning out human."

Raucous laughter.

The same juror: "How do you know when a lawyer is lying?"

An old lady: "His lips are moving."

Another: "A lawyer is a liar with a permit to practice."

And another: "If an IRS agent and a lawyer were both drowning and you could save only one, would you read the paper or go to lunch?"

Scott finally interrupted the revelry.

"Hey, I went to law school. I get to tell the jokes."

The jurors' laughter died down, but their smiles remained.

"I take it you people don't care for lawyers?"

All twenty-nine heads shook emphatically.

"You hate lawyers?"

All heads nodded emphatically.

"Why?"

An older man: "Because lawyers don't know the difference between the truth and winning an argument."

An older woman: "Because lawyers think being clever is the same as being smart."

A young woman: "Because a lawyer will tell you the sky is green if that'll help his case."

A young man: "Because lawyers are greedy."

Bobby: "Yeah, and they're—"

"Bobby!"

Scott turned to the jurors. "And he's a lawyer!"

The jurors were chuckling again.

Ray Burns stood. "Your Honor, if Mr. Fenney is through with his stand-up comedy act, perhaps we could—"

"Sit, Mr. Burns," the judge said.

Ray Burns sat. Scott addressed the prospective jurors.

"Okay, I think we've established that all of you hate lawyers. And that's okay. We deserve it. But my client doesn't. You can hate me because I'm a lawyer, but don't hate her because you hate her lawyer. Her life is in your hands. Give her a fair shake. Can you all agree to that?"

The smiles were gone, replaced by sober expressions. Every single juror nodded.

"All right, now I need to ask you a few questions. First, have any of you participated in voir dire before?"

One young man with a nose ring raised his hand and asked, "Is that like when there's four?"

"Four what?"

"Four people. You know, like ménage à trois plus one."

From behind, Judge Buford's weary voice: "You're excused."

The man rose, shrugged, and shuffled out of the courtroom.

Scott said, "Any of you *not* heard about this case?"

No one raised a hand.

"All right. My client is a prostitute and a heroin addict. You all know that, right?"

Their heads nodded.

"Again, I ask only one thing of you: Don't prejudge her. Don't assume. You don't know what another person's life is like until you've walked around in her shoes awhile. Ms. Jones is not here today because she's ill. She's suffering withdrawal sickness. How many of you smoke?"

Eight jurors raised their hands.

"Imagine if you had to quit cold turkey."

319

They nodded.

"Have any of you ever retained a prostitute?"

No hands were raised, but one man glanced around.

"Sir?"

"I ain't never retained a hooker, but I had sex with one."

The judge: "You're excused."

Scott thumbed through the jurors' questionnaires and stopped at one completed by a high school football coach. Most football coaches considered themselves smarter than the general population because they understood the definition of pass interference. But one other predisposition of football coaches gave him pause. So he turned to juror number 28 and said, "Coach, who's the greatest running back ever produced by the State of Texas?"

Without blinking, the coach asked, "Negro or white?"

The judge: "You're excused."

After the coach had left, Scott turned to another juror, an older man whose sunburned face told Scott he worked outdoors.

"Sir, in response to question number eleven asking how far did you go in school, you answered twelve miles."

"Yes, sir, we lived in the country, so that's how far we had to go."

"Uh, well, the question means, you know, what was the highest grade level you attained?"

The man seemed genuinely embarrassed. "Oh, hell, I'm sorry. I made a B once."

The judge: "You're excused."

Scott now turned to an older woman clutching a big purse in her lap and wearing a worried expression.

"Ma'am?" She looked up. "Ma'am, is there anything that would interfere with your serving on this jury?"

"Will I be home in time for *Oprah*?"

The judge: "You're excused."

On the drive home, Bobby said, "Will I be home in time for *Oprah*? That was a good one."

Scott had struck seven prospective jurors and Ray Burns nine. The twelve jurors who would determine whether Shawanda Jones would live or die had been selected and seated for the trial that would start on Monday: there were seven men and five women; six were white, four were black, and two were Hispanic; there was a teacher, a nurse, a carpenter, a dental assistant, a car salesman, two housewives, a mechanic, a junior college professor, a contractor, a bartender, and a grocery store clerk.

Scott said to Bobby, "Do you trust Karen?"

"Yeah, why?"

"I'm worried Dan Ford planted her."

"You mean as a spy?"

"Yeah, to learn our strategy."

"What strategy? *Prayer?*" Bobby smiled. "Don't worry, Scotty, she's not a spy."

"How can you be sure?"

"Remember a few weeks ago, in the pool, I said I'd probably never have sex again?"

"Yeah."

"I was wrong."

"You mean . . . ?"

"Yeah. And no girl would have sex with me just for money. Believe me, I know."

Money could not make the rape go away. The physical pain was gone, but the mental pain would never leave Hannah Steele.

It was a beautiful afternoon in Galveston. The sun was warm, but the sea breeze was cool against her skin. Hannah was strolling down the seawall, seventeen feet above the beach. To her left, across the boulevard, were restaurants, bars, gift shops, and beach-front

321

condos and hotels; to her right was the sandy beach and beyond that the Gulf of Mexico, a body of brown water whose swells rolled ashore and broke into small waves that died in the sand around the feet of kids wading at the water's edge. Their parents were sitting in chairs under colorful umbrellas that dotted the beach in both directions as far as Hannah could see. Other kids were building sand castles or hunting for seashells, and a few surfers were trying to find waves strong enough to provide a ride, but without much luck.

Hannah liked to walk the seawall.

Her therapist said it was good for her to take these walks and to realize that all around her life went on and that her life must as well. But Hannah always focused on the kids; her therapist said she would have children one day, but Hannah didn't think she would ever be able to have sex again. Clark McCall had destroyed her life.

And now his life was over.

She had tried not to feel happy when she had heard about Clark's death. But somewhere deep inside her she hoped he had suffered. Now she was the accused woman's only hope, Mr. Fenney had said. Her only hope. So she would fly to Dallas on Sunday. It would be her first trip back since she had left.

Could she do it?

Could she go into that courtroom and sit up there and see Senator McCall and tell the world what Clark did to her? *He kissed me . . . he touched me . . . I said no . . . he said yes . . . he slapped me . . . hit me . . . once, twice, three times, harder each time . . . he was wild-eyed, crazy, strong . . . he pinned me down . . . pulled my panties down . . . pried my legs apart . . . yes, I fought him . . . but he was too strong . . . he pushed into me . . . the pain . . . the pain . . .*

The pain would never go away.

She had gone to SMU on a dance scholarship. She loved to dance. She had not danced since that night. The rape had changed her life. She hadn't been able to get over it, to get on with her life. Her therapist had convinced her that testifying at the trial might

322

be just the closure she needed to move forward. She almost walked into a man.

"Excuse me," she said.

"Hello, Hannah," the man said.

Hannah looked up at the big bald man in front of her and started to cry.

The only open chair was next to Penny Birnbaum.

Scott and Bobby had returned home and eaten lunch with Louis and the girls. Scott had then driven the Jetta to the title company that was closing the sale of 4000 Beverly Drive. The receptionist led him to the small conference room where he would sign over his home to Mr. and Mrs. Jeffrey Birnbaum.

Penny was smiling and patting the seat of the empty chair.

Scott introduced himself to Joy, the closing agent sitting on the near side of the table next to Jeffrey, who was poring over the stack of documents like a jeweler over a new batch of uncut diamonds. Scott walked around the table, sat next to Penny, and scooted his chair up under the table. Before he had settled in, her right hand was on his left knee.

"I still need to measure for furniture, Scott," she said.

She was wearing a sundress that accentuated her round breasts and narrow waist. Her hand moved up to Scott's thigh and began closing in on his crotch. He reached down, grabbed her wrist, and placed her hand firmly in her lap. She pushed out her lips in a pouty face. But when he released her wrist, her hand returned to his thigh like a spring-action screen door slamming in place. She smiled.

Joy pushed a pile of papers across the table to Scott and began reciting the numbers shown on the closing statement.

"Three-point-four million sales price due to the seller, less deductions for the loan payoff, two-point-eight million principal plus twenty-four thousand eight hundred ninety accrued interest, the title policy premium, nineteen thousand, miscellaneous title company charges for the escrow fee—"

"Two-fifty?" Jeffrey said.

Joy said, "Standard charge."

"But there's no escrow."

"We still charge the fee."

"But—"

"I'll pay the two-fifty, Jeffrey," Scott said.

He wasn't in the mood to argue over a $250 charge in a $3.4 million deal. Even with that deduction, Scott would net over $500,000 from the sale. After paying taxes and closing on the little starter home by SMU, with the rest of his 401(k) and the $67,000 from the yard sale, he'd have enough to start a new life.

He removed Penny's hand again and whispered, "Stop!"

Across the table, Jeffrey and Joy were huddled over the buyer's closing documents, more voluminous because of the mortgage documents between Jeffrey and his bank. Scott's thoughts drifted back to that day three years ago when he had signed similar mortgage documents to purchase this very home, but before he could get very far he felt a soft whisper in his ear: "I'm not wearing any panties."

Penny pulled back and their eyes met. Her eyes dropped and led his down. She twisted slightly in her chair and spread her legs a little and slowly slid the end of her dress up to reveal her tanned lower thighs, her smooth upper thighs, and finally that lovely intersection of thighs and torso. Scott inhaled sharply. She wasn't lying.

Scott felt the blood rush southward. He began signing the closing papers as fast as his hand could scribble his signature: the closing statement, lien affidavits, nonresident alien certification, tax proration agreement, and the deed conveying his dream house to Jeffrey Birnbaum et ux Penny Birnbaum. Scott's hand trembled when he signed *A. Scott Fenney*. He pushed the deed across the table to Jeffrey. And with that, his dream home was gone. He felt as if he had handed over his manhood.

But he knew he hadn't because Penny had a firm hold on his manhood below the table. Scott's face felt hot, whether from the emotion of signing away his home or the movement of Penny's hand, he couldn't say. All he knew was that he had to get out of this closing fast, so he scratched his name on the final document, the temporary lease by which he would lease the home back from the Birnbaums for ten days, enough time to vacate the premises. He pushed the paper across the table to Jeffrey, who glanced up from his stack of documents and at the lease, then at Scott and Penny and back to Scott, his eyes narrowing with suspicion.

"What the hell's going on?" he said.

Scott froze, as did Penny's hand.

"Uh, what do you mean, Jeffrey?"

Jeffrey picked up the lease. "Ten days? It was supposed to be seven."

Scott exhaled with relief; Penny's hand went back to work.

"Jeffrey, you moved up closing to today."

"Well, can't you get out sooner? We're ready to move in."

"No, Jeffrey, I can't. I've got a murder trial starting Monday—you might've read about it. That's a little more important than you getting into my house a few days earlier."

"It's not your house anymore, Scott."

Jeffrey said it with the arrogance of a man completely unaware that at that very moment his wife was massaging another man's penis.

That night, after prayers, Pajamae asked Scott, "So those twelve people are going to decide what happens to Mama?"

"Yes, baby, they are."

"Do you trust them, Mr. Fenney?"

"Well . . . I don't know them well enough to know whether I trust them or not. I hope they can find a way to be fair."

Pajamae said, "I'm going to pray for them."

"The jurors?"

She nodded. "Mama always says to pray for other people, so they do the right thing. Like she said I should pray for you."

TWENTY-FIVE

WHEN SCOTT WOKE UP on Sunday morning, his mind instantly filled with fear. The trial would begin in twenty-four hours: Was he a good enough lawyer to save Shawanda? For the last eleven years, when he needed help, Scott had always gone to Dan Ford. Now he needed help and his thoughts went to Butch Fenney: Son, when you need help, hit your knees.

Scott rolled out of bed, put on his shorts, and hurried down the hall and up the stairs to the third floor. He found the girls on the bed. Pajamae was fixing Boo's cornrows.

"Get your clothes on, girls, we're going to church."

Boo's mouth fell open.

Louis led the way up the sidewalk to the front entrance of the small church in East Dallas and Pajamae said, "I wondered why y'all never went to church. Mama and me, we go every Sunday. I figured maybe white people just didn't go to church."

"Why didn't you say you wanted to go?" Scott asked.

"Wouldn't have been polite, Mr. Fenney."

Scott Fenney had attended church regularly with his parents, but after Butch died, he'd lost any enthusiasm he had for religion. Why would God take a good man like Butch Fenney? But he still attended church with his mother until she died. The last time he had entered this church was for his mother's funeral.

The preacher had nothing on Big Charlie.

Before they had parted back at the stadium that day two weeks ago, Big Charlie had said, "When God gives you a gift, it doesn't mean you're special. It means you're blessed."

Scott finally understood what his mother had meant when she had said he had a gift and she didn't mean football. He knew that his entire life had led him to this one moment, to this trial, to Shawanda Jones. The judge was right: She needed a hero. She needed him. And he needed her. But it had been a long time since Scott Fenney had been someone's hero. And he honestly didn't know if he had it in him to be a hero now.

He glanced down at the two little girls sitting next to him. Boo and Pajamae turned their eyes up to him, the way he had often turned his eyes up to Butch in this very church. He remembered his father's words again, and he slid forward and knelt.

And he prayed for help.

A mile away, Bobby Herrin was sitting in his dingy office drafting a trial brief. The front door was propped open because the landlord didn't turn on the air-conditioning on Sundays. He inhaled and caught the scent of cheap cologne. He looked up. Standing in the door was a white man, bald, burly, and thick-necked. Delroy Lund.

Carl's more thorough background check on Delroy Lund had revealed a DEA career checkered with reprimands for unnecessary use of force. Carl said he was digging deeper, but he hadn't reported back yet.

Bobby tried to maintain his composure, but flinched when Delroy reached into his coat.

"Don't try anything, Delroy! I yell out, Joo-Chan will come over—and he knows karate!"

Delroy chuckled. "That gook knows how to make donuts—but not on Sunday. You're all alone, Herrin."

But Delroy didn't pull out a gun; he pulled out an envelope. Bobby exhaled with relief. Delroy tossed the envelope on the desk. Bobby opened it; inside was a check made payable to Robert Herrin, Esq., for the sum of $100,000. Bobby suddenly felt better about his standing in the legal profession: finally, he was important enough to be bribed. He examined the check.

"Bank check issued by a Cayman Island bank. That's cute, Delroy. Not traceable back to McCall."

"We ain't stupid."

"That's open for debate."

"Here's the deal, Herrin. That little fuckup Clark ain't gonna cheat his dad out of the White House, alive or dead. So you got a choice: take the money and get out of town or get arrested."

"For what?"

"Dealing drugs."

"I don't have any drugs."

"You will when I'm finished. I'll call my buddies at the DEA and they'll bust your ass."

"With your record at the DEA? I don't think so. I'll tell them you planted the drugs, take a polygraph, and they'll arrest you. So, what, McCall thinks Scotty can't defend her without me? Scotty doesn't need me."

"He proved that before, didn't he?" Delroy grinned. "You're the only conscience he's got, according to Burns."

Bobby replaced the check and tossed the envelope to Delroy.

"Get out."

"You're making a big mistake."

"Won't be the first time. See you at the trial, Delroy."

"Sorry, I can't make it."

"Sure you can." Bobby picked up a subpoena, wrote *Delroy Lund* in the witness blank, and tossed it to Delroy. "You're served, asshole."

As soon as the word was out of his mouth, Bobby knew he had pushed Delroy's button—and that he shouldn't have. Delroy bent over and picked up the subpoena from the floor. He glanced at it; his face changed. He came over to Bobby, grabbed Bobby by the shirt, and yanked him halfway out of his chair. Delroy's mouth was about six inches away from Bobby's face when he said, "You little mother—"

"Hey, *hombre!*"

Standing in the door was Carlos Hernandez. Carlos was six feet tall, weighed maybe one-ninety, and was dressed for church: black leather pants, black pointed boots, a black tee shirt tight on his muscular tattooed arms, and two-inch silver bracelets on each wrist. His black hair was slicked back.

"Get your stinkin' hands off my lawyer, gringo!"

The two men glared at each other. Finally, Delroy chuckled, released Bobby, walked a few steps, then turned back.

"Oh, your star witness took her check. She figured a vacation was better than being fish bait in Galveston Bay."

Delroy laughed as he walked out the door past Carlos's mean face. When he was gone, Carlos broke into a big grin and said, "Good thing you got me bail, huh, Mr. Herrin?"

"Yeah. Thanks, Carlos."

Carlos held out a twenty-dollar bill. "From my mother."

"Can we go see Mama?" Pajamae asked.

Scott opened the car door for the girls and said, "Sure."

The drive from the church in East Dallas to the federal building in downtown took only minutes on the vacant Sunday morning streets. Louis stayed outside in the car. Scott and the girls went inside and rode the elevator to the fifth floor. They were escorted to the small bare room and waited for Shawanda. When she entered the room, she hugged Pajamae and Boo. Then Scott hugged her.

When he released her, he held her shoulders and said, "Shawanda, don't be afraid of what might happen at the trial. With Hannah Steele testifying, we've got a fighting chance. And if we lose, we'll appeal all the way to the Supreme Court."

Shawanda smiled softly. "I ain't scared, Mr. Fenney. People like me, we been on the wrong side of life long enough to know what to expect in a courtroom. But most of all, I ain't scared 'cause you my lawyer."

An hour later, they arrived back home to Bobby's car parked in the driveway and Bobby sitting on the back steps smoking a cigarette. Bobby said, "Hannah Steele's disappeared. McCall bought her off or Delroy scared her off; either way she ain't testifying. We're screwed."

TWENTY-SIX

Scott parked the Jetta in an open lot two blocks down from the federal building. There was no shade to be found, so he lowered the windows an inch hoping the inside temperature wouldn't rise high enough to melt the dashboard, then he climbed out. The girls followed him, both wearing the best outfits Rebecca had purchased for Boo at Neiman Marcus. Pajamae had on a white sundress with black polka dots and a wide-brimmed white hat; Boo wore a light blue sundress with a matching hat. They looked like two little Southern belles—except for the cornrows.

Scott pulled his handkerchief from his back pocket, removed his glasses, and wiped away the sweat already accumulating on his forehead. He then replaced his glasses, put on his coat, locked the car, and picked up his briefcase. He paid the attendant ten dollars for all-day parking, and then they walked up the street. Scott felt like he always did right before a game, his body alive with nervous energy, particularly when the opponents he would soon face were bigger, stronger, and meaner.

He looked down at the two little girls walking in front of him. Boo was the love of his life and Pajamae had become like a second daughter to him. They were excited, as if they were going to the zoo instead of a murder trial, chatting and giggling—until they turned the corner onto Commerce Street.

Then all three of them froze. Hundreds of people were gathered at the front entrance to the federal building: local, network, and cable TV vans lined the street, their satellite dishes and camera crews ready to capture and transmit breaking news; several dozen police were keeping the peace. It was the media circus Buford had promised.

"A. Scott, who are all those people waiting for?" Boo asked.

"Me."

He pulled the girls close and forged ahead. When they were spotted, the cameras and reporters came rushing forward like the kicking team rushing downfield to tackle number 22 returning the opening kickoff. Scott would rather have faced those foaming-at-the-mouth football players than these crazed reporters wanting a sound bite for the evening news. They stuck microphones in his face and shouted from a foot away:

"Is Shawanda claiming self-defense?"

"Will other women testify that Clark raped them?"

"Are you gonna call the senator to testify?"

To all of which Scott answered, "No comment," and pushed ahead. But then they went after Pajamae, sticking microphones in her face and shouting at her:

"Do you think your mother killed Clark?"

"Where will you live if she's convicted?"

"Do you still love your mother?"

Scott got mad. He shoved the microphones and cameras away.

"Leave her alone!"

But Pajamae had stopped dead in her tracks. Her head was tilted up at the last reporter, an odd expression on her face, and she said in the softest voice: "Of course, I love my mama."

Her words struck the reporters silent. A little black girl had embarrassed the media circus into submission. The crowd parted and allowed Scott and his two little girls free passage into the courthouse.

They got off the elevator on the fifteenth floor and walked down the hall and around the corner to Judge Buford's courtroom, where Delroy Lund was sitting on a bench, reading the sports pages. They hadn't seen each other since that day at the Village, but Delroy only glanced up at Scott and then back at the newspaper, without comment or expression. Per his subpoena, Delroy was legally obligated to sit outside the courtroom for the duration of the trial, waiting to be called inside to testify.

Scott pulled the big double doors open and escorted the girls into the courtroom, up the center aisle to the front row, and as he was pointing out where they should sit, he glanced back at the second row and found himself staring at United States Senator Mack McCall and his wife. And they stared back. Scott thought he noticed the senator's right arm come up slightly, as if he were going to reach over and shake Scott's hand, a politician's habit, but the senator pulled back. Scott's eyes fell on Jean McCall; she looked straight into his eyes and her eyebrows rose slightly, as if asking a silent question, then she recrossed her legs, left over right. The movement drew Scott's eyes down to her short skirt, and she looked away, but ran her hand down the length of her smooth thigh. Scott was turning his head back to the girls when he noticed Dan Ford. His former senior partner, mentor, and father figure was sitting next to Jean McCall with a grim expression. Dan broke eye contact with Scott and looked down, slowly shaking his head.

Scott got the girls settled in on the jury side of the spectator section. He wanted the jurors to see the defendant's daughter and think, *How could the same person be a loving mother and a cold-blooded murderer?*

"Oh, that's a nice touch."

Ray Burns's smart-ass voice. Scott turned to his adversary, but Ray just shook his head and walked to the prosecution table. Bobby and Karen were already seated at the defendant's table.

"Clark McCall was lying on the floor of his bedroom, writhing in pain after being kneed in the groin, when the defendant, Shawanda Jones, walked over to him, grabbed his hair, yanked him up, stuck the barrel of her .22-caliber pistol to his forehead, and pulled the trigger, killing him instantly. Then she stole his money and his car. Shawanda Jones murdered Clark McCall, a federal official, during the commission of a robbery. That is what the evidence will show. And that is why I will ask you to return a verdict of guilty and a sentence of death."

Assistant United States Attorney Ray Burns turned away from the jury, walked from the podium back to the prosecution table, and winked at Scott, knowing that he had just made a very effective opening statement, telling the jury exactly what he would prove and knowing he could back up his words.

"Mr. Fenney," Judge Buford said.

Scott stood and glanced at the spectator section crowded with gawkers gathered to witness a trial the likes of which Dallas had never seen. At the back of the courtroom were the groupies, old men who came to the courthouse each day like other old men went to the golf course. Next up were several rows of the general public who had lined up outside before daybreak to get a seat. Then came five rows of reporters taking notes and courtroom artists sketching portraits. Then came an assortment of lawyers and state court

336

judges who viewed the trial as continuing legal education. And finally there were Senator McCall and his wife, McCall staring holes in Scott's skull, Jean just staring, and Dan Ford shaking his head. Directly in front of them, Boo and Pajamae sat like two little prim and proper Highland Park girls, knees together, hands in their laps. He looked at Boo and she smiled and gave him an emphatic thumbs-up. He wished he shared her confidence. He walked over to the podium and faced the jury. He would not dispute the government's evidence. He would only dispute the government's conclusions.

"Shawanda Jones is a prostitute and a heroin addict. She's not present this morning because she's sick; she's suffering withdrawal. Judge Buford permitted me to make you aware of her illness so you would not hold her absence against her. If you remember, at jury selection, I asked only one thing from each of you, and that was to give Shawanda a fair shake."

There was a time, not that long ago, when a black defendant could not get a fair shake in a Southern courtroom; when a complete stranger could walk in off the sidewalk and, without knowing anything about a case, instantly pick out the defendant, the only black person in the courtroom; when a jury of a black defendant's "peers" would be white men. But the times had changed and so had the law. Scott now looked into the eyes of the black and brown and white men and women sitting in the jury box—the teacher, the mechanic, the nurse, the bartender, and the others— and wondered if they could be fair.

"You hold her life in your hands. Listen carefully. Think for yourself. Be fair."

Dallas Police Officer Eddie Castille swore to "tell the truth, the whole truth, and nothing but the truth so help me God" and sat in the witness stand. Castille was in his midtwenties, Hispanic, a

337

young cop eager to please, and still under the impression that he could make a difference on the streets of Dallas. He was the prosecution's first witness. Ray Burns addressed him from the podium.

"Officer Castille, what is your position with the Dallas Police Department?"

"Patrol officer."

"Were you patrolling the Harry Hines vicinity of Dallas on the afternoon of Sunday, June sixth?"

"Yes, sir."

"And during that patrol did you come upon an abandoned Mercedes-Benz?"

"Yes, sir."

"Please tell the jury what you did next."

"I saw the vehicle parked on a side street and pulled up to it. We don't generally see cars like that in the Harry Hines area, except at the strip joints. The vehicle was unoccupied, so I ran the plates. Dispatch came back, said it hadn't been reported stolen, said it was registered to a Mack McCall."

"As in Senator Mack McCall?"

"Yes, sir, that's what dispatch said, but I didn't know who that was."

That brought light laughter from the courtroom and a self-deprecating shrug from the senator.

"And then what did you do?"

"The registration address was in Highland Park, so the duty sergeant said he would call Highland Park PD and have them go over to the residence."

"And did that end your involvement with this case?"

"Yes, sir, other than waiting for the car to be towed to impound."

"And what time was this?"

"Approximately one P.M."

"Thank you, Officer Castille. No further questions."

Judge Buford turned to Scott, who said, "No questions, Your Honor."

"Mama, you okay?"

Instead of going out each day for lunch, the defense team had decided to eat lunch with the defendant. So they were now in the small bare conference room, eating the ham and cheese sandwiches the girls had made that morning. Scott pulled his coat off the chair back and wrapped it around Shawanda's shoulders. His client was having chills again.

"Yeah, baby."

"Why can't you have your medicine?"

"Don't know."

"Mama, the jury people keep looking over at me."

"That 'cause you so pretty." She warmed and she said, "How the trial going, Mr. Fenney?"

"Nothing much this morning, Shawanda."

"Mama, that Mr. Burns, he's a little prick. He stood right up there and lied to those jury people. He told them you killed that McCall boy, just like he meant it."

"He did, baby."

After the lunch break, Ray Burns, the little prick, called Sergeant Roland James of the Highland Park Police Department as the prosecution's second witness. Sergeant James was one of those middle-aged cops who had long ago made his peace with the fact that he wasn't going to make a difference, so he would just ride out his shift until his pension kicked in. He testified that he had been on duty on the afternoon of Sunday, June 6, and had taken the call from the Dallas PD regarding the McCall Mercedes-Benz. He had arrived at the McCall estate at one-thirty P.M.

"Sergeant James," Ray Burns said, "when you arrived at the McCall residence, did you notice anything out of the ordinary?"

"No, sir—except that the front gates were open."

"What did you do?"

"I drove in, went up to the front door, and rang the doorbell several times. No one answered. I tried the door, but it was locked. So I walked around to the back of the house and found the back door open. I stepped inside the residence and called out, but no one answered."

"What did you do then?"

"I commenced searching the residence, the ground floor first. Nothing was disturbed, and I found no one. I walked up the stairs to the second floor, started on the west wing. I found the body in a bedroom in the east wing."

"What body was that?"

"White male, naked, gunshot wound to the head, lying on white carpet soaked in blood."

"Was the body that of Clark McCall?"

"Yes, sir."

"You knew that from having met Clark McCall on a prior occasion?"

"Yes, sir."

"Did you check the body for vital signs?"

"No, sir."

"Why not?"

"From the appearance of the body, there was no question that the victim was dead and had been for some time. I didn't want to contaminate the evidence."

"And was that in accordance with your police training?"

"Uh, well, no, sir. That was in accordance with O.J.'s trial. They accused those L.A. cops of contaminating the evidence. I wasn't going there."

"So what did you do?"

"I stepped out of the room and called headquarters, talked to the chief. He called in the Feds. The FBI."

"Thank you, Sergeant James. No further questions."

Scott stood and went to the podium.

"Sergeant James, why did your chief call in the FBI?"

"He figured they had jurisdiction."

"Over a murder?"

"The victim was a federal official."

"You knew that at the time, when you were standing in his bedroom door?"

"Well, no, sir, I didn't know that. I guess the chief did."

"But you knew who the victim was?"

"Yes, sir."

"And how did you know Clark McCall?"

"Well, Clark McCall, he, uh, he had a history with us."

"A record?"

"Yes, sir."

"How long have you been with the Highland Park PD?"

"Twenty-three years this December."

"And had you ever personally arrested Clark McCall?"

"Yes, sir."

"On how many occasions?"

"Three that I recall."

"For what?"

"Disturbing the peace."

"What was he doing?"

"Drinking in public, when he was in high school."

"Is that all?"

"Drugs."

"Is that all?"

"One time he was standing naked in the SMU fountain."

"Was he ever arrested for a sexual crime?"

"Not that I'm aware of, sir."

341

"Was a complaint ever filed against Clark McCall alleging a sexual crime?"

"Not that I'm aware of."

"So, bottom line, your chief called in the Feds because he knew the victim was the son of Senator McCall?"

"Yes, sir. And because we'd never worked a homicide in Highland Park."

The next witness for the prosecution was the FBI agent first on the scene, Agent Paul Owen, fifty, ex-military with a soldier's bearing and haircut.

"Agent Owen," Ray Burns said, "you arrived at the McCall residence at what time?"

"Approximately two-thirty P.M."

"And what did you do?"

"I entered the residence, which Highland Park PD had secured, and went upstairs to the crime scene. I observed the victim's body lying on the floor. I commenced documenting the crime scene, and I called in the Evidence Response Team. They arrived at approximately three P.M."

"You were in charge of the investigation?"

"Yes, sir."

"And did you process the crime scene?"

"Yes, sir, we collected the evidence."

"And what evidence did you collect?"

"We cut out the carpet under and surrounding the body to obtain blood samples. We collected hair next to the body, fingerprints, various pieces of clothing, personal effects, the sheets off the bed, drinking glasses, a .22-caliber bullet imbedded in the floor, a .22-caliber pistol, and the body."

"And what did you do with this evidence?"

"The body went to the Dallas County medical examiner. The

rest of the evidence went to the FBI lab at Quantico, Virginia, for analysis."

"Did you conduct a luminol test to locate blood elsewhere in the room?"

"Yes, sir, we did."

"And did you find blood elsewhere?"

"No, sir."

"So the victim died where he was found?"

"Yes, sir. The body had not been moved."

"Did you immediately run a check on the fingerprints?"

"Yes, sir, we did that in Dallas."

"And did you get a match?"

"Yes, sir. The fingerprints on one of the drinking glasses and the pistol belonged to the defendant."

"Shawanda Jones?"

"Yes, sir."

"What did you do then?"

"We obtained an arrest warrant for Shawanda Jones."

"Did you make the arrest?"

"No, sir. I sent Agent Edwards."

"What did you do next?"

"I called next of kin."

"Senator McCall?"

"Yes, sir. I informed the senator that his son had been murdered in their residence."

"And what did Senator McCall say?"

"He asked how his son had been killed."

"And did you tell him?"

"Yes, sir."

"All right. Back to the crime scene, Agent Owen. Were photographs taken of the crime scene?"

"Yes, sir."

Ray Burns stepped over to Scott and handed him the four photographs he would show the jury. The crime scene photos had been the subject of heated pretrial arguments over their prejudicial effect on the jury. Burns wanted to introduce two dozen photos, but the judge had approved only these four, one of which was particularly graphic. Scott handed the photos to Karen, who was sitting next to him. She inhaled sharply. He forgot she hadn't seen the photos. Which reminded Scott; he twisted in his chair, caught the girls' attention, and gestured that it was time for them to lower their eyes. He knew the photos were coming and had discussed it with them on the drive over that morning. He told them to stare down at their feet until the photo show was over.

"Agent Owen, would you look at your computer screen and identify the photo being displayed to the jury on the overhead screen?"

Agent Owen turned in the witness chair to view the computer screen. Scott kept an eye on the jury box.

"This is the view of the crime scene from the bedroom door, as I first observed the scene. The bed is directly in front of the door, the bathroom over to the right, and the body over to the left. Only the victim's legs are visible in this photo."

"This is an accurate representation of the crime scene?"

"Yes, sir, it is."

The next photo came up on the overhead screen.

"Agent Owen, can you identify this photo?"

"This is a close shot of the bed, evidencing that it had recently been, uh, occupied."

"And is this an accurate representation of what you saw?"

"Yes, sir."

"And this photo?"

"The bathroom, and it is accurate."

"And finally, this photo."

A collective gasp went up in the courtroom. In the jury box, the two housewives averted their eyes, the bartender grimaced, and the car salesman stared. Ray Burns had displayed his climactic photo, a close-up of Clark McCall's body, his eyes open and vacant, a hole in his forehead, his head in a pool of blood.

"This is a close shot of the victim's body. He was naked, no wounds evident except about the head. There is apparent swelling around the right eye, some scratch marks on the face, and the entry wound in the left forehead."

Scott turned to the girls. They were staring down at their feet as instructed, but Pajamae's hat brim rose slightly; she was peeking. Scott snapped his fingers at her; she looked at him. Her expression said it was too late. She had seen the photo.

Ray allowed the gruesome image to sink into the jurors' minds before saying, "No more questions."

For the next thirty minutes, Bobby cross-examined Agent Owen about the toxicology reports, which showed alcohol and cocaine in Clark McCall's blood, so that the jurors would leave the courtroom that day with something on their mind other than the crime scene photos. After he passed the witness, Judge Buford adjourned for the day. Scott, Bobby, Karen, and the girls returned home; Senator McCall held a press conference on the courthouse steps. The senator spoke with the confidence of a man who knew his words would not be contradicted by Hannah Steele: "Clark was the kind of son every man dreams of having."

"Now, Scotty, don't get depressed," Bobby said through a mouthful of Chinese takeout. "The first day of a criminal trial is always bad. At least he didn't surprise us with anything."

"I'm not depressed about the prosecution's case, Bobby. I'm depressed about our defense. We've got nothing!"

They were at their designated places on the kitchen floor and the girls were at theirs.

"Carl's still working the case."

"Where the hell is he?"

"Del Rio."

"What's he doing down on the border?"

Bobby shrugged. "With Carl, you give him full rein and don't ask questions. He always finds something."

"I hope he finds something soon, Bobby, 'cause this isn't looking good."

Bobby stuck a little spare rib in his mouth, worked it over, pulled it out clean, and said, "Shit, Scotty, don't worry about today. Tomorrow's gonna be a lot worse."

Boo and Pajamae were already in bed when Scott entered their bedroom to say prayers.

After prayers, Pajamae said, "One night, a man got shot outside our apartment. When the po-lice came, Mama and me, we went outside. The dead man, he had a white sheet over him. I always wondered what he looked like, that dead man. Now I know."

"Pajamae, you promised not to look."

"I'm sorry, Mr. Fenney, but I had to. They're saying my mama killed that man. I had to look. But she didn't do it. You believe her, don't you, Mr. Fenney?"

Scott looked into her big brown eyes and lied, "Of course I do."

346

TWENTY-SEVEN

THE NEXT MORNING Scott and the girls walked unimpeded into the federal building. The reporters did not shout questions. Instead, from a respectful distance the cameras silently recorded the entrance of Shawanda Jones's lawyer and their daughters, dressed in smart short outfits, color-coordinated from head to toe. Boo, who had steadfastly refused to wear these outfits despite Rebecca's continuing threats, had meticulously selected their wardrobes; she knew it was important to look good for Pajamae's mother.

They again walked past Delroy Lund, looking like he hadn't moved since yesterday, except that he was holding the current day's sports section. They again entered the courtroom to heads turning their way, as if craning to see a bride's entrance into the church. They again walked to the front row, where Scott deposited the girls for the morning session. And Scott again exchanged glances with the McCalls and Dan Ford. Apparently his former senior partner wanted to witness his protégé's final defeat.

Scott soon learned that Bobby was right. The second day of the trial was a lot worse than the first day. The prosecution's first witness was the FBI agent who had made the arrest. Agent Andy Edwards, forty, professional in every way, testified on direct examination by Ray Burns that he had arrested Shawanda Jones at approximately six P.M. on Sunday, June 6, at her apartment in South Dallas; that he had advised her of her Miranda rights; and that his agents had executed a search warrant for her apartment, finding and taking into custody heroin packets, clothing, ten hundred-dollar bills, and a blonde wig.

He further testified that he had taken her to the federal detention center and that she had given a voluntary written statement admitting that she had been with the victim the night of Saturday, June 5, that she had engaged in sex with him at a mansion in Highland Park, that they had fought, that she had hit him, that she had taken the keys to his Mercedes and the thousand dollars he owed her, and that she had abandoned the car on Harry Hines Boulevard.

As Ray Burns left the podium and walked to his table, his eyes met Pajamae's; she made a face and stuck her tongue out at him. Ray just shook his head, but two jurors, the dental assistant and the teacher, smiled. So far the girls were the best thing the defense had going for it.

Scott stood and began his cross-examination.

"Agent Edwards, what was Ms. Jones doing when you arrived at her apartment?"

"Sitting on the front steps playing with her daughter."

Scott pointed to Pajamae in the first row.

"Is that her daughter?"

Agent Edwards looked at her and said, "Yes, sir, I believe she is."

"Did Ms. Jones attempt to run?"

"No, sir."

"Did she resist in any way?"

"No, sir."

"Did she exhibit the demeanor of a murderer?"

Ray Burns jumped out of his chair. "Objection. Calls for speculation."

Scott turned to the judge: "Your Honor, Agent Edwards is an experienced FBI agent who has arrested . . ." He turned back to the witness: "How many murderers have you arrested?"

"Dozens."

Back to the judge: "Who has arrested dozens of murderers. He knows the demeanor of a murderer."

"Overruled."

"Agent Edwards, did Shawanda Jones exhibit the demeanor of a murderer when you arrested her?"

"No, sir."

"Did you tell her she was being arrested for the murder of Clark McCall?"

"Yes, sir."

"And what did she say?"

"Who?"

"Ms. Jones."

"No, sir. That's what she said. 'Who?' I said Clark McCall and she said, 'Who?' "

"She didn't know who Clark McCall was?"

"Apparently not."

"And when Ms. Jones gave her written statement, did she personally write the statement, in her own hand?"

"No, sir. We had a stenographer take it, then type it up. Ms. Jones read it, I read it to her, and she signed it."

"I notice that in her statement she does not admit to killing Clark McCall. Did you ask her?"

"Yes, sir, I did. She denied it."

Ray Burns next called FBI Agent Wendell Lee, the crime lab analyst, to testify as to the results of his analysis of the evidence taken from the crime scene. Agent Lee was methodical, like an accountant giving a quarterly report. Burns took him through the FBI procedures for accepting evidence, logging it in, and maintaining an unbroken chain of evidence to prevent mix-ups. Then he got to the specifics.

"Agent Lee, the blood collected from the carpet removed from the crime scene was Clark McCall's blood?"

"Yes, sir. DNA tests were conclusive."

"The clump of hair, who did that belong to?"

"Clark McCall. Also confirmed by DNA tests."

"And what part of his body did that hair originate from?"

"His scalp." Agent Lee put his hand on his scalp above his right eye. "From this region. It was yanked out by the roots."

"What about the clothing?"

"We examined a blue polo shirt, jeans, and sneakers. Nothing was found on the clothing."

"And the bedsheets?"

"No semen was found on the sheets. We did remove a condom from the body with ejaculate present."

"Did you find anything else on the sheets?"

"Yes, sir, pubic hairs that matched Clark McCall's and synthetic blonde hair fibers."

"And did you match these fibers?"

"Yes, sir, we matched them to the blonde wig seized from the defendant's residence."

Ray Burns removed the blonde wig from a plastic evidence bag and held it up like a dead skunk.

"This wig, labeled government's exhibit fifteen?"

"Yes, sir."

"What about the fingerprints?"

"Fingerprints were lifted from the drinking glasses, bathroom countertop, the pistol, and the vehicle. All prints matched either Clark McCall or Shawanda Jones. The prints on the murder weapon matched only Shawanda Jones."

"Were there any unidentified prints?"

"No, sir."

"All right. Now to the murder weapon. The .22-caliber bullet retrieved from the bedroom floor—you ran ballistics tests on it?"

"Yes, sir. It was fired by the .22-caliber pistol found at the crime scene."

"So the bullet that killed Clark McCall was fired from Shawanda Jones's gun?"

"Yes, sir."

"No further questions."

Scott walked to the podium. "Agent Lee, the defendant's clothes were seized during the search of her residence, correct?"

"Yes, sir."

"Was Clark McCall's blood found on any of the defendant's clothes?"

"No, sir."

"Wouldn't you expect to have found his blood on her clothing if she had shot him at point-blank range?"

"Not if she was naked when she shot him."

After that disaster, Scott did not cross-examine Dr. Victor Urbina, the Dallas County medical examiner, who testified next as to the cause of death—"gunshot wound to the head"—and the time of death—"approximately ten-thirty P.M., Saturday, June fifth"—and the entry and exit wounds and angle of the bullet's path through the brain. He figured that cross-examination would only extend the time the evidence was in front of the jury, which couldn't be favorable to his client.

———

That day's picnic lunch featured egg salad sandwiches prepared by Pajamae Jones, wrapped in foil and kept cool in a cooler, along with Vanilla Coke, her favorite. After Scott summarized the morning's testimony for Shawanda, Pajamae said, "Mama, I stuck my tongue out at Mr. Burns."

"Pajamae, that ain't nice."

"Neither is he. You should hear the things he's saying about you, Mama. Your ears must be burning!"

"Shawanda," Scott asked, "are you feeling better? Up to testifying?"

"When?"

"Tomorrow."

After lunch, FBI Agent Henry Hu, a forensics expert, took the stand. After agreeing with the testimony of Dr. Urbina as to the angle of the bullet's path through Clark McCall's brain, Agent Hu, in a long, painstaking, and detailed direct examination, proceeded to offer his expert opinion as to how he believed the murder occurred, according to the forensics evidence and with the help of a graphic exhibit on which was depicted a human figure, halfway between lying down and kneeling up, and standing over him another human figure, holding a gun to the victim's head. Measurements were noted around the perimeter of the figures, with lines drawn to show various heights and angles and a dark line showing the path of the bullet from the gun, through the skull, and to its impact point in the floor. Dr. Hu pointed to the exhibit with a metal pointer as he testified.

"The victim was in a semi-kneeling position when he was shot. We believe that because, as you can see here, the bullet's path through the skull must align with the point at which the bullet impacted the floor. The victim was seventy-one inches tall. If he were standing when shot, the twenty-eight-degree downward angle of the bullet's path through the skull would require that the perpetrator hold the gun overhead and then shoot at a downward angle, a physically difficult act"—Agent Hu demonstrated the difficulty for the jury—"or that the perpetrator be unusually tall.

"So, if the victim were kneeling, the point of entry—his forehead—stands only fifty inches above the floor, still a little high. But if he's in a semi-kneeling position, as if he were getting up off the floor, with the point of entry approximately forty inches above the floor, which is the approximate height at which a normal-sized person would hold a gun in front of him, like this, give or take several inches"—Agent Hu again demonstrated for the jury—"then the bullet's path through the skull and the point of impact in the floor align precisely."

The jurors nodded in agreement with his analysis.

"We also know that the victim's hair was ripped out by the roots, which requires great force. This leads us to conclude that the murder occurred as follows: the victim was on the floor of the bedroom. The perpetrator grabbed the victim by the hair on the right side of his scalp and yanked him up to approximately forty inches off the floor. The perpetrator placed the barrel of the gun to the victim's forehead over his left eye and shot the victim. The force of the gun's discharge knocked the victim to the floor—which is consistent with the location in which the body was found—and extracted his hair from his scalp."

Clark McCall was a rapist, but he had died a horrible death. By the time Dr. Hu completed his testimony, the jurors were somber. Their sympathies may have been with the little black girl sitting in the front row, but they had to face facts; and the facts pointed to her mother as the murderer of Clark McCall. Ray Burns could barely suppress a grin when he stood and announced, "Your Honor, the prosecution rests."

Scott noticed that Ray turned and caught Senator McCall's eye; the senator nodded at Ray, obviously pleased with the prosecution of his son's killer. No doubt, he had told Ray Burns he would never forget this, particularly if Ray's name should ever come before the United States Senate for confirmation to a high government office.

Dan Ford caught Scott's eye; his ex–senior partner's expression asked a silent question: *You gave up your career for a murderer?*

Judge Buford adjourned for the day. Shawanda Jones's defense would begin at nine in the morning. Now all Scott had to do was come up with a defense.

Dinner on the kitchen floor was like a funeral reception.

"Everything Hu said is true," Bobby said, "except it doesn't prove Shawanda's guilt. Problem is, she was in that room with him that night, they fought, and her gun was the murder weapon. So any reasonable person would assume she did it. And without Hannah Steele to back up a claim of self-defense—which is unavailable so long as Shawanda refuses to admit to shooting Clark—we can't ask the jury to acquit her on that basis."

"So what's left?"

"We've got to answer one question for the jury, Scotty—what they want to know: Who killed Clark McCall? If Shawanda didn't, who did? Who came into that house right after she left, before Clark could get up off the floor and get dressed, picked up her gun, stuck it to Clark's head, and pulled the trigger?"

Scott shook his head. "Have you heard from Carl?"

"He'll call when he gets something."

"Well, he's got twelve hours to save us. Right now all we've got is Shawanda, her word against the evidence."

Pajamae said, "Mama's going to testify?"

"Yes, honey. She has to."

"What's she gonna wear?"

"I hadn't thought about that."

"We saved some of Mother's things at the yard sale," Boo said, "for Pajamae's mother. For when she gets out."

Scott turned to Karen. "Will you help the girls pick out some clothes?"

"Sure."

"At least she'll be nicely dressed."

They ate the take-out Mexican food in silence now. Scott absentmindedly watched the girls eat, wondering how Pajamae would handle life with her mother on death row and then life without her mother after the execution, when he noticed something: Boo was holding her fork in her left hand.

"Boo, come over here."

She got up off the floor and stepped over to him. Scott took the aluminum foil wrapping from his entrée and fashioned it into the shape of an *L*. An aluminum foil gun. He placed it on the floor.

"Please pick that up."

Boo frowned. "What's it supposed to be, a gun?"

"Yes."

She shrugged, leaned down, and picked up the foil gun with her left hand.

"Now grab my hair."

She stood directly in front of him and with her right hand grabbed his hair above his left eye.

"Now point the gun at my forehead like you're going to shoot me."

She put the barrel of the foil gun to Scott's forehead, above his right eye.

Bobby said, "Clark was shot above his left eye."

"By a right-handed killer."

Seeing Boo hold her fork with her left hand, Scott had remembered his first meeting with Shawanda, when she had held his pen with her left hand.

"Pajamae, your mother's left-handed, isn't she?"

"Yes, sir, Mr. Fenney, she sure is."

TWENTY-EIGHT

"THE DEFENSE CALLS FBI Agent Henry Hu."

Ray Burns was out of his chair.

"Your Honor, Mr. Fenney declined cross-examination of Agent Hu yesterday; now he's calling him as a defense witness?"

The judge looked at Scott: "Mr. Fenney?"

"That's exactly what I'm doing, Your Honor."

"Proceed."

Scott had been so sure that his client had killed Clark McCall that he had failed to ask a basic factual question of the government's forensic expert: Was the murderer right- or left-handed? He had been so sure his client was lying that he had failed to even consider that she might be telling the truth. Now, for the first time since he had been appointed to represent the defendant in *United States of America versus Shawanda Jones,* Scott knew his client was innocent. Shawanda Jones did not kill Clark McCall.

But then, who did?

Agent Hu took the stand, with the judge reminding him that he was still under oath, and Scott said, "Agent Hu, your testimony yesterday was quite illuminating, and I mean that as a compliment."

"Thank you."

"If you don't mind, I'd like to reenact for the jury the manner in which you believe Clark McCall was murdered."

"Certainly."

"My cocounsel, Mr. Herrin, will assist. Bobby, if you'll kneel on the floor."

Bobby walked over and knelt in front of Scott.

"Now, Agent Hu, your testimony is that Clark was halfway between lying and kneeling on the floor like Mr. Herrin is here when he was shot, correct?"

"Yes."

"And the killer was facing Clark, as I am now, correct?"

"Yes."

"And the killer grabbed Clark's hair on the right side of his scalp, like this?"

Scott grabbed Bobby's hair with his left hand.

"Yes."

"And the killer than stuck the gun to Clark's forehead above his left eye, like this?"

Scott fashioned his right hand like a gun and stuck his index finger to Bobby's forehead.

"And the killer then shot Clark?"

"Yes. That is how I believe the crime occurred."

"Well, I agree with you. But doesn't this demonstration prove something else, something important about the killer?"

Agent Hu frowned. "I'm sorry?"

"The killer was right-handed."

Agent Hu's expression revealed his realization. "Yes, most likely the killer would have been right-handed."

"The killer grabbed Clark's hair with his left hand and held the gun with his right hand, correct?"

"Yes, that would be correct."

"One other thing, Agent Hu. The medical examiner testified that there was a contusion around Clark's right eye, as if he had been hit with a fist."

"Yes, there was."

"As a forensic expert, is it more likely that the person who hit Clark's eye was right- or left-handed?"

"Left-handed."

"So the person who punched Clark McCall was left-handed, but the person who shot him was right-handed?"

"Yes, that would be the most likely scenario."

Scott called FBI Agent Edwards to the stand again.

"Agent Edwards, you testified that you arrested the defendant?"

"Yes, sir."

"And that you took her statement?"

"Yes, sir."

"You typed what she said?"

"Yes, sir."

"And then she read it over and signed it?"

"Yes, sir."

"With which hand did she sign her statement?"

Agent Edwards thought for a moment, then said, "Her left hand."

The jurors had yet to see the defendant in person. They had seen her mug shots and pictures in the newspapers and on television, but they had not seen her. And they needed to see her and hear her, to listen and watch as she denied killing Clark McCall. Scott knew he had to put Shawanda on the stand, the Fifth Amendment to the Constitution notwithstanding, but he wanted to give her the best possible chance of success. So he had done two things: he had persuaded the judge to allow her methadone treatment, and he had kept her out of court until this moment.

Now all eyes—those of the judge and the jurors and the prosecutors and the spectators—were focused on the door at the side of the courtroom, anxiously awaiting the arrival of Shawanda Jones. Boo and Pajamae and Karen had been allowed in her cell—after being searched by a female guard—to help Shawanda get dressed. They had come into the courtroom a few minutes ago. Boo gave Scott another thumbs-up.

The door opened and a murmur ran through the room. Shawanda did not look like the heroin addict Scott had seen earlier that morning; she looked stunning and young. Scott had forgotten she was only twenty-four, the heroin had aged her so. But today she had recaptured her youth. She was wearing Rebecca's navy blue suit, Rebecca's high heels, and Rebecca's makeup; her hair was fluffed lightly and brushed smooth; her eyes were sharp and alert. She looked at Scott and smiled. Shawanda looked like Halle Berry on a very good day.

The jurors' eyes followed her as Ron escorted her over to the defendant's table and pulled out her chair. She sat daintily and Ron pushed her chair in. She turned and looked at each juror, one by one, and they looked at her. Their first impression was a good one. Scott glanced back at the McCalls: the senator's face revealed his worry, Jean's face her jealousy. Beside them, Dan Ford's face showed renewed interest in the proceeding.

Scott stood and said, "The defense calls Shawanda Jones."

Shawanda stood and walked to the witness stand, took the oath, and sat down. Scott stood at the podium.

"Ms. Jones," he said, "are you left-handed?"

"Yes, sir."

"Did you kill Clark McCall?"

"No, sir, Mr. Fenney. I did not."

"All right, Ms. Jones, let's talk about your life. Where were you born?"

"In the projects."

"The projects in South Dallas, same place you now reside?"

"Yes, sir."

"What was your mother's name?"

"My mama, she was called Dorena."

"What was your father's name?"

"Mr. Fenney, you know I don't know that."

"Your mother and father, they weren't married?"

"No, sir. My daddy, he was a white man my mama worked for. She cleaned his office."

"Okay, so you were born illegitimate?"

"No, sir, I was born in a hospital, Parkland."

"Uh, okay. You never knew your father, correct?"

"No, sir."

"You grew up in the projects?"

"Yes, sir."

"Your mother died when you were thirteen?"

"Something like that."

"What did she die of?"

"No doctor."

"No, I mean, did she die of cancer or what?"

"No, sir, she died 'cause she ain't got no doctor. She fall over and we call for the ambulance and no one come."

"And so you raised yourself."

"Yes, sir."

"And you fell in with a bad crowd."

"Only crowd we got in the projects, Mr. Fenney. People got nothing to do, they get in trouble."

"And you got in trouble."

"Eddie, he my trouble."

"Eddie was your child's father?"

"Yes, sir. White man selling dope in the projects, seen me one day, when I was fourteen. He like what he seen, so he give me some dope and I let him touch me."

"And Eddie gave you heroin?"

"Yes, sir."

"And you became addicted at age sixteen?"

"Yes, sir."

"And by that time you were a prostitute?"

"Yes, sir."

"Why?"

Her eyes dropped. "Mens, they think they gonna find all they been missing in they lives between Shawanda's legs. Ain't so." She looked up. "It the only thing men ever want from me."

"Ms. Jones, do you have a daughter?"

"Why, you know that, Mr. Fenney. She staying with you."

The teacher and the housewives smiled. Scott turned to Pajamae behind him and gestured for her to stand. Pajamae stood, the most innocent expression imaginable on her face.

"Is she your daughter?"

"Yes, sir, that my baby."

Pajamae turned to the jury and curtsied. Now every juror was smiling. The kid was good.

They broke for lunch before beginning Shawanda's testimony about the night Clark McCall was murdered. Shawanda was not sitting on the floor with the girls, but at the table with Scott and Bobby and Karen, being very careful not to spill tuna fish on her Neiman Marcus suit.

"We've got a really pretty outfit for you to wear tomorrow, Mama," Pajamae said from the floor.

"How I do, Mr. Fenney?"

"Fine, Shawanda. But the hard part's this afternoon."

"Think they gonna believe me?"

He thought no but said yes.

"Ms. Jones," Scott said, "let's go back to Saturday, June fifth. Did you take heroin that day?"

"I was alive, so I must have."

"You took it every day?"

"Two, three time."

"So before you went to work that night, you injected heroin?"

"Yes, sir. Make it easier that way."

"Make what easier?"

"Sex."

"All right, then Kiki, another prostitute, came by and the two of you drove over to Harry Hines Boulevard?"

"Yes, sir, our regular location."

"And you waited for men to come by?"

"We never wait too long."

"And did Clark McCall come by?"

"Yes, sir, but I don't know him. He just a white boy in a black Mercedes."

"And he offered you one thousand dollars to spend the night with him?"

"Yes, sir."

"Oh, before Clark, did you, uh, work for another client?"

"No, sir, I don't work for no one. I'm self-employed."

"I mean, did anyone else pay you for a sex act that night?"

"I give a blow to a cop, but he don't pay."

"You engaged in oral sex with a police officer?"

"Yes, sir, Mr. Fenney, that way he don't bother us. Me and Kiki, we take turns with the cops. They freebies."

"Okay, so back to Clark McCall. You got into his car and he drove you to his mansion in Highland Park?"

"Yes, sir."

"And you went inside?"

"Yes, sir."

"And upstairs to his bedroom?"

"Yes, sir."

"Tell the jury what happened then."

Shawanda turned to the jurors and told them the story of that night without shame or guilt, just as a matter of fact. That she and Clark engaged in sex, after, that is, she made him put on a condom—"I can't get that AIDS. I gotta take care of my Pajamae"—that he became rough, started slapping her, calling her nigger, that she scratched and punched him in the eye and kicked him in his balls, that he fell to the floor, and that she took her thousand dollars and his car keys, drove herself back to Harry Hines, and abandoned the car.

"And Clark McCall was alive the last time you saw him?"

"Yes, sir, he sure was, cussing me like a redheaded stepchild."

"What did you and Kiki do then?"

"Go home, go to bed."

"What did you do the next morning, Sunday?"

"Got up, fixed breakfast for Pajamae, go to church."

"You went to church?"

She had a bemused expression. "Mr. Fenney, without sinners, no need for churches."

The jurors smiled at that remark.

"And what were you doing when the FBI came to arrest you?"

"Sitting outside on the stoop, watching Pajamae."

"Did you know why they were arresting you?"

"They say for killing some man. I said, I don't kill no one. They don't believe me."

"No further questions, Your Honor."

Ray Burns nearly knocked Scott down, he was in such a hurry to cross-examine Shawanda.

"Ms. Jones, you're a prostitute, correct?"

"Yes, sir."

"And a heroin addict?"

"Yes, sir."

"And you were with Clark McCall the night he was murdered?"

"That what the police say. I don't know when he be killed."

"He picked you up for sex, is that correct?"

"Yes, sir."

"He offered you a thousand dollars for the night?"

"Yes, sir."

"You got into his car, a Mercedes-Benz, correct?"

"Yes, sir."

"He drove you to his home?"

"Yes, sir."

"You went upstairs, he gave you alcohol to drink?"

"Yes, sir."

"He removed his clothes, you removed your clothes, and you and Clark McCall engaged in sexual intercourse, correct?"

"Yes, sir."

"And then you hit him in the eye?"

"Only 'cause he slap me and call me nigger."

"And you kicked him in the groin?"

"No, sir, I didn't kick his growing, I kick his balls."

"Okay, his balls."

" 'Cause he be coming after me again."

"And then you grabbed your gun and you shot him?"

"No, sir, I didn't shoot no one."

"You know your gun was the murder weapon?"

"I don't know no such thing. You say that."

Ray Burns picked up the .22-caliber pistol.

"This is your gun, isn't it?"

"Yes, sir."

"And why do you carry a gun?"

"You live in the projects, you die of old age waiting for the police to come when someone trying to get in your place."

"You shot Clark McCall, didn't you?"

"No, sir. I didn't shoot no one."

"And you stole a thousand dollars from him?"

"No, sir. I earned it."

"And you stole his car?"

"No, sir. I borrowed it, to get back where I belonged."

"To flee the scene of the crime?"

"To get away before he hit me again."

"And you went home to your daughter like nothing happened?"

" 'Cause nothing happened."

"Ms. Jones, do you really expect this jury to believe you?"

Shawanda looked at the jurors and said in a soft voice: "No, sir, I don't expect no one gonna believe me."

On his way upstairs to tuck the girls in for the night, Scott stopped at the small TV on the kitchen counter where the late news was replaying the day's events at the trial. An artist's sketch of Shawanda was on the screen. The reporter said that the defendant was quite beautiful and had comported herself well on the stand. The jurors, he said, were attentive and respectful and, by the end of the day, thoroughly confused by the idea of a killer who was probably right-handed and a defendant who was certainly left-handed. "If Shawanda Jones didn't kill Clark McCall," the reporter asked, "who did?"

Upstairs, Scott was leaning over the bed, tucking the girls in, when Pajamae said softly, "Mr. Fenney, I know what my mama does now, with her tricks."

"You do?"

She nodded. "Mama lets them touch her private parts, put their private parts in hers. That's what sex is, isn't it, Mr. Fenney?"

"Yes, it is."

"Why, Mr. Fenney? Mama always tells me never ever to let a boy touch my private parts. Why does she let men touch hers?"

"It's like you said, Pajamae: she loves you, but she doesn't love herself."

"Mama, she's had a sad life, hasn't she, Mr. Fenney?"

"Yes, she has."

"Now I know why she's so sad always. She's never had anyone who loved her all over, not just her private parts."

"No, she hasn't."

"But she looked pretty today, didn't she?"

"Very pretty."

"Pretty enough to marry?"

Boo sat up. "A. Scott, we want to live together, with you and her mother. Wouldn't that be a wonderfully happy ending?"

Scott sat on the edge of the bed. So many times he had fudged the truth with Boo, but after three days of a murder trial, she and Pajamae could handle the truth.

"Girls, happy endings happen in fairy tales, not in real life."

TWENTY-NINE

SHAWANDA LOOKED equally stunning the next morning in Rebecca's tan suit. Scott was standing beside her in the courtroom, all eyes on him but his eyes on her. She had told him the truth. But Scott was her lawyer and he knew, as all lawyers know, that the truth seldom prevails in a court of law. Bobby was right. When the jurors retired to decide Shawanda's fate, they would ask each other one question: If Shawanda Jones didn't kill Clark McCall, who did? They needed an answer. But Scott didn't have an answer. He didn't even have a clue.

So he went fishing. When a lawyer takes a deposition in civil litigation and doesn't have a clue, he goes fishing. He asks every imaginable question and then some, hoping the witness will slip up and tell him something he didn't know. It never works. But Scott threw out his fishing net anyway.

"The defense calls Mack McCall."

Ray Burns exploded out of his chair. "Objection. Senator McCall is not on the witness list."

"That's true, Mr. Fenney," the judge said. "Do you have a good reason for calling a witness who is not on the list?"

"Yes, sir. Mr. Burns is trying to have my client executed. I'd like to keep him from doing that."

Judge Buford's mouth turned up in half a smile. "Very well. Overruled."

Senator McCall slowly rose from his seat in the second row of the spectator section, adjusted his coat and tie, and walked past Scott without so much as a glance. After taking the oath, he sat in the witness chair as if he were having his portrait taken.

"Senator McCall, your son had a history of alcohol and drug abuse, is that correct?"

"Clark had some problems with substance abuse, but he had overcome them."

"Did he also have some problems with rape?"

"I'm sorry, I don't understand the question."

"Do you know a woman named Hannah Steele?"

"No, I don't."

"Have you ever heard that name, Hannah Steele?"

"No, I haven't."

"Have you ever paid money to someone named Hannah Steele?"

"No."

"Are you aware that Hannah Steele filed a criminal complaint against Clark a year ago, alleging that he had beaten and raped her?"

"I'm not aware of any such thing. Do you have a copy of this complaint?"

"Senator McCall, did you pay Hannah Steele five hundred thousand dollars to drop her rape complaint against Clark and move out of Dallas?"

The senator stared directly at Scott and did what only a politician could do better than a lawyer. He lied.

"Of course not."

"Did you pay six other women to drop their rape complaints against Clark?"

"Do you have any names to go with your allegations, Mr. Fenney? You made these false statements on national TV, but you have no evidence to back up your allegations, do you?"

Scott glanced over at Dan Ford. His former father figure and senior partner sat there without any outward acknowledgment that a U.S. senator was committing perjury. Dan Ford knew the women's names because he had personally paid off all seven. But, as Scott well knew, the attorney-client privilege allowed an attorney to hide his clients' misdeeds, everything from letting lead leach into a river to committing perjury in a federal court; so Dan Ford remained silent. Scott turned back to McCall.

"Answer the question, Senator."

"No, I did not pay other women."

"Did Clark have an apartment in Washington?"

"Yes, he did."

"He lived there when he was in Washington tending to FERC business?"

"Yes."

"Did you expect Clark to attend your campaign kickoff on Monday, June seventh, in Washington?"

"Yes. He said he'd be there."

"Did you know Clark had come to Dallas on Saturday, June fifth?"

"No. Not until the FBI called."

"Were you surprised to learn he was in Dallas?"

"I was surprised to learn he was dead."

"Clark returned to Dallas often?"

"Yes. He didn't like Washington."

371

"Clark would just fly back to Dallas on a whim, without telling you?"

"Yes. Clark was . . . impulsive."

"And when he was in Dallas, he lived in your Highland Park mansion?"

"Yes."

"Do you know Delroy Lund?"

"Yes, I do."

"Is he an employee of yours?"

"Yes, he is."

"What does he do for you?"

"He's my bodyguard."

"Is that all he does, provide physical protection?"

"Sometimes he carries my luggage. Bad back."

"Does he bribe witnesses for you?"

"No, he does not."

"Did he bribe Hannah Steele for you?"

"No, he did not."

"Did you send him to bribe my cocounsel, Bobby Herrin?"

"No, I did not. I don't even know who Mr. Herrin is. Would you point him out?"

Bobby was not at the defendant's table. He had gotten a message on his cell phone and had run out of the courtroom at the first opportunity.

Ray Burns stood. "Your Honor, is Mr. Fenney going to spend the morning insulting the senior senator from Texas or is he going to ask questions relevant to this murder case?"

"Do you have an objection, Mr. Burns?"

"Objection, irrelevant."

"Overruled." The judge turned to Scott. "Mr. Fenney, please tie the senator's testimony to this case."

Scott was thinking, *I wish I knew how*, when the courtroom

doors opened and Bobby entered. He gave Scott a time-out gesture. Scott asked the judge for a fifteen-minute recess.

Scott walked out of the courtroom with Bobby and down the corridor to where Carl Kincaid was leaning against the wall and holding a large yellow envelope. Carl was long and lanky and wore a plaid sports coat over a golf shirt. When they arrived, Carl handed the envelope to Scott. Scott removed and examined the contents. Then he looked back at Carl.

"You know what this means?" Scott asked.

"I think I do," Carl said. "He's dirty."

"How did you get all this?"

Carl smiled. "I won't tell you how to bribe judges if you don't tell me how to do my job."

When the court reconvened, Scott knew how Senator McCall was tied to the murder of his son: by his bodyguard.

"Your Honor, the defense calls Delroy Lund."

"You have no further questions for Senator McCall?"

"No, sir."

"Very well."

The judge nodded at the bailiff, who went outside. When the courtroom doors opened, Delroy Lund strode in like the ex-Fed he was. He was a big man and carried an attitude with him; clearly he was a cop who had banged a few heads together in his day. He walked up to the witness stand and took the oath. Then he sat down, leaned back, and crossed his legs, right ankle over left knee, like he owned the damn place. Scott saw his effect on the jurors: before he had said one word, they hated him. Which made at least thirteen people in this courtroom who hated Delroy Lund.

"We meet again, Mr. Lund."

Scott first elicited from Delroy his background: He was fifty-one years old, born and raised in Victoria, Texas, college at Texas A&I, street cop in Houston for three years, then twenty years with the DEA, working in South Texas, fighting the war on drugs. Divorced, no children. Six years ago, he had retired to Senator McCall's payroll.

"Mr. Lund, did you ever frame a suspect?"

"Nope."

"Ever plant dope in a suspect's home or car?"

"Nope."

"Ever beat up a suspect?"

"Nope."

But his eyes said yep. And the Hispanic and black jurors saw the truth in his eyes.

"You ever kill anyone?"

"Yeah."

"How many?"

"Nine I'm sure of."

"Might be more?"

"When you're in a firefight with the Mexican drug cartels, you don't stop to count."

"Did you ever kill anyone up close and personal, face-to-face?"

"Yeah."

"When and where?"

"Laredo, 1994."

"What were the circumstances?"

"I was a DEA agent. He was a drug trafficker. He didn't want to go to jail. He pulled a gun on me, I shot him first."

The jury knew Delroy Lund was capable of killing.

"How did you feel afterward?"

"Happy. He was dead; I was alive."

"Mr. Lund, that wasn't the only time you killed someone up close, was it?"

Delroy's eyes narrowed. "You talking about Del Rio?"

"Yes."

"I was completely exonerated."

"Being no-billed by the grand jury isn't the same as being exonerated, Mr. Lund. It only means there wasn't sufficient evidence to prosecute."

Ray Burns stood. "Objection. Irrelevant. Your Honor, Mr. Lund is not on trial here today."

Scott said, "Maybe he should be."

"Overruled," the judge said.

Scott turned back to the witness. "Mr. Lund, what happened the night of March thirteenth, 1998, in Del Rio, Texas?"

"I shot a suspect during a confrontation with drug dealers."

"You shot a sixteen-year-old boy."

"He looked older."

Scott picked up Carl's envelope, removed the documents, and placed them on the podium. When his background check of Delroy Lund had revealed reprimands for unnecessary use of force, Carl had decided to dig deeper. He found more dirt.

"Mr. Lund, the internal DEA incident report—"

"That's supposed to be confidential. How'd you get that?"

"Sorry, attorney-client privilege, Mr. Lund. As I was saying, the internal DEA report states that on the night in question, you approached a group of Mexican nationals, approximately a dozen boys and girls, outside a bar in downtown Del Rio after observing them selling drugs. At least that was your story. Witnesses said you were drunk and propositioned one of the Mexican girls."

"They lied."

"In any event, an altercation ensued and when it was over, you had shot and killed an unarmed sixteen-year-old boy."

"He was going for a gun."

"The report says no gun was found at the scene."

"His *amigos* took it when they ran off."

"Did the boy mouth off to you, Mr. Lund, is that how the confrontation started?"

"The suspect refused to obey my orders. He got in my face. Things got out of hand."

"Things got out of hand?"

"Yeah. It happens."

"It seems to happen a lot with you, Mr. Lund. Your record shows nine deadly shootings, numerous other questionable discharges of your firearm, a dozen reprimands for unnecessary use of force, internal affairs investigations for freelancing, running interdiction operations without agency approval—you put together quite a career at the DEA, Mr. Lund."

Delroy shook his head with disdain. "Civilians. Mr. Fenney, the war on drugs ain't gin rummy at the country club. Mexican drug cartels are violent and ruthless narco-terrorists. They've killed over a hundred women in Juárez, many of them young American girls. They've kidnapped and killed dozens of American tourists in Nuevo Laredo and dumped their bodies in the Rio Grande. They've murdered border patrol agents and Catholic priests who spoke out against them. They own the police throughout Mexico and those they don't own they kill. You want people like them running around Dallas? People like me, Mr. Fenney, we keep people like them on their side of the river."

"That may be true, Mr. Lund, but the fact is your superiors at the DEA grew tired of your practices, didn't they?"

"Bunch of desk jockeys who couldn't cut it on the border."

"Shortly after that incident in Del Rio, you were forced to retire from the DEA?"

"Yeah. By bureaucrats more concerned about getting promotions than results. I got results."

"You got results with Hannah Steele, too, didn't you?"

"I don't know what you're talking about."

"Mr. Lund, did you bribe Hannah Steele to absent herself from this trial?"

"Nope."

"Did you threaten to make her fish bait?"

"I don't fish."

"Answer the question."

"No, I did not threaten anyone."

"Do you know Hannah Steele?"

"Nope."

"Did you attempt to bribe my cocounsel, Robert Herrin, to drop out of this case?"

"Nope."

"You didn't offer him a hundred thousand dollars?"

"Nope."

"Did you know Clark McCall?"

"Yeah."

"What did you think of him?"

"Honestly?"

"Why not, we're in a court of law."

"He was a little fu . . ." Delroy stopped and glanced past Scott to Senator McCall.

"A little fuckup? Isn't that what you called Clark? Isn't that the term you used to describe him?"

Delroy looked back at Scott and said, "He was a real nice boy."

"A real nice boy who liked to beat and rape girls?"

"I don't know anything about that."

"Where were you on the night of Saturday, June fifth, of this year?"

"D.C."

"Washington, D.C.?"

"Yeah."

"You're sure?"

"Yeah."

Scott picked up another document from Carl's envelope. "Mr. Lund, I have a copy of a first-class plane ticket from Washington to Dallas, flight number 1607 on American at eight-twenty-three A.M. on Saturday, June the fifth, in the name of Clark McCall."

"So?"

Scott picked up the next document. "So I also have a copy of another first-class plane ticket from Washington to Dallas, at eight-thirty A.M. on the same day, flight number 1815 on US Airways. It has your name on it."

Delroy didn't blink an eye. "Must be a mistake."

"You think there's another Delroy Lund running around out there?"

"You never know."

"Clark's flight was booked at four-thirty-seven P.M. on June fourth. Your flight was booked twenty-eight minutes later. You had someone in Clark's office keeping tabs on him, didn't you?"

"Nope."

"May I see your driver's license?"

"What?"

"Your driver's license, would you please produce it?"

The slightest hint of unease invaded Delroy's dark eyes. He leaned slightly to his left and reached around to his right back pant pocket. He pulled out his wallet, removed his license, and somewhat reluctantly held it out to Scott.

"Your Honor, may I approach the witness?"

Judge Buford nodded. Scott walked over, took the license, and walked back to the podium. He compared the license to the next document.

"Mr. Lund, you're sure this isn't your plane ticket?"

"Yeah."

"And you're sure you weren't in Dallas on June fifth?"

"Yeah."

Scott held up the document. "Well, then how do you explain this rental car agreement with Avis at the Dallas airport dated June fifth with your signature and driver's license number on it?"

Delroy uncrossed his legs. His eyes turned down. His expression did not change, but his jaw muscles began flexing rapidly, like he was grinding his teeth into chalk. A thin sheen of sweat glistened on his broad forehead. He was lying and everyone in the courtroom knew it. He knew that they knew it, and that he was on the verge of a perjury charge. But Delroy Lund hadn't gone toe to toe with Mexican drug lords without having brass balls. His faced turned up, he looked Scott straight in the eye, and he said, "You know what, now that you remind me, I was in Dallas that day. I forgot."

"You forgot?"

"Yeah, I forgot."

"Okay, Mr. Lund, we'll go with that. You arrived in Dallas on Saturday, June fifth, at eleven A.M. and you left Sunday afternoon on US Airways flight number 1812 at four-fifty-five P.M.?"

"Sounds about right."

"So why did you come to Dallas for just thirty hours?"

Delroy grinned. "To get laid. To pick up a two-bit hooker"— he gestured at Shawanda—"like Blondie there and get laid."

"Mr. Lund, do you usually carry a handkerchief?"

"Yeah. Allergies."

"May I see it?"

He reached back, pulled a handkerchief out of his pocket, and held it out to Scott.

"Keep it."

Scott walked over to the defendant's table to get a pad and pen. He looked at Shawanda and froze . . . her hair was brown. Not blonde like the . . . Scott glanced over at the prosecution table . . . wig. The wig she had been wearing that night was blonde. Delroy just called Shawanda "Blondie." Delroy had been there that night.

Delroy Lund murdered Clark McCall.

Scott's adrenaline pump kicked in like an overdrive. His mind started working fast. The murderer was sitting in the witness chair ten feet away, but Scott had nothing to tie this man to that crime. Delroy Lund was an experienced lawman; he had left no incriminating evidence at the crime scene. Scott's only hope was to get Delroy to confess on the stand, to break down and blurt out the truth, to tell the world that he had murdered Clark McCall. A Perry Mason moment. A moment lawyers dream of. A moment that happens only on TV and in the movies.

Scott walked over to the witness stand and placed the pad and pen in front of Delroy.

"Mr. Lund, would you please sign your name?"

Delroy shrugged, picked up the pen with his right hand, and signed his name.

"You're right-handed, Mr. Lund."

"Yeah, so what?"

"So the FBI's forensic expert testified that the person who shot Clark McCall was right-handed. You're right-handed, the murderer was right-handed. The murder occurred in Dallas on June fifth, you were in Dallas on June fifth."

"Ninety percent of the people in this room are right-handed. And more than that were in Dallas on June fifth."

"Yes, but none of them had a reason to kill Clark McCall, did they?"

"You'll have to ask them."

"I'll ask you: Did you kill Clark McCall?"

The judge was studying the witness when Ray Burns stood to object. "Your Honor—"

"Sit, Mr. Burns," the judge said without removing his gaze from Delroy. Ray sat. "Answer the question, Mr. Lund."

Delroy said, "No, I didn't kill Clark. Why would I want him dead? I work for his dad."

"Who wants to be president."

"So?"

"So if it became known that his son used cocaine and engaged prostitutes and maybe even raped a few girls, Senator McCall's chances of getting into the White House would be about as good as the defendant's, isn't that true?"

Delroy snorted. "Give me a fuckin' break."

The judge: "Mr. Lund, watch your language."

Delroy said, "Hell, if having a screwup for a kid was a motive for murder, half the politicians in D.C. would've already killed their kids. I don't know nothing about rapes, but you think Clark was the only politician's kid out drinking and doing drugs and other stuff their daddies want to keep quiet? The town's full of 'em, rich kids who had life handed to them on a silver platter then shit on it."

"Mr. Lund, why did you decide to get laid in Dallas on June fifth?"

Delroy shrugged. "Most beautiful women in the world are in Dallas."

"That may be true, but you work for Senator McCall in Washington. Certainly you could have found an acceptable prostitute in the nation's capital so you could remain in town, especially since two days later, on June seventh, the senator was scheduled to announce his campaign for the presidency. But instead of staying in D.C., you came to Dallas on June fifth to get laid, on the same day Clark came to Dallas? Mr. Lund, did you come specifically to kill Clark?"

Delroy sighed. "I said, I didn't kill Clark."

"Then why did you come to Dallas? Why did you leave Washington two days before Senator McCall's big day? Why did you fly down to Dallas to pick up a prostitute instead of staying in Washington and protecting the senator—"

It hit Scott.

"That's it, isn't it?"

"What?"

"It's just that simple, isn't it?"

"What are you talking about?"

"You didn't come here to kill Clark. You came to Dallas to protect Senator McCall."

"I don't know what the hell you're talking about."

"Mr. Lund, what usually happened when Clark was in Dallas?"

"I give, what?"

"He got in trouble. He always came home to get into trouble. Fact is, Clark was smart enough to get in trouble *only* in Dallas, because here his daddy could buy his way out of anything. The McCall name means something in Dallas. The McCall money can buy anything in Dallas—even seven rape victims."

"Like I said, I don't know anything about that."

"And the last thing Senator McCall needed right before he announced for the presidency was Clark getting arrested, and not just for drinking or drugs—like you said, that's common. But getting charged with rape, that's not so common, is it? Particularly for the son of the next president. The press would go into a feeding frenzy, maybe even dredge up the other girls. The senator had spent millions to keep Clark's past hidden so it wouldn't ruin his political future. And now the presidency was his, he had a commanding lead in the polls, his dream was about to come true . . . and what was the only thing that could lose the White House for him before he had even won it? A rapist for a son. That would do it. That would destroy Senator McCall's dream, wouldn't it?"

Scott pointed back at the senator in the spectator section.

"When Senator McCall learned that Clark was coming to Dallas right before his big announcement, he sent you here to follow Clark, to keep him out of trouble."

Scott held up another document from Carl's envelope.

"Clark had booked a return flight to Washington on June sixth at three-twenty-one P.M. so he would be back for his father's campaign kickoff. The senator knew that if Clark was flying to Dallas just for a Saturday night, that meant only one thing: his demons were calling again and he was answering. He was coming home to get drunk and stoned and pick up a girl. And the senator knew what usually happened when Clark's dark side took over—exactly what he couldn't let happen. He couldn't wake up Sunday morning and read that his son had been arrested for beating and raping another girl in Dallas. So he sent you to Dallas to make sure that didn't happen. Your job was to wet-nurse Clark, to be his guardian angel, to keep him out of trouble and out of the press. You came to Dallas to protect Senator McCall from his own son."

Delroy's eyes again looked past Scott to McCall. Scott turned to McCall as well, and what he saw surprised him. In the senator's eyes and on the senator's face Scott saw that he had it exactly wrong. He turned back to Delroy.

"The senator didn't send you, did he? You freelanced this one. You ran this operation without his approval. Why? Why didn't you tell the senator? Did you think it best to keep him out of the loop? Did you just not want to bother him right before his big day?" Scott shook his head. "Either way, you came here to make sure Clark didn't screw things up for his father. That's why you came to Dallas on Saturday, June the fifth, isn't it, Mr. Lund?"

"No."

"You flew to Dallas, you rented a car, you followed Clark that night, didn't you?"

"No."

"You followed him down to Harry Hines where the prostitutes hang out, didn't you?"

"No."

"And there you watched Clark pull his Mercedes over to two black girls, one wearing a red wig, the other a blonde wig, isn't that right?"

"No."

"The girl in the blonde wig got into Clark's car, didn't she?"

"I don't know."

"That girl was the defendant, wasn't she?"

"I don't know."

"Then why did you just refer to the defendant as 'Blondie'?"

"I . . ."

"Her hair isn't blonde, Mr. Lund, it's brown. She hasn't worn her blonde wig since that night. She's been in jail, Mr. Lund."

Scott stepped to the prosecution table, removed the blonde wig from the evidence bag, and handed it to Shawanda.

"Your Honor, may the defendant put on the wig?"

"Yes."

Shawanda pulled the wig on. Scott returned to the podium and pointed at Shawanda.

"Mr. Lund, you saw the defendant wearing *that* wig *that* night—that's the only way you'd know to call her 'Blondie.' You saw her get into Clark's car. You followed them to the McCall mansion in Highland Park. You parked out of sight on the estate. You figured Clark couldn't get into too much trouble with a black hooker. Oh, he might slap her around, but what's she gonna do, call the cops? She wasn't an SMU coed, she was just a hooker. So you sat outside while Clark had his fun.

"But then you saw the defendant drive off in Clark's Mercedes. You ran inside and upstairs to Clark's bedroom and you found Clark lying naked on the floor and holding his balls. And you . . .

you laughed at him. The little rich boy got kneed in the balls by a black hooker, that was pretty damn funny. So you laughed at Clark. You mocked him. Did you call him a little fuckup?"

"I wasn't there."

"Clark didn't like that, did he, someone like you mocking him? You were just an employee, and employees don't mock Clark McCall. So he cursed you. You outweighed him by, what, a hundred pounds? But the alcohol and cocaine made him brave and getting beat up by a hooker made him mad, so he cursed you just like he cursed her. And then he . . . what? What else did he say to you? What could he say that would make you want to kill him?"

Scott snapped his fingers and pointed at Delroy.

"He threatened to get you fired. He was gonna tell Daddy and get you fired. Now, maybe he could, maybe he couldn't, but you couldn't take the chance. Because what would you do if he did get you fired, go back to the DEA? Not with your record. Your job prospects weren't exactly bright, were they, Mr. Lund? Hell, if you got fired, your best hope for a job would be as a security guard at Wal-Mart. Delroy Lund, former big-shot DEA agent chasing Mexican drug lords on the border reduced to chasing shoplifters in a parking lot. That was your future without Senator McCall, wasn't it? And that pissed you off, didn't it, that little rich boy lying naked there on the floor, threatening your future? That little fuckup!

"Things got out of hand again, didn't they, Mr. Lund? Clark got in your face just like that Mexican boy in Del Rio. Rage took over. You wanted desperately to kill Clark McCall. You saw a pistol lying there on the floor. You pulled your handkerchief from your pocket. You wrapped it around the pistol and picked the pistol up with your right hand. You stepped over to Clark. You reached down with your left hand and you grabbed the little fuckup's hair and yanked his head up. Then you put the gun to his forehead above his left eye. And you pulled the trigger. You killed

Clark McCall just like you killed that Mexican boy in Del Rio, didn't you, Mr. Lund?"

Delroy's eyes again went to Senator McCall. Scott turned and watched as bodyguard and senator stared at each other for a long moment; then McCall's eyes dropped. His face sagged and he suddenly looked old, either from the realization that his own bodyguard had murdered his son or that his dream of living in the White House was over for good. Scott returned to Delroy.

"You thought the defendant would be blamed. Her gun, her fingerprints, but you didn't know one critical fact. You didn't know she was left-handed. That's what happened that night. Things got out of hand and you killed Clark McCall. Didn't you, Mr. Lund?"

Scott paused. All twelve jurors were leaning forward as if bracing against a wind. Judge Buford had turned in his chair and was focused intently on the witness. Ray Burns's expression said he knew his coveted Washington assignment had just been lost. Bobby and Karen and Shawanda were practically on top of the defendant's table. Dan Ford's elbows were resting on the back of the pew in front and his hands were folded, as if praying. Boo and Pajamae were holding hands like finalists in a beauty pageant. The entire courtroom was waiting to hear Delroy Lund confess to killing Clark McCall. Scott decided Delroy needed a little push; he decided to get in Delroy's face.

He grabbed the crime scene photo of Clark McCall from the defendant's table and asked the judge for permission to approach the witness. When the judge nodded, Scott walked to the witness stand and dropped the photo in Delroy's lap under his now downcast eyes. Then he got in Delroy's face.

"Come on, Delroy, admit it! I know you killed Clark! This jury knows you killed Clark! Even the senator knows you killed Clark!"

Delroy's face was red and sweaty. His breathing became faster and labored. His blood pressure was rising, causing the veins in his bald head to protrude like blue ropes against his white skin. His meaty hands closed in on the photograph in his lap and crumpled it into a ball, mashing it mightily as if trying to pulverize the memory of Clark McCall into pulp. Scott knew things were about to get out of hand; Delroy's rage would soon take over and he would scream: *Yeah, I killed Clark! Yeah, I killed that little fuckup!*

But when Delroy's big bald head finally turned up, his eyes were defiant. He said, "Then prove it."

"The defense rests, Your Honor."

Ray Burns tried to save his Washington job by calling FBI Agent Henry Hu to the stand again and eliciting somewhat reluctant testimony that a left-handed person could have fired the murder weapon with her right hand. When Ray sat down, Scott stood and picked up the nearest document.

"Your Honor, may I approach the witness?"

"Yes, Mr. Fenney."

Scott walked around the defendant's table and toward the witness stand, and at the last moment, stumbled on an imaginary obstacle, tossing the document to the floor next to the witness stand. As Scott righted himself, Agent Hu, courteous as always, got out of the chair, took two steps, leaned over and picked up the document. Standing no more than two feet from the jury box, Agent Hu held the document out with his right hand.

Scott said, "Agent Hu, are you right-handed?"

Agent Hu realized his silent testimony, that he had picked up the document with his right hand because that was the natural thing to do, what anyone would do, even Clark McCall's killer. He smiled slightly.

"Yes, I am."

"No further questions."

Karen and Bobby were cooking pasta in the kitchen, the girls were taking their baths, and Scott was slumped on the floor, mentally and physically exhausted. Bobby opened the refrigerator, pulled out two beers, walked over to Scott, and held one out to him.

"No matter what happens tomorrow, Scotty, you've done right by her."

"Thanks, Bobby. And just so you know, I did this for Shawanda. Not to get back at Mack McCall or Dan Ford. For her."

"Thanks for telling me that, Scotty. I needed to know."

"I know. And thank you, Bobby."

"For what?"

"For doing this, being part of this, working your tail off even though you're not getting paid."

The beer halfway to his mouth, Bobby froze: "I'm not getting paid?"

After prayers, Pajamae opened her eyes and said, "Mr. Fenney, I don't want that McCall man to be the president."

Scott smiled. "Me neither."

"And that Delroy, he's a bad man, isn't he, Mr. Fenney?"

Boo said, "He killed Clark?"

"He is and he did."

"Is he going to jail?"

"I don't know." Scott stood. "You girls go to sleep. We've got another big day tomorrow, closing arguments, maybe a verdict."

"Mama might get out tomorrow?"

"She might. But she might not."

Pajamae thought about that, then said, "Thanks, Mr. Fenney."

"For what, baby?"

"For caring about my mama."

Scott removed his glasses and wiped his eyes. "Pajamae, my life is better now because of your mother. And because of you."

THIRTY

A SCOTT FENNEY, ESQ., stood before the twelve members of the jury and said: "When I was a boy, my mother used to read her favorite book to me at bedtime, *To Kill a Mockingbird*. You might've read it or seen the movie. It's the story of a little girl and her father, a lawyer named Atticus Finch. He was an honorable man and an honorable lawyer, unusual even back then, in the 1930s when the story took place.

"Every night my mother would say to me, Scotty, be like Atticus. Be a lawyer. Do good. She even named me after him, Atticus Scott Fenney. Well, my mother's dead and I'm a lawyer, but I'm no Atticus Finch. I haven't done much good. I made a lot of money, but I didn't make my mother proud.

"But that's another story.

"Or maybe it's the same story. Because this story, our story, the story playing out in this courtroom, is also about making your mother proud.

"See, in the book, Atticus was appointed to represent a black man named Tom Robinson. Tom was accused of beating and raping a white girl. Atticus showed the jury that the girl had been beaten by a left-handed man because the right side of her face was bruised, but that Tom's left hand was disabled due to an accident years before. Atticus proved that Tom didn't do it. And Atticus also showed the jury that the girl's father was left-handed and a mean drunk to boot. Well, everyone in the courtroom knew that Tom didn't commit the crime and that her father did. But the jury, twelve white men, convicted Tom Robinson anyway, just because he was a black man.

"Now, that story took place in Alabama in the thirties—in a different time and a different world, back when the color of law was black-and-white. But our story is taking place seventy years later, in Dallas, Texas. The world's a different place today, things have changed—not everything and not everywhere and not enough, but in our courts of law things have surely changed. Judges have changed. Juries have changed. The color of law has changed. It's no longer black-and-white. My former senior partner told me the color of law is now green. Today, he said, the rule of law is money. Money rules. And he's right. Lawyers use the law to make money, politicians sell the law to special interests for money, people sue each other for money. Everywhere in the law, it's all about money—except one place. Right there where you're sitting, in that jury box. You're not here for money. You're here for the truth.

"And what is the truth of this story? The first truth is, Clark McCall was murdered by a right-handed person, a person strong enough to yank him up off the floor, mean enough to stick a gun to his head and look him in the eye when he pulled the trigger, and experienced enough in the ways of murder investigations to know how not to leave incriminating evidence behind. The truth is, Delroy Lund murdered Clark McCall.

"The second truth is, Delroy Lund followed Clark to Dallas,

followed him down to Harry Hines, saw him pick up the defendant wearing her blonde wig, and followed them home to Highland Park. When he saw the defendant driving off in Clark's Mercedes, he went inside. He found Clark alive, naked and holding his privates after being kicked in the groin by the defendant. He laughed at Clark and Clark got mad. Clark cursed Delroy, Delroy got mad, and Clark got killed. Things got out of hand, and Delroy killed Clark.

"And the third truth is, Shawanda Jones is innocent. Clark McCall was killed by a right-handed person. Shawanda Jones is left-handed. She didn't do it.

"That's the truth. That's what the evidence shows. We've proved that the defendant is innocent and we've answered the question this trial presented: Who killed Clark McCall? Now there's only one part of this story left and you've got to write it: the ending. How is this story going to end? Like *To Kill a Mockingbird*, with an innocent defendant convicted just because she's black? Or are you going to write a new ending, where the color of law is not black or white or green, where truth and justice prevail even if the defendant is poor and black?"

Scott paused and glanced over at the judge for a long moment, then turned back to the jurors. He said: "Ladies and gentlemen, before Judge Buford appointed me to represent the defendant, I thought I was a winner in the game of law—and that's how I viewed the law, as just a game. When I tried a case, I wanted to win. I wanted to beat the other lawyer. It wasn't about truth or justice; it was just about winning . . . and money. But I was wrong. The law isn't a game. It's not about winning or money. It's about truth and justice . . . and life. Today, it's about the defendant's life.

"This case has given me a chance to do something I had never been able to do before as a lawyer: make my mother proud. I hope I did that. I hope my mother is finally proud of me." He paused. "And I hope you'll make your mothers proud of you, too."

The judge instructed the jury at 11:45. The jurors retired to the jury room for lunch and deliberations, Judge Buford to his chambers, Shawanda to her cell, and Scott, Bobby, Karen, and the girls to the house on Beverly Drive.

Scott had waited for jury verdicts many times in his career, all in civil cases where only money was at stake. While waiting for his last jury verdict, he had spent the time back in his office calculating alternate bills for his client, one at a straight hourly billing if they lost, and one with an added bonus if they won. Clients won or lost, but the lawyers always won.

This case was different.

It wasn't about money; it was about Shawanda's life. Twelve people were deciding whether she would live or die, whether she would spend the rest of her life in prison or free, whether Pajamae would have a mother or a memory.

The court clerk called at 1:30. The jury had a verdict.

"Ms. Jones," Judge Buford said, "please rise."

Shawanda Jones and her three lawyers stood and turned to the jury. Several jurors, black and brown and white, had tears in their eyes, as Shawanda did in hers. Scott felt Shawanda's hand next to his, trembling, her entire body shaking. He put his arm around her shoulders and pulled her close.

The foreperson of the jury handed the verdict to the bailiff who handed it to the judge. Judge Buford put on his reading glasses, gazed at the piece of paper, then raised his eyes to the defendant.

"In the matter of *United States of America versus Shawanda Jones*, the jury finds the defendant not guilty."

Shawanda sagged and would have fallen to the floor if Scott had not caught her. She buried her face in his chest and embraced him.

He held her tightly, his tears mixing with hers. Boo and Pajamae ran to them as the courtroom erupted in cheers and shouts and applause. The jurors hugged each other, reporters crowded Scott and Shawanda, Ray Burns sat at the prosecution table shaking his head, and Bobby and Karen kissed like newlyweds. Senator McCall pushed his way through the crowd and out of the courtroom. Dan Ford sat shaking his head in wonderment at the turn of events. Shawanda whispered in Scott's ear, "That a righteous name, Atticus."

Scott turned to the bench and his eyes met Judge Buford's. The judge nodded at Scott and Scott nodded back.

Shawanda Jones was free. Half an hour later, they finally made their way through the mob of reporters and cameras and to the sidewalk fronting the federal building. Dan Ford was waiting there. Scott sent Shawanda and the girls ahead and walked over. Dan held out his hand and Scott took it.

"Scotty, my boy, you are one fine lawyer."

"Dan, I'm not your boy anymore."

"Yes, well . . . look, Scotty, Mack won't be in the White House now, so why don't you come back? You can have your old office, I'll fix things with Dibrell and the bank, you can buy another big house, get the Ferrari back . . . you can go back to your old life—with a substantial raise, say a million a year. Not bad for a thirty-six-year-old lawyer. What do you say?"

There was a time. And a place. And a lawyer.

But they were no more.

"Dan, I'm just not the Ford Stevens type."

Scott turned away from Dan Ford only to find his path blocked by another familiar face: Harry Hankin.

"Harry! How you doing, buddy?"

During his four-year tenure as a member of the country club, Scott had played golf with Harry most Saturday mornings—and usually won a hundred bucks from Harry most Saturday mornings. Harry fought a wicked slice. They shook hands, and Scott threw a thumb back at the courthouse.

"You got a trial?"

Harry Hankin was the premier divorce lawyer in Dallas, admitted to the membership of the country club only after his written promise never to represent a member's wife.

"Uh . . . well . . . no." Harry glanced down at his shiny shoes, then back up. "Here."

Harry held out a thick document, almost as if he were embarrassed. Scott took the document and his trained eyes immediately found the caption: PETITION FOR DIVORCE.

"I wanted to do this personally, Scott, so I could explain."

"She filed for divorce?"

Harry nodded. "Trey, the pro, he hired me—or he's paying me. He's already won a tournament, a million bucks, so he can afford me."

Scott almost laughed. "We played golf how many times, Harry? A hundred? And you're taking money from the guy my wife ran off with?"

"I couldn't say no, Scott—he cured my slice."

Scott laughed now. "Well, sure, Harry, straightening out your golf swing, that's pretty goddamned important."

"You thought so once." Harry turned his hands up. "Look, I'm sorry, Scott."

"Is she happy?"

Harry shrugged lamely. "I was married to a woman like her. With them, you never really know."

"Does she want Boo?"

"What?"

Scott held up the petition. "Does she want custody of Boo?"

Harry shook his head slowly. "No. She said the PGA tour is no place for a little girl. And she said you need Boo more than Boo needs her."

Scott started to walk away, but stopped when Harry said, "Scott." Scott turned back to the divorce lawyer. "I'll take his money, Scott, but I'd never take your girl."

The two lawyers locked eyes, and Scott recalled that some years back, Harry Hankin had lost his own children in a bitter divorce.

"Thanks, Harry."

Scott caught up with the others a block down the street, where Louis was leaning against his old car and Shawanda was turning in circles, her arms spread, her face to the sky, a young beautiful woman, her tan skin radiant in the sun's reflection. Pajamae and Boo were watching and laughing joyously. Scott smiled at the sight. It was without question the best moment of Atticus Scott Fenney's legal career.

Boo said, "A. Scott, they want to help us move."

"Boo, I don't think Shawanda wants to spend her first free day in three months helping us move."

Shawanda said, "Yes, I do, Mr. Fenney. Me and Pajamae, we come tomorrow. Louis, he bring us over."

Louis walked over to Scott and they shook hands.

"You a good man, Mr. Fenney."

"Thanks, Louis, for watching the girls. For everything." To Shawanda, Scott said, "Look, I want you to go into rehab, okay. I'll pay for it."

"Thought you ain't got no money?"

"I sold my house. And I want you to work for Bobby and me, we're gonna start a firm. I want you and Pajamae out of the projects."

"Thanks, Mr. Fenney, for being my lawyer. And for caring about me."

Shawanda smiled and reached up and touched his cheek and gazed at him in the oddest way, as if memorizing his face. She stretched up and he leaned down and she kissed his cheek.

"I ain't never gonna forget you, Mr. Fenney."

And he would never forget her. And when Scott Fenney returned home, he would be greeted by enchiladas and Consuela de la Rosa, who had just arrived by bus from the border—the INS had granted her green card "out of the blue," Señor Gutierrez had said when he called her that morning. He did not know how and he did not know why and she did not care; she only knew that now she would always live with Señor Fenney and Boo, her *familia*. And later that night when Scott Fenney tucked his daughter into bed and kissed her good night, she would smile up at him and say, "See, A. Scott, there are happy endings in real life."

EPILOGUE

T HE GIRLS SQUEALED with delight.

Four months later, Scott was sitting in his pajamas and robe on the couch in the small house over by SMU and smiling as the girls opened their presents early on Christmas morning.

Their lives had been irrevocably changed.

This Christmas, he didn't have a wife and Boo didn't have a mother. Rebecca had left and never come back. Every few weeks, he still found Boo crying quietly in bed, and he had cried when the divorce became final. But they were both doing better now. He was sure he wouldn't marry again, despite Boo's attempts at match-making; she said her teacher had a really big crush on him. Ms. Dawson did seem nice at carpool.

But Boo now had Pajamae and Pajamae had Boo. They attended fourth grade at Highland Park Elementary where Pajamae was the only black girl and Boo the only white girl with cornrows. They were like sisters, and would be when the adoption was final.

Scott had Bobby and Bobby had Karen and Consuela had Esteban and they were having a baby who would be an American citizen. They had married a month ago in a traditional Mexican wedding in the Cathedral Santuario de Guadalupe Catholic Church in downtown Dallas. Scott gave the bride away and Boo was her maid of honor.

Scott also had Big Charlie back in his life. He often brought his girls over to play with Boo and Pajamae. But they no longer talked about playing football in the old days; they talked about raising kids in these new days. Scott Fenney and Charles Jackson were fathers now and that was good enough.

Scott lost the state bar election to a big firm lawyer in Houston. He now practiced law with Bobby and Karen on the second floor of an old Victorian house renovated into office space and located just south of Highland Park. The Fenney Herrin Douglas law firm represented the thirty homeowners whose residences were being condemned by the city to make room for Tom Dibrell's hotel; and they were preparing a class-action suit on behalf of the residents of the South Dallas projects against the city for violation of federal fair housing laws. Louis had gone door-to-door signing up residents; Scott's suddenly lofty reputation in the federal judicial system had allowed him to resolve all of Louis's outstanding issues with the Feds. Bobby still represented his regulars from the Mexican bar in East Dallas; charges against Carlos Hernandez were dropped due to prosecutorial misconduct. He was training to be a paralegal and acted as translator for their Hispanic clients. Scott wore jeans to the office, ate lunch once a week with the girls in the school cafeteria, and played hoops with Bobby and John Walker at the YMCA.

His office faced due south and offered a nice view of the downtown skyline. He could sit at his desk and see Dibrell Tower out his window. Karen's ex-secretary at Ford Stevens told her that the firm would close out the year with record profits. Dan Ford sat on top of his world, perfect but for the fact that vandals had repeatedly slashed the tires of his Mercedes-Benz in the parking garage, while Sid Greenberg sat in Scott's former office, drove Scott's former Ferrari, and practiced aggressive and creative lawyering for Scott's former client.

Oddly enough, Scott felt no satisfaction when Frank Turner filed a $10 million sexual harassment lawsuit against Tom Dibrell on behalf of the blonde receptionist; or when Harry Hankin filed a divorce petition against Dibrell on behalf of Tom's fourth wife alleging infidelity and seeking over $50 million in community property; or when the Environmental Protection Agency filed suit in federal court against Dibrell Property Company and Thomas J. Dibrell jointly and severally seeking $75 million in costs required for the cleanup of lead contamination on the fifty-acre tract of land located adjacent to the Trinity River.

Scott did feel relieved when Delroy Lund was arrested and charged with the murder of Clark McCall and obstruction of justice in the Shawanda Jones case; Hannah Steele agreed to testify. Mack McCall withdrew from the presidential race but was elected senate majority leader; soon after, he was diagnosed with prostate cancer. Ray Burns was now an Assistant U.S. Attorney in Lubbock. United States District Court Judge Samuel Buford remained on the bench in Dallas.

Right after the trial, Scott had moved Shawanda and Pajamae out of the projects and into a rent house near Highland Park. He paid for Shawanda's drug rehabilitation; she fought hard and gave it all she had, but she couldn't break the hold heroin had on her. Two months after the trial, Shawanda Jones injected heroin into her right arm, drifted off to sleep, and never woke up. Pajamae missed her mama very much, but said she's in a better place now where she doesn't need her medicine to be happy. She prayed for her mother every Sunday morning when Scott took the girls to church.

Scott had begun reading a new bedtime book to the girls: *To Kill a Mockingbird.* They loved Boo Radley.

THE ABDUCTION
Mark Gimenez

The emotionally gripping follow-up to *The Colour of Law*.

When hotshot lawyer Elizabeth Brice turns up to collect her daughter Grace from football practice, the coach tells her she needn't have bothered, as Grace's uncle has already picked her up. The only problem is – Grace has no uncles.

And so begins a furious race against time to save Grace from unknown kidnappers. Grace's internet geek father John leads the search, forced to unite with his terrifying wife and even more terrifying father Ben, a battle-hardened Vietnam veteran. Somehow they must find Grace before it is too late. But secrets from the past make the little girl's survival more uncertain with every passing minute . . .

A riveting, action-packed thriller, *The Abduction* will have you on the edge of your seat from the first page to the last.

'Try it . . . firmly in the John Grisham mould'
Daily Mirror

THE PERK

Mark Gimenez

A grieving widower gets caught up in the politics of his Texas
hometown when he returns to make peace with his father.

Beck Hardin returns to his Texas hometown – and his estranged
father – after the death of his wife leaves him with two children to
raise. The town is still reeling from the murder of sixteen-year-old
Heidi, whose father – Beck's old college friend – asks Beck to help
him find Heidi's killer before the statute of limitations runs out.

Meanwhile, Beck is pushed into becoming town Judge, and he
makes some powerful enemies amongst the rich white landowners
when he refuses to condone their treatment of the Mexican workers
of the town. As events escalate, the landowners carefully plot
their revenge . . .

'Gimenez has gone from strength to strength'
Daily Mail

THE GOVERNOR'S WIFE

Mark Gimenez

Bode Bonner is the Republican governor of Texas. He has everything he ever wanted: money, power, influence. But something isn't right in his life – everything feels too settled and easy. He longs for one more moment of excitement, one more challenge.

Lindsay Bonner is Bode's wife, and she's bored too. Bored of Bode's womanising, bored of the endless cocktail parties and receptions. She is desperate to break free of her bland, wealthy Texan lifestyle.

And that moment comes when she saves a poor Hispanic boy's life. From that moment on, nothing will be the same for Bode and Lindsay Bonner. Their lives are about to change in ways they could never have predicted . . .

Filled with dramatic and ingenious twists and turns, this is an addictively readable novel that delves deep into the dark heart of Texas.

'A gripping story, well told'
Literary Review